"So. What can I do for you, Li

"It came to my attention that problem here, one that I have some experience with, being in the navy—"

"You're a doctor?" I interrupted. "A medical doctor?"

"Well, yes," he agreed, blue eyes dancing.

"Well, no," I said flatly. Slowly I sat straighter, watching his eyes. "And my guess is that you aren't even in the navy. My guess is that I should call security and have you tossed off the property."

The blue eyes flickered only slightly, less of a movement than a darkening of the color, a graying out, an emotional recognition of failure. Veiled hostility. Suddenly the blue eyes were not quite so attractive.

"What are you? Reporter? Not television—the hair's too short and the uniform fits too poorly. Press?" I nodded. "A tabloid?" I let the questions sound like the insults they were intended as.

One fist tightened on the arm of his chair. Hostility unveiled as a slow smile spread across the lower half of his face. He didn't like me and wanted me to know it. Most people couldn't carry on a conversation with facial expression alone. This guy could.

"Why the charade? I mean, just for argument's sake, until security gets here to escort you away?"

He blinked. Slowly, he moved his eyes toward the phone/intercom and let them rest on the brightly lit red button that showed our conversation was being monitored. For an instant, the threat of violence sizzled on the air. His mouth snapped closed, blue laser eyes stabbed me in sudden fury and Lieutenant Montgomery Leander simply got up and left.

GWEN HUNTER

PRESCRIBED DANGER

MIRA®

ISBN 1-55166-916-1

PRESCRIBED DANGER

Copyright © 2002 by Gwen Hunter.

All rights reserved. Except for use in any review, the reproduction or
utilization of this work in whole or in part in any form by any electronic,
mechanical or other means, now known or hereafter invented, including
xerography, photocopying and recording, or in any information storage or
retrieval system, is forbidden without the written permission of the publisher,
MIRA Books, 225 Duncan Mill Road, Don Mills, Ontario, Canada M3B 3K9.

All characters in this book have no existence outside the imagination of the
author and have no relation whatsoever to anyone bearing the same name
or names. They are not even distantly inspired by any individual known or
unknown to the author, and all incidents are pure invention.

MIRA and the Star Colophon are trademarks used under license and registered
in Australia, New Zealand, Philippines, United States Patent and Trademark
Office and in other countries.

Visit us at www.mirabooks.com

Printed in U.S.A.

To Tamar Myers, Marisa's favorite author,
and my dear friend.
You have been a source of inspiration
both in my literary endeavors and in my spiritual walk.
Thank you for your positive outlook
and hopeful expectations.

ACKNOWLEDGMENT

Though I drew on Chester County, South Carolina, and its hospital blueprint for inspiration and information, Dawkins County, its citizens, its employees, its hospital and its patients are entirely fictional. I have tried to make the medical sections of *Prescribed Danger* as realistic as possible. Where mistakes may exist, they are mine, *not* the able, competent and creative medical workers in the list below.

FOR MEDICAL HELP:
Laurie Milatz, D.O.
Susan Prater, O.R. Tech and sister-in-love
Amy Killian—infection control, Chester, South Carolina
Rudy Pate, R.N., DHEC, South Carolina
Henry Nunnery, Clemson extension office, South Carolina
Isabel Pittman, R.N., Chester, South Carolina
Amy Proctor Williams, R.N., BSN, Chester, South Carolina
Marc Gorton, registered Respiratory Therapist, Chester, South Carolina
Joan Strait, Lab Manager at Chester County Hospital
Susan Saunders—for being there at any hour of the day or night!
John Saunders, M.D., for answering questions
Steve Vassey—for DHEC help

Sgt. Garry Leveille of the Charlotte, North Carolina Police Department

As always, for making this a stronger book:
Miranda Stecyk, my editor
Jeff Gerecke, my agent

South Carolina Writers Group—my local chapter—for all the help in making this novel work. Thanks for bleeding all over its bits and pieces.

Robin Breeden, Dawn Cook, Craig Faris, Norman Froscher, Jason Gilbert, Melissa Hinnant, Ed Johnson, Bob Lynch, Misty Massey, Todd Massey, Virginia Wilcox

Prologue

According to my mother, I had breeding, good genes and the right to success. Of course, my mother said that during one of her many drunken binges, and so it was something I took with a grain of salt. She was a Rheaburn, of *the Charleston Rheaburns,* but had married beneath herself, had a baby within five months of the marriage, been quickly widowed, and then taken up with a bottle of Jack Daniel's. The Rheaburns could have forgiven her the marriage—after all, the man had the good sense to die quickly enough—but it was the baby and the Jack that caused her disgrace. I was that baby, and I have been paying the cost of her rebellion ever since.

The price has been a peculiar sort of aloneness. I tend to stand back and watch as others interact, rather than joining in myself. I spend a lot of time evaluating and assessing people and situations, which makes me a good diagnostician, a quick thinker, and someone who reacts instantly in times of stress or trouble. It's a personality trait that makes me a capable ER physician. It also makes me a bit of a cold fish.

That last is the opinion of Miss DeeDee Stowe, the woman who took me under her wing, taught me all I ever knew about family and friendships, and put me through medical school. She also killed a man and maimed three people, but insists it can't really be held against her. She was under a bit of strain financially at the time. Miss DeeDee is now a ward of the state, occupying a private room in our state mental facility, the price of her fatal financial negotiations. She is a bit of a cold fish herself, I suppose.

One good thing came of my isolated upbringing, and that was my ability to make and keep friends. I value friendships, and work hard to keep them fresh and strong. It was this gift for friendship, combined with the ability to keep a clear head and diagnose obscure medical conditions, that led me to the murderer of Leon Hawkins....

Leon's death was a bad one. No easy passing in his sleep. Not even a quick bullet to the brain. And the manner in which he died led me to some strange and incorrect conclusions before the truth was finally known.

His story and his death reminded me of one of my mama's drunken aphorisms—''Things aren't always as they seem.''

1

STORMS, POKÉMON AND TORTURE

Lightning tripped the breaker. The overhead fluorescents died, throwing the ER into blackness. In theory, the backup generator was supposed to prevent blackouts, but the reality was often something different. Just outside of my range of hearing, thunder boomed, more a vibration of the foundations than a sound. The old building groaned as wind battered the southeast side. Water poured through lighting fixtures and into buckets procured by the roaming security guard. The rattle of metal was soothing, like the sound of rain on a tin roof. I paused mid-suture, waiting for the lights to be restored or for someone to bring me a flashlight. Beneath the sterile drape, my three-year-old patient whimpered. "Mom?" he said, his voice quivering.

"It's okay, Charlie," I said, knowing I was soothing both mother and son. "Almost done." I could hear his mother swallow. When the lights finally flickered back on, I made a point of not looking at her, but kept my expression cool and professional as I tied off the last suture and sat the toddler up. "All done. See?" I turned his leg so Charlie could see the neat row of stitches that replaced the gaping laceration and shooting streams of blood.

"Wow!" he said. "Look, Mama! I got a creepy-crawly crawling up my leg!"

I grinned at him. The neat row of stitches did look like a many-legged bug. "Not so bad, and for being a big boy, you get five stickers." I held out my hand, fingers splayed. "Want Pooh or Pokémon?"

"Both," he said promptly, and then laughed through his tears. He was a cute kid, and I ran my hand across his short, curly hair as I left the room, knowing that one or another of the nurses on duty would see to the stickers and his mother's instructions for wound care.

I stretched, moved into the break room and sighed, then poured a cup of raspberry-cream-flavored coffee and picked up my copy of the *New England Journal of Medicine,* opening it to an article pertinent to gastric lavage in the gut-shot gang patient—not that the *Journal* writers would ever put it so baldly. Anne and Zack, the RNs on duty tonight, were puttering around in the drug room, counting tablets, capsules, and vials of various drugs. I was alone with the police scanner, listening to reports of storm-tossed mayhem, bored enough to actually consider filing and painting my nails with the clear polish Anne had left on the break-room table. It had been more than a year since I'd bothered, however, and there was no sense in putting my cuticles into shock.

The lights went out again. In the strange dark, I heard someone crying, the sound muffled and choked.

My only other patient, diagnosed with lower lobe pneumonia, had been admitted but was still waiting for a room on the medical floor. She also had a bad case of grief. Her husband had died in the last week, leaving her alone and mourning herself to death in that dry-eyed form of grief where everything simply shuts down and the mourner feels nothing.

I had examined her, tried to get her to talk to me, and been rebuffed. She had been willing to accept my medical help but not my more personal concern, turning her face away when I asked about her emotional state. But now she was crying.

The lights finally flickered back on, and I stepped into the treatment room. The woman, Regina—her last name was gone from my memory—was weeping, her dark-skinned face buried in the thin hospital blanket. Putting down my coffee, I pulled up a chair and slowly sat, bending forward so our faces were level. I wasn't much good in counseling sessions, but I understood pain, and my patient was in agony. I held out a hand, pulled gently at the blanket.

Regina moaned, her red-rimmed eyes focusing on mine, her mouth opening and closing at each painful breath. With a sudden jerk, she took my hand, her icy grip transmitting her desperate grief. "Want to tell me about it?" I asked.

"I found him," she moaned. "I found him hanging there."

I blinked. I hadn't understood that her husband had committed suicide. I gripped her hand tighter, enfolding the frigid flesh in my warmth.

"He was so heavy. I couldn't lift him good. And he—" she sucked a tear-wet breath "—dead. He dead." Fresh sobs tore through her. After a moment she looked up. "I got up top and my friend Louise, she went back for a knife. We cut him down. And he fall. I still hear that sound. Him falling. Heavy, big man, onto the rock. He hurt his head when he fall. Thump sound, like a melon breaking. My man dead. My man dead."

There was nothing I could say. Nothing. Regina rocked, and I held her hand. Motioning to a passing nurse, I ordered a strong sedative, and stayed by Regina's side until it took effect. When the woman's frail body relaxed, uncurling from the tight ball beneath the blanket, her eyes fluttering into sleep, I slipped my hand free and found my cold coffee. But I stayed with her until the nurses took her to the floor.

Even at 8:00 p.m., there were no more patients. No crying babies, no drunks, no mothers-to-be with phantom pains for me to diagnose and treat. Just a freak spring storm weather

forecasters were referring to with awe. The storm had settled
in over the upper part of the state as if it intended to stay.
Back in the break room with a fresh cup of coffee, I listened
to the scanner reports a flooding in the lowlands, as creeks
and ponds expanded their banks to include neighborhoods
and roadways. Mud slides threatened as hillsides weakened
by too much April rain gave way. Nature seldom listened
to the projections of engineers on hundred-year floodplains
and storm runoff.

South Rocky Creek, which normally wound its peaceful
way behind the hospital property, was taking over the doctors' parking lot, and I had been forced to park uphill from
the hospital to protect my little BMW through the night. It
was a mess out there.

High winds were taking off roofs and downing trees all
over the state, shutting off electricity for tens of thousands.
Vinyl siding torn from houses was flying in the wind, shattered windows were letting in rain by the bucket, buildings
were lying flat. Bridges were being washed out and electrical lines whipped in the wind, throwing sparks and starting
small fires that the rain quickly damped. Phones were out
throughout the piedmont region of the state.

According to the radio, Charleston, where I was raised,
was heavily damaged. DorCity, my adopted home, had also
been hit badly.

I was intimately familiar with the condition of the town,
having just made the run from my house through DorCity
to the rural hospital. I thought my toy-size car might take
up wings and fly away a few times, but I had made it in
under my estimated time. And truth to tell, I was glad to be
in the hospital instead of my old, bungalow-style home,
which might be reduced to matchsticks by morning if the
hundred-year-old oaks that surrounded it decided to give in
to the wind and crash down. Even my dogs hadn't wanted
to stay home through the storm, so I had left them with the
cop across the street for the night. Mark Stafford was half

boyfriend, half annoyance, but he loved dogs; Belle and Yellow Pup were safe there, with his half-dozen hunting dogs in their brick-lined shelter.

When the storm finally passed over, the small rural ER would fill up with typical Thursday night problems, as well as stress-induced heart attacks, babies being born too early, minor injuries, and accident victims who couldn't wait to get out and ride around to see the damage. The latter were fools, a danger to themselves and the rescue personnel out doing their jobs, and I would likely tell several so by morning. It was the perk of being a doctor. I could tell strangers the truth and they had to take it. I sipped at the coffee, now cool enough to drink.

The ambulance service air-lock opened with an ear-popping whoosh. Humid air and shredded leaves blew in, but no one entered. Just the wind, too strong to hold the doors shut one moment, then reversing directions, becoming too strong to force them open at all.

The lights flickered again, blackness and light like a strobe above me. The elevator was out, and the high winds had closed the second floor, where pediatrics and obstetrics were located. The patients had all been moved to the medical wing. Three pediatric patients and one jaundiced baby. No OB patients. Those would have to go to Ford County tonight and all weekend, as the OB/GYN was out of town. Dawkins boasted exactly one doctor who delivered babies, and Michelle Geiger was in New York at a conference.

The hospital was not a modern monstrosity, a solid rectangular block of stacked hallways and units, but a haphazard U-shaped construction put together over the years on cheap county land. Units went every which way, with ICU heading south, the medical floor facing east, and the nursing center situated down a long connecting hallway back around to the south. Surgery was a new section to the north. All parts of the building, both old and new, were being battered as the wind groaned overhead.

Behind me, the EMS scanner crackled to life. "Dawkins County Hospital, this is Unit 52. Come in." It was an EMS unit, out in this storm. I wandered closer to hear what patient would be brought in.

Anne picked up the mike and depressed the button on the side. "Unit 52, go ahead."

"Dawkins, we have two patients. First is a white male, age twenty-four, with multiple contusions, abrasions, bruising over large portions of torso, abdomen and groin area. Bruising on both wrists, possible broken fingers on both hands. Patient is a victim of assault." Anne sighed as she took notes. "BP is 125 over 85, pulse is 105 and tachy. Temp is 96.5, say again, 96.5.

"Patient two is Asian female, age twenty-two, also victim of assault, para 1, gravida 2, six months gestation." I moved closer, not sure I had heard correctly. A pregnant patient who had been beaten? I hoped the assailant wasn't the man with her in the ambulance. That was never a good situation. "This patient also has abrasions and shallow lacerations to limbs, chest and abdomen. BP 145 over 95, pulse 125, with very tachy episodes up to 175. Temp is 94.2. Repeat 94.2 Patient appears to be in early labor. Copy that, Dawkins?"

"We copy," Anne said. She was writing furiously, but paused to glance over her shoulder at me and shake her head. I had heard the emergency medical technician correctly. She was pregnant and had been assaulted. Her body temperature was low and her heart rate was high—"tachy" was medic speak for tachycardia.

"Patients were immersed in Prosperity Creek for a number of hours and have swallowed a large amount of creek water. Possible aspiration of same. Copy all that, Dawkins?"

"We copy," Anne said, shaking her head again.

"Dawkins, you might like to have the sheriff's department on hand at hospital. They have not been notified. Unit 52 out."

"We'll call them in," Anne said. "Dawkins 414, all clear." She replaced the mike and stood, grimacing at me. Neither one of us liked this. We had an assaulted female in labor with a six-month fetus and no OB/GYN on hand. We were supposed to ship all pregnant patients out.

Anne was a medium woman: medium brown hair and brown eyes, medium build, middle age, medium height. But in an emergency, she was great. Already she had moved into the treatment room with the OB table-bed to pull out supplies I might need.

"Anne?" I called. When she stopped and looked back over her shoulder I said, "Call them back. Ask them if the road to Ford County is open. See if they can take both patients there."

"Not possible."

I looked up at the dry tone and surveyed the cop standing there in a rain slicker and black combat boots. I hadn't heard Mark come in. "Seventy-two is closed, two bridges out. I-77 is down for the next six hours at least, with accidents." Anne snorted and went on into the treatment room where I could hear the crackle of plastic being torn.

"We have three separate situations with tractor-trailers flipped over," Mark continued. "Two on 77, one on Highway 9 just outside of town. HazMat has been called in for the Highway 9 accident, by the way. Guy was trying to head north through this wind carrying a load of sulfuric acid. Thought he'd drive around the mess on 77 and hit the interstate again up in Ford County. Bad decision."

"Lovely," I said. I hadn't delivered a baby since med school. I wasn't the maternal type. And if there were any burn victims from the acid spill, I would get them. With this wind, there was no way to fly anyone out to burn or trauma centers.

"Ain't it?" Mark said. "Now it's covering the road, running out of the ditch banks, and flowing toward the creeks. Fun time in the old town tonight."

I wasn't sure if he was kidding or not; cops think the strangest things are fun. To Anne, I said, "Get me a mag sulfate drip. If we need to slow down contractions I want it ready." To Mark I said, "You're dripping all over the floor."

He grinned, a drop of water sliding down his forehead, getting caught in his thick brows. "You gonna mop up after me?"

"Not in this lifetime."

He laughed, leaned forward and stroked my head, his hand damp against my short black hair. Mark didn't believe in public displays of affection. Neither did I. "Have to hit Highway 9 and see if I can help out." He smiled broadly, as if he thought that standing around in a violent storm, surrounded by flowing sulfuric acid, would be a fine thing. "Be sure to call the deputies on your assault. But if you need me, call the dispatcher. I'll come back."

I was touched but wasn't about to show it. Our relationship hadn't made it to the point of sharing many vulnerabilities yet. Probably never would. "Yeah. Thanks. And by the way, you were right. I do need a truck to handle this kind of weather. It's real nasty. Be careful out there."

"I know of a truck for sale. We'll talk."

"Oh. Whoopee."

Mark laughed at my lack of enthusiasm.

Resigned, I followed him into the air lock, a big, burly, out-of-uniform cop with a gun on his hip, a second one on his ankle beneath his jeans, and an ugly orange slicker still dripping with water, the word *POLICE* in huge capital letters on front and back.

Mark pushed against the outer doors and air sucked through, swirling leaves inside. Under the ramp, a branch swept past and the outer doors shook with wind and pressure changes. Without a word, Mark thrust the outer door open and shoved his body into the tumult. He was still grinning, green eyes gleaming, as he drove away in his dark green

Jeep, and I knew he was having the time of his life. He unbent enough to toss me a wave.

The sky was dark, ripped with purple clouds, lit with flares of lightning. Debris, tossed like failing kites, whirled along the ground, only half visible in the dying light. Rain slashed like warm butter knives, beating at the hospital's brown stucco sides. A cat, drenched and miserable, ran into the covered breezeway and shook herself. She crouched at the sight of me, wary, cautious. When I didn't move, she relaxed and lifted a paw to lick away the rain. Her affected air of unconcern only partially hid the hyperalertness caused by the storm.

From the road in front of the hospital, a pair of headlights turned into the lane, red lights flashing above. Wind rocked the ambulance from side to side. Even the heavy conveyance was too small to fight the storm. Engine roaring, it pulled up under the ramp and stopped beneath the covered ambulance bay. The cat scuttled back into the storm, tail down.

The driver door opened and Mick Ethridge hopped out, his wet hair slicked to his skull. He was just a kid, still too young to drink legally, but old enough to take the paramedic exam. Last I heard, he was still waiting for the test results.

"Hey, Doc! We gonna need a wheelchair," he shouted, over both engine and storm.

I stepped through the inner doors and shouted back down the hallway, "Anne, Zack, get a wheelchair!" Not waiting to see if they heard, I went to the back doors of the ambulance. Wild wind grabbed my lab coat and tried to pull it from me. Horizontal rain wet my scrub suit and soaked through to my legs. An overweight EMT jumped down, wedging the doors open. I peered past him inside.

There was blood in the back of the unit. A lot of it, pooled in the smooth floorboard. A man, his long, soaked hair draggling forward over his face, sat hunched in the corner seat, almost invisible in the poor light. Lying limp on the stretcher was a young woman, a waiflike thing who looked little more than a child, her small belly pushing against her wet dress.

"When did this start?" I couldn't tell if Mick heard me or not, my breath whipped by the wind.

Zack came through the air-lock doors, a wheelchair before him. He stopped, his face lit by flickering fluorescent lights and shadow. Black skin grayed by lightning. Huge eyes. "What a storm!" he shouted happily.

Mick nodded back, jumping into the unit and assisting the paramedic inside. "Started not more than two minutes ago, Doc. Pressure's dropping."

The EMS crew transferred the woman first. She was covered in mud, wet to the bone, and was in heavy labor, bleeding profusely. "Vitals," I shouted as we moved to the air-lock doors.

"BP dropping. Last time I took it, it was 90 over 45. Pulse 90. Pupils equal and reactive. They were in the water all day, Doc. Through the entire storm." The air-lock doors gave, Anne holding the inner doors open for the stretcher.

"Why?" I shouted.

"They been kidnapped, Doc. Tortured. For four days."

2

I WOULD HAVE KILLED HIM WITH MY BARE HANDS

We took the patients to separate rooms, placing the woman in the room with the gynecological exam table, its steel stirrups and poor padding the best we could do. I knew instantly that the mother was in distress. She was straining and pushing. And I didn't like the amount of blood trailing down the hallway in her wake.

"See if you can call someone in to help with this, Zack."

"The phone lines are—"

"Try," I said shortly. Bending over my patient, I saw the bruising on her ankles and wrists. Shackle marks, the skin over her bones rubbed raw and bleeding. Inflammation was days old, pus collected in the cracks of wound and skin. Her mouth was raw, the redness a stark line about three inches wide reaching around her jaw. Duct tape had held her mouth closed. She coughed, the sound long and retching, wet.

"I want cops here *yesterday*. Let's get a line going. Get me a CBC, chem seven, magnesium, two blood cultures, and I'm going to need some blood cross-matched," I said, ordering IV fluids and a routine battery of tests for both trauma and infection. Anne took her blood pressure as I spoke. It was falling, 80 over 50. I didn't like this at all. She was losing blood fast. "Temp?" I asked.

"Up to 97.8, pulse 100 and very fluttery."

The patient coughed. A bloody mucoid film stained her lips, which she wiped with the back of her wrist. I didn't like the look of the sputum. It wasn't a typical symptom in anyone, and with childbirth, it indicated an underlying health concern, but I had more immediate problems to deal with.

I snapped on latex exam gloves and smiled at my patient. "Hi. I'm Dr. Rhea Lynch. Can you talk to me? When are you due?"

The woman moaned, a long, low sound full of anguish. "Three months." Her teeth started chattering. Her whole body was racked with sudden tremors.

A lab tech entered behind me. I glanced up. "Amanda, get her typed for four units of blood. On second thought, I want a unit of type-specific ASAP." I didn't think I would have time to wait for a cross-match. I hated to give un- crossed blood to anyone, especially a woman of childbear- ing age, but at least I could give ABO and Rh specific units and not cause problems down the road with possible future pregnancies. "Rainbow her, okay?"

"Yes, ma'am." Amanda pulled out an extra set of multicolored tubes, drawing plenty of blood for later testing.

My hands roamed the patient's abdomen as I spoke, her wet dress no hindrance to my sense of touch. She was rigid with strong contractions. I followed the contours of the baby's body beneath the mother's skin. She was under- weight by at least twenty pounds and the baby was tiny. I guessed about four pounds, maybe three and a half. The baby was turned head down, his legs curled in place at the front of his mother's body. I couldn't tell about his arms without doing a full exam.

Changing gloves for a sterile pair, I said, "I've got to check you, okay?" When she nodded, I inserted my gloved hand to do a quick exam, sliding into her as gently as I could. There was too much blood to see anything, so I would have to work by feel. The patient's cervix was fully effaced, fully dilated. Magnesium sulfate wouldn't stop this birth. Nothing would. The baby was coming.

"Guys, let's get her in the trauma room," I said. "I can't work in here. Too crowded."

"Her husband's in the trauma room," Anne said. "The leak in the treatment—"

"Move him. This baby is coming. Get someone down here with a heated incubator, a baby monitor, the works." I placed the earpieces of my stethoscope into my ears and listened to the woman's heartbeat and breathing. I couldn't hear the baby's heartbeat. I feared it no longer had one.

Beside me, Anne was trying to find a vein for another IV. The EMTs had started one in the field, but if we had to give meds and blood, the patient would need another.

"Zack," I shouted out the open door, "where's my help?"

"I got a deputy going for the on-call peds doc, Dr. Haynes. You gonna need a surgeon?"

"*Stat.* Send the rescue squad for Statler. And after they get him in, send them back after Wallace." Another thought surfaced and I stuck my head out the door, looking up at the EMTs standing at the desk. "You know where Dr. Statler lives?" They nodded. "Well?" I said lifting my brows. They left in a rush as I walked to the nurses' desk. Lights flickered overhead again, throwing the ER into black night. "Call the squad for Wallace," I said as soon as I had light. Zack nodded, moving for the emergency radio. My pregnant patient screamed. I could hear her husband shouting in the trauma room. "Zack, get me Trish!"

"Already on her way." Zack was coolly dialing the phone as he spoke, handling the phone and the radio at once.

I needed the nursing supervisor. Trisha Singletary had probably delivered more babies than I had. She handled all OB situations between the hours of 7:00 p.m. and 7:00 a.m. until Michelle Geiger could get here. The doctor lived five minutes away. Sometimes that was too long and Trish handled the delivery.

"What are their names?"

"Mel Campbell and Lia Yi Campbell," Zack said. "No ID. Claim the guys who kidnapped them took it all, along with their jewelry, cash and credit cards," Zack added, holding the phone to the side.

"Okay." I took a deep breath and let it out.

Entering the trauma room, I took one of Mel's hands. He was screaming for his wife, begging for her, his eyes wild, dark misery swirling in their depths, torment that I didn't want to explore—but then, I had always been a coward. "Mel?" He pushed me away with bandaged hands. I noted that his wrists bore the same kind of wounds as Lia's. Shackle marks. Bruises covered his arms and face in various shades of purple, blue, yellow and green. I didn't have time to react to the signs of torture on his body; I had to deliver his baby. Still, a sick feeling sat heavily in the pit of my stomach.

"Where is my wife? I want my wife!" he roared.

"Mel, I'm a doctor." I restrained his hands, and he hissed with pain as I touched the broken fingers. "Your wife is in the next room." Zack came in behind me and pushed the man back down on the stretcher. "Mel, tell me what happened. I have to know so I can help her. Help Lia, understand?" A hint of reason began to clear away the fog in his eyes. "I'm a doctor and I'm here to help," I repeated more slowly.

Mel struggled to sit up, a spark of comprehension on his face. "A doctor?" I nodded to Zack to let him rise. He grabbed at my left hand with both of his own and held me tight. Broken bones grated against my own flesh "You're a doctor? Oh, God, you got to help her. They..." His blue eyes scrunched up in pain as a raw sob tore through him. "They held her down...and hit her. Over and over." His voice broke. "I couldn't stop them. I couldn't get free."

Below the bandages, the nails of both of his hands were ripped off into the quick, red mud caked into the edges and cuticles. The nails had not been pulled out, but had been mangled some other way. The man was exhausted, his face lacerated, ravaged by torture, lack of food and hours in the creek.

Gently, I stroked his head, which was bowed over my left hand. "Mel, did they hit your wife in the abdomen?"

He nodded and sniffed. Looked up into my face. "Over and over. Afterward, she *said* it was never hard. Just enough to hurt. But over and over, you know? She's six months pregnant. She's gonna lose him, isn't she?"

"The baby is coming. I don't know if it will survive, but we're going to do all we can to save it. Understand?"

"Yes. Yes, I understand."

"Has she seen a doctor? An obstetrical doctor?"

He looked blank for a moment, then his eyes cleared. "Last month. Dr. Geiger. She was fine. Taking her vitamins, getting her exercise. They did an ultrasound. The baby was doing great. It's a boy."

"Any allergies?"

"No. None. She's healthy as a horse. That's what Dr. Geiger says."

"Okay. Dr. Geiger's not in town. I am going to have to deliver this baby because there isn't time to get Lia to Ford County. Zack, here, is going to get some permits for you to sign, so I can deliver the baby, and then move you to another room so I can have this one for Lia. Okay?"

"Where's Dr. Geiger?" Mel's eyes had widened again, fear like a fresh wound on his face. He looked like an old man, yellowed bruises like jaundice. His lips were split and swollen.

"Zack will tell you all about it. Zack, get me a baseline CBC and tell the lab to rainbow him, just in case," I said, telling the lab to again draw extra tubes of blood. "Get a chest." I listened to his chest as I spoke, the bell of the stethoscope moving and pausing, my other hand on his chilled, water-wrinkled flesh beneath the muddy, soaked shirt. His lungs sounded a little wet. "Get a couple blood cultures. Let's get him out of these wet clothes and into some warm blankets. You been coughing, Mel?"

He shook his head no.

"Has Lia?"

"Yeah. Since we got into the water. You got to help her."

"I intend to. You listen to Zack here and do what he tells you. We're moving you now."

"Why?" he asked, the fear back in his eyes.

"The light's better in here and Lia needs it." I needed to get back to my critical patient, but I hesitated and took Mel's hands again, not to offer comfort, but to examine his nails. There was blood caked in the mud and abrasions, and fresh blood seeped in the nail beds. "Mel, did you dig with your hands? In the ground?"

"Yes. Last night they left my cuff loose. I dug under the wall and crawled out." His voice changed as he spoke. Some of the fear vanished. "I found a hoe and widened the space. Crawled back in and got Lia free. We made it to the creek. They never saw us." He looked up at me, his eyes hard for an instant, his voice guttural. "I don't know if they had a guard. They wore masks. I don't even know who they were. But if they had left a guard, I would have killed him. God forgive me, I would have. With my bare hands."

I understood that this was more than a statement of fact. Mel had made peace with the homicide he had been willing to commit. He had been ready to murder if necessary to save his wife. I patted his wrists. "Mel, I'm going to be busy for a while working on your wife. If you yell and scream, you'll distract me. Can you be quiet?"

Mel nodded, his eyes calmer, more reasonable. He had something he could do for Lia again, even if it was simply staying silent. He needed that lifeline. This man clearly loved his wife, would swim oceans for her. It was a feeling

I had never experienced. "Good. Because if you keep carrying on, I am going to have problems concentrating. And Lia needs my total attention."

"I'll be good." He laughed suddenly at his own words, a slightly hysterical sound. A little boy, promising anything to avoid a spanking. And then the hysteria was gone. "You just concentrate on Lia." I smiled and left the room. Zack pushed the stretcher out into the hallway behind me and into the far treatment room. Mel was quiet.

I entered Lia's room. Trish was there, along with Anne, a Doppler in her hand as she listened for a baby's heartbeat on the woman's abdomen. Looking up, she shook her head. No heartbeat. Lia coughed again, depositing more of the blood-smeared sputum into an emesis basin. The sputum was not solid blood, which would indicate a pulmonary embolus, a clot in her lungs; it looked too dense for that diagnosis. This was thick and purulent. I needed a chest X ray, but knew I wasn't going to get it before the delivery.

I said, "We can move her now. Vitals?"

"Better," Anne said. "Pressure is 90 over 75 and stable, pulse is 90 and regular. She's had a half liter of fluid and, with the hot blankets, her temp is up .5. She's conscious and alert times three. I started another line and put her in Trendelenburg." Trendelenburg was the position of Lia's gurney, her head lower than her feet, so blood would move with gravity to the upper part of the body, helping to temporarily stabilize her pressure.

"Good. A lot of this could be dehydration, then," I said. "Contractions?"

"Hard." Anne looked up at me "We have about ten good minutes if we're lucky. And she's still bleeding. Ready to move her?"

"Yes. Let's go." Like a well-schooled team, we secured all IV lines and raised the handrails, kicked the brakes off the gurney, leveled it and rolled Lia out into the hallway, down to the trauma room.

While I watched, Trish settled the gurney into its place beneath the big exam lights and rearranged the O_2 cannula on Lia. Blond hair wisped around her face as she worked. She had cut her hair in the last week. I liked it. "Blood is on the way," she said. "I'll sign for it and hang it. We've got two more patients, but I told the switchboard to hold noncriticals." Zack pushed the door to the hallway closed. Angry voices ringing at the ambulance entrance were cut off. Whatever it was, Zack could handle it.

"Doc, you should see this." Anne lifted the hospital gown that had replaced Lia's wet, stained dress. Exposing the patient's chest, Anne pointed. Over the bruises was a tattoo, crude and uneven, the kind created by hand with ink taken from a ballpoint pen. It was fresh, the lines swollen and inflamed. "She says the guys who held them did this."

It was a star. Or a pentagram. I bent closer. The star was six-sided. Not witchcraft, then, but more like a Star of David. The kind Jews had been forced to wear in Hitler's Germany.

Leaning over the woman, I looked into her eyes for the first time. I took the opportunity to complete my earlier exam and shined a penlight into her eyes to check pupil reactions. She had beautiful eyes, deep brown and fringed with heavy lashes. Both pupils were equal and reactive. "Hi, Lia. It's Dr. Lynch. Are you half Asian, half Jewish?"

"No. The nurse asked me that," she said between puffs of breathing. "My daddy's…Italian-American. He met my mama in…Korea. And Mel's mostly German and Irish. Baptist, both of us. The guys who…" She moaned and paused a moment, turning her face away, breathing in quick pants. "The guys who did this to us kept calling him Jewish, though. And called me a gook." She coughed again, harder, the sound like wet linen ripping. Definitely an atypical sound, like nothing I had ever heard.

"Lia, I have to ask you this. Did the men…did they assault you in any other way besides hitting you?" I asked.

"No." Lia's eyes filled with tears but she faced me squarely. "I thought they were going to…rape me…but they…said I wasn't good enough for them to touch me…." The words were strangled as a massive contraction hit her.

"Check her, Trish?" I asked as I started my sterile wash under nearly scalding water.

"She's crowning, Doc," Trish said, her face intent. Lia screamed, a low and guttural sound, with the effort of pushing the baby from her body. "Dr. Rhea, I feel a loop of… We have a prolapsed cord." I could hear fear in her voice. Lia began to grunt, pushing.

"Keep your hand in place," I said, speeding the wash. "Keep steady pressure on the baby's head. Don't let it move."

"It's not going anywhere."

Prolapsed cord was rare but dangerous as hell. If the baby moved, pulling the cord wrapped around it, the placenta could yank off the uterine wall and cause massive bleeding.

Pulling on a paper gown, settling a face shield over my head, and snapping sterile gloves in place, I kicked the exam stool until it settled between the patient stirrups. Trish eased out of the way, her hand steady. Anne adjusted the light, pulling my face shield down over my eyes.

When I inserted my hand beside Trish's, there was a rush of blood. The light was a nice touch, but no help. I'd be working by feel alone.

3

NO FEMALE DEITY...A PAINFUL ATROCITY

The baby's head was slippery, a loop of cord curled around its ear and shoulder. I followed the coil, unwrapping it as I went. Lia's screams gurgled into heavy panting as another contraction began. My hand was prisoned against her cervical walls. The lights went out. Murphy was working overtime to prove his law. Five long seconds later they flickered back on.

My fingers slipped. Again. Finally, as the contraction eased, I got the cord loose and followed it down the length of the fetus as the tiny body was pushed out of its mother.

Lia screamed.

Trish and I caught the baby. A fetid scent filled the room. The baby was dead. Had been for a while. The afterbirth quickly followed, a gush of blood accompanying it. Panic shuddered through me. *How was I going to control this bleeding?*

"Blood hanging and running," a voice said beside me, "line opened wide. I'm going to put a pump on it."

"Start another unit," I grunted. The blood flow slowed as I watched. It was no longer bright red. It turned slightly darker as it emerged from Lia's body. Not arterial but there was a lot of it. Way too much... "Pitocin, ten units IV, ten units IM, and methergine, 0.2 mgs, IM,'' I said. The drugs would slow Lia's bleeding. I hoped.

"Bleeding's slowing,'' Trish said. I blew out a hard breath, feeling my heart slamming against my ribs.

"Pitocin's going,'' Anne said. "I'm going to see if I can stop Dr. Haynes. Doesn't look like we need him now. You want I should stop Dr. Statler, too?''

I checked Lia again, then removed my hand, the movements gentle, slow. The blood flow continued to decrease. I heaved a huge sigh of relief. "Yes, please,'' I said to Anne. "Things look fine here for the moment. Wallace, too. I think we've got it under control.'' It would have been a very different thing had the baby been alive and the blood arterial. I would have needed the extra hands. "Vitals.''

"Seventy-five over 50. Pulse 95 and dropping but strong. Respiration dropping, 27 right now,'' Trish said.

I bent over Lia, holding my hands to the side so the sight of blood wouldn't shock her. It looked like a lot of blood, even to me. "You awake, Lia?''

She nodded, the motion jerky and rough. A sob escaped her, as strangled as her breathing had been. "He's dead, isn't he?'' I hesitated for an instant. When I didn't answer she turned away.

I pulled the gloves off, hating the cowardice that seized me at her question. How do you tell a mother that her child is dead? "Vitals every fifteen, increase the fluids. Measure her output,'' I said to the nurses. I wanted to know if Lia's kidneys were functioning. "And get her some more heated blankets. I want her warm.''

Trish said, "Yes, Dr. Rhea.''

The bleeding had slowed dramatically. Lia's legs quivered with exhaustion, shock, and cold, as long tremors gripped her cramped muscles. Covering her with a blanket, I arranged it so that she was still exposed slightly. She was miserable, but her bleeding had to be monitored.

I stripped the blood-saturated gown from me. Removing

the plastic faceplate and walking to the far side of the make-shift birthing table, I sat beside the bed on a footstool, which brought my head to Lia's eye level.

"Lia?" She rolled her head away. I plunged in. God, I hated this. "Lia, you're right. Your baby didn't make it. I'm so sorry." Lia cried openly now, her sobs soft and broken. I took her hand, stroking the bruises that ran up her arms, indication that she had fought her manacles. "Lia," I said softly, slowly. "Your baby was a boy." She didn't respond. "I'm going to have the nurses clean you up now, and—" the name was gone "—your husband can come in for a while." I stood, not prepared for this sort of thing.

I had hated obstetrics as a med student. When other students came away gushing and excited at witnessing their first birth, I just remembered Miss DeeDee's comments about the birthing procedure. *"It is totally undignified and a sure indication that the Creator is indeed male. No female deity would have permitted such a painful atrocity."* Sometimes I even agreed with her.

"I want to see him. My baby."

Looking quickly at Trish before I answered, she shrugged. The look said she could make the baby look acceptable. "We'll need cultures," she said. She was telling me that the baby had been dead long enough to have bacteria growing on it.

Nodding at my patient, I said, "Give us a sec to clean him up, Mrs. Campbell. And to get your husband in here with you. You should be together right now."

Softly, for the nurse's ears alone, I added, "Do the cultures. And arrange to have a post done. When you clean up Lia, let's get a few cultures on her. I want to swab the cervix. Treat it as a wound, not just for GC. And see she gets a set of three sputum cultures. I don't like that cough. As soon as her husband has seen her and the baby, get me a chest X ray. I want to see it ASAP."

Trish nodded, writing on the bedsheet to keep up with

the list of orders. "And tell the lab if she's Rh-negative, I want her given a dose of Rhogam now, and retest her Rh in the morning for mixed field reaction. I don't want today to interfere with future pregnancies. Clean up her wounds and treat with antibacterial ointment."

"I'm Rh-positive," Lia said, her voice dull. I didn't respond and didn't change my orders. Sometimes a patient had no idea of her own blood type.

Moving up beside me, Anne began the tedious and delicate procedure of collecting the cultures and cleaning up the child for viewing. He would be washed, then wrapped in blue absorbent pads and blankets for the parents to hold. To begin the grieving process.

The door behind me opened. A deputy stuck his head inside and took in the room at a glance. My patient was still uncovered. *"Out!"* I said. He closed the door, his dark-skinned face reddening. Anne reopened the door and slipped in. "Sorry," she said, referring to the interruption.

As the door closed on the hallway I heard more voices and saw uniformed men. Zack had let patients into the other rooms. Deputies milled at the desk.

Going quickly to work, Anne washed Lia with a weak solution of betadine, and began the process of cleaning up the blood. Trish took vitals again. Her blood pressure was rising, and her pulse was steady at 82. I hadn't had time to notice that the heart monitor had been hooked up. Lia's heart rate was a neat, normal sinus rhythm. It looked like I could admit Lia to the medical-surgical wing instead of the ICU.

Mentally I went over the things I had done for my patient, and tossed the last pair of gloves into the biohazard trash. "Call me if you need me." Bending over Lia I said, "As soon as they can, the nurses will call your husband. You can see the baby together. Did you have a name picked out?"

"Melvin George Campbell III," she said softly.

I stroked her head. "That's a fine name. After his daddy?" She nodded, tears coursing into her hairline. "Everything feels fine inside of you. Of course, we'll have to have Dr. Geiger recheck you when she gets back in town, but I think you are physically healthy, Lia. I know it doesn't help right now, but you can have another baby. You can probably start trying in a few months."

"Thank you, Doctor."

Her tilted, dark eyes glistened with despair, bleak and empty; I felt something twist inside me at the sight. "I think it would be wise if you and your husband received counseling, too. You have been through a horrible time. Lost your baby. Think about it."

"We have a great preacher now. Not like the last one. He's a spirit-filled man of God. He can help us," she said.

"Good." I left the room, paused in the hallway and took a breath. What a night. Stepping around a bucket half filled with leaking rainwater, I went to the nurses' desk. The deputy who had stuck his head into the room turned quickly to me.

"Sorry, Doc. I didn't mean to—"

"It's all right, Steve." I made a point of learning every cop's name. I never knew when I might need one for something. It was a selfish attitude, but unruly, drunk or mentally ill patients, or patients who became violent following illegal drug use, were common and that meant I often needed the services of cops in their official capacity. "You can talk to her in a few minutes."

"We've called in the state cops, too. There will be a lot of SLED boys wanting to question her."

"Don't tire her out. If a nurse tells you to leave, do it or I'll bar you all from her room. Pass that along to the state boys, too. And why are you calling them in?"

"You ain't been keeping up with news, Doc?"

"Not lately," I admitted. I took the local paper, but the *Dawkins Herald* didn't offer much more than local reports.

The cost of hog feed. Farms going belly-up. Any law in state legislature or before Congress that might affect local farming or industry. There were four or five papers still rolled and rubber-banded on my kitchen table.

The deputy bent toward me. "There have been a series of hate crimes in Charlotte in the last few weeks. A neo-Nazi group moved in and has been attacking mixed-race couples like them. Beatings. A few rapes." Steve's voice was tight with anger. He stood flat-footed, a hand on his belt near his weapon. It was a stance I had learned to recognize during my tenure in ERs in various parts of the country. I watched his eyes, the hollow-eyed look of a man at war. "They drop them off at a desegregated Charlotte church, naked, bound and with the words 'Nigger lovers die' or 'Gook lovers die,' or whatever, spray-painted or written with indelible markers on their chests. This situation is close enough to fit a pattern."

"No six-sided stars, like a Star of David?"

"Seen a few, here and there. Sheriff's looking into it. Why?"

"My patients, the ones you came to take statements from, were forcibly tattooed."

The cop's dark eyes gleamed. "I'll let the sheriff know."

I patted Steve on the shoulder, preparing to go see Mel. I hated to tell him the news, but the sooner the better.

"The FBI was called in to Charlotte a couple days ago, too. They might have a few questions to ask. Especially after the lynching."

I turned back slowly, my hand frozen on the cop's shoulder. "Lynching?"

Steve nodded. "Oh, yeah. My daddy seen one back in '63 in Detroit. This was just like then. Black man hanging off Cutter's Bridge over Prosperity Creek." Steven's lips were hard. "Name of Leon Hawkins, local man. Good job, was in the armed forces, National Guardsman—in that unit with one of the new doctors, what's his name?" When no one answered, he said, "Got three kids, is a deacon in his church. Know him?"

I shook my head no, but turned and flipped quickly through the pile of patients' charts, looking for Regina's. And there it was. Regina Hawkins. *"I found him…. I found him hanging there."* Her husband hadn't committed suicide. He had been killed. Murdered. The fact buried itself in my midsection like a fist.

"'Course, we got the bastard that done it this time. Ain't so easy for a white man to get away with killing these days. We got brothers in law enforcement."

"Good," I said, forcing away the cold feeling that had knotted inside me. "I met his widow. She found him. Nobody deserves that kind of grief."

"Yeah, we got him. Richard Ellis is in the county lockup," a second voice said. "AWOL marine, recently joined a so-called survivalist 'Patriot' group in the southwest part of the county. Ellis ain't been in lockup ten minutes before two of his Aryan goons beat up a black kid. Had to be segregated to avoid a riot." The speaker wore deputy black and combat boots stained with mud. Muscles bulged against the sleeves of his uniform shirt and the neck opening over his tie, the kind of muscles created in a gym instead of by nature. Malcom Haskins glared at me, dark eyes hard.

"Patriot groups?" I asked.

"Thinly disguised white-power groups."

"I thought the KKK was kicked out of Dawkins County years ago."

"They were. But a rose by any other name still stinks of hate crimes," Malcom said. "There's a compound in the western part of the county that Ellis and some other white-power groups use as a training facility. Learning how to kill unarmed blacks in the name of self-defense. There's speculation that Ellis is a member of the Charlotte group, but the FBI hasn't found a tie-in."

"Shoulda left them Aryans mixed in," Steve said with a

tight grin. "Don't think they'd a lasted long. Saved the tax-payers some money."

"We had the FBI and a lieutenant from the Naval Investigative Service underfoot for two days to determine whether Ellis and his pals were part of the Charlotte group and they still got it all wrong. We coulda saved them the effort and just told 'em all these white-power groups got ties to one another. They splinter off constantly, like rotten wood. At least the NIS will take the sumbitch off our hands. Hope they hang his sorry ass, begging your pardon, Doc. Neo-Nazis every one."

"Yeah. Well, don't forget that not all whites are Nazis," I said dryly.

Malcom grinned with mischief. "You're all right, Doc. Ever date a black man?"

"Nope. Never had a black man look at me twice. Too skinny," I said without missing a beat. I had learned to hold my own with man-talk back in med school. A woman had to have certain skills to survive that experience.

"You come to lunch at my mama's on Sunday. She'll fatten you up. And my Arlana will find you a good man to warm your bed."

"*Your Arlana* would skin you alive if she heard you refer to her like that. And you tell your mama I'll take her up on the invitation anytime. Just call me."

"You best tell Arlana to keep her matchmaking skill to herself or you'll have Mark Stafford climbing your butt," Steve said. "'Sides. No need to waste time finding a good brother for the doctor. I'll volunteer anytime. I like a tall, bony woman what got no hair."

I sighed, a wry smile hovering at the corners of my mouth. "Thank you ever so much. I am truly flattered."

Both men laughed. I stand over five feet nine, with short black hair and black eyes. My best feature is my long legs. The "tall, bony woman what got no hair" comment wasn't far off the mark.

I entered Mel's room. This time I had a chart to look at, a proper chart with data on his condition. I was no longer flying blind. My patient, Melvin George Campbell Jr., was running a fever now, his temp at 101.2. Half hidden behind a privacy curtain, I watched him answer questions from Sheriff C. C. Gaskins and considered my patient. He and his wife had been in the creek all day. Hypothermia might have been covering some type of infection, something they may have picked up from the dirty water. I made a note to start prophylactic antibiotics on both.

"I couldn't tell what they looked like, Sheriff. They were all in masks. But I can tell you it was the same four each time. All white. All clean shaven. One had a scar on his mouth that curled up this way." Mel drew a line with his hand from the left tip of his lip to the middle of his nose. I wondered for a moment how he saw a scar if the men wore masks, but I had missed a large part of the narrative. "And we got names on each. Lia and I spent nights making it a point to remember as much as we could about each one of them. I wish we could tell you more."

"Be glad you never saw their faces, son. The fact that they wore masks at all meant that they hadn't made up their minds yet to kill you both," Gaskins said. "We'll get men to head upstream from the point where you got picked up, but Prosperity Creek is pretty well mapped out, and I can tell you right now there are half a dozen places could be like what you described. And with the smaller creeks that join in with Prosperity, we may never find it. Not unless you can give us more to go on."

I sat down on a stool in sight of the sheriff, who nodded at me. "I'll want to ask some questions of you both again later, especially about them tattoos the men put on you and your wife, but first, the doctor here wants to examine you." Mel turned his intense gaze on me.

"Not too many questions now, Sheriff, if you don't mind. Just the basics. They both need sleep and medication." I glanced at Mel and smiled. "Your wife is fine." A look of profound relief crossed his features before he closed his eyes. The action seemed to shut out the world for a moment.

"The baby?" Mel asked, opening his eyes, hope mirrored there like a blue sky.

I shook my head, the sick feeling settling deep inside me again. Why had I ever wanted to become a doctor? "He didn't make it," I said gently. "I'm sorry, Mel. But Lia is fine. Physically a little battered up, like yourself, but she will heal. I know it doesn't help now, but you *can* have other children later on."

Mel murmured "Thank you." For some reason the gratitude disconcerted me. I hadn't done much. They had saved themselves from a horrible experience, one I had heard only bits and pieces of. Awkwardly, I again patted his hand.

"I've recommended counseling for both of you. You went through a lot in the last few days." I turned to the sheriff. "I need to admit both patients. You want to sit a deputy on them, in case someone nasty finds out that they're here?"

The sheriff nodded, stroking his chin. "I'll leave Malcom with them, but I got to say, it's possible we already got most of the men involved in lockup."

"Richard Ellis?"

Gaskins nodded. "And most of his Patriot group. That might be why the ones who kidnapped them didn't leave a guard on these two. Because they all ended up in jail. But I won't take no chances. They'll have protection."

"Good. I'll put them in a semiprivate room together to save you using two deputies. And do me a favor, Sheriff Gaskins? Tell the state cops to heed the nurses. If I say rest and no questions, I mean it. These people are exhausted. You can question Mel all you want in the ER. Once they get to a room I want them left alone. You can talk to them both in depth tomorrow."

The sheriff flashed his political mile-wide smile and

winked at Mel. "Never piss off medical people. They say jump and I say 'How high, ma'am?'"

"Exactly," I said. "You never know when I'll be the one digging a bullet out of your backside, and you want me to use plenty of painkiller."

4

I GOT SOME LUNGS—YOU'LL HEAR ME

When I stepped out of Mel's room, I spotted Douglas Byars, the doctor on call to admit medically unassigned patients. His hair was plastered to his skull, his clothes damp. It was pretty clear that Douglas hadn't used an umbrella. I was still a bit damp myself from standing under the ambulance hood. He lifted a hand to motion me over and ended a conversation with the cops. While Steve and Malcom put their heads together and conferred, Douglas picked up a chart. It was Lia Campbell's.

"Nice storm," he said, by way of greeting. "I parked up next to your BMW to keep my van from floating downstream. And it's a *heavy* mother."

"I thought about tying my car off to the maple tree but didn't have enough rope. What brought you in?"

Douglas wiped a trickle of rainwater running across his brow and shook it off onto the floor. There was a small puddle at his feet. "Stream behind my house is way up and the phone lines are down. Emily and the kids are at her mother's in Tallahassee, so I thought I'd bunk in here tonight in case I was needed. I have flood insurance, and if the house floats away, at least I'll be safe. Who do I see about getting a room?"

"Trish can handle it for you. She's in with your patient." I nodded to the chart.

"They tell me this—" he paused, as if searching for a word for a moment "—situation…may be racially motivated. Cops finish talking to them yet?"

"No. She's pretty banged up."

"Kidnapping and torture?" His voice was disbelieving. "Why?"

"Shackle and ligature marks on ankles and wrists. Defensive bruising on arms and hands. Abrasions and bruising consistent with prolonged assault. They say it lasted about four days. My guess is that her baby has been dead about that long, but I've ordered a post mortem to be sure. And your female patient has a nasty cough, maybe resulting from being in the creek for hours. As to why? The couple is racially mixed—the woman is part Asian."

Douglas shook his head, still skeptical.

"This doesn't look like something they conjured up, Douglas. I have to say it looks like the real thing."

Douglas sighed. "We never had things like this in Dawkins County when I was growing up. Even desegregation went smoothly. I just don't understand."

"That's 'cause you're white, Doc. We see it all the time," Steve said, leaning across the nurses' desk. "And the lynching on Cutter's Bridge is part of it."

"I thought the state police ruled that an isolated incident, not a hate crime," Douglas said, tucking the chart under his arm.

"Like I said. You're white. You don't see it like black folk do."

Cutting in before the conversation became counterproductive, I offered to go over Lia and Mel Campbell's charts before I saw the other patients who were waiting. Douglas and I spent a few minutes covering the events of the last hour. I suggested an antibiotic for Lia and left the two in his hands. Picking up the rest of the charts, I went to work.

I had a kid with a sore throat and a drunk someone had picked up on the side of the road and brought to the hospital. I sent the child home with Tylenol and Robitussin, over-the-counter medicines the child's mother could have used and saved a trip to the ER. The drunk I handed over to the cops. His blood alcohol was 252, more than two and half times the legal limit. High enough to be arrested, not so high I had to admit and watch him. I had no compassion for drunks. My mother's drunken binges had taught me well.

As I worked, my faint nausea began to dissipate. Having patients I could actually help eased the sick sense of worthlessness and uselessness that had gripped me when I delivered the stillborn child.

In a treatment room waited Shareeka Warden, my third patient since the birth. She was a three-year-old, mixed-race child with beautiful dark skin, huge green eyes, and kinky, curly blond hair who showed symptoms of bronchitis. Her Caucasian mother, who looked no more than sixteen, was holding her, patting her back with one hand while holding an O_2 mask to the child's face with the other, trying to help her breathe.

The child had been waiting for more than an hour while I dealt with the more critical patients. Zack had ordered X rays, a complete blood count to rule out sepsis, and turned on the oxygen. The pulse-oximeter on the child's finger showed both pulse rate and oxygen levels were normal. I signed the orders as if they had been mine from the beginning. It wasn't standard procedure, but then, nothing about tonight was.

I checked the chart, read the CBC results, which were nonremarkable and listened to Shareeka's chest. Looking at the X rays, which did not show pneumonia, I asked the mother a few questions. The child's address was the women's shelter in Ford County. When I asked her mother about the address, she told me she had been forced to move out.

"The people was nice and all to me in the shelter, but they can't let no one stay more than fifteen days. I couldn't find me a place by then so I had to leave." She patted her daughter on the back, her hand moving gently on the child's warm skin. "My mama said I could stay with her, but she done changed her mind. The street ain't so bad," she assured me, "till the storm, and then Shareeka got so sick. It's warm outside and all. And last night I found us a warehouse we can stay at, with a creek behind where I can get bathwater for Shareeka and me. They some good people there, too, staying with us."

I had a feeling that anyone who didn't turn this child-mother away was considered good people. "There's nothing I can do about finding you a place to stay tonight," I said, watching her pale, blunt fingers comb through the kinky curls, "but I figure I can find a reason for you to remain in the ER until the storm blows over and social services can be contacted. You may have to wait in the lobby, but you'll be dry and safe and can catch a few winks on the chairs." I wasn't sending them back out into this storm. Ms. Warden appeared immensely relieved and thanked me. I wanted to ask how old she was, but didn't. That was a situation for social services.

It seemed like a straight-up diagnosis requiring antibiotics and a breathing treatment, but as I wrote orders on the patient's chart, Shareeka's breathing suddenly grew labored and her lips began to turn blue. At first there was just a tinge of gray, then a strangled breath later, they were almost purple. The tiny pulse-ox showed O_2 levels dropping alarmingly fast.

"Doctor?" Ms. Warden said, alarmed.

Quickly, I pushed her aside and pressed the bell of the stethoscope to the child's chest. I heard rales, a soft, wet flutter of lungs filling up with fluid. Only moments before the lungs had sounded clear. Now Shareeka was short of breath, wheezing, diaphragm retracting to drag in air. The change was remarkable. I had never seen SOB hit so fast.

I turned up the O_2, took the mask from Ms. Warden's hands and replaced it on her child's face. Shareeka began to breathe easier as the increased oxygen did its job. "Hold the mask firmly in place," I instructed the shaky mother. "You're doing fine." Opening the door to the hallway, I yelled, "Zack! Get me a repeat chest X ray and arterial blood gasses. And get Respiratory Therapy down here. I want a breathing treatment *now*."

Returning to the stretcher, I watched her breathe. I didn't like the look of the toddler, but had to wait for the X ray to determine a diagnosis. We had no acute care pediatric ward in Dawkins, and there was no way to fly anyone out tonight. It looked like my night for problem situations.

As the pessimistic thought settled into me, the lights went out again, going through a syncopated flash sequence before the power was restored. In the dark, I could hear my patient's rasping breath. It sounded frighteningly obstructed.

After ten minutes on oxygen and with breathing treatment going, Shareeka seemed to stabilize. I left her with the respiratory therapist and Dora Lynn, the X ray tech. "Get me that chest film as soon as the treatment has stopped, and call me if there's a change in her condition," I said.

"Don't worry about that. I'll holler," Dora Lynn said. "I got some lungs. You'll hear me. Come on, baby, you sweet thing, we'll see what's happening inside you, yes we will. Come on, Mama, you come help us push her stretcher down and hold her still."

I liked Dora Lynn. She was fast and competent and had a way with kids. But I could hear Shareeka wheeze as they went up the hall. Then she coughed, a long moist sound. Like the sound of wet linen being torn. I stared after her, puzzled at the sound.

My last patient was one Shackleford Lamb Sexton, referred to by one and all as the Reverend Lamb. He had cut his hand on a chain saw, moving a fallen tree off a roof on his new "Lamb of God" complex out near I-77.

I blotted the preacher's left hand on sterile cloths and looked it over. "He'll need a few stitches. Ethilon," I added, asking for the type of suture material I wanted, "and clean it up a bit more, if you don't mind, Zack. Anyone ever tell you to stay out of storms, Reverend?" I asked as I pulled back against the edges of the wound. It was a ragged laceration across the palm of the hand, but there appeared to be no nerve or tendon damage.

"The Lord looks after his own, Dr. Lynch," he said. "I fear no wind when the Lord is with me. For the Lord will send angels to carry me and minister unto me in time of peril."

"Uh-huh," I said, turning the hand over one last time. "Flex," I commanded. "And did He feel it necessary to tell folks to go inside when it's raining and blowing seventy-mile-an-hour gusts out? I think there's an old saying—'Fools rush in where angels fear to tread.'" I looked up at the man for the first time. He didn't look like a preacher, in jeans and plaid work shirt, sleeves rolled to his elbows. He had a stubble of beard, mud-smeared work boots, and a mass of curly red chest hair through which a gold chain peeked. Except for the fanatical gleam in his eye, he looked like a lumberjack going through a midlife crisis.

"I am indeed a fool for the Lord, Doctor. Have you ever seen my television show, *The Lamb of God?*"

It sounded like the religious babble my mother had listened to while she sat in a drunken stupor and pickled herself to death. I smiled tightly, said I would be back in a few minutes, and left the Lamb of God to Zack.

Out in the hallway, Sheriff Gaskins and half a dozen cops stood, most holding cups of coffee, gathered around the nurses' desk. Retreating to the break room for a caffeine jolt, I poured a cup of fresh brew, added two packets of sugar and a dollop of whole milk from the fridge. Stirring it with the communal spoon, I drank down half. It scalded my tongue and tasted like charred tree bark. I wondered which cops had finished off my pot of raspberry-and-cream coffee.

"Doc, you got a minute?"

I sat and offered the sheriff the other high-backed chair. Sheriff Gaskins was the highest elected law enforcement official in the county. A politician through and through, he knew how to kiss babies and press the flesh with the best of them. A good ol' boy from way back. I had always wondered, however, how he got elected, what with the nose hair sprouting from his nostrils. Dark and coarse as nettles, it drew the eye like a three-car pileup on a highway. I always had to force my gaze to remain at eye level.

Gaskins settled into the chair with a sigh and pushed the door closed behind him. I sipped the coffee and waited, surprised at his need for privacy.

"These two who claim they were held captive. You believe them? I mean, the whole entire story?" He clasped his hands across his stomach, looking relaxed yet concerned. Perhaps I was a tad cynical, but it looked like a well-rehearsed bit of body language. Campaign trail choreography.

"Yes. Why?"

Gaskins sighed again. I had the feeling he used that sigh as a political move, but I didn't rise to the bait. I sipped the coffee and waited, offering nothing.

"Well, their stories don't match. Not exactly."

"How so?"

"He says, she says, you know?" When it was clear that I didn't, Gaskins went on. "He says there were four, all masked. She says there were three most of the time, four some of the time, and one took his mask off. He says they went by names of Bill, Jessie, Stew and Ace. She says two had different names, and it was a fifth man who tattooed them both. He says they never got a close look at them. She says they all had blond flat tops. Now, how did she see that if they wore masks? He says they never left the shack where they were kept. She says the men let them out late on the second day and made them clean out the buckets they used to…uh…relieve themselves in. Only thing they both agree on is that the shack was one room with a dirt floor and the place stank, depending on which way the wind blew."

"They've been through a lot, Sheriff."

"Real bad stink." He looked up at me, nose hair twitching. I didn't know whether he meant the place where the couple had been held, or the stink of the mismatched stories. Finally he said, "I reckon they have. And then again, maybe not. I got enough trouble in this county without some kids making up stories based on troubles taking place in the jail and in Charlotte."

I lifted an eyebrow. "Ligature marks, location of defensive wounds, signs of methodical torture. The woman lost her baby. The six-sided stars tattooed on their chests indicative of racially motivated beatings. They clearly were battered. Kept manacled for several days. Their body temps were abnormally low, in keeping with the part about spending the day in a creek. They didn't do it themselves. They were systematically beaten and tortured. What else would you call it, Sheriff?"

"Now don't go getting riled, Doc."

"I'm not *riled,* Sheriff," I lied. "And I don't see what their ages has to do with it." Abruptly, I understood what the sheriff's problem *really* was. I should have been polite but I was tired, and so charged in with both feet. If I was wrong, I could apologize later.

"You might want to take this situation seriously, Sheriff. If your local situation turns out to be tied in with the Charlotte situation, deal with it. You'll still be the sheriff when all the feds go home." Mama was likely turning over in her grave, and Miss DeeDee probably woke up with indigestion. I could hear them both now. *"A lady would never chastise a person in authority....''* Well, I didn't feel like a lady. I felt like a doctor who had seen several patients, all suffering the violence of racism.

"If this is a hate crime and you do nothing, the media will be all over you. I can see the headlines now. 'Dawkins County Sheriff Has Racial Problems' would be the most polite.'' The grocery store checkout tabloids would put it "Redneck Sheriff's Racial Hatred,'' but I kept that one to myself.

C. C. Gaskins turned a bit red in the face for a moment, pursed his lips and looked at me under bushy brows. "There *have* been a few tattoos like that star showing up in the jail for the last couple months. A couple stories about beatings in DorCity.'' I could tell he was deciding whether he would accept what I had said or offer argument. "Humph,'' he said at last.

"Exactly,'' I agreed.

5

THE LAMB OF GOD

I finished my coffee and ate a bagel I found in the freezer. It was freezer-burned and stale, but a generous spoonful of strawberry cream cheese made it palatable. I had left the bagel there weeks ago; I had no idea who had left the cream cheese, but I taped two quarters to the lid to pay for my theft. A fresh cup of coffee in my hand, I walked up the hall to X ray. My films should be ready.

Douglas Byars was standing in the darkened X ray office, one hand on his chin, the other wrapped around his skinny waist. "You see these?" he asked, pointing to the films.

"Not yet. What've we got?"

"Lia Campbell. Look at her lungs."

I stepped in front of the view box and studied the chest X ray carefully. There were dark and light patches on the film, and long filamentlike shadows that had no correlation with normal lung tissue. Both lungs were filled with fluid and signs of infection, a clotted-cream mass that would surely be fatal if not corrected in hours.

"Tuberculosis?" I asked. I had been right on top of the woman, breathing in her aspirates and any contagion she might have.

"I ordered a set of AFB cultures and a stat AFB stain, but I imagine it will be morning before I get that. The lab is backed up pretty badly and the third-shift guy can't get in at all. I don't know what this thing is, but I want a stat gram stain as soon as I have a fresh sample."

I understood why Douglas wanted an AFB work-up. The X rays could have come from a case of untreated, end-stage tuberculosis, a disease isolated by AFB—acid-fast-bacilli—testing. "Looks like something out of a Third World country," I said.

"Doesn't it," Douglas said, his expression hidden in the dark of the room. "I decided to leave the Campbells together in the same room for now because they've been together all along. Whatever she has, he probably does, too."

I nodded, agreeing that sometimes the emotional needs of a patient outweighed the standard medical precautions.

"They need each other tonight," Douglas added, "but come morning I'm separating them. Maybe put her in isolation. Meanwhile, I've changed her antibiotic cocktail." He handed me Lia's chart and I scanned the list of antibiotics. Levaguin topped the list.

"I had the nurses clean that tattoo wound on her chest," he continued. "The infection is worse than it looked. I ordered wound cultures and dressing changes...." Douglas paused. "When you were in the delivery, did you see the boils around her vulva?"

I looked at him quickly. "No. But there was an awful lot of blood." I thought quickly back to the moment when Trish had adjusted the light in our makeshift delivery room. In the few moments when there had been decreased blood flow, I had seen nothing that I would have classified as boils. "Douglas, I'm sure I didn't see anything like that."

"Well, she has them now. Started small, but they seem to grow as you watch them."

A dark shadow appeared at the doorway. It was Dora Lynn, with a sheaf of films in one hand. "You need to see these, Doc." Something in her tone alerted me and I took Shareeka Warden's chest X rays with a feeling of trepida-

Gwen Hunter

tion. "You might want to stick around," she added to Byars.

Shoving the films into the bare space in the lighted view box, I scanned the films. The sense of trepidation became pure dread. I didn't know what I had here, but I didn't like the look of it.

"Huh. Looks just like the picture of my patient," Douglas began, but a commotion interrupted him.

Out in the hallway stood the Reverend Lamb, one hand on Shareeka's chest, the injured one held in the air, praying loudly. "Oh *Gowud,* hear this, your *ser*vant. *Heeeal* this child, this innocent one, so abused by the evil of the world." The preacher had stopped Zack, blocking the stretcher on which Shareeka lay, and started what looked like a healing service in the hallway. "The *mixed* blood of her *unmarried* parents has brought her—"

"Hey. Lamb!" Ms. Warden said. "What you doin' with my baby!"

I moved quickly to the stretcher, intercepting just as Shareeka's mother arrived.

"You get away from my baby. Take your hands offa her!"

"But I'm only praying for her to be hea—"

"I said, you get your hands offa her! You done had one chance to help with my baby. When I came to you for help, you turn me down! You and your pure—"

"Ms. Warden, Reverend Lamb—" I started.

"Reverend, my white ass! Him with his 'purity of the races' and putting down folk don't believe like him! You tell him to get his hands offa her. He ain't nothin' but trouble."

Shareeka coughed, the now familiar sound of tearing wet linen, and with a retching sound, deposited a blob of blood-streaked mucous on the Reverend's curly chest hair. Shareeka started screaming, her airway cleared. Her mother grabbed her up, running into the treatment room, and Zack turned quickly away, his face suffused with laughter.

It was all I could do not to join him. Byars, beside me, had no such compunction and chuckled softly. The Reverend Lamb of God glared, turned a dozen shades of red, all in the beet family, bent over and shook the blob off his chest, gagging as he did. With no other words he was gone, out into the storm, his untreated, lacerated hand of no consideration at all.

"Seems like the Rev draws the line of Christian charity at hockers." Douglas said.

"Wimp," Zack said, wiping the bloody mass off the tile.

"Douglas," I said, interrupting their sophomoric comments, "I don't like the sound of her cough. It sounds just like the Campbell girl's. Come see this."

I led him back to the darkened office and pointed to Shareeka's X rays, placed beside Lia Campbell's. "This is that child's films taken not fifteen minutes ago. These are the previous ones."

"Okay. So she has pneumonia now."

"In two hours? Zack ordered them while I delivered your other patient's fetus."

"Somebody must of screwed up. Look here and here." He pointed to two hazy whitish patches on the newest set of X rays. "This didn't develop that quickly. It's not possible."

"*Dr. Rhea!*" The alarm in Anne's voice was unmistakable. I sprinted down the hall to Shareeka's room, Douglas close on my heels. In the treatment room water poured in a strong stream through the lighting fixture into the bucket. The lights flickered again.

Shareeka lay gasping. "I want Respiratory down here again *stat* for another treatment, 100 percent O_2, and get ready to bag her," I said. The child was blue, and when I touched her she was on fire, her pulse weak and far too fast. Anne slapped a mask over Shareeka's face and the soft hiss of oxygen came on. The child's mother was crying, both hands over her mouth in panic. Suddenly, Shareeka's breathing stopped altogether.

Anne punched the ambu bag onto the mask and pressed several times, trying to force air into the child. "Nothing," she said. "Nothing's going in."

I took Shareeka's head in my hands and tilted it back, forcing open her mouth. I could see no obvious obstruction. "Intubate?" I asked.

"Let's do it," Douglas said.

I picked up the child and together we ran to the trauma room. Shareeka's young mother screamed after us, an agonized sound, shut off by the trauma room door.

Anne directed the overhead directional light at the child's head. Zack opened a child's ET kit as Anne slapped leads on Shareeka's chest for a heart tracing. "I haven't tubed a kid this small since residency," Douglas said, referring to the process of putting a breathing tube down a patient's throat, past the vocal cords, into place deep in the chest.

We would have to rearrange for me to do it. There wasn't time. I nodded at him. "Go for it."

Quickly I extended the child's neck, her head tilted back at the requisite angle. Douglas placed the laryngoscope blade into her throat. The stiff metal implement wasn't sharp, looking more like an elongated shoehorn than a knife as it disappeared into her throat. With a quick, practiced flip of his wrist, Douglas inserted it fully. "Got it," he said, wonderingly. I offered him the suction tube and he pushed it through. "Suction." Then, "Nothing's happening."

"Sorry, Doc." Zack turned a small knob on the wall. "Now?" he asked. The suction began to gurgle, removing the sputum clogging the child's airway. The substance was thick, the sound almost ratcheting. Blood and thick pus bubbled up through the tube.

Douglas ran the suction tube up and down inside the ET tube. The child's entire chest was clogged. I glanced at the pulse-ox. The readings were horrid. Suddenly the suction was clear, sucking air instead of sputum. "Yes!" he said.

"O_2 at a hundred percent, a set of blood gasses, and get that child's ambu bag Anne had," I said, watching for movement of Shareeka's chest. It remained still.

"Coming."

I heard doors opening and closing, plastic wrappers ripping, and felt drafts around my ankles as the RNs moved. Anne shoved the smaller ambu attachment onto the ET tube and began to squeeze the bag, forcing air into the child's lungs. The respiratory therapist appeared and took over bagging as enough hands for the emergency arrived after the fact.

"Sorry, Doc," she said, picking up the pulse-ox. "I had a patient with—"

"Don't worry about it," I interrupted. "Let's get a treatment," I told her. "And what does the pulse-ox show?"

"Not good," she said. "Seventy-two percent." My patient's oxygen levels should have been at or near ninety-nine percent.

I checked my watch. I guesstimated it had been about two and half minutes since the child last had air. We were reaching a critical time for brain damage, and as I watched the monitor and the movement of the child's chest, the number on the pulse-ox went up. Seventy-five percent. Then seventy-eight. "Nice job on the tubing, Douglas."

He held out his hands for my inspection. They were shaking. "You're the ER doc. Why didn't you do that?"

"You were at the head of the bed. Luck of the draw."

I watched the child's color. Watched for any sign of spontaneous respiration. Still none. "It's awfully stiff," the RT said. Little air was making it into the lungs.

Douglas listened to the child's chest. "Really poor air sounds."

I repositioned the ET tube.

"Got it." After a moment, Douglas said, "Good air

sounds on the right. Still poor on the left. We need an X ray for placement.''

"Called for one already," Zack said, as he pulled aside Shareeka's diaper. "You want to draw the gasses?''

I nodded and took the small plastic syringe in my right hand, the alcohol swab in my left. Carefully, I wiped the child's groin area and placed my left fingers over the femoral pulse. It was dangerously fast. I glanced at the heart monitor. Her rate was 183. By feel, I isolated the artery and inserted the needle. Bright red blood instantly filled the syringe, which I handed off to a technician to run as I applied pressure to the puncture site.

"We have spontaneous respiration. Look. There.'' Douglas said. The child was indeed trying to breathe on her own. Between pumps of the ambu bag, the tiny chest tried to lift. As I watched, Shareeka began to pinken up, and the pulse-oximeter read eighty-two percent. Air was getting to her lungs and heart and starting to reoxygenize her body.

I sighed with relief. Of course, the hard part now was the decision of whether to put the child on a respirator. We had no Peds ICU. Children in this condition were routinely flown out of the county to Spartanburg or Carolinas Medical in Charlotte. I had to speak to Shareeka's mother. I could hear her sobbing in the hallway.

A tech handed me the test results from the blood I had drawn. They were horrible, but since Shareeka was breathing now, they seemed irrelevant. I nodded and handed them back. "Thanks.''

Douglas sighed and pulled a three-legged stool beneath him, half sitting, his legs outstretched. His tension was almost palpable. "I'll start a line,'' he said. "You got me an IV tray?'' Anne passed him a yellow tray with a handle in the center; it was filled with needles, syringes, Jelcos, and other paraphernalia. Bending over the child's arm, he tied on a tourniquet and began to search for a vein.

"It's getting hard to bag her again,'' the RT said. I

watched the woman's hands. They were straining as they pushed the small bag closed, forcing air into the child's lungs. I lifted a tiny foot and checked the temp and color. Blue and hot, which was weird in itself. I expected blue and cold. Again, I didn't like the look of things. The child's pupils were equal and a little sluggish, her reflexes hyper.

As Douglas searched for an IV site in one arm and Anne in the other, I listened again to Shareeka's chest sounds. I could hear thick mucous move in both chest and airway. Her heart rate was too rapid to get an accurate count, but the heart monitor now estimated it around 225. SVT—supraventricular tachycardia.

"She could be hyperkalemic," I said. "I want new blood gasses, a chem-seven, and a sputum culture with a stat gram stain. We need to know what's causing this.

"Zack, get on the phone to Spartanburg. Let's see if we have a bed there. Call the highway patrol and see if they can provide us a way to the county line on good roads and handle a relay on to Spartanburg. If anyone knows which roads are clear it would be them."

Anne suctioned as I spoke. The sputum was bloodier. She pulled a small bit out, placed it in a sterile plastic collection tube, and passed it off to a lab tech who had materialized at my elbow. "*Stat* like yesterday on that gram stain. And I want to see it." She nodded and left. "Douglas? Any luck?"

"Not much," he muttered, head bent over the small arm. "One tiny vein. Maybe. But even if I get it, drawing blood may ruin it."

"Nothing here," Anne said. I glanced at the monitor. The heart rate was still high at 247. The information from the other machines was no better.

"Yes!" Douglas said, looking up from her hand. He had hit the small vein on his first attempt.

"You should have gone into pediatric medicine," I said.

"I did. Did two years of residency until I got my wife pregnant. Had to stop."

"Now he tells me. So much for griping about the ET tube," I added, quickly attempting another femoral stick for the blood gasses.

Douglas shrugged and drew off three CCs of blood before taping the line in place and starting the fluids. "It's been a few years."

"An escort with the ambulance might be a good idea. Douglas, I'll go with them if you'll cover here for me. Money's good." I handed off the blood gas syringe to an empty hand.

He laughed. "I haven't covered an ER since my student days. I'm a little rusty."

"Not to judge by that tubing."

"I did do a fine job, didn't I? But you're right. We can't keep her here. I'll flip you for the honor."

Fresh hands took over the job of pumping the ambu bag. A strip of paper was thrust into my hand. The blood gas results. The patient was slightly acidotic, her pH too low, her carbon dioxide too high. No big surprise.

Behind me a portable X-ray machine whirred into the room. I slipped into a lead apron provided by the X-ray tech and moved out of the way. Within seconds, we had an X ray of Shareeka's chest, but it would have to be developed. That meant time, and time was not something this child had. What had caused her to digress from a happy bouncing baby with a little fever and a slight shortness of breath to this flaccid thing with lungs like an end-stage tuberculin patient of the 1800s? All in a matter of less than two hours?

"We got problems." Douglas pointed to the heart monitor.

The SVT had disappeared from the screen. There had been a sudden drop in heart rate and the child now was in a ventricular rhythm of 150. As I watched, the rate dropped quickly—120…100…90. "We need to shock her," Douglas said.

"I'm having trouble here," the new RT said. "Nothing's going in."

"She's going to code," I said wonderingly.

"Doc," Zack said, his head in the doorway. "Lab called. Said the potassium was 7.8. They are repeating but—"

The sound of the heart monitor alarm cut him off. Asystole Flatline.

The record later showed that we had shocked Shareeka twelve times. I officially called the code at 11:23 p.m. Shareeka Warden was dead.

With the back of my wrist, I scrubbed the hair off my forehead and turned away from the small body. A bad case of the "If only's" set in immediately. If only I had allowed Haynes to be brought to the hospital. If only I had started Shareeka on IV antibiotics the moment I saw her second chest film. If only I hadn't laughed along with the others when the child spit on the Reverend Lamb. If only I didn't have to walk out that door and tell her child-of-a-mother that her daughter had died in my hands. A slow anger began to burn but I quickly damped it. The ER was no place for a doctor to lose control.

"I want a postmortem. Call in the pathologist and get it done in the morning. I don't care if he did intend to take a four-day weekend, I want this PM right away."

"He's out of town already, Doc. Left right after work. I have an on-call man from Newberry who can maybe come in tomorrow, if the roads are clear," Amanda said softly, her eyes on the still form before us. Dressed in purple surgical scrubs, her blond hair pulled back in a ponytail, Amanda crossed her arms and shook her head as if denying the sight of the dead child. "I have a grandkid about her age."

"We did everything…everything we could, Rhea,"

Douglas said, stripping off his gloves with a muted snap. "We both saw the X rays. Whatever acted on this child, it was fast. And for all we know she was immuno-compromised. Amanda, do we have enough blood in the lab to do an HIV tomorrow?"

"Can do." She turned away from the child and passed me a sheet of computer paper. "You got a gram positive cocci and four-plus white cells in the sputum."

"Could it be strep pneumo?" I asked. Streptococcus pneumonia was the causative agent in many sudden-onset pneumonia deaths. Jim Henson, the creator of the Muppets, was said to have died of pneumonia from this fast-acting bacterium. It was relatively easy to spot on a gram stain— the little, purple-staining, round bacteria all appeared in pairs and were bullet-shaped.

"No bullets, Doc. And all appear singly."

"I want to see the smear," I said, "as soon as I talk to her mother."

I washed my hands free of the blood that had become smeared on them during the code. I hadn't worn gloves. There had not been time. Blood deeply lined the crevices of my fingerprints, thicker in the cuticles. I remembered Douglas's comment about HIV and checked for minute cuts and tears in my flesh as I soaked. My skin looked fine, but I couldn't get all the child's blood off my hands. Finally I gave up and smeared cream on my rough skin.

Weariness and defeat settled about my shoulders like a shroud. I had lost her.... Defeat was a familiar feeling, one that haunted me any time I had to tell a patient's family that my efforts hadn't been enough. That I hadn't been able to play God and bring the dying back to life. The last year felt like a series of failures, one after another, dominoes falling through the months. Personally, professionally—in every area, there were gaps that stood out, dark shadows in my memory. Now, for the second time in one night, I had failed. "God, I'm getting maudlin."

"Ma'am?"

"Nothing, Zack. Would you put Ms. Warden in my office, and then clean up the body as much as you can. She'll want to see her daughter." I knew the tubes and IVs would have to remain in place. They were part of the postmortem. But at least the blood the child had coughed up at the last could be washed away or covered with sheets.

Zack nodded, opened the door and went out into the hallway. I could hear the soft sobs of the distraught mother. *She knew.* They always seemed to know. And then she seemed to strangle on something. She started coughing. Once again I heard the distinct sound of wet linen tearing and I knew my night of dealing with horror wasn't over.

I told Donnalaura Warden her daughter had died, and admitted her to ICU after looking at a set of chest films. They were patchy with fluid and the strange filamentous shadows we had seen in her daughter's X rays. Douglas Byars and I came up with an antibiotic cocktail strong enough to kill off anything known to man, had it mixed in the pharmacy, and started it on Donnalaura and on Lia Campbell and her husband, who were both coughing and experiencing shortness of breath. Outside, the storm continued to rage, the creeks to rise and winds to blow. The lights still flickered, the tinny sound of water falling into pails odd in the medical environment.

My feeling of dread and exhaustion were smothering. Although I had done all I could, I knew that I had not done enough. In my heart, I feared that not all of the patients I had admitted would survive. Whatever bug this was, it was nasty.

6

By 1:00 a.m. I had cleaned out the ER, seen a total of eleven patients for a variety of complaints, three of them MVAs, car accident victims. Joy-riding idiots had ended up wrapped around a tree, three feet into a stream that had outgrown its flood-level banks. It relieved my sense of apprehension to tell the driver that he was more dense than the tree he'd hit. If I could have put "general stupidity" down as his diagnosis, I would have, but such plain talk is frowned upon in medical circles. I like to think he left my ER a pained but wiser man. I refused him painkillers for his battered body. He'd been drinking so I had a sound medical reason. It still felt good.

I had just finished the last lecture when the phone rang. Someone called out that it was for me. Like most people, any time the phone rings after midnight, I get edgy. Ready for something bad to have happened. Ready for fearful words of dread. To catch my breath, I poured a cup of coffee and sat before answering.

"This is Rhea Lynch."

"Rhea dear. So good to hear your voice." I sucked down a boiling mouthful of coffee. Choked on a strangled expletive. Coughed. Tears gathered as I tried to catch my breath. It was Miss DeeDee, her tone dulcet over the snapping and popping of the wind-damaged lines. "Are you all right, dear?"

Thoughts flashed across my mind like overlaid transparencies in a *Gray's Anatomy*. *Did she climb over the wall and escape?* But Miss DeeDee would never do anything so uncouth as to possibly expose her backside to the help. What idiot had let her get to a phone? She was supposed to be heavily medicated and under lockdown in the state mental ward, not free to roam. *Had she tried to find Marisa?* I had not been far off the mark with the dreaded expectations.

"Miss DeeDee?" I asked, knowing it was she, but still choked on coffee and the sound of her voice. "Who let you use the phone this late?"

"Good *evening,* Rhea dear." Miss DeeDee was nothing if not proper. I sloshed hot coffee onto the tender patch of skin between thumb and index finger at the reminder.

"Good evening, Miss DeeDee," I said, hissing with pain, still coughing, punished and prodded into my manners, a young girl again at Miss DeeDee's social graces lessons. But this time I was grown, and a flare of anger rose in me as I found my voice. I didn't much care if she heard my hostility, either, a sure breach of proper etiquette. "How...*interesting* that you called. Rather late for a *social* call," I said, not above a little social-graces-needling myself. "How are you?" I put the cup down and sucked at the scalded skin. The patch was red but not bad enough to need treatment.

"I'm quite well, dear. And in answer to your question, just the most darling young man let me phone out. Theodore Jamal Green is his name, and he is putting himself through medical school on loans and work here. I'm going to help him, secure his loans, that sort of thing, just as I did for you."

"How much did he lose to you?" I asked dryly. Miss DeeDee had a gift with cards and poker. She could beat anyone anytime, and she was a master at sleight of hand. In other words, she could cheat like a pro.

Miss DeeDee chuckled, her own voice as dry as mine. "One must not bury one's talents under the sand, Rhea dear."

"Mmm," I said, committing to nothing, sipping coffee delicately over my blistered throat and waiting. Miss DeeDee would not waste a precious, illicit phone call on Theodore Jamal's future plans, no matter how wonderful he was. Unless he was in hock to her for several thousand and he was paying off his debts by the minute. Feeling catty, I asked, "Do they let people in the loony bin secure loans?"

The silence on the other end of the phone was frigid, if short-lived. Miss DeeDee had a purpose and couldn't risk me hanging up on her, so she ignored my jibe. "I called hoping you could assist me in a small endeavor."

I knew it was silly, but I turned the receiver and looked at it as if it were crazy. "Assist you?" I repeated. "Me?" Miss DeeDee, after all, had tried to kill me....

"Yes, dear." Miss DeeDee paused, a tone I had never heard before entering her voice. I couldn't identify it over my own incredulity. "I have an opportunity to move into a private hospital, a very nice one with whirlpool baths in the rooms, mattresses without crinkled plastic covers, real linen, and a three-star chef. But the judge is not going to be very agreeable without your assent."

Private hospital? Maybe the phone really was bonkers. "Miss DeeDee, the state's not going to pay for that. And I'm certainly not going to pay for it. My guess is that you would have to cover some of the costs of such a move, and you don't have any money left. Or not enough to get you into a swank place."

"Don't be crude, dear. You are a well-educated young woman and need not resort to unrefined vocabulary such as *loony bin* and *swank* to make a point. However, I have been allowed access to a computer and to my finances while here—as long as I do not attempt to visit a gambling site, you understand."

"Yes, ma'am." I blinked at the *ma'am*. It was habit and the motions of respect I had not intended to show her. Not ever again.

"The result is that I have done quite well in the stock market. I have more than enough to pay the entire cost of a private hospital, and still continue investing to recoup my estate. I have even put a bit aside for Eddie's higher education. He'll need some help, and the dear boy has called me twice in the last few weeks."

I ground my teeth at the mention of Marisa's stepson. That was another person who would never have access to Marisa again if I could help it.

"I am even hoping to be able to repurchase the farm for Marisa and her baby."

A slow burn began in the back of my brain.

"Rhea, dear—" she paused "—how is Marisa?"

And then I recognized the tone in DeeDee's voice. Fear. Something close to pleading. Not emotions Miss DeeDee had ever experienced, or at least acknowledged. She wanted something only I could deliver, and accepted the probable hopelessness of her request. Because of Marisa. Miss DeeDee's niece. My best friend.

I swallowed hard, forcing down the anger. "Marisa...is learning how to speak again." I fought for breath that was suddenly scarce in my burned, aching throat. "Marisa is learning how to walk again. Marisa is learning how to wipe herself again." I couldn't keep the quaver from my voice. Closing my eyes on the overhead fluorescents, I gripped the arm of the chair. "Marisa is pregnant, in rehab, and has the communication skills of a three-year-old. I haven't talked to her in months. That's how Marisa is. Thanks to you."

Miss DeeDee sucked in a breath. Perhaps to remind me to be polite. Perhaps in shock. But she stayed silent. She wanted out of the state mental hospital and that meant asking favors of me. Silence widened between us, phone line crackling and spitting.

I finally found a breath and felt the fury begin to recede. Marisa knew where her Aunt DeeDee was. I had told her, the one time I talked on the phone to her. Her reaction to the news had been one word mumbled over and over in horrible agitation. "Pammy. Pammy. Pammy."

I hadn't understood what she was saying and her agitation had increased until an aide took the phone and told me what Marisa was saying. "Family. Family. Family." She didn't want DeeDee in a mental hospital. She wanted her free. I focused on the near distance, seeing nothing.

I remembered the word *family* now as DeeDee waited, mute, wordless. Only because Miss DeeDee held her tongue was I able to reply to her entreaty. Not as I wanted to reply, but as Marisa would want me to.

"You…have the judge call me, Miss DeeDee. I'll tell him….I'll tell him that I think you deserve to be put anywhere you can pay for, as long as you aren't set free. I'll tell him what you want him to hear. This time. But that's all. When it comes time for you to be released on bail, that I'll fight to my last breath. Are we clear on this, Miss DeeDee?"

"Oh, yes," she said softly. "We are quite clear. Thank you, Rhea."

"Have a happy Easter, Miss DeeDee."

"You too, dear. Goodbye."

I held the phone in my scalded hand, swallowed past the ache in my throat and closed my eyes to stop the tears that threatened. I was sure they would sear like acid if I actually let them fall. Miss DeeDee had been like a mother to me. When my own mother had been dead drunk passed out on the floor, Miss DeeDee and Marisa had picked me up in her current black Caddy, taken me to the lovely house on the Battery and fed me imported black tea and scones, or cucumber sandwiches and punch, or smoked salmon on toast points with spring water. The fire had burned with hickory and cedar, and scented oil lamps had cast a soft glow on antique furniture.

"A lady lifts only one or two sandwiches onto her plate at a time. A few nuts, a mint. And she eats slowly, with delicate, tiny bites, like so." Middle-aged mouth chewing, lips firmly pressed together.

"But what if the lady is hungry?" I asked, balancing the punch cup on my knee. "What if her stomach is growling?"

"A lady's stomach never growls. A lady is, in fact, *never* hungry in public. A lady is eating because she is being entertained, not stuffed." Amused blue eyes sparkling, Miss DeeDee tilted her head. "Actually," she said with a conspirator's smile, "a lady eats a good meal before leaving home."

"Can it be PB & J instead of fish?"

A strange look crossed Miss DeeDee's features, identified in later years as shock, followed by pity. And then she smiled.

"This salmon is a bit strong. Marisa, don't you think we should offer our honored guest a lunch with a bit more substance before we continue with lessons on afternoon tea? So it would be more realistic?"

Honored guest? Me? I put down the toast point and set the delicate punch cup to the side. My stomach rumbled, which I guessed meant that I was no lady. Mama hadn't remembered to pick up food at the store, only beer.

"How about roast beef on rye with cold steamed asparagus? Girls?"

I didn't know what rye was, and asparagus was green, but I was willing to try it. I was hungry. "Yes, ma'am. Thank you, Miss DeeDee."

She had inclined her head like royalty and smiled at Marisa and me. Little girls learning about life, safe and protected in Miss DeeDee's care. At least for a time.

And then Miss DeeDee had come upon hard times, losing

her entire fortune gambling in Las Vegas. To recoup her financial position before it became obvious to the nonbanking world, she had hired several local thugs and had them hold Marisa down while she shoved an ice pick into her brain. She then blamed the assault on Dr. Steven Braswell, Marisa's husband, and Eddie Braswell. While I was trying to save Marisa's life, DeeDee had been busy trying to get legal custody of the vegetative Marisa and the Stowe family trust fund, and silencing the hoodlums she hired to help her with Marisa.

The phone was sweaty in my hand, the high-pitched beep a reminder of the time and place. Hanging up, I went to my call room, took a long, hot, steamy shower, rubbed myself down with jojoba oil, then threw myself onto the narrow bed and tried to find sleep.

I was wide awake, however, and jumpy, as if I hadn't gone for a run in days. So instead of relaxing, I got up, pulled on a fresh scrub suit and brushed my short black hair. Worried black eyes stared back at me from the polished stainless-steel mirror as the brush ran front to back, front to back, ruffling the strands.

I needed lipstick to camouflage my paleness, but hadn't brought any. Shrugging as if answering a question, I left my call room and meandered the halls, stopping in the cafeteria to catch the updated weather on the muted television bolted to the ceiling. The storm was still violent, and a very wet news anchor I had not seen before was standing in front of a raging creek lit by headlights. The back bumper of a car protruded from the muddy water, and I didn't need sound to know that the car had been swept off the road. Emergency vehicles were at work trying to pull the car from the creek. Rain spotted the camera lens. The anchor's hair and clothes were plastered to him, as if he had given up any attempt to stay dry.

Leaving the cafeteria with a Diet Coke, the only thing

left in the machine, I checked on the patients I had admitted to Douglas Byars. None was doing well.

Douglas had moved Lia and Mel to the ICU, in separate rooms and in total isolation. Lia was on a ventilator. Her lungs had shut down entirely, but she seemed to be responding to the antibiotics and Douglas hoped that she would be breathing on her own in a few days. The state cops were giving him a hard time about not being allowed to question the couple, but Douglas held firm.

I made it to the lab, then, to see the smears I had ordered made of Shareeka's exudate. Amanda, working overtime for the third-shift worker, who had been trapped inside his mobile home by rising creek waters, had made a series of smears on the sputum samples brought down on Lia, Donnalaura and Mel. Douglas had planned to gram-stain the smears himself, but had not had time.

I glanced at the smear Amanda had reported to me in the ER. Like she said, it was full of pus, the microscopic white cells I expected to find in the sputum of a pneumonia patient. The predominant organism was tiny, purple-stained cocci. Thousands and thousands of them. Millions.

She was right. It didn't look like streptococcus pneumonia. Since I had nothing to do, I stained the rest of the smears for Amanda and left them to dry before wandering down to the ER to sit and sip hot chocolate.

I needed to know what the gram stains showed, but sitting in the lab and staring at the unfinished slides wouldn't help them dry. Gram staining was a simple procedure. A minuscule quantity of sample was smeared on a sterile slide, allowed to dry and exposed to two different stains, iodine and alcohol, for specific lengths of time, rinsed, and then allowed to dry again. The result under a microscope could be spectacular. Gram-positive organisms would appear dark purple, while gram-negative organisms would appear fuchsia. Depending on the shape and color of the organism, a doctor could order a certain type of antibiotic and be reasonably sure it would target the group of bacteria causing an infection.

I had worked in a lab to pay part of my way through medical school. Miss DeeDee co-signed the loan that paid my tuition, but the cost of books and lab fees and living expenses still had to be funded somehow. I had to eat. I cleaned Miss DeeDee's Charleston home two times a week and worked various odd jobs. I worked as a waitress for all of four days before I insulted some stupid patron who wanted to complain about the pecan pie. Worked in a car wash drying windows, until I said something less than conciliatory to a city council member who wanted to complain about streaks. The woman had a cat. Cats have oily paws, and the prints had baked in the sun for days. I wasn't sure what she expected, but even then I couldn't perform miracles.

So I took a job working nights in a reference lab, mostly doing antibiotic-level testing and electrophoreses, the specialized test that allowed a doctor to diagnose diseases of the blood, like sickle cell. The lab job was perfect. I could study when it wasn't busy and I didn't have to deal with patients. And I learned a few skills here and there that stuck with me years later.

Back in the ER, I listened to the police scanner as I sipped more hot chocolate, following the action as city and county worked to clear debris, open roads, rescue people stranded by flood waters, and move inmates from one flooded wing of the county lockup into a dry one. It meant crowding one hundred and nineteen county inmates into a space built for less than thirty, but at least they would be dry. There would probably be lawsuits about the primitive and overcrowded conditions, but that was tomorrow's problem.

At exactly 2:00 a.m., as I sipped my second cup of cocoa with miniature marshmallows floating on top, the police scanner screamed to life with amplified feedback. Zack sat straight up in his chair. Anne gasped.

"Attention all units! Attention all units! We have armed men, repeat *armed men*, in the LEC. We need backup! We need—" Gunfire sounded over the scanner. Screams. The sound was cut off.

"Joke?" Anne asked as the silence continued unbroken.

"If so, someone is out of a job," Zack said. The LEC was the Law Enforcement Center, a combination jail, city and county law office, and courtroom. If prisoners had taken over...

"This is Unit 214, dispatch." The dispatcher did not reply. "Dispatch, this is Unit 214, come in." The silence continued. After a moment, the scanner crackled to life again. "Attention all units, this is Unit 214. Converge on the LEC. Repeat, converge on the LEC. Until further notice, this is considered an armed takeover and jailbreak. You are to proceed with speed and caution to the LEC, to my vehicle. Do not approach the LEC until my word. Repeat, do not approach the LEC until I give the word. Check in all units and give ETA to the LEC."

One by one the city checked in. The two off-duty officers checked in. And then the county checked as well. There were fourteen units in the county and city combined and each unit made itself available to Unit 214. Unit 214 was Mark Stafford, my sort-of-boyfriend, one of the county's two captains. Whatever the situation at the jail turned out to be, Mark was preparing to go in and take command.

I walked outside to gauge the weather conditions. The rain had stopped for an instant, but the wind was still gusty and strong, the storm building a last grand grab for control of the piedmont. No rescue or medic choppers would be flying out tonight. If there was a gun battle, all the patients would be mine. I shivered in the wet wind. The stray cat was nowhere to be seen. I hoped it had found a dry place to wait out the storm.

Back inside, I made a batch of strong coffee, and then a second batch. Douglas joined me in a cup and sat down in

one of the squeaky break room chairs. He looked haggard
and the expression deepened as the scanner continued to
crackle with terse comments from cops gathering at the
LEC.

Using police codes as often as plain speech, Mark called
for the state boys, asking for SWAT teams from the capital.
The storm would delay their arrival. He made sure every
cop was wearing a Kevlar bulletproof vest and had enough
ammo, and even requested that cops send home for extra
firepower if they had it. He called in EMS to wait with them.
Three units responded. Adrenaline and testosterone were
flowing fast in the county.

My own heart rate had accelerated, and I wondered how I
was going to get a surgeon into the hospital if one were
needed, how many bleeding patients Douglas and I could
handle at one time, and how many units of O-negative blood,
the type that could be given to anyone regardless of their
own type, were available in the blood bank. Dawkins County
hospital was small, and there were times when we were lucky
to have four units on hand.

At some point in the long hour that followed the takeover,
Mark stopped using police codes and I understood that he
intended for the armed men in the jail to know certain
things. The police radios were being monitored in the LEC
by the hostage-takers.

The men responsible for taking over the jail were using
the county's emergency communication system, too, relay-
ing demands and taunting the cops barricaded outside. At
one point, a man calling himself Barney bragged that he had
shot a deputy and was watching the man bleed to death. In
the background we could hear screaming. I wondered how
many of the prisoners, deputies and dispatchers were female.
And what their medical and emotional situations would be
when this was over.

The hostage-takers demanded money, a helicopter,
twenty-five hot pizzas and a case of vodka. Police were

alternately ignoring the demands and promising the moon, but trying their best to keep the armed men talking. An interesting dance. I didn't recognize the negotiator's voice but it was mellow and smooth, like aged bourbon and hickory smoke.

At about two-forty, they added a new request to the list. They had a man down. He was bleeding. They wanted a doctor. A shock of electricity went through me. If the cops agreed, I would be that doctor.

Almost instantly the ER phone rang and I answered. "Emergency Room, Lynch."

"Rhea, it's Mark. We got a problem here."

Fingers tightening on the arm of the chair, I said calmly, "We've been listening to the scanner. What do you need?" Two bodies appeared at the door to the break room. Douglas leaned closer, his eyes on mine, lips a tight line.

"Then you heard."

"They want a doctor. That would be me." My heart missed a beat and tumbled into motion again. Fast and irregular.

"No. I want a set of scrubs, a black bag and stethoscope, and a white lab coat. I'm sending a man to the hospital to get them. You remember Jacobson?"

Relief sagged through me. Mark was sending in a cop as a decoy. "Yes."

"I need a set of scrubs that might fit him if he was wearing a vest. Can you help me?"

"Consider it done," I said. "Good luck." The phone went dead.

I looked up at the group standing in the doorway. The numbers had grown to include Trish and Amanda from the lab. "Trish, the cops are sending a man in disguised as a doctor and they want us to outfit him. Jacobson is about the size of Dr. Statler if you add, say, ten pounds. The vest will add another ten or so. Can you—"

"On my way." She turned and jogged off. "I'll get a lab

coat that will work, too," she finished from down the hall-way.

I had an old bag in my trunk and, braving the squall, I ran for the parking lot.

Wet through by the time I was back inside, I shook my-self and the bag, splattering droplets of rain. The storm was winding down, the winds noticeably less strong. I knew Mark. He was timing this action—whatever it was—to the storm. He would use everything and anything to accomplish his ends. I knew. I had played handball with the guy a few times. He was sneaky. It was a character trait that would serve him well tonight.

"Anyone got an old stethoscope they want to contribute to the cause?" I asked.

Zack handed me a pink one that had been hanging on the back of the break room door for months. "Broken. So is this BP cuff. Think it matters?"

"No. But let's make this look real. Add whatever you think he might need."

"Bandages?" Douglas asked. "I have a reflex hammer the cat chewed on in the car. And an old reference book or two."

"Sounds good to me."

Douglas took off at a run. From under the ambulance portico, lights flashed. The cop courier was here. It was Steve, drenched to the skin, his face grim. We loaded him down with supplies and he took off from the emergency ramp like he was on fire.

The scanner was silent for a long time as my mind imag-ined the turmoil inside the jail. The possible injuries. The supplies I would need when this finally came my way. When Amanda wandered through a bit later I asked about the sup-ply of O-negative blood.

"Only four units, Doc. But we have nine O-positive, and we can give that to most any male. Might make Rh antibodies in them and maybe a delayed reaction…'' Her voice trailed off.

''Fine. Type specific if possible, then. Use the O-neg only when absolutely necessary. You need to call in any help?''

''Like who?'' she asked with a wry grin. ''Even I'm not supposed to be here.''

''Good point. Maybe we'll get lucky.''

Over the scanner came Mark's voice. ''We are sending in the doctor. He is to be treated with utmost respect. If he is injured, I will make sure that the one responsible will face prosecution for this takeover.''

My breath went still at the raw threat in his voice.

''I hope I make myself clear.''

I gripped the arms of my chair, holding on.

''Yeah, whatever.'' The words sounded slurred. I wondered if Mark had delivered the case of vodka to the armed men in the LEC and in the same instant knew he had not. Not Mark. Middle-of-the-road Mark. Straight-and-narrow Mark. The men holed up in the LEC were getting their first and only demand met. The supposed doctor.

The phone rang and Douglas took the call, murmuring a moment and then agreeing. ''Be right there.'' He hung up. ''I have a Regina Hawkins with pneumonia. You admitted her?''

I nodded.

''She's coughing up blood. I have to go check on her. But you need me, I'll be back ASAP.''

''Douglas?''

His brows raised in question.

''Wear a mask. Especially if the lungs sound like wet linen tearing.''

''You think…'' He stopped, not saying what I hadn't said. Superstition. *Don't say bad things and bad things won't happen.* Almost an ER credo.

''I don't know, but take precautions. All of them. You have kids.''

He nodded and jogged up the hall. It was against the rules for hospital workers to run or jog. Everyone was breaking the rules tonight.

Over the scanner there came two clicks. Sharp and distinct. I had dated Mark long enough to know that two clicks meant go ahead. The cops were putting into motion whatever they had planned. I felt the coffee and hot chocolate burble uneasily in my stomach.

7

WANT FRIES WITH THAT?

Nothing more came over the scanner. Trish and I sat in the break room, me drinking coffee, Trish practically swimming her way through a two-liter Diet Coke. Nerves, both of us. Minutes passed. I kept hearing the screaming in the background, the memory-sound shrill beneath scanner static.

At 4:47 the EMS radio buzzed, Zack picking up on the mike even before it finished its unpleasant blare. I stood and went to the door, propping myself against the frame.

It was Buzzy, an EMT. Cool and methodical, he gave the patient info over the radio. "We got three patients. First patient is a fifty-six-year-old black male with a gunshot wound to the left arm. Entrance and exit wounds both noted, and bleeding is controlled. BP is 147 over 97, pulse 82, respiration is 15. Second patient is a forty-seven-year-old white female, victim of assault. Multiple lacerations and contusions, possible broken right wrist and arm. BP is 175 over 120, pulse 110, respiration's 18.

"Third patient is a twenty-two-year-old Asian male, signal 45." Buzzy's voice had changed suddenly, becoming sharper edged, and I knew that this last patient was a prisoner, not county emergency personnel. And he was drunk, as evidenced by the signal 45. Drunks were not Buzzy's favorite type of patient. I smiled at the irritation in his voice.

''Patient has signal 14 wounds to torso and abdomen, stab wounds are fleshy only, no penetrating wounds.''

Buzzy continued to give vitals and I looked over at Anne. She was setting up the treatment room with the OB/GYN table for the second time tonight. The victim of assault... Possibly the same person who had been screaming over the radio? I hoped not. Of all the things I hated most about ER medicine, sexual assaults were at the top of the list. With Michelle Geiger out of town, this patient also would fall to me. Much as I liked her, Geiger was quickly falling out of my favor.

Trish was setting up the trauma room for the gunshot wound and the stabbing wounds. Zack finished taking the radio report and looked over his shoulder at me for any orders. I shook my head but walked closer. ''Ask if there are any more patients coming.''

Buzzy answered my question himself. ''Tell the doctor no more patients. Because the storm broke, we have two going out by chopper any minute now, and one LEO coming by POV for a broken right index finger.''

I nodded. One LEO by POV meant one law enforcement officer coming by personally owned vehicle. Cop talk. EMS talk. They were almost as bad as med speak, the incomprehensible gibberish spoken by doctors to one another. ''ETA?'' I asked, adding my own little part to the accumulated babble.

''ETA twelve minutes.'' Buzzy, still working a three-way conversation.

I nodded again and moved to the trauma room, placed the orders for Ethilon and staples for the drunk. If he was sufficiently drunk, I would go with staples and forgo the time-consuming stitching and local anesthetics. If he was conscious and violent, he might still get staples. If he was polite, and if his wounds were not too extensive, he might get a stitches-and-staples combo, stitches where scarring would show, staples where it was less important. "Want fries with that?" I murmured, and grinned at my whimsy.

The overhead loudspeaker sounded, the switchboard operator's voice loud and distinct. "Code 99 to PCU. Code 99 to PCU. Code 99 to PCU."

"When it rains it pours," Trish said. I was thinking along those lines but with a silent expletive attached. I draped my stethoscope around my neck and pulled on my white lab coat. Trish glanced at me as I started down the hall to the arrest in the Progressive Care Unit. ER doctors always answered a Code 99—an arrest of either respiratory or cardiac function. Hospital policy. "Right behind you, Doc," she said to my retreating back. "Anne, you and Zack okay?"

"We're fine. If we need you, we'll call."

"Doc? Wait up," she said, sounding breathless.

I slowed for her to catch up. "You might want to try a few aerobic exercises," I said, noting her huffing breaths and high color as we rounded the corner past the Radiology Department.

"I use the Abdominizer and ThighMaster to keep toned, but you can't catch a man by running," she winked. "All those ugly, long muscles in place of this rounded womanliness." She ran a hand over her hip and buttocks. "Besides, I have other things to do with my days. All those men and so little time," she sighed wickedly.

I knew when I was being razzed. I was a runner, covering a minimum of five miles a day, almost every day. "You could walk or swim," I said mildly, not rising to the bait. "Golf, if you walk the course, or tennis. Ride a bike. Ride a horse."

"I'd rather ride a man," she said slyly, and I laughed. I had walked right into that one and shook my head. Then I slowed. We had reached PCU, and the sounds coming from room five were horrible.

Nurses and techs in full personal protective equipment, their masks, gowns, face shields splattered with blood,

milled around in the doorway and the hall just outside.
Bright light spilled from the room. A negative pressure unit
hummed, drawing in clean air from the hallway, filtering
out bacteria from the air in the room and expelling the
cleaned air. Harsh breath sounds and a wet cough echoed
over the nurses' voices shouting orders. The sound of tearing wet linen. Then the breath sounds stopped.

I grabbed a mask and passed one to Trish, quickly tying
the paper straps in place. Shaking out a blue gown, I
dressed, peeking into the room. Douglas Byars was directing
a bloody spectacle, walking over sheets that had been
stretched over pooled blood, ordering medications, and extra
lines started. And now, bending over the head of the bed,
he was trying to get the black, middle-aged patient intu-
bated.

It was Regina Hawkins, the woman I had admitted earlier
in my shift. She'd had a little pneumonia, but nothing like
this. The dread that had been growing all night blossomed
into an icy panic. The fear Douglas and I hadn't spoken
aloud shot through my mind.

A belated alarm sounded, the thin warning bell that sig-
naled a patient was not breathing. "Need help?" I asked.

He glanced up from her open mouth. "Yeah. I need
X-ray vision to see past the blood in this woman's trachea.
I can't see anything."

I leaned across the nurse starting a new IV in the brachial
vein located at the elbow and tilted Regina's head back.
Instantly a gush of blood shot out of her mouth and Douglas
dodged to the side. Trish, appearing at the far side of the
bed, took her head from me and turned it to the side, allowing the blood and what looked like hunks of tissue to expel
harmlessly to the floor. Behind me someone gagged, and I
felt my own gorge rising.

As soon as the rush of blood subsided, Trish nodded to
me and I took Regina's head, moving it to the proper position for intubation. "See the cords?" I asked.

Douglas grunted. A moment later he shoved the tube in and stood. I let her head go and placed the bell of my stethoscope over the patient's chest as someone attached an ambu bag to the tube at her mouth. Quickly, a hand compressed the bag. "Good breath sounds," I said after listening to four complete breaths. "X ray for tube placement?"

"In the hall."

"Rhea. Look at the monitor," Douglas said.

I stood straight and stepped back. The heart monitor showed V-tach. Ventricular tachycardia. And then, suddenly, she straight-lined. Asystole.

"Shock her. Two hundred." Douglas stepped back and Trish ripped the remnants of the patient's hospital gown away, slapping two gel pads in place over her chest. Applied the paddles.

"Clear!" she called. Glancing down the bed to make sure all stepped back, she pressed the triggers. The patient's body jumped as the electrical charge shot through her. The heart monitor showed no change.

"Charge it again—three sixty," Douglas said, calling for a max charge of three hundred and sixty joules. "And administer epinephrine, one amp IV push, and atropine one amp IV."

Trish glanced at the nurse handling the bulky defibrillator. When the woman nodded, Trish said again, "Clear." The patient jumped, this time noticeably higher with the stronger charge. Still no change.

The instant the patient settled on the bed, Gloris, a nurse from ICU, added the epi to the IV line.

"Start compressions."

Gloris handed off the next syringe to another nurse and bent toward the patient, placing her hands in the center of Regina's chest, and began compressions. The angle was awkward, the bed too high. A stout woman, Gloris was huffing instantly. "Lower the bed," she said. "Or get me a stool.'' The bed began to hum, dropping steadily. "Better,'' she said.

"Dr. Lynch, they need you in ER.''

I looked around, recognized the face but couldn't find a name. And then remembered. My gunshot wound, my assault, my knife wound. Douglas Byars cursed. "Go on,'' he said. "We've got it here.''

I nodded, moved to the door and stripped off the bloody paper gown and mask. I didn't realize until then that the patient had vomited on me at some point. Balling the bloody PPE, I stuffed the gear into a red biohazard bag, stopped at the sink and washed carefully, checking my face in the mirror over the sink. No visible blood, but I bent and washed my face, too, wishing for stronger soap and maybe some Betadine to kill more germs. Whatever this condition was, it was fast-acting and dangerous. I wasn't taking chances.

Behind me as I left the room, I heard Douglas ordering two heart drugs. And then, "Shock her again.'' But I think we both knew it was hopeless.

My twenty-two-year-old drunk was unconscious, then became combative in his few moments of awareness, so I had him strapped down while I stapled his wounds closed. He would have some fine scars to show off in a month or so, to go along with the almost healed, uneven, six-sided star tattooed over his left shoulder blade. A jailhouse tattoo, exactly like the ones worn by the Campbells when they were admitted. This one, however, had been applied days ago, and showed no signs of infection.

The female victim of assault had not been raped. It seemed the leader of the jail takeover had made certain that no one was injured once the county and city employees were hostages. She was sent home with instructions for icing her black eye and other bruises. The sheriff's deputy with the gunshot was lucky, too. It was a clean wound, in and out, with no damage to the major vessels, tendons or muscles. He'd be sore but that was about all.

And then there were the patients that I hadn't expected. Seven black inmates who had been beaten during the jail takeover. As Zack and I treated the contusions and lacerations of the two most injured, we overheard them talking about the event, describing the white guy who had led the takeover and then allowed his men to segregate the other prisoners by race.

"Cold sumbitch. Eyes like ice. Jist sitting there, watching while them others beat me. Little smile in him, too. Like he liked watchin' as much as beatin'."

"Got it in for the brothers. You hear his name?"

"White-power shit. Ow! Watch it there, bro. That hurts!"

"Sorry," Zack said, his dark face tight. "But it's supposed to hurt. Means it's working."

"You a doctor? A *black* doctor?"

"A nurse," Zack said shortly, placing a wad of gauze soaked in Betadine over a shallow, bleeding cut. "Hold this. Put pressure on it."

A massive black hand covered the bandage. "Ellis. Dickhead Ellis," the complainer said. Both men laughed. "And I hope some brother do to him what his boys done to that kid. Ain't never seen nothin' like that." Zack moved on to another patient. I had heard enough, and left the room.

Ellis. The man who had killed Leon Hawkins. I patched the prisoners up, ordered painkillers where necessary and sent them back to lockup.

Suddenly things were quiet again, the ER empty and silent but for Zack and Anne restocking shelves and counting drugs, finishing up the miscellany of paperwork that is the bane of the medical profession. I rinsed out the coffeepot and wiped down the counter then tucked Anne's clear polish into her carryall bag with my own ragged, unpainted nails and chapped hands. I wandered back to the desk, at loose ends, stretching as I moved. My muscles were stiff after the last eleven hours.

Standing there, arms propped on the counter, I caught a glimpse of Douglas Byars walking into the Radiology Department's film-viewing room. He had a sheaf of films in one hand, and was raking the other through his hair. The ends stood straight up. Without asking, I knew Regina Hawkins had died.

Slowly, remembering the word still unspoken between us, I walked up the hall to join him. There were several X-ray view boxes in ER but the film-viewing room in Radiology was built specifically for examining multiple numbers of X-ray films. The room was long and narrow with a twelve-foot-long lighted view box on one wall, clips above to hold X rays in place, a table and four chairs for small conferences. Douglas looked up as I entered. Almost angrily, he shoved several films into the clips. There were five different films, none of them looking as if they belonged to the same person.

"Regina Hawkins when you admitted her around seven-thirty last night." He tapped the first film, his voice rough as cold brick. "Regina Hawkins when we x-rayed her for tube placement." He tapped the second film.

The lung tissue showed drastic changes, light and dark patches that were evidence of blood infiltrating the lungs, or perhaps a sudden massive buildup of white blood cells and bacteria. Long strands, filamentous and branching, stretched to every part of the lungs. It looked as if someone had filled Regina's lungs with cottage cheese and tar, and then, with a shaking hand, streaked them out with a brush.

"Did you know that her husband was lynched just a few days ago?" I jerked, nodded. I knew. "She discovered the body," Douglas said, his voice dead and toneless, "hanging from a bridge. Almost was drowned herself, getting him down. Hurt her back trying to lift him."

"Yes. She told me...."

Douglas seemed to draw himself up and stood straighter for a moment. "She was still in asystole at the time I got the X ray, and I called the code shortly. She was gone long before that." He pointed at the next film, the doctor taking over again from the man.

"This one is Lia Campbell on admission. This is Lia now, or—" he checked his watch "—say a half hour ago. By now, her lungs could look like Regina's. Whatever this bug is, it acts fast."

"Doesn't look like congestion," I said, "or massive infarction. Putrefactive necrosis?"

He nodded. "I took a look at the first sputum you collected on Lia. It now has three layers. Stinks so bad even the vent fan in the Micro Department didn't clean it all out of the room. I mean really foul."

"Three layers?" I struggled to remember. Necrosis of the lungs was rare, a secondary condition to some other inflammation of the lung, and with the stringent antibiotic therapies administered today, we didn't see it often. But the sputum of people with necrosis separated into three layers. "Top frothy, middle serous, bottom purulent and reddish green," I finally recalled.

"Yeah. I think something is breaking down the lungs themselves. It looks like the alveolar tissue is practically melting. Look here." He pointed to the cardiac depression, the indentation in the left lung where the heart rested in Regina's last film. "It looks like it may even be eating its way out of the lungs into the chest cavity. We have hemorrhage, congestion, maybe even a pneumothorax trying to form here as the lungs dissolve and air leaks out next to the chest wall."

"Not anthrax. The symptoms are all wrong." I took a deep breath and said the word we had both avoided. "Ebola?"

"Looks like it. Sure as hell looks like it. But if so, what is the gram-positive cocci that the lab saw earlier? And where in blazes would an Ebola come from? I'd expect to see Ebola in a city that has a zoo or a research facility. Not out here in the boonies.'' Douglas lifted his gaze from the evidence of epidemic and met mine. ''I called Emily and the kids. Told them to stay put in Tallahassee for a few days. Didn't tell them why. Don't want to start a panic. But…''

''Yeah. But.'' I stared again at the films, the fascination of horror pulling my attention back. ''Have you seen the smears?''

''No. No time. And Amanda hasn't had time to make them, let alone had time to look at them. Said she saw some in the lab, though. Yours?''

''Let's go take a look. See if we see Ebola.''

Wordlessly, as if we were walking to a funeral, we moved to the lab. Not liking the silence, I broke it. ''I didn't notice any smell when I made my smears. And I didn't use the hood,'' I confessed.

In cases of dangerous airborne bacteria, all lab and diagnostic work was performed in full protective suiting, with a negative-pressure hood overhead, pulling the disease organisms out of the room and through filters, away from the breathing passages of the workers. And because no one could ever know when a particular sample would prove deadly, all microbiology work was supposed to be carried out beneath the hood. I had been in direct contact with patients and the bacteria-filled samples themselves, without protective gear, without the hood that was in the microbiology department.

''Smell may come later, as the sputum sits. Or it may be a result of the lungs' breakdown, coming later in the progression of the disease.''

''But from now on, we take all precautions.'' I pushed open the lab door and frigid air flowed out. The clinical laboratory was kept as cold as possible due to the large number of computers and delicate equipment kept there.

Douglas nodded. "I had housekeeping come in early. The walls and every piece of equipment in Regina Hawkins's room are being washed down with Clorox and hot water. Twice. I put all the other pneumonia patients under the most strict isolation possible. I'd ship these patients but I doubt anyone will take them."

"Probably not."

The slides I had made and stained earlier were dry and I put the first one on the viewer of the binocular microscope. Hundreds of white cells met my eyes, the polymorphonuclear white blood cells called segs or polys, stained red and purple.

"We have polys," I said, telling Douglas that the killing pneumonia was bacterial and not viral in origin. "And we...do not have an Ebola." I could feel Douglas almost sag with relief. "We have a few gram-negative rods and a four-plus gram-positive cocci in clusters and chains."

"Strep? Staph? A staph is causing *this?*"

"I don't know what else to call it," I said, scrolling through the millions and millions of cells and bacteria. I changed slides, looking at another patient's sample. It was almost identical to the first. "But whatever it is, we'll have an ID in a couple days. We can ID this on site and not have to send it out to a reference lab."

"Code 99 to PCU. Code 99 to PCU. Code 99 to PCU." The words blared over the loudspeaker.

"Lia Campbell." With the words like an epitaph Douglas Byars was gone.

8

Lia died shortly after I got to her room. On the floor around us, beneath the sheets thrown for safety, tissue and blood was splattered and being squished beneath the nurses' ridge-soled running shoes. A sputum sample had been sent to the lab, and Amanda had stopped all other jobs to set up the cultures and report the gram stains. Douglas, haggard and spent, bent over the patient's chart, carefully detailing notes and running through the code information again and again, questioning nurses and even me on what we had done, and who had been where in the room at what time.

We needed documentation of everything. Especially if this organism proved to be contagious person to person...making this the beginning of an epidemic.

Mel Campbell was distraught, and though it could possibly interfere with his prognosis, Douglas administered a sedative and requested that Gloris stay with him until it took effect. Mel had been in the room down the hall from his wife and had known Lia was dying. After all he had done to save her and his baby, it hadn't been enough. He had screamed and begged to be allowed to go to Lia during the code, and an orderly had been forced to sit with him, holding his broken hands and praying with him as he once again waited helplessly while Lia suffered.

I peeked into his room. Gloris was wearing a mask, one hand adjusting the controls on a negative-pressure unit, the other hand holding Mel's bandaged one. She was a good nurse, one of the few who managed to reach a high level of experience without losing her compassion.

Amanda, who had left the Micro Department to help with the code, told Douglas that the tattoo wounds on Lia's and Mel's chests were caused by gram-negative rods—not the gram-positive cocci we had been expecting. Two organisms? It was rare, but not unheard-of, and after this night, I was ready to believe almost anything.

Mel's minister came in just after sunrise and was told to dress out in complete PPE, looking surprised to be forced to wear gloves and mask, gown, blue hat and paper shoe coverings. Even with the extra precautions, he was determined to stay with his parishioner, praying and grieving. I didn't know much about preachers, but this one was a deal more sincere and dedicated than the Lamb of God had been. I couldn't imagine the Reverend Lamb in the room with Mel, unless Mel had been a big contributor to his church and his wallet needed praying over. Mel seemed anything but rich.

I left the war zone of the PCU and headed back to the ER, patting Douglas and giving him my home number as I went. "Call me if you need anything," I said, sounding as ineffectual as I felt.

"I may need you when I call Infection Control this morning," he said, lifting his head. His eyes were bloodshot, dark circles shadowing them, skin pulled tight across his long, bony face, like the face of a man starving to death. "They may want your take on all this. And I may check with the CDC Web site to see if anything like this...pneumonia, for lack of a better diagnosis, is being reported anywhere else. You ever been to their site?''

"A few times," I said. "It's confusing when you first use it, but then, CDC is a pretty big organization. I got a handle on it after a few tries. You may want to look at the NETSS Web site too." NETSS, or National Electronic Telecommunications System for Surveillance, was the electronic notification part of the National Notifiable Diseases Surveillance System, a fairly new system for tracking specific disease patterns nationally. It was supported by CDC staff, and its weekly data updates were available to health organizations.

"If the phone lines aren't down, I'll give it a try. But I'm more familiar with CDC's site." Douglas's voice was exhausted.

The Center for Disease Control and Prevention was a massive, federally funded agency consisting of doctors, bacteriologists, statisticians, inspectors, theoreticians, geneticists, virologists and specialists of every variety, all gathered under one header for the purpose of recognizing, identifying, tracking and treating disease in the United States. When a state health department found a contagious organism they couldn't handle, CDC was the bastion of knowledge and federal intervention they contacted.

In this world of fast travel, mutable microbiological organisms and increasingly ineffective antibiotics, doctors needed all the help they could get. CDC was the sanctuary for the white knights of health care.

"I'll be home or on the cellular," I said. "Call me if you need anything."

Sighing, Douglas nodded and returned to the chart.

Back in the ER, I had a patient waiting for me. It was a paramedic, Mick Ethridge's partner Sam Tooley. Sam and Mick had been on the run that brought in Mel and Lia Campbell and Sam had sudden onset flu symptoms. I ordered a chest X ray, had blood work drawn and waited an hour with him to see if he developed a cough, then repeated the chest film.

There was no change. No sign of dark filaments or cottage-cheese-like crud starting to build, no sign of pneumonia or necrosis similar to the cases I had seen overnight. Still, I gave him a prescription for the strongest oral antibiotic I could before sending him home with my phone number in his pocket. We didn't know how Lia's, Regina's and Shareeka's bacterial organism was passed. It could be person-to-person, or perhaps through creek water, or maybe via insect vector, like heartworms were in dogs and malaria was in humans. We didn't know. And I couldn't admit every patient I saw simply because of a sense of building hysteria.

I was ready to get out of the hospital, understanding in a small way how posttraumatic stress syndrome could debilitate a war-zone doctor. The human mind wasn't accustomed to horror. Though I had seen more than my share of emergency room traumas, disease and death in my residency in Ohio, it had been a while. I had grown complacent.

When I gave my report to Wallace, my replacement on the twelve-hour day shift, I knew I wasn't the only one to have become nonchalant about the medical aspects of working in a small rural hospital. Wallace, my titular boss, was one of the Chadwicks, a prominent mixed-race family in the county. Wallace and his wife Pearl were both half white, half African-American, and fully beautiful people. Just the story of my night had him gaping, greenish eyes wide in his dark face. The unexpected concern of an impending epidemic didn't help his reaction.

Wallace leaned against the counter, his lean form tensing as I spoke, his eyes moving from my face to the ER that was his responsibility for the next twelve hours. I could see him checking out the walls, the floor, wondering if the place needed a full biohazard decontamination before any more emergency patients were admitted. When I finished speaking, he shook his head, thanked me and dialed housekeeping.

As I gathered my things to make my way out of the ER, the outer doors blew open and the Reverend Lamb Sexton breezed in to the department, followed by Wallace's temporary ER second-in-command, Dr. Taylor Reeves. Reeves was working the emergency room with Wallace until his patient base grew enough to support him, a common activity among doctors new to a town, who were not taking over or joining an existing medical practice. Currently, there were three new local doctors providing full- or part-time ER coverage, some of whom I hadn't met.

Sunlight and a fresh wind followed the men in. The storm had passed and the Reverend wanted his wound sewed. Looking at Wallace, I just shook my head and held up two hands to show how long the wound had been left untreated. It had been far too long, much more than the four hours medically acceptable for closing a laceration. The wound would have to heal all on its own. It would leave a nasty scar.

Before Wallace could pass along the info, one of the office staff—I thought she worked in admitting—came into the ER and approached the Reverend.

"Reverend Lamb! Reverend Lamb! Oh, my God! It *is* you! Oh, my God! I just got to ask you something. I just got to! Oh, my God!"

I didn't know if she was calling on God or calling the man God. Either way, it looked like it could be either entertaining or a problem, and I paused as I stuffed my lab coat into the overnight bag I always carried. Taylor joined me in the corner, watching the scene in the hallway as he poured a cup of coffee.

"Sister," Lamb said, placing his unhurt hand on her head, a huge sparkling college-style ring seen for an instant before it was buried in the stiff, sprayed, unmoving tresses. "I perceive you are a child of the Spirit. Are you living a holy and unblemished life? One pure and unsullied before the Lord?"

"I am, Reverend, sir. I am a firm believer of purity, and I contribute my time and my tithe to the ministry faithfully."

"Speak your question, my child."

"Tell me about the prophesy! My sister Pauline was at the church during the storm and said you were taken with the Spirit and prophesied!"

"Indeed I was, my child." The Rev bowed his head and closed his eyes in solemn agony, as if the experience of prophesy was a burden too heavy to bear. "I was taken by the Spirit and, like John, the future was opened to me. I saw the last days, which are *these* days," he said, his voice drawn deep into melancholia, his words slow and sweeping, as if he were addressing an entire congregation and the massed millions of TV viewers and not just the admissions clerk. I wondered if this was practice, a rehearsal before the big opening night.

"I saw..." The word was drawn out, as the Rev's anguish deepened, "I saw the *final battle* between the forces of Christ and the forces of the Antichrist... I saw the protection of *angels* for the holy who were gathered at the compound..." His voice raised in holy ecstasy, and despite myself, I shivered. "And I saw *death* and de*struc*tion as *plague* took the whole world in its grip."

The Rev looked down at the smaller woman. "Sister, do you believe?"

"Oh yes, Reverend," she gushed. "I *do* believe. I wear my symbol of the Lamb every waking moment." She grabbed a gold charm at her neck and held it up for display. "Every waking moment. But Reverend!" the clerk gasped, and gripped Lamb's injured hand. He didn't flinch but again stared at the damp ceiling tiles over his head, as if mesmerized by the circular rain stains made by the storm. "Reverend Lamb, the compound isn't *finished!* It isn't *ready.* Does that mean that the plague is gonna wait a few years?"

"No, sister. The plague is coming *now.* Today. And the compound will be finished by the *holy* who gather there for *protection* and *sanc-tu-ary.*" He paused. "Then, together, as the world dies around us, we will *finish* the compound. *We* will become the 144,000 who survive the onslaught of death. And the 144,000 will finish the compound." His voice rose again. "And the *promise* of *Zion* will be *fulfilled!*" he thundered, raising his clenched fist at the damp ceiling.

"The great cities of the world...will *die!*" he ended on a whisper before his voice again rose. "Charlotte, New York, Atlanta will be among the first to succumb, followed by Los Angeles, the city of fallen angels! The cities who have turned against the Lord will be *taken!*" The shouted words were sibilant echoes in the empty ER.

I found that I couldn't look away from the tortured face. The shiver that had taken me worsened. I thought my teeth might chatter. Beside me, visible in my peripheral vision, Taylor Reeves stood stiffly, his eyes not leaving the scene.

"The *despised* of heaven will pass away...as the *sword* of the *Lord's vengeance* falls! Listen to me, sister. Bring your earthly goods and worldly possessions, especially food and nonperishables, into the compound this week. *Today! Be saved!* Come to the compound and be one of the 144,000 or—like the people of Noah's time—be locked away forever!"

Relief washed through me. The spell the Reverend Lamb was weaving broke and cast me aside. That was the ticket— bring all your worldly possessions.... The Reverend didn't have any prescient vision of plague. He hadn't foreseen the pneumonia I had been dealing with in the ER suddenly sweeping the whole world. He just wanted people's money.

Picking up my bag, I glanced up at Taylor. A good-looking, very fit man in his late forties, Dr. Reeves was new to the hospital, and we had not found time to become acquainted. I had heard that he ran, and considered for an instant asking him to join me on my usual five-mile run, but his expression changed my mind. He looked royally PO'd, as if someone had stepped into his personal space and made themselves at home, despite being asked to leave.

"See you," I said instead. Taylor caught my arm as if to stop me, then pulled back his hand quickly.

"Sorry," he said, nodding to me finally, as if just now noticing that we shared a room. His face still set in tight lines, he asked, "Want to update me on these pneumonia patients you got in last night?"

"Not really," I said with a tired smile. "Wallace has all the particulars. You can get what you need from him. How'd you hear about it, anyway?"

Irritation flashed across his face. "A nurse called me—at 5:00 a.m. on my day off—to ask about getting additional negative-pressure units for the patients. But please, don't let me detain you," he said, gesturing with his coffee cup toward the door.

I could tell that he did indeed want to detain me, but I smiled in apparent relief, said my thanks, and headed out. I was done. And I would rather run alone any day than with a sour-faced, ill-humored person like him.

Wallace grinned at me and followed me to the parking lot. "Got to you, didn't he? The Lamb, I mean."

"A little. For a minute or so," I admitted, looking up at the blue sky, squinting at the golden ball of sun sitting above the horizon. It glinted across my car, parked on the low hill where last night's rising flood waters couldn't wash it away. Somewhere nearby, a bird that had survived the high winds began to sing. "He's good. Don't let him hear about the pneumonias or he'll use them as fuel for his end-of-the-world fire."

"He's been saying the same thing for a year, calling for purity, talking about death and destruction and the fall of the cities, and then begging people to join him in his new city out near I-77." Wallace crossed his arms and followed my gaze into the sky. "The spring floods are part of the destruction, the tornadoes last year were part of the destruction. Next thing that goes wrong and he'll be calling for the mother ship and killing off his followers. Of course, there's another side of the man," he said reluctantly.

"What side?"

"He donated over $200,000 to the hospital for indigent care last year. And he opened a soup kitchen in DorCity."

"Him?" I didn't mean to sound incredulous, but that's the way it came out. I couldn't see the Reverend dipping soup. And then the image of the man dressed in work clothes, damp from the storm and bleeding from hard work, came to mind. Perhaps I wasn't being entirely fair.

"The man's a humanitarian. Sort of. In his own unique way." Wallace glanced at me, his expression claiming he was only trying to be fair.

I snorted. "He's all yours. And so is your sourpuss Reeves."

"Thank you, kind lady," Wallace said wryly. "Thank you so much. The good doctor does look to be in a ripe mood, don't he though?"

Leaving Wallace standing in the lot looking up at the sky, I drove home. Pulling into the drive at the little bungalow-style house I was currently purchasing, I was met by the dogs, Belle and her four-month-old pup, Yellow Pup. I wasn't the one who named the puppy and had no idea what we would call him when he was fully grown, but I simply refused to call him Yellow or Yeller, so had settled temporarily on Pup. Belle, a long-haired black lab-setter mixed breed, weighed in at eighty-five pounds. Her yellow-haired pup was already a monster-to-be at forty pounds. He had feet like snowshoes.

The two dogs romped in the yard with a bird dog, a blue-tick hound and a long-eared bloodhound, splashing and running in wild circles around the car as I eased down the drive. Mark must have come home at some point in the last few minutes and let all the dogs out. They were too excited to have been loose long. Not wanting mud tracked into the house, I left them all playing.

It was a wise decision, as Arlana had left a note with strict instructions to keep the dogs off the furniture, out of my bed and away from her clean floors. She also informed me that she had installed a phone line in the kitchen and purchased a phone for it. The bill was attached to the note with payment instructions. I wondered if all housekeepers were so bossy, and decided that my friendship with the almost-grown-woman had spoiled any attempt on my part to be in charge. Arlana was like the tides. An unstoppable force of nature.

Discovering that I had power, I checked my e-mail, all twenty-seven of them, and made replies where necessary. Amelia's mother had colon cancer, Wes's sister had gotten married, Shirl had bought a new car—no big surprise, as Shirl drove for stress relief, pleasure and in place of food when she was dieting. Charlie Goldfarb's dad was retiring from his position at the Pentagon, and Cam was delayed because of the storm. He and Marisa were stranded in Duke, where Cam was doing his neurosurgical residency and Marisa was undergoing rehabilitation, and they couldn't fly back until after the storm passed. The storm, at last news, had headed north, then stalled again near the tri-city area where Duke was located.

I felt my heart wrench. I missed my best friend, even

though the injury to her brain meant we couldn't talk in the same way we had for the previous twenty years of our lives. I had expected her to be back, though logic—if I had bothered to use that small part of my brain—insisted that no one but a fool would fly in the kind of storm that had damaged the state.

The other e-mails were from various friends across the nation, all offering information or advice or both. Most either told me to find a new man, now that my ex-fiancé John and I were permanently apart, or told me to stay footloose and fancy-free. A few offered a cousin or co-worker as a prospective date/mate. My friends seemed to think I was lonely.

So far I had told none of them about Mark. I wasn't ready to admit that he might be more than just a good friend. Mark hunted. Mark raised dogs. Mark was a cop, for God's sake. And Mark was a local good-ol'-boy, albeit a fairly well-off good-ol'-boy with an excellent pedigree, if you listened to his mother. But Mark wasn't suave, debonair John Micheaux...who had jumped ship when his family came calling. I put the thought of Mark aside in order to finish reading the e-mails from my well-meaning friends.

I was good at making friends, maybe better than good. It was a gift. And I had a lot of good friends. Steadfast, stalwart friends, to be a little melodramatic. But Marisa was my best friend. And Marisa wasn't here. Which may be a good thing, until I knew more about the putrefactive pneumonia that caused necrosis of the lungs and killed in hours.

My body knew it was overdue for a run, but I ignored the creaking ligaments and stiff joints. Disgruntled and blaming my feelings on Marisa and Cam being stuck in the medical center near Duke, I made a cup of camomile tea and wandered my house. I liked the relatively new pleasure of it being both clean and attractive. I wasn't much of a housekeeper in my own place, perhaps because of having to keep Miss DeeDee's Charleston manor so spick-and-span while taking premed. Until Arlana entered my life and home, I had lived in a disorganized, damp, slightly moldy pigsty.

Arlana—my new housekeeper, decorator, advice-giver and friend—had done a great job with window treatments, rugs, pillows, new living room furniture, and especially the decorated bedroom. Arlana had a gift for finding just the right things for me. Nothing frilly, nothing lacy, nothing leather, nothing yellow, nothing plaid. Everything soothing to the eye, in shades like blush, ecru, stone, slate.

At loose ends, I took a hot shower. Exhaustion finally claimed me and I fell asleep on the bed, remembering to toss back the comforter. Arlana had informed me after the first time I slept on it that the comforter was for sleeping under, not on. And she had assured me that I would not be allowed to live like PWT—Poor White Trash.

The phone rang at noon, the tinny, soft *brrrr* waking me from uneasy dreams. It was Sam Tooley's wife, Josephine, sounding frantic. It took a moment for me to recognize the name but only an instant to recognize the noise in the background. A cough like wet, tearing linen and the rough burbly sound of rales. Sam, who had been both in the presence of the Campbells and near the creek where they had been found, had the pneumonia.

"Josephine, did Sam start on the antibiotics I prescribed?"

In a voice almost too soft to hear, she said, "No. The pharmacy wasn't open till nine and he—" her voice trailed off, then picked back up again after a moment, even softer "—and he felt a little better by the time he went to bed. He said not to wake him. So I didn't. He thought he would be fine if he started on it this afternoon."

Anger washed through me. Noncomplying patients really ticked me off. Especially when it might mean their lives and they expected me to pick up the pieces and put them back together again. Humpty-Dumpty had surely been noncomplying and not simply clumsy. Controlling my frustration as best I could, I said, "Josephine, he should have started the meds. I thought I made that clear. He is very sick now. *Very* sick." When Josephine said nothing, I ordered, "Meet me at the ER. Now."

The tone of my voice convinced her and she slammed down the phone even as she was directing her husband to get to the car.

I dressed in record time, throwing on sweats and sneakers, made sure the dogs had water and food in the back hallway and that their doggy-door was still loose and not swollen shut by the rain, and ran for my car. The hospital parking lot wasn't far as the crow flies, but country roads have a tendency to weave and twist. Still only half awake, I made the trip in record time, the tires on my BMW gripping the turns almost desperately.

Wallace looked up at me as I jogged into the ER, surprise etched on his face. "'S up?" he asked, green eyes wary as he tried for humor and failed.

"Sam Tooley. He here yet?"

"No. Why?"

I motioned him into the triage room and pushed the door shut, although not completely, or the wags would have us sleeping together. "Sam Tooley was on the Campbell call."

"The pneumonias? The man's been put on the vent today. Doesn't look good."

"Oh, no." I shook my head, my thoughts still caught in the swamp of dreams. "I thought he…" I stopped. That too had been a dream. Gathering myself, I took a deep breath. "Well, Sam came by this morning with flulike symptoms. I did two chest films on him over the course of an hour and they looked fine. Now he sounds like the patients did who died. Like his lungs are ripping apart. He and Josephine are meeting me here. Okay if I take care of him?''

"Off the clock?'' he asked, amused. "Off the clock, you can do anything you want.''

"Thanks. I'm pulling the chart from this morning, then, and taking him straight in. Is there a room available?''

"Place is empty. Help yourself.'' Out in the hallway, we heard the now-familiar cough. Wallace's brows went up. "That yours?''

"That's mine. And I'm wearing a mask to treat him. You hear that sound today and I suggest that you wear one, too.''

Wallace nodded and followed me at a safe distance as I greeted Sam and Josephine.

Sam Tooley looked better than I expected. His color was good, his chest X ray looked fairly clean—nothing like the films I had seen the night before—and his blood gasses were nearly perfect. Still, I didn't like the cough and called Sam's personal physician to see if he would admit the man to isolation.

It took a little persuasion, but he finally agreed. Sam was admitted to the medical unit under strict isolation, and I sent Josephine to the drugstore to fill prophylactic prescriptions for her entire family. If this bug was contagious, and I had no reason to think it wasn't, then I wanted everyone associated with it on antibiotics just in case.

This time I made certain that she understood the gravity of the situation, telling her that some of the people who had contracted this pneumonia had died from it. Hearing that, Josephine promised that she would take the meds immediately and make certain that her kids did, too. As an afterthought, she added, "And I intend to have our preacher come pray for Sam and lay on the Hands of Healing. If nothing in the world will help my husband, then prayer will. The Hands of Healing will. I know. They healed my cousin Betty of cigarette addiction last month.''

The way she said it sounded like the "hands" were written in capitals, but I didn't ask. Nor did I tell her that if Betty had only been addiction-free for a few weeks then she might not be exactly healed. There were places I didn't want to go, and faith was one of them. Marisa was faithful, and thanks to her I knew every old-fashioned gospel song ever sung. But faith hadn't kept Marisa safe when a member of her own family wanted to harm her, so I didn't know how much help it would be to Sam.

As I was taking my leave to find my bed again, it suddenly occurred to me to ask, "Your preacher? Who is he?"

"The Reverend Lamb of God," Josephine said with fervor.

"Ah," I replied. And on that inadequate note, I left the hallway outside of Sam Tooley's room.

9

CLEAN MIRACLES

Shareeka Warden's distraught mother had been admitted to the hospital and I couldn't remember her name. Could not remember if I had even heard her name while treating Shareeka. But before I left the hospital to find my deserted bed again, I wanted to check up on her. Douglas Byars had admitted her after Shareeka died, and with a little help from the hospital switchboard, I located the patient on the medical-surgical wing, only one room down from Sam Tooley. Shareeka's mother's name was Donnalaura Warden. One word, Donnalaura. I liked it. But I didn't like her condition when I stuck my masked face into the room. Didn't like it one bit. In fact, after one glimpse at her gray face, I tore off the mask and went looking for Byars. His patient was dying.

Working like the well-oiled team we had quickly become, Douglas and I went to work. Transportation to PCU was fast, Donnalaura receiving vital sedation as we moved so that her survival instincts would not prevent us from inserting a tube down her throat the moment we arrived on the unit. It wasn't possible to intubate a patient who was fighting. Well, it might be possible, but it wasn't smart. Being put on a ventilator was terrifying.

Unlike Regina Hawkins, this patient had not reached the

point of cardiac difficulties or breathing out blood, and the antibiotics had already eased the wet-tearing-linen cough. But she was weak, and her lungs were full of fluid that her body had not yet thrown off. With the vent to assist, she stabilized quickly as the machine took over the primary job of the lungs and exchanged oxygen and medications for carbon dioxide. Within twenty minutes she was out of immediate danger. Things were suddenly looking up, and Douglas, dead on his feet, went home to sleep.

I realized that I could go home, too. Instead I sat at the PCU desk and stared across the hall to Donnalaura's room. Loss of sleep was hanging heavily on my tired brain. My body felt both wired and sleep-heavy at the same time, though the sense of dread that had taken hold earlier may have added its own weight. If this was an epidemic, even a treatable one, we could be in trouble. Dawkins was a large rural county, a place with more cows than people, more pigs than people, and certainly more cultivated fowl than people. What we didn't have was a boundless supply of space or personnel. Without a doubt, when word and fear of the contagion spread, we would begin to have massive sick-outs. Employees with children at home would not be taking the kids to a nursery while they went to work. Nurseries were the primary source of contagious childhood disease. Parents, the immuno-compromised, the fearful, would be staying home. We'd be short-staffed and overrun with panicked patients.

And yet, there was no proof of an epidemic. What we had was a very small outbreak of something. With Donnalaura stabilized, I headed to the microbiology lab. I passed Dr. Reeves in the hallway, his hands clasped behind his back, his gaze on the floor at his feet as he walked. He didn't see me at all, and so didn't speak. I didn't interrupt his deep thoughts, as he might have been thinking through a cure for the common cold or herpes simplex, or trying to figure out where the next negative-pressure unit was coming from. Never bother a man deep in his thoughts or his beer. Another lesson learned in med school.

One of the first things I did when I came to Dawkins was to familiarize myself with the lab, what tests were done stat, which were done daily, which were sent to reference labs. And where every department was located. Most hospitals are built with specific needs in mind and when the needs and technology change, management has to find ways to make space for the new. In Dawkins, the micro lab—which was also called bacti, short for bacteriology department— was at the end of the hallway beyond ICU, a goodly walk from the rest of the lab.

In the cramped, noisy space, I found Bess, staring into a microscope. She didn't look up when I entered. Instead she waved me to a chair. "Hi, Doc. Been expecting you."

I was surprised. "Why?"

"You discovered our little critter and you're the only doctor in the county who hasn't come by to see it."

By *critter*, I assumed she meant the bacteria that had killed several patients, but I knew her emphasis wasn't on the germ. "You mean *doctors* found this hole in the wall?"

"Ain't it amazing? Found it and actually asked questions. Not that I can tell them much." She glanced quickly up from the 'scope. "It's still too early."

"What does it look like?"

"Like a strep. There's not enough to do a confirmatory yet. It's slow-growing."

"It didn't look like a strep pneumo on the slide. That's the only strep I know of that could kill so fast."

Bess shrugged, put aside the slide she had been looking at and slipped another under the lens. "Plates are in the incubators on the far left and the far right, if you want to see 'em. Culture numbers are in the book," she said, her voice vaguely disinterested.

Bess was busy, so I made myself at home, looking up the sputum cultures in the bacti book and then pulling the plates from the incubators. She was right. The plates showed a little discoloration, but no actual colony growth. I figured we might have seventy-two hours before this critter, as Bess had called it, was identified. I wondered if Donnalaura Warden, Mel Campbell and Sam Tooley would last till then.

There was nothing to be learned here and sleep pulled at me, so I said my goodbyes to Bess, who mumbled something in response, and slipped back into the hallway. Wanting to inform Wallace how Sam was doing, I stopped at the ER. The emergency scanner was crackling with crises, and he and several employees were gathered around, discussing the current problem.

In spite of the drenching storm, Killan's Mill, an old mill-turned-warehouse out near Prosperity Creek was on fire. Several squatter families living in it had somehow managed to set the thing ablaze. Volunteer rural firefighters were on the scene, had used up the water in the holding-tank truck, and were now pulling water from the swollen creek. But fire had engulfed the building and, with the blowing wind, was too hot for firemen to get close.

There was no evidence of injuries at the site and Wallace could handle a few small burns and any smoke-inhalation patients. I decided that I was unnecessary and left, drove home in a sleepy half daze and fell into bed. I was beat.

I woke at five to the sound of someone knocking on my bedroom window. Groggily, I lifted my head and focused on the sound. The dogs weren't barking. If they hadn't been dog-napped, poisoned by drinking some neighbor's hydraulic fluid or antifreeze, or garroted by a mad strangler who also happened to know about the broken doorbell, then it was either Mark, DeeDee, Marisa or Cam. As DeeDee was in the state mental facility, and Marisa and Cam were still near Duke Medical Center at the rehab clinic because of her injury, that left Mark. I pulled the pillow over my head. Maybe he'd go away.

The house had no functional front doorbell, which I thought was a grand thing, as it kept me free of door-to-door types. Friends knew not to bother with the front and came to the back. This friend apparently knew I was sleeping. And didn't care. He knocked again.

I pulled myself from the bed, tapped back on the window without looking out and went to the bathroom. No matter who it was, even if it was the mad strangler, he could wait while I emptied my bladder, brushed my teeth and hair, pulled on jeans and T-shirt, and stared in the mirror for fifteen seconds. I seldom bothered with makeup, but I always looked to see just how much I needed to. Today was a bad one. I had dark circles and pillow-case-wrinkles. Perfect for the mad strangler.

Feeling a bit more presentable, I went down the back hall to the door and peeked out. Belle and Yellow Pup were running circles around a woman...Marisa.

Yanking open the door, I leapt down the few steps and into her arms. We squealed like schoolgirls, arms around each other, dancing in circles. Belle and Pup raced around us whuffing with joy. Their women were together again. For the dogs, the whole world could be falling apart, but if Marisa was home, then all was well. I felt that way, too. A strange pain—half lump, half sound—caught in my throat. She had been gone for months.

I pulled away, my eyes searching out details and trying to see the whole picture at once. Marisa was home. Really home. She was standing in my yard, under her own power. She was looking at me. And seeing me. The last time I saw her, she was little more than a vegetable.

Her hair was brushed into a gleaming blond chignon, her makeup so perfect I couldn't see anything but peaches-and-cream, her dress was stylish, managing to hide the fullness of her pregnancy, and she looked...wonderful. Just simply wonderful, the dark circles and pallid skin of her recuperation were gone. I gripped her arms. My best friend in the whole world was back.

I don't know where the tears came from. Maybe I was PMSing. Maybe it was lack of sleep. But tears welled and fell so fast that I had no control. Through their blur, I touched her face, which smiled back at me, I stroked her hair, and lastly, when she gripped my lost and wondering hands and pulled them in, placed them on her belly. A hard kick met my palm. "Oh, God," I screeched, jerking away, hands out in shock.

Belle barked at my shriek. Marisa laughed. It was a sound I hadn't heard in months. "My baby," she said proudly. And I stared at her. Her tinkling laugh rang out and she patted my face, amused at my expression. At the request of her therapist, I had visited Marisa at the rehab center only once in the months she had been gone. She hadn't spoken then, but had mimed and pointed and managed to make herself understood. It hadn't been conversation like I wanted and needed, but it had been more than I expected.

I sniffed hard, fighting the pain in my throat. "You talked."

"I...can. Shom...some," she corrected, sounding pleased.

"Oh, my God. Look at you. And you can talk." My hands patted her belly again and roamed over her half professionally, half in awe as the dogs wound themselves around our legs in joy.

"Sunshine," Marisa said happily as she slipped an arm around me. "Shunshine...you are my Shunshine," she sang. I realized she was singing to me. "You make me...happy when skies are gray...." She laughed, her eyes sparkling.

Sunshine. That hated nickname from grade school. Yet Marisa had remembered such a tiny detail and managed to communicate it. I could live with the name. I hugged her back. "Sunshine," she said again softly. "My Sunshine."

"She's been practicing that song so hard she ought to be able to sing an opera in Carnegie Hall."

Without letting go of my friend, I turned and spotted Cam standing in the trees, leaning negligently against an old oak, black eyes glittering, ebony hair tossed back in unruly abandon, dark clothes blending with the shadowed trunks. Holding out my arm, I welcomed him into the huddle and held him close.

"You did this, didn't you," I said to Cam. "You and that hateful, wonderful place you took her to that was so blasted far away, and that wouldn't let me talk to her on the phone. You gave back her speech…her words." I would have said more, but my voice met a clog and stopped.

"Yeah. The center is pretty fabulous," he said, his mouth near my ear, breath warm on my skin. "But I have to warn you, she didn't get back everything. Somewhere along the way, we lost the gentle, tender Marisa and got left with this."

Marisa, laughing, pulled back and swatted Cam.

"See? She hits now. And opinionated as hell."

Marisa hit him harder, still laughing. "Don't curse," she said.

"What did I tell you?" Cam pulled her fair head forward and kissed Marisa's brow. "I got to go, girls. You're going to be too busy shopping to need me around." When I stiffened, Cam and Marisa both laughed. "I told you. Still same Rhea-Rhea. Still *loves* to shop."

"I'm just a bit busy right now," I said, thinking about the hospital and how wonderful it was to have an epidemic to keep me busy and out of the malls Marisa loved so much. "I don't have—"

"—time to shop," Cam said with me. "And you have to make time. Risa needs baby things."

"Why didn't you—"

"Make time to shop with her in Raleigh? We did. And

brought back so much stuff we nearly didn't get off the ground.''

Marisa punched him again, her brows pulled together in mock anger.

"See? Vicious woman. Violent as hell." Cam pulled away from the three-way hug before Marisa could punch him again for the forbidden word and sauntered back toward the woods. "I'll be back in a few weeks. Sooner if she goes into early labor. I have a long weekend off next month and I intend to spend it here." Pausing, he turned back to us, his eyes on my face. "You ever get a guest room bed?"

"No. Why?"

"Well, if you don't want me sleeping with you, I suggest you get one."

I knew he saw my blush, was waiting for it, and I stuck out my tongue at him, offering him that picture of me to take back to Duke. Better that than anything else he might have spotted in the instant his words penetrated.

"Have fun shopping, Marisa," Cam said with a devilish laugh, all white teeth in his dark, olive-skinned face. "Be sure to take plenty of ammonia capsules to wake Rhea at the end of the day." He flipped us a wave and hopped across the creek, jogging into the trees toward Marisa's house.

"He likes you," Marisa said sweetly when he was gone.

"Of course he likes me," I snorted. "If I had an overbite like a horse, ears like a mule and a butt like a dairy cow he'd still like me. I'm female." Hooking her arm, I pulled her toward the house. "But he's in love with you. Remember? Moon-faced, suffering Cameron Reston, crying his heart out over the only woman he would ever love, who married his arch rival Steven Braswell?"

Marisa resisted, halting, blue eyes intent on me as she searched for words in her damaged memory. "Before…me. Not now me." Her free hand made little circles in the air then touched the scar at her left brow.

I understood, though I hated what she was saying. The

universal symbol of a person who was crazy or had scrambled brains, with the addition of the location of her assault. She wasn't what or who she had been before the penetrating trauma and resulting brain damage. Marisa knew that. The weird part was that Marisa accepted that change with such equanimity. Such peace.

"Not me now. He likes you."

"Good," I said, ignoring the little jolt of shamed pleasure that warmed me at her words. "Come in. I want you to see something."

Marisa resisted again, this time looking in distaste at the house. After a moment, she found the word she was searching for and spoke emphatically. "Dirt!"

"Not now," I teased. "Not anymore. Come on in."

"Clean?" Marisa looked at me wonderingly, a spark of mischief in her gaze. "Miracles."

10

Marisa and I toured the house, Marisa cooing and oohing at the decorative changes, the clean bathroom tile, the new furniture. She was especially impressed at the new, larger windows installed throughout the house, part of the price of the sales negotiation with the current owners, who had no takers until I came along. They were, in the parlance of the Realtor, *highly motivated to sell.*

I had provided them with a list of repairs and improvements soon after my offer was made, and many of the requests had been met, including real tile on the kitchen floor, new countertops in kitchen and baths, and a total paint job inside and out. We were still negotiating on the new roof and the insulation, and I figured if I got even half of the repairs made, it was a bargain. I loved the house and would have bought it in the condition I found it. I was smart enough not to tell them that.

After the tour, Marisa and I had coffee. Real coffee, Marisa's first cup with caffeine since her injury. She held the mug in both hands, just as she used to, allowing the warmth to sink in as she inhaled the fragrance of the Kenyan beans and real cream. When she finally sipped, it was almost anticlimactic, though she groaned with pleasure under her breath, causing me to grin.

"You tell Cam or Miss Essie that I let you have real coffee, and it'll be the last time," I warned. "Understand?"

Eyes still closed on her second sip, Marisa nodded.

"I'll buy a bag of caffeine-free for later."

Marisa's eyes popped open in alarm.

"And every time you come over for coffee, we'll pour some down the drain so Arlana doesn't tell Miss Essie I'm cheating. And only two cups of the real stuff for you a week. I'm not risking your brain any more than that."

Marisa's eyes sparkled blue fire. If a jewel that shade of dark blue could be discovered or manufactured, it would take the world by storm. The lump I had found in my throat when I first saw her returned, but I didn't let Marisa see my distress. If she could accept what had been done to her, then I could, too. Even if it killed me.

Marisa took my hand, her grip communicating her latest urgency. "Rhea-Rhea."

"Yes, Risa?" I squeezed her hand in encouragement.

"Eddie?"

I sighed, closing my eyes. Did Marisa remember the attack? Eddie was Marisa's stepson, and had been one of the young men implicated in her attack. One of the ones who held her down while Miss DeeDee shoved an ice pick into her brain. How much should I tell her? Mentally, I cursed Cam for flying off and leaving me to deal with this one.

Marisa shook my hand. "Eddie!" she insisted.

Opening my eyes, I said, "Eddie's in jail, Risa." At her blank look I said, "He assaulted a teacher in Ford County. And a young girl…" More softly I added, "And you." Marisa's eyes filled with tears, disbelieving. "You don't remember, do you?"

"No. Eddie?" Her eyes asked me to recant, to deny.

I nodded slowly. "Eddie."

"And Miss DeeDee. They hurt me. Together?" A tear slipped down the perfect arc of her cheek.

I leaned my head in and touched her temple with mine. "Yes. They did."

Marisa put down her cup, pushed me back a bit to make firm eye contact, took my hand and placed it on her belly, her other hand still clutching mine. "Family," she said firmly. "Family."

I nodded, tears misting my own vision. "Family. Miss Essie, you, me and baby makes four."

"And Cam," she said, wiping her eyes and face.

"And Cam," I agreed.

Marisa sniffed, lifted her coffee cup and held it up as if for a toast. I raised my cup, clinked it to hers, and we both drank. A solemn pact had been made.

"So what's the latest on the due date?" I eyed her tummy, sticking up under full breasts, her coffee cup now resting on it as if it were a table. "And what's the sex? Don't tell me you refused to ask."

Her smile returned, blindingly beautiful. "Baby in two weeks, or three," she said with ease, words she spoke often, with pride. "Stupid doctors can't decide for sure."

I laughed. Marisa had been to medical school with me, and dropped out to marry Steven. Her stupid-doctor remark was directed at me. "Because *this* stupid doctor took so long to notice you were pregnant?"

Marisa grinned again. "And I know what it is. Boy or girl."

"As in opposed to dog or cat? Cute, Risa. You didn't let them tell you?"

"No," she said with finality.

"So what color are we supposed to shop for? Green?"

Marisa put down her mug and clapped her hands. I had just agreed to take her shopping. Then her face clouded and she took a deep breath. Placing her hands on her stomach in that protective way most pregnant mothers had, she stared at me. I was made to understand that what she had to say was important.

"I can not...talk so good. Now. Baby need talker. Helper. English."

I wasn't sure what she meant. "You want me to talk around your baby so she will learn how to speak properly?"

"No. English."

"I don't speak English well enough?"

Marisa shook her head.

"Thanks," I said, amused rather than insulted. I spoke with a Charleston accent, Southern to the core. Not good enough for Marisa's baby, it seemed.

"English helper," she repeated, her eyes demanding me to understand.

And suddenly I did. "You want an English nanny!"

"Yes!" Marisa's beautiful smile spread over her face. "You get one."

"I'll make some calls. I'll bet there's a doctor around here somewhere who knows how to find a nanny service."

"No Cockney talk." And I was impressed with the easy way her mouth formed the word *Cockney*. Marisa had been practicing this speech for a while.

"You want a nanny who speaks like the royal family, not like Eliza Doolittle, I take it?"

Again, an emphatic nod.

"Why not ask for one who speaks French and Spanish, too," I said waspishly. And I should have kept my mouth shut, because Marisa thought that was a great idea.

I sighed. "Shopping for stuff isn't good enough for you. Now you want me to shop for people, as well."

She stood and came around the small table that had been a gift from Miss DeeDee before she went bonkers, bent and put her arms around me. I hugged back.

"Okay. You win."

"Good. Now I have to go," she said sweetly, forming the words carefully. "Thank you for a pleasant afternoon."

I couldn't help myself. I chuckled. And Marisa laughed with me. God, it was good to have her back.

*   *   *

I was off from the ER on a rare Friday night, and at loose ends. Marisa slept ten or twelve hours a night and was clearly tired when I walked her back to her house on the other side of the still-swollen creek, so visiting her was out. Cam was flying back to Duke. The dogs were too worn-out to play, sitting on the back stoop, tongues lolling, Pup lying across Belle as if she were a pillow. Both needed a bath, stinking like the wet dogs they were in the early April night.

I had to admit that I was almost lonely. I seldom experienced loneliness, enjoying good music or a good medical journal as much as other people's company, but tonight was different somehow. I wanted to be around people. Maybe see a movie. Something.

I sipped the last cup of Kenyan coffee and thought about a run, but I was also feeling lazy. Without dislodging Pup, Belle clawed her way to my foot on the stoop and nosed it. She wanted to be scratched and I obliged. "That's a good Belle," I murmured, taking comfort in her presence as night fell and the temperature began to drop.

Spurred on by the rain and unseasonable warmth, frogs had come out of hibernation in the creek out back, and several sang out throaty calls. Somewhere nearby a horse neighed, hooves clopping on damp ground. Some neighbor's mount loose after the flood. I wouldn't go looking for it, but if it came into the yard, I'd tie it off and call the sheriff. Loose livestock was always a problem after inclement weather. The darkness grew thicker, my cup colder. Belle snuggled closer and I let her, stink and all.

I was on the verge of calling Mark to come over for takeout when I heard him in the drive, lights cutting the blackness as he pulled to a halt. The dark green Jeep purred in place, Mark's head hanging out the window, face cut into planes of light and darkness by the reflection of headlights.

"A woman after my own heart. Two hunting dogs and a cup of hot coffee, waiting on the back porch for her man."

I snorted. "Belle is not a hunter, and Pup is too tired to

breathe. The coffee is both cold and nearly gone, and I was watching the sun set, not waiting on you. But I am hungry. Let's go eat.''

"How convenient. My wish is your demand."

"Cute. Let me get my bag." I shoved Belle off my lap and went into the house. The dogs stretched to their feet and went to greet Mark. He always carried dog treats. I brushed my short black hair, put on a smear of blush and lipstick, changed shirts, as Belle had left her scent all over me, and put on clean sneakers. All spiffed up for a date. Took me all of five minutes. As a last thought, I grabbed a light jacket and spritzed on a spray of Red, by Giorgio. The perfume was in case Belle's scent was worse than I expected, not for Mark. At least that's what I told myself.

I climbed into the Jeep, shut the door and belted myself in as Mark pulled down the drive. The tired dogs went back to the stoop and flopped down. Night and the hum of tires on asphalt surrounded us. "So," I said, opening the conversation with a one-word zinger.

"You smell good."

"Thanks. It was perfume or dogs." Another man might have been insulted at my laconic comment. Mark laughed.

"Dogs or perfume. I like both about the same."

"Yeah, well, these particular dogs had been in the creek all day and smelled like wet gym socks. You want to tell me about the jail takeover? I thought for a minute this morning that I was going to have to go inside."

Mark glanced at me from the corner of his eye. "You thought I'd let you go in there?"

"No. Not really. But it crossed my mind." I *had* thought just that, but it wasn't what he wanted to hear.

"You haven't been listening to the news?" When I shook my head, he went on. "A neo-Nazi arrested for lynching a man started a riot when we got all the prisoners crammed in one wing of the lockup. Man by the name of Richard Ellis. Been in jail two days or so, awaiting pickup by the navy. Grabbed the opportunity and the confusion of moving all the prisoners and took over. Shot a few people, beat up a few others, mostly other prisoners when they didn't do what he wanted. We're still looking for him.''

"He got *away?*'' I didn't mean to sound so surprised, or so insulting, but Marisa was home alone with Miss Essie, and the seventy-something-year-old woman was not going to be much protection for my brain-damaged friend if bad guys decided to come calling for supplies and help at her door.

"SLED was on the scene.''

"Oh. Of course. The *state* boys let him get away.'' Now I did mean to sound insulting, but Mark only grinned. He was entirely too happy about this.

"Matter of fact, yes. They took over the operation when they got there. Our man inside was ready to spring the trap and let us all in, when the lieutenant in charge mixed up his signals. Only Grace of God kept anyone from getting killed, but Ellis got away. And the NBC helicopter got it all on tape.''

Now I understood the grin. Mark had video proof that SLED—State Law Enforcement Division—had screwed up. It was enough to make any small-town cop happy.

"And Ellis?''

"Is footloose and fancy-free with a dozen guns and a massive manhunt going on for him, down in Lancaster County, where he was spotted only an hour ago,'' he added as if he thought I was worried about possibly seeing an armed-and-dangerous man on the side of the road.

"So why aren't you taking part in this bicounty manhunt?''

"Uh,'' he grunted, sounding remarkably like one of his hunting dogs. "The Lou I mentioned? Well, his feet somehow got tangled up in mine and he fell. And his jaw accidentally hit the back of my hand on the way down.'' Mark looked at the knuckles of his right hand and made a fist as if to see that it still worked.

"You tripped the man, hit him with your fist, and he fell," I said dryly.

Mark glanced at me again, smug and happy in the dash lights. "That's not what the witnesses say."

"Who all happen to be your men."

"You know, come to think about it, they *were* all Dawkins men." And the grin grew wider.

I sighed. Men and their games. "So, tell me about this Ellis. He beat up some of my patients this morning, so I already know his methods."

"Ellis beat them up, or his men did?" Green eyes probed mine as if this was an important distinction.

"Ellis watched. And enjoyed the show."

Mark nodded. "Record of hate crimes," he said thoughtfully. "Kicked out of the Citadel for various race-based actions on younger underclassmen. Enlisted, and then caused problems in the marines after Desert Storm. Later he was convicted in court-martial for hitting a superior officer. Black officer, of course. Served part of his time, had some kinda religious conversion, and then escaped, along with a couple other men. They killed a guard on their way out of the stockade. One of his friends and he were accused of assaulting a Jewish couple in New York City in 1997. Attacked a gay couple in the same city a few nights later. Arrested, then both set free before the NIS could get there. Paperwork snafu. But they were gone, of course.

"In early 1998, a man fitting his description was caught with several vials of anthrax on a train in Washington, D.C., heading for the Potomac, not that the anthrax could have been dispersed through water. The vials were covered in Arabic writing, and were tied to half a dozen different Middle East terrorist groups. We don't know what he had planned to do with it, but it couldn't have been anything good. Got away, again, but Secret Service kept the vial."

Mark paused as he pulled in behind a logging truck and then turned off the main road into a parking lot. I hadn't asked where we were eating and really didn't care, but the restaurant wasn't familiar. "Sottise?" I asked, realization dawning. "Is that *French?* In *Dawkins?*"

"Means *foolishness* or something. We got a menu at the department last week. You're not dressed to eat inside, but we can eat on the porch. Al fresco."

My mouth watered. "I would eat in the yard out back if I had to." I hadn't eaten really good food since I got to Dawkins, no insult intended to the very fine steakhouses, fish camps, home-cooking establishments, sandwich shops and fast-food places boasted by the county. But when I was engaged to John, we ate *well.* John had been a more-than-great cook. He had trained under some of the finest chefs in New York each summer, paying for the opportunity to work under the demanding taskmasters to learn the art of Continental cuisine. I couldn't cook worth a darn, but I *loved* to eat. In that respect we had been a match made in heaven. I was suddenly famished.

"Group of men caught on a bank video beating and robbing an Asian couple in Atlanta, one of whom happens to look a lot like him. And in jail here in Dawkins, his men caused trouble promoting the killing of 'retards, mutants, spooks, chinks, Hebes and other people of color.' His words, not mine. And claiming that race wars are coming. Personally I'm glad he's gone. Hope he runs into a brother with a big gun and a bad attitude real soon."

"Huh?" I asked.

"Ellis." Mark looked from my face to the restaurant's neon marquee. "Hungry?"

I ignored the look of false innocence on his face. "If this place is any good, I will be working extra to pay for all my meals from here. Do they deliver? God, I have *missed* good food." I unbelted and started to open my door.

Mark laughed and caught my hand. "Keep your seat. Our reservations aren't for a half hour."

"We have reservations?" I looked down at my jeans. "I could have dressed."

"You own anything other than jeans?"

I stared. He was serious. "You've never seen me in anything other than jeans?"

"Nope." He seemed interested in the possibility, his green eyes warm. Maybe too warm. I slid my hand from his.

"I have clothes. In storage somewhere in a guest room for the most part. But I have a few things in the closet." Clothes I had worn to the many parties given by and for John and me the months after we were formally engaged and living in Charleston, where dressing was part of the everyday social life. Just before we broke up. Clothes far too elegant for Dawkins. But now... "I even have dresses," I added as he looked at my jeans-clad legs. "And high heels," I concluded, lifting my nose in the air.

"No kidding? Any legs under there?"

"Keep your prurient curiosity to yourself." I crossed my legs modestly.

"Want to see the department's new toy?" he asked, changing the subject.

I wasn't certain about the segue from my legs to toys, but I was interested, anyway.

Mark reached around behind the seats and hefted a black-and-gray contraption into my lap. It looked heavy but wasn't, made of lightweight plastic shaped into some kind of boom microphone, parabolic dish and video camera in one. He nodded to the restaurant, pursed his lips in anticipation and flipped a switch on the instrument. A light blinked before achieving a steady red glow. "We got this on loan from a police-surveillance supply company. This and a little robot for the bomb squad. We can listen to almost anything inside. Sound waves bounce off the window and are picked up by the mike.''

"Don't people have legal rights to privacy?"

"Not all people."

I could feel the reaction to his comment stretch across my lips. This could be fun. Our arguments usually were, though Mark had informed me we didn't argue. We discussed. I could have argued the point, but it wasn't worth it. "According to the Constitution, people have rights," I said, my tone both mild and provocative.

Mark lowered my window, hefted the equipment up and aimed it at the restaurant. Ignoring me. Voices, scratchy and overlaid with kitchen sounds, tinny piano music, and the sounds of cutlery, filled the car. Adjusting the volume, Mark glanced at me with a prankish grin. "Have to practice. And the Supreme Court okayed these little babies—and similar gewgaws—for investigative purposes by certain law enforcement groups."

"Gewgaws? How...Southern," I said with a straight face.

"You mean *redneck*," he clarified, chuckling.

From the restaurant came the sounds of an argument, sotto voce, between the couple in the front window. The woman swallowed, leaned forward and said, "You weren't staying late at work. I called Darrell and asked."

"You called my boss to check up on me?" the man said, sitting back. He was young and good-looking, in a blond, Nordic sort of way. "You little bitch."

"Oops," Mark said joyfully. "Bubba done got caught."

"Stuff the outraged dignity," the woman said. "You're screwing around on me again, aren't you? Who is it this time? Some little—"

"I'm not screwing around on you. And keep your voice down."

"Don't tell me what to do!" she snapped.

I reached over and flipped the switch. The sound stopped.

"Privacy," I said. "And I don't care what the Supreme Court decided."

Mark sighed. "You take all the fun out of it."

I nodded, a half smile in place. "I've been accused of that before."

"And if they were two child pornographers planning a new movie with six-year-olds? Do they deserve privacy, too? Or what if it was drug dealers sitting there? Planning on distributing near a school, or planning on bringing in a trainload of cocaine?"

I lifted my brows and let my smile widen. This was an old argument, debated often with new stimulus. And while I got the feeling that he wasn't telling me everything he knew about the use of the new toy, I wasn't averse to a good debate. "You can play around with situational ethics all you want. I'm not interested in listening in to a couple having marital problems," I added dryly.

"You want law enforcement to protect you from trouble but you don't want us to do whatever is necessary to accomplish that. You want to sit in a little ivory tower and let us cops take all the risk," he baited, eyes glinting, half smile hidden by his new mustache.

"Risk? Don't give me that," I said, only half jesting. "You boys on the *thin blue line* love taking risks. Adrenaline junkies, all of you. If they didn't pay you, you'd *still* do it."

"But you still get to sit back all safe and sound, taking for granted that we'll be there in the event of trouble."

"What I want to take for *granted*," I said languidly, trying to keep my grin from widening, "is that you won't be playing cops and robbers without any restraint. I don't want you invading the privacy of someone to practice with your new toy. I don't want you to cross over the legal boundaries."

Mark laughed, and I shook my head. "I'll convert you some day."

"My conversion to a love of guns, guns and more guns isn't likely. I spend too much of my time patching up holes left by their bullets."

After a moment, Mark said appreciatively, "Situational ethics? That's a new one."

"I try." My stomach growled. The smells coming from the restaurant had surpassed wonderful and become heavenly. "But we've had this, ah, *discussion* so often I'm running out of new ways to win it."

Mark shook his head. "Win? You? Are we talking about the same, ah, *discussion,* I just heard?"

"Yes. The situational ethics threw you. You had no comeback for it. So technically I won."

Mark checked his watch again and settled back in his seat. I tried to control my hunger. "By the way, Eddie Braswell's out of jail," he said.

I sat up, the French restaurant and the enticing smells wafting from it forgotten. Eddie hadn't gone to trial for the assault, and likely never would, though he had served time in another assault, this one on a teacher. "Out of jail? When? Is he living with Steven?"

Dr. Steven Braswell, Marisa's soon-to-be-ex-husband, was gone from the county since the assault on Marisa had been uncovered, but he was still pulling strings. He was working in the Ford County hospital, living with the woman who had broken up the Braswell marriage. Personally, I thought the doctor should be in jail for allowing his wife to vegetate after she was injured, but the Dawkins County prosecutor had disagreed and Steven was a free man, able to meddle at will. It had been only a matter of time before he got Eddie out on good behavior or parole or whatever they let people out on in this state.

"Three days ago. He was converted in jail by the Reverend Lamb of God. Baptized and everything. Ever hear of him?"

"The Lamb? Oh, yeah. I met him even." At Mark's

raised brow, I said, "Patient confidentiality, but he cut his finger. Waited a bit too long to come in to have it closed. Had a prophecy service right there in the ER. Tell me about Eddie."

"Too bad he didn't cut it off. Bleed to death. Anyway, Eddie now sports a flattop, army fatigues and a gold necklace of some sort they all wear. Lives at Lamb's compound out on the edge of the county. He quotes scripture like a preacher, but I don't think it all comes from the Good Book. The kid's still loony, but Marisa seems to be safe from him. And a contact I have in Ford County says Dr. Braswell hasn't been in communication with him. Steven is still being a good boy, and staying out of Dawkins and away from Marisa, as per the judge's order."

I smiled, knowing what he had done but wanting to hear it from him. "And?"

His brow went up again.

"And...you knew he was out of jail but didn't tell me until you checked him out because you knew I'd worry about Marisa."

Mark shrugged, diffident, but not at all uncomfortable.

"Thank you. I would have worried, as much about Steven as about Eddie." Leaning over, I kissed his cheek. "Now feed me or I'll start taking bites out of your Jeep. I'm starving."

11

THE TAIL STOPPED WAGGING

The meal was superb, with both nouvelle-cuisine and more traditional dishes made with heavy cream and cheese and wine, all served under the awning as a fresh wind blew up and the piano player ran through a series of old blues tunes my mother would have loved in her sober days. I ate until I was stuffed, and then forced down dessert and coffee with Bailey's Irish Cream liqueur. I could have stayed until they closed, but we both had to work the next day, so we left just after ten, walking arm in arm back to the Jeep.

Maybe it was the wine, a rich cabernet sauvignon that went wonderfully with the beef. Maybe it was the liqueur that spiked my last cup of coffee. Or maybe it was the memories of happier times with John after a grand meal he had prepared for us. Whatever it was, when Mark backed me up to the cold metal of the Jeep and leaned himself against me, I melted into him. He tasted of coffee, with a faint tang of wine and chocolate. His mustache was bristly and very un-John.

I kissed him back, shivering as the sharp wind cut into me through the light jacket. And felt ancient heat rise as he pressed closer. But I didn't let it take me. I held down the need, the want, the desire to hold and be held. And when the kiss gentled, I carefully pushed away. Mark rested his face near mine, breathing deeply.

"I'm going to convert you some day," he whispered, bringing a different meaning to our earlier debate. I could only nod. He likely would.

Later, when I entered my cold house and greeted my dogs in the back entrance, I wondered why I was holding Mark off. Why I didn't just take what was offered and make my empty life full. John wasn't coming back. And if he did, I couldn't trust his promises or plans. So I wasn't saving myself for John.

Bending, I scratched behind Pup's ears as Belle laved my chin with her tongue. "Good babies, yes, you are. Good Belle and Pup." I stood, only a little woozy from the meal and Mark's kiss.

And remembered Marisa's words from the afternoon. "He likes you." Fourth-grade tease, like a note from a boy in the back of the class. Cameron Reston liked all women. Adored them, in fact. Worshiped them to the point that he couldn't settle down to any one for very long, no matter how much he claimed love and devotion. And for me? Friendship is what he had always offered. At least I had something no other woman ever had from him, and unlike the numerous women in his life, including the live-in girlfriend I remembered from a few months earlier, our relationship seemed permanent.

No, Cam wasn't for me. Not now, not ever. And Mark? He wasn't a third choice out of three. I sighed. He was his own unmeasured sum of untested significance. And I simply couldn't. Not just now.

My beeper sounded, a soft single chirp in the bedroom. Turning on a light, I found the beeper on the bedside table and checked it. A hospital number flashed on the LED readout and the time the call came through. At 10:00 p.m. Calling the hospital, I asked for the extension. An ICU nurse answered.

"Hi, Gloris. Someone called me? This is Dr. Lynch."

"Yeah, Doc, hold on for Dr. Byars."

"Rhea?" His voice sounded worried, and something constricted inside.

"Douglas. What's up?"

"I just wanted to update you on our patients."

"Bad?"

"The worst."

I sat on the bed and pulled the comforter over my legs. I was going to have to turn on the heater tonight. The unseasonably mild weather was gone. "Tell me."

"Donnalaura Warden expired this evening at 7:02," he said steadily. I picked at the cream-and-ecru cloth of the down duvet cover, soft as suede beneath my fingers. "Same cause of death as her daughter, but I'm sending her to Columbia for a medical PM to verify. Sam Tooley is on the vent, and it looked touch-and-go for a while, but he's stabilized. Mel Campbell..." Douglas sighed, exhaustion in every breath. "Mel won't last the night. But we have no confirmed new cases, and it looks like this may be it."

"Have you been home since this started, Douglas?" I asked softly.

"Nope. Except to shower and change and wash some clothes. I figured I had been exposed to whatever this is. Why turn it over to another doctor and risk spreading it around?"

"No confirmed new cases?"

He hesitated. "We have three new bronchitis and pneumonia patients, all rescue squad members and firefighters."

"Causative agent?" I asked, lapsing into the med-speak doctors used to talk to one another.

"That's a problem. We have nothing to go on, even on the patients who expired. Multiple organisms. That grampositive thing we saw on the gram stains. It's beta hemolytic and slow-growing. The others are gram-negative and resistant to everything. We have a pseudomonas—unspeciated so far—an *E. coli* and a salmonella,'' he said, listing three common bacteria. "In most patients we have all organisms to one degree or the other. And because the gram-positive is the predominant organism in all cases, I'm beginning to think the others could be contaminants. The lab is trying to work up the cultures, but with nothing much growing, what can we do? We can't send it off to a reference lab and expect back results any time soon.''

"That gram-positive organism,'' I said thoughtfully. "You said it's beta hemolytic. Could those properties be contributing to the bleeding?'' Beta-hemolytic organisms literally ate and digested the blood in special blood-based media in a lab. "What if this is a weird new strain that is causing bleeding through some interruption of the coagulation cycle, say, through hemolysis?''

In my mind, I could picture tiny round bacteria attacking the lung cells, exposing veins and arteries, first causing blood to clot, then to bleed.

"I don't know, Rhea. I just freaking don't know.''

I could hear cloth scrape against cloth and knew he had lifted his arm to scratch his scalp in frustration. Belle padded into the room, Pup nipping at her ankles as if to herd Mama along.

"If it was causing some kind of coag problem we'd be seeing petechiae,'' he said, referring to the tiny purplish pinpoint spots beneath the skin that many patients developed when their bodies could no longer regulate their own blood-clotting cycle, "and the PT and PTT results would be going up. Nothing like that is happening, though I'll run a fresh PT and PTT on Mel. Hold on.''

I could hear Douglas, his voice muffled by his hand over the phone, as he gave the order to a nurse or lab tech to draw blood for the tests. A PT and PTT, prothrombin time and partial thromboplastin time, were two of the most basic tests used to evaluate a patient's ability to clot blood. If my half-baked theory was correct, my gram-positive organism would be making the patients' clotting times increase, allowing them to bleed out with the slightest injury internal or external. Not that I expected a positive result to confirm my hypothesis. If this bug was causing patients to bleed out there would be other symptoms, just as Douglas said, and there weren't.

"Okay, Rhea. I just wanted you to know. I hear you're on in the morning, so get some sleep. When you get here I may take a break for some shut-eye. That is, if I can convince you to cover for me for a few hours."

"I'll be glad to. Why don't you try to grab a few hours tonight."

"If I can. See you."

"Sure."

The phone went dead and I replaced it on the table. "Belle, you and Pup stink to high heaven." The big black dog rested her head on my thigh and wagged her tail, eyes pleading for permission to get on the bed with me. Pup danced at her feet. "Time for a bath." The tail stopped wagging. Belle's expressive eyes widened and a small whine escaped her.

"No arguments. Come on, dogs. We're taking a shower."

I stripped, threw on a pair of old jogging shorts and T-shirt, herded the two dogs into the big beige-tiled shower and slid the door closed. I might not be able to do anything about John, Cam or Mark, or about Mel, Donnalaura and Sam Tooley, but I could take care of the awful smell of two stinky dogs.

Saturday dawned clear and cold, and I burrowed back under the blankets. I had forgotten to turn on the heat the night before; the bedroom was warmed by the heated air from the blown-dry dogs. Without new insulation in the walls, the house warmth had escaped. Belle snuggled against me, making little snuffling noises. At least I hoped it was Belle. I lifted the edge of the covers and spotted her long black ear on the pillow next to mine. The dogs were not allowed on the bed, but I was too sleepy to make her get off. Today was wash day, anyway. Arlana would change the sheets and take everything to the laundry in town, mumbling about rich people who paid to have their laundry done instead of buying a washer and dryer and doing the labor themselves.

When the snooze control came back on, I rolled out of bed and pushed Belle out the other side. Skipping a shower, I was dressed and at work by 7:00 a.m. On little sleep, I was facing a twenty-four-hour shift, *and* covering for Douglas Byars, but it was my fault. I had the chance for an extra hour of shut-eye, but had spent it washing and blow-drying two oversize dogs. If I hadn't been so persnickety about the stench...

The morning went well. Douglas spent it sleeping in the doctors' call room; I spent it worrying about the possibility of more pneumonia patients, which was a waste of time. I didn't even see a cough, and the patients already admitted seemed to be stable, or even a bit better. When I had a free moment, I walked to the lab.

Amanda was tinkering with the innards of a big machine in the Chemistry Department. The hood of the machine open like the hood of a car, exposing all sorts of pumps and cams and tubing. It looked terribly boring to me, but she seemed entranced. When I greeted her, she grunted, the sort of grunt that meant *wait a minute, can't you see I'm busy?*

So I waited. Shortly, she lifted her blond head, put down a screwdriver and looked at me quizzically with eyes that were a strange shade of brown, sort of gold with brown flecks. She was leaning against the open machine, watching me, appearing patient, busy and interrupted all at once. Somehow, I gathered that now wasn't a good time to be invading her domain.

Since she didn't speak, I did. "Morning. Broken?"

"Very. Don't be ordering any cardiac work-ups anytime

soon," she said, sounding exasperated. "You can't have them, 'cause this mean ol' mother broke down and quit."

"Okay. Can you tell me any more about the pneumonia cases?"

"Not much, Doc." She stood and went to the sink to wash her hands, glancing back at the machine, still perturbed. "We've got a problem trying to ID one of the gram-negative organisms. We know it's a pseudomonas just from looking at it, but it comes back twenty-five percent probability of four different species. It'll be sent to the reference lab in Charlotte, but it may take them till the middle of next week, with the holiday and all."

At my blank look, she supplied, "Easter. It's Easter weekend, Doc." Teeth flashing, she added, "Where you been? Lose track of time?"

"I guess I did," I said ruefully. I had known that Marisa was coming home for Easter. Just the night before, she had informed me in that broken, gentle way she now had, that I was taking her to church. It wasn't like I could turn her down, but I hadn't remembered that this Sunday was Easter Sunday. "So what about the other organism? The gram-positive?" I said, returning to the present.

"Still TYTR." Too Young to Read.

"Any idea when?"

"No, ma'am. And I'd appreciate it if you would pass that along to Dr. Chadwick, Dr. Reeves, Dr. Byars, and all the other doctors you may spot this morning. Every single one of the on-call doctors for the entire three-day weekend has been in here asking. And I can't help. I'll make a general announcement when I know something. Call all a y'all," she said, with an affable Southern emphasis.

"If you'll just tell me, I'll be glad to let the others know when you have something."

Amanda looked pleased. "Well… Thanks, Doc. 'Preciate that. You're a peach."

"'Welcome." I patted the open hood that pointed to the

fluorescent lights overhead. "How 'bout letting me know when I can have cardiac work-ups again."

"You got it. Oh, and Doc? Since we 'rainbowed' all the patients we stuck when they were admitted, Dr. Byars asked me to run PTs and PTTs on the Campbells, and they show the same thing. Normal PTT results, with higher-than-normal PT results. Instead of a normal twelve seconds to clot, they're all running near twenty. Kinda weird, but not life threatening."

"Oh," I said. "Curious. Thank you."

Feeling that I had somehow rescued the reputation of all medical doctors in Amanda's mind, I wandered away. Easter Sunday. Great. Just great. And I would be taking Marisa to church. Did I have a dress hanging in my closet? One that was suitable for Sunday Mass, or whatever it would be? Or was I going to have to shovel through the boxes of clothes in the guest room for something else? And—God forbid—iron it?

"Doc?"

I stopped just as I reached the door.

"Those two people, the Campbells?"

I nodded.

"The infected tattoos are all growing the same things."

"Multiple organisms?"

Amanda nodded. "Preliminary reports indicate we've got a pseudomonas, an *E. coli* and a salmonella."

"Really? Hmm," I said. "All that?"

Amanda shrugged and went back to her broken machine.

Three different organisms. And all three were organisms routinely found in the intestinal tract....

The ER was empty and I was bored. Picking up a cup of vile ER coffee, I wandered the hallways, sipping and thinking, or rather, not really thinking at all. Just letting thoughts come to me. Mel and Lia had been in a creek. During a storm that flooded the whole county. Before that they had been held prisoner. Tortured. In a small shed with a dirt floor. And a foul smell came across on the wind from time to time. And a pseudomonas was in their lungs and on their skin, along with a salmonella. Both enteric pathogens. Regina Hawkins had stood in or near a creek and cut down her hanged husband. And Donnalaura and her child had been living in a warehouse…and a warehouse had burned down near a creek. Creek water had been used to put out the fire. And rescue workers and volunteer firemen were there….

Swerving, I went back to ER and the huge county map hanging on the wall. It was wrinkled, faded and out of date by a decade, but it was the only map I had. I found the pickup point where Mel and Lia had been discovered crawling out of the water. The secondary road where they had been picked up crossed over Prosperity Creek. That rang a bell, coinciding with the warehouse fire location.

Finger tracing the narrow, wandering, twisting blue line of creek, I followed the waterway north and west. Quickly, I lost all consciousness of scale. Prosperity was a major runoff for the county and was intersected by dozens of other, smaller, unnamed waterways. It was a wet maze only hinted at on the old map. But it was here. I knew it. If only I could figure out what *it* was.

Whatever I thought I knew about the creek was important but remained clouded, lost in the depths of my mind. And yet, as I stared at the map, my fingertips began tingling.

The foul odor the Campbells had described taunted me with an almost-knowing. Foul odor and enteric pathogens.

And then I knew.

Whirling, I went to the phone and dialed Mark's cellular number from memory.

"Eeee-yellow," he said on the fourth ring.

"Pink. Or is it blue? Listen," I said. "Is there a pig farm upstream from the location of the point where the Campbells were picked up? There are—and were—enteric pathogens in the lungs and wounds of them both."

"Well, ain't that jist dandy to know all 'bout them path things." I could hear laughter in the phrase, and redneck humor in the words. "Why, I'm jist proud and pleased to hear a that. Yur a fine lady doctor, yes you are, ma'am. And I do *love* a smart woman, I do."

A frisson of heat passed through me at the accent he put on the word *love*. "Smart aleck." I turned away from the hallway to hide my pinkening cheeks from Zack, who looked up at my tone, dark brows raised in amusement. "Enteric pathogens are germs that live in and/or attack the intestines of humans. And that live in the intestines of pigs and hogs and cows. And with the storms and high water we've had, we could have had a pig-poop-pool or whatever you call them fill up and overflow into the creek. No farmer would contact any agency if he thought he could get by without doing so. The paperwork alone would be enormous. He'd just fix the problem and hope no one noticed.

"But," I continued, "Mel and Lia swam in the creek, and the warehouse burned on the creek and creek water was used—"

"Hang on a minute, Rhea. I'm tracing the creek." The amused redneck vernacular was gone. In the background, I could hear official sounds of the law enforcement center, paper shuffling, a scanner, voices. "Looks like it branches at least twice," he murmured, "but...hang on."

The receiver was partially muffled. "Mayleene!" he shouted to someone at the LEC. "Is McHewell's farm near one of the branches of Prosperity Creek...? Yeah, and...? Think so...? Get a county car out there code three and ask old Mack if his hog waste lagoons are overflowing. And give DHEC a call and report a possible overflow. See if someone from Infectious Waste is available to do a fast inspection.

"If McHewell gives you any guff, let me know and I'll ask for a warrant. Yeah, the Campbell couple. Hell, I should ask for a warrant, anyway."

The sound was restored. "Lady, if you're right, I'll buy you supper."

"At Sottise?" I couldn't keep the craving out of my voice and Mark chuckled.

"Glutton."

"Gourmand," I corrected.

"Whatever. Sottise it is. I'll get back to you."

I waited with little grace, knowing that it might take a few hours to get DHEC—the South Carolina State Department of Health and Environmental Control—out on a holiday weekend. I saw a few patients to pass the time. A laceration, an MVA—car wreck—an earache, a wasp sting with minor allergic reaction…the usual for a rural ER. Fortunately it wasn't deer season, with its attendant rifle shot wounds, broken limbs from falling out of a deer stand with a case of Schlitz in the bloodstream, and more gunshot wounds. I hated hunting season.

Six hours later, a grim-faced Mark trudged into the ER, sat down in my favorite chair and sighed. He was muddy, wet to the knees, and didn't smell particularly pleasant. I washed my hands and sat across from him, nursing my tenth, or so, cup of coffee. I really had to give up the stuff. "And? Do I get dinner out?"

Mark nodded and laid his head against the tall back of the chair, eyes closed. "Dinner, dessert, wine. Even that nasty coffee stuff you like so much."

"Bailey's is not nasty. It's a treat."

Mark's lips curved up slowly, his eyes still shut, and suddenly I remembered the kiss. My face heated and I was glad Zack was not in the room to observe. I was blushing entirely too much these days. And I didn't blush. Ever.

Mark's smile slowly faded, and as I watched, he settled into the chair, his bones seeming to melt and reform into the shape of the vinyl cushions. Sighing again in a long, drawn-out breath, he spoke, his eyes remaining closed, his voice worn and thin. He was exhausted. "Old Mack McHewell tried to keep my deputy off his property. One quick warrant later, me and a half dozen deputies, a few HazMat guys, a fellow from animal control and a woman VIP from DHEC's Infectious Waste Department converged on the site and took out his fence, sedated about ten dogs and started quartering the acreage.

"Of course we discovered the two pig sh—ah, *hog waste lagoons,* that had overflowed on the north edge of Old Mack McHewell's property into the swollen creek. The HazMat people are still having loads of fun cleaning up the site, and the DHEC woman is taking cultures for your enteric pathogens up and down the waterway for miles. She, and whatever teams she calls out to investigate, will be in rubber hip waders for days."

A faint, hard smile lit his features for an instant. "She was right impressed that a good ol' country boy like me knew what the hell an enteric pathogen was. I quoted you, of course. Sounded like I really did know what I was talking about." Mark's mouth twisted down in a self-deprecating smile.

I watched him and waited. Knowing he wasn't through.

"Meanwhile, no one had seen anything that could have been the place described by Mel and Lia Campbell. Until I got to wondering about that Patriot camp that Ellis was involved in. It was upstream a ways and across the creek from Mack's place, but within walking distance if you didn't mind a short, muddy hike. So, I drove to it and tramped around. Place was deserted. Hasn't been used in days."

He sighed, closed his eyes. "I found a few trails, mostly animal trails, some used by hunters. And one well-traveled path that crossed the creek."

I grew still, listening, seeing Mark move through the woods in my mind's eye.

"I put on my own yellow plastic rain gear and hip boots, just in case I happened upon some of your pathogens...."

Mark smiled, a somber sort of smile. "Crossed the creek in a shallow place, back toward Mack's farm. I could see some of the HazMat team working upstream. Finally found the hut where Mel and Lia were held." His voice sounded tired and tattered suddenly, and I couldn't read the expression on his face, though the fine lines around his eyes were deeper, darker. "Old feed shed, with newly attached doors, bars on the windows, and big metal hooks set into the support beams. And chains and handcuffs still lying there…"

I shook my head, though his eyes were shut and he couldn't see.

"Mess of a place. Like something out of Vietnam, according to Ralph—Sergeant McMurphy. And he should know. Prisoner of war for about six months back in the seventies…"

Needing to do something with my hands, I drank more coffee and waited for Mark to continue. Eventually he took up his narrative, his words slower and slightly slurred.

"All located near a branch of Prosperity Creek, just as the lady doctor surmised. Old Mack says the hut used to hold feed and a tractor and such, but has been abandoned for about four years. He claims he had *no idea* it had been used as a prison and torture chamber. Oh, *my*…" Mark quoted, his tone vaguely sarcastic.

"'Course, I don't believe him." One lid lifted, exposing a green iris surrounded by bloodshot whites. "I got an investigator talking to him now. And we'll hold him overnight. Let him think it through. My guess is that about two or three this morning, when he has to use the facilities and realizes that a jailer and half a dozen prisoners are watching, some with intense and salacious interest, he'll suddenly remember a detail he forgot." The tired smile slid off his face and his eyes again closed.

"The legal system doing its job…. Kinda reminds me of the…*lagoons*…at McHewell's. But it works…in its own slow, limping, aromatic way.'' Mark's voice trailed off. I thought he might be asleep.

"Thank you," I said softly. He'd figured it out. Other cops might not have bothered.

"Welcome," he murmured. "Dinner on me..."

I smiled and stood, leaving the break room and pulling the door closed after me. It was near evening, and a nap seemed smart to me, too. As the door closed, I heard him mutter.

"Goddamn prison...what it was...torture chamber... I'd a killed the sonabitch...."

I had to agree. I might have, too.

12

DOUBLE-GLOVE AND A RED FORD TRUCK

My twenty-four-hour shift seemed to dwindle down to nothing at 1:00 a.m. and I went to nap. Mark had left hours earlier, nodding to me on his way out the door. I was running a code at the time and couldn't stop to say goodbye. Some things are simply more important than good ol' country boys who love smart women....

Douglas Byars had arranged with housekeeping to change the sheets on my bed and I fell into the crisp—okay, stiff and rough—linen, asleep instantly. I got a good three hours before I was disturbed again. When the ER nurse called me, I knew it was bad. Before she even spoke, I could hear the patient wheezing in the background. Shortness of breath.

"Doc, we—"

"On my way, Anne. Asthma or COPD?"

"Mild COPD. Firefighter," she said

"Everybody wears surgical masks," I said. "Get a set of gasses and respiratory down to do a treatment. Then I want a chest and a cup of fresh coffee."

She laughed. "Got the coffee going, respiratory's on the way and the lab's standing by."

"I meant it about the masks," I said. Anne's laughter

drained away. "Everybody. All employees, on every SOB or cough until further notice."

"Yes, ma'am."

It was telling that she didn't ask why. Word was getting around. The problem was growing.

Minutes later, my stethoscope beneath his shirt, I listened to the patient's lungs, which sounded both rubbery and grinding, like typical COPD, chronic obstructive pulmonary disease, not like the vicious, seemingly malevolent condition I feared. But the patient was running a fever of 102 and was shivering, and I figured he had pneumonia. I had only one question for him.

"Were you at the warehouse fire near Prosperity Creek?"

He nodded, the motion jerky with chills.

I wrote two sets of orders, one for shipping him to a bigger hospital in the state capital, the other set of orders as if I were going to admit him to Douglas Byars, including the same antibiotic cocktail Mel was on, and my now standard isolation order. Even if this patient wasn't admitted, I wanted him on the antibiotic. Outpatient IV therapy for six days. The nurses were going to be thrilled, as ER personnel handled such orders on weekends and holidays when the outpatient department was closed. I wasn't going to be too terribly popular if this one wasn't a keeper or a shipper. Having done all I could at the moment, I sat and drank coffee as I waited for the X rays.

Someone had alerted Douglas, or he had radar. Looking like death warmed over, he appeared minutes later, his steps slow and trudging, dark circles beneath his eyes, a heavy beard marring his jaw. With only a nod, he fell onto the vacant break-room chair, air whooshing from his lungs and the cushion with the same force. Looking like the limp bag of bones Mark had mimicked earlier, he sprawled loosely and closed his eyes.

Without being asked, Anne found a package of razors

kept on hand for prepping patients, and tossed them on the table between us. "Razors, Doc. You look terrible. And there's soap and towels in the doctor's lounge. I know. I checked." Douglas nodded his thanks and his agreement, too tired to speak.

Finally, as our new patient was being wheeled back down the hallway, he found the energy to say, "Mel just died."

Mel. Died. Not the patient. Not expired. *Mel just died.* The simple phrase was evidence that Douglas was getting too involved. Was losing the distance he needed to hold his emotions in check, to see the patients and their conditions as puzzles to be solved, was growing too tired and too engrossed to be a good doctor. But I said nothing.

"And now I hear we got another one. Firefighter."

"No. *I* have a COPDer with possible pneumonia."

"So far. So damn far."

Until this weekend, I had never heard Douglas curse. This made three times. At least. "Go home, Douglas. Get some sleep. For about a week."

"I'm pulling call," he said, eyes still closed. His lids looked like they were too heavy to lift. "Called the other physicians and told them to stay home, enjoy the holiday. Told wife and kids to…stay at her mother's."

"Doc," Anne said. "You may want to take a look at the patient's arms. He's getting a rash. Fever had dropped to 100.5, and now is going back up."

In the next room, the patient coughed, a rough vibration, like a serrated electric knife rending meat. A ripping, wet, by-now-familiar sound echoed down the hallway.

Douglas and I were up in the same instant and converged on the man. He was unconscious and turning blue. Douglas turned up the oxygen and I hooked up a pulse-ox device to the patient's left index finger and called for the antibiotic cocktail I had ordered in the admit orders. Then added, "Masks. Everyone."

Anne had one hanging around her neck and passed out masks to Douglas and me with a look that said *you said everyone*. While I hadn't worn a surgical mask earlier, contrary to my own order, I now tied mine in place and noticed that Douglas did the same.

I stared at the pulse-oximeter. The man's O_2 levels were dropping, his pulse increasing.

"I want a repeat blood gas and blood cultures times two, and I want to see the chest film. Can you bring it in here?" I asked Brian.

"Yes, ma'am."

I checked the man's reflexes. His right side was hyper-reflexive; his left showed marked changes, very slow reactions to stimulation. Stroke?

"Rhea. Look at this."

I looked where Douglas pointed and saw the rash the nurse had mentioned earlier. It was a reddish, flat smear on the surface of the patient's skin. Douglas pressed one and the color disappeared. Then it reappeared, darker for an instant as it slowly faded to the original shade of red.

We were living in a nightmare, a circular, spiraling one that kept repeating a theme with ever more frightening variations.

"Let's get him admitted," Douglas said. "Full isolation, everyone in hepa-masks, foot protectors, gowns and double-glove. Just in case." Double-glove. In med-speak it was a verb, meaning put on double sets of gloves.

I had to agree. Either this patient had something else in addition to the respiratory condition, or this disease was mutating. Fast. With hepa-masks—tight-fitting masks that would filter out almost anything biological—and double sets of gloves we could contain this. Maybe.

"I want a PT and PTT. No—make that a DIC work-up," Douglas said, changing his order to more comprehensive testing of the blood-clotting cycle. "And a CT scan of his head and his lungs. Who's on for Radiology?'' he said, asking which doctor would be performing and reading the CT scan.

"Chris Russell," a nurse answered.

"Get him in. And I'm calling hospital in-house Infection Control again. We need isolation and negative-pressure units to deal with this bug, whatever it is."

"DHEC needs to be informed about this." I said. "Maybe someone from Health Hazards Evaluation. I don't know, exactly. But I can call the message number and they can get the proper department to call me back."

"Yeah. And hospital administration," Douglas said without looking up. "I don't know who's on call in-house. Nursing supervisor handled that call yesterday. And we might need CDC," he finished. Douglas's face was flushed and pale all at once, stress making him look vulnerable and far too young. "I checked their Web site several times within the last two days. They've got nothing like this bug listed. Nothing."

"Let's go one step at a time," I said.

I dialed the emergency number for the on-call Infection Control nurse. Her line was picked up by an answering machine, and though I left a message, I assumed she was out of town for the holiday. I knew there would be a call sheet for the person covering for her, but I didn't see it.

Alarm began to percolate in the depths of my mind. Feeling the urgency of the situation, I looked up the county number for DHEC. All I got was a message machine and a promise to call me back. It was likely that the officers were still processing the samples collected on the creek today. They had a bigger problem now, and I needed the number for whoever was covering Epi Call for the county. Epi was short for epidemiology, and that person carried a beeper at all times, as well as a special book called the Epi Book Bag, a bag with every conceivable contact number, every com-

prehensive procedure and protocol for any infectious disease
scenario ever imagined or experienced. And I was imagining
several already, none of them good.

Paging the nursing supervisor, I was happy to discover
that Trish was working. In her own vernacular, she agreed
to ''notify the necessary hospital PTBs and DHEC VIPs.''
The Powers That Be and Very Important People at the
county and state level. She also promised to call Dr. Reeves
and ask about the extra negative-pressure units he had told
her he was trying to find. Vaguely, I remembered that
Reeves had been called in the morning of the first outbreak
of pneumonia. I didn't know what special contacts he had
with medical equipment companies, but anyone who could
get us more equipment would be a godsend. I went back to
the new patient.

With a small sterile lancet, I cut into one of the flat reddish places on the firefighter's arm, made a sterile slide and
collected a culture. Because Douglas had taken over the
more important aspects of treatment, I took the sample to
the lab, gram stained it and read it myself. There were lots
of red blood cells, very few white blood cells and thousands
of tiny gram-positive cocci. Whatever had attacked all my
other patients' lungs was now in this man's skin.

I wondered if the brain-bleed was something peculiar to
this patient—some predisposition to stroke we didn't know
about. Did the patient have previously undiagnosed high
blood pressure? A preexisting aneurysm? Or was this a new
turn of events? The disease presenting itself in a new and
frightening way? Perhaps the bacterium was multiplying in
his brain as well, leaking blood and causing him to stroke-
out.

I had a sudden mental picture of the man as each little
reddish place on his skin began to seep blood, soaking
through the sheets onto the floor as he lay there, blood flow-

ing from every orifice. His brain a mushy mass of blood and infection.

Running back to the ER, I told Douglas what I had found. He had already received back the DIC testing, which investigated all parts of the blood-clotting cycle, looking specifically for Disseminated Intravascular Coagulation—a condition that caused first clotting in a patient and then massive bleeding—hoping to rule out the very picture I had formulated.

The results were consistent with the previous patients' results. Moderately elevated PT and normal PTT. The additional testing showed an increased bleeding time, and moderately decreased platelets. But nothing that pointed to the specific diagnosis of DIC. That meant that the abnormality appeared to be minor and was present in only one part of the blood-clotting cycle. It was nothing that needed emergency treatment, at least not under ordinary circumstances. If it didn't self-correct, I might have to treat for it, but because we knew so little about this disease, I didn't want to risk it.

"I want this man out of here," Douglas said. "I want him flown to Richland or to CMC or anywhere. But I don't want him here."

"You think anyone would take him?"

"No. I don't." Douglas looked up with a fierce grimace on his face. "Not even the Veteran's Association, and I just found out he's a vet. Can't get him stable enough to transport him now. Look at his pressure."

I glanced at the screen of the computerized monitor, showing pulse, oxygen levels and blood pressure. It was down, way down from when I first saw him. And the rash was worse. "Bleeding out under his skin? Even without DIC?" Leaning forward, I pulled down an eyelid and checked his color. The white of the eye was lined with swollen veins, and the tissues surrounding the eye itself were very red. Not typically bloodshot, nor a typical feverish picture. Something different, peculiar.

"I should have known it was you spoiling my holiday weekend."

Turning, I spotted Chris Russell, the hospital radiologist, standing in the doorway, already dressed out in paper gown, gloves, mask. His brown eyes gleamed with good humor, in conflict with his words.

"Sorry," I said, smiling beneath the hospital mask I wore. "But we've got something nasty here."

"So I've heard," he said. "Fill me in. But I've already got to say, I can't recommend contrast for this patient, so your results aren't going to be as specific as you wanted."

"I'll take what you can get," Douglas said, holding out a hand and shaking Chris's gloved one.

"Dr. Lynch?"

I looked at the door and the nurse calling to me. It was Anne, her hepa-mask firmly in place.

"We got another one."

"Give me a sec. I need my hepa-mask. Douglas?"

"I'm fine. Go." He didn't even look up when he spoke. Instead he began to lay out for Chris the type of patient we had been seeing all weekend. His hands were steady, but his voice was shaking, and a fine sheen of sweat glinted on his forehead. As he spoke, the good humor faded from Chris Russell's eyes.

Rummaging around in my bag, I found one of the special hepa-masks. It was green, of thick fabric, and shaped around the outer edges with bendable wiring. This one had been shaped to my face and tested for leakage months before at a hospital employee health fair. Every doctor had one. No doctor ever expected to need one.

I pulled the two elastic bands over my head and pressed the mask in place. Breathed deeply several times to test the fit. It still seemed snug. Double-gloving, I went to the next room. It turned out to be two patients. Mother and child. Both were breathing with painful, coarse-sounding breaths. And both had flat, reddish rashes over all the exposed skin. I wanted to howl. Out in the hallway I could see Dr. Reeves as he talked with the supervisor. I hoped he had found some extra negative-pressure units. It looked like we would need them.

Between Douglas, Chris Russell and me, we admitted all three patients by 6:00 a.m. The CT scans Chris ran of the firefighter, and then of the lungs of the mother and daughter were little help. They showed what we had already deduced. Massive infection and bleeding. The beginning of a fast-acting necrosis, as though the lungs were dead and rotting at unbelievable speeds. The firefighter's brain scan looked like something had turned his brain to mush. His wife and family were gathering in the chapel, stunned and grieving.

The hospital was totally out of isolation rooms. The mother and child went in a room together. The firefighter went into the room vacated by Mel Campbell. It still smelled of Clorox, which had been used to wipe down the walls and furniture, floor, bedframe and mattress.

People I seldom saw were moving purposefully down the hallways wearing casual clothing, wrinkled jeans and T-shirts, sneakers or running shoes—clothes they had pulled on in a hurry as they were woken from a sound holiday sleep and called in stat. I saw the hospital administrator and his assistant, the director of nursing, the in-house infection control nurse and a woman in smelly, half-dried jeans whom I took to be the infectious waste coordinator from DHEC. I guessed that another stranger wearing DHEC ID was the Epi Call person.

It was Easter Sunday morning, and though everyone had planned, prepared and tested for such an emergency, no one was experienced with them. And no one wanted to believe that they were facing such a case now. There was a thinly cloaked air of fear in the hallways, present in the tight lips and downcast eyes of employees. Who would be next? How quickly would the next mutation present its unforeseen set of symptoms? And how long before this bug learned to transmit itself person-to-person and became a raging epidemic?

I was off duty in an hour. I had pulled my twenty-four-hour shift. I was tired. But instead of gathering my things and heading home, I went to the hospital MODIS room— oddly unlocked, but then things weren't exactly normal today—and dialed up the system. MODIS was the Medical Online Diagnostic Interface System—part Internet, part closed system with several major hospitals and medical institutions hooked up, sharing the mental resources of the specialists. With it, I could talk to someone at CDC, the Center for Disease Control in Atlanta.

It was early, but I knew that Shirl would be at work before dawn if she was on call and would check her e-mail if not. I got her on the first try.

"Epidemic Intelligence Service. Dr. Shirley Adkins here," she said, her English accent crisp and precise.

"You mean *the* Shirl Adkins? The intrepid medical student who flashed the entire Hornets basketball team in the Charlotte airport terminal while in medical school?"

"Charlotte Douglas *International* Airport, if you please, and I was on wager. I won out twenty quid with my little paps and took home almost as many autographs," she said, half in London street slang, half in her usual patrician accent. "Rhea-Rhea?"

"That's me," I said, pleasure in both syllables. "And man, am I glad you're in."

"Problem, luv?"

"Big one. And it may be growing." Carefully I filled her in on the details of what I believed could be the beginning of an epidemic. And yet, as the sequence of events came from my mouth, the situation sounded less critical than only hours before when I helped admit three patients. Rather than asking for official help, I closed my soliloquy with careful statements and two questions. "I'm not officially asking CDC in on this because it isn't my responsibility, though I imagine hospital administration or the state health department might, later on today. I'm calling you out of curiosity. So, do you think I have a problem or am I nuts? And do you have any suggestions?"

"What steps have you taken thus far?" she asked, ignoring my questions. Shirl was an EIO, an Epidemic Intelligence Officer of CDC, and approached problems like mine from that distinctive perspective.

"DHEC, and in-house so far. We can't get the causative agent to grow, so I can't get you cultures."

"Not good," she said thoughtfully. "It sounds like you could have a mutated strain of strep A. Perhaps it needs some type of enriched media to grow in vitro."

"Of course," I breathed. "Like potato or something." Some virulent organisms needed something special to grow outside of the body, like media made from potatoes or—

"What's the weather like there?" Shirl asked, interrupting my thoughts.

"No better than Atlanta, and the entertainment is nil, except for this little French restaurant that just opened. And I'm not calling you in, Shirl. Not yet."

"I understand the political schematics of small-town hospitals, as well as big-town and state health organizations, Rhea. I'll be patient for the official queries. But I have a few days' scheduled holiday starting the end of this shift." She pronounced *scheduled* as a *shed* sound in the first syllable. I smiled into the phone.

"Think you might come?"

"It's a definite possibility. I'll ring you back. Meantime, I'll send a courier to pick up the cultures you have so far.

See what we can do with them here. Professional courtesy and all that rot.''

I gave Shirl my home phone number and my work schedule, chitchatted for a moment about med school and who was where and with whom, who was pregnant or looking for a new love, though we never seemed to mention either her love life or mine. Finally we hung up, Shirl to find a courier to pick up Dawkins County's problem bug, me to report in and head home. I had a date with a preacher, a congregation of Easter worshippers and an old friend still recuperating from a head wound.

As I neared the ER, I slowed. A man in navy officer's blues stood at the desk, a new briefcase at his left heel. The uniform was a bit tight, as if he had recently gained a few pounds around the chest and shoulders. He had a shorter-than-regulation, quarter-inch buzz cut, wore spit-shined black boots showing a faint rim of dried red mud around the thick soles, and stood with strict military bearing. His half of the conversation reached me. Being nosy, I leaned against the wall near the office shared by shift doctors, crossed my arms and listened in.

"I understand your legal requirements regarding patient confidentiality, but it is possible that I, or my department, could help.

"No, we saw no reason to bring subpoenas at this time.'' I could hear the amusement in his voice, a voice used to command but willing to negotiate. Slightly condescending. "I'm here in a mostly unofficial capacity because we heard about the bacteria you people pulled out of the creek. We have some experience with wet germs.''

Wet germs? I wanted to laugh. Whatever he was, he wasn't a doctor. He didn't have the lingo, the patter, the "if you can't dazzle 'em with disputations, then rule 'em with rubbish'' mentality. A doctor would have already been tossing out the medical terminology, offering something in the way of education as a proof of identification, and making a nurse follow him down the hallway.

Why the navy? My fingertips started to tingle, a sure sign something was wrong, but I had no idea what.

"All we need, to see if we can help, is a listing of who seems to have the germ, and where they were when they picked it up."

A soft-voiced negative reached me, just a bit louder than a moment ago, a hint of irritation in the tone. This had been going on for a while.

"It really wouldn't take much of your time. If I could just speak to your doctor."

"Maybe I can help," I said.

As he turned, the man's blue eyes blazed down the hallway. Hawklike, intense, he assessed me in an instant and dismissed me just as quickly. "Thank you, nurse, but I really need to talk to a *doctor*."

Anne's head peeked around the corner just as the man spoke, then disappeared, but not before I saw her wicked grin. Nurse, my rear end.

I did laugh then, a bit unpleasantly, uncrossed my arms and stood straight. "You are speaking to a doctor. *Dr.* Rhea Lynch. Come on into my office." It wasn't phrased as a request.

Without waiting for his reply, I turned my back, entered the small cubicle-size office, slipped into the white lab coat that was always left hanging handily behind the door and sat down behind the slightly battered, wood-grain-laminated desk I called mine when on duty. It looked official, authoritative, if not exactly high style.

When the man entered and closed the door, I cocked my head and studied him at close range. Weathered face, early forties, fit. He looked like he ran twenty miles a day, drank coffee like the sailor he professed to be, and was used to command. Good-looking in a weathered, experienced sort of way. I could see women in any port city of the world drooling at the sight of him. It was those blue eyes. They focused on me and smiled. "Lieutenant Montgomery Leander." He bent across the desk and shook my hand. "Ma'am. Sorry about the misidentification."

I glanced at the insignia on his uniform as he sat. I had no idea what a lieutenant's bars or stripes or whatever looked like, but something didn't feel right. The tingling in my fingertips increased. "What can I do for you?"

"As I was just telling your colleague—"

"Nurse."

"I beg your pardon?"

"Anne is a nurse, not my colleague."

"Of course." Leander sat straighter in his chair, if that was possible. Feeling snippy, I slouched lower in mine. The lieutenant bent and placed his briefcase on the floor, his arms straining the fabric at the seams.

Where was his hat? Didn't officers in blue have to wear a hat? They did on the TV show *JAG*....

And then I knew what my fingers and my subconscious mind had been trying to tell me. The ill-fitting uniform wasn't the result of too many pastries. It simply wasn't his.

Without giving myself away, I leaned across the desk, yawned elaborately and propped my chin in one hand. With the other I flicked on the intercom. Anne, at the desk, could now hear every word.

"So. What can I do for you, Lieutenant?"

"It came to my attention that you may have a little problem here, one I have some experience with, being in the navy—"

"You're a doctor?" I interrupted. "A medical doctor?"

"Well, yes," he agreed, blue eyes dancing.

"Well, no," I said flatly. Slowly I sat straighter, watching his eyes. "And my guess is that you aren't even in the navy.

My guess is that I should call security and have you tossed off the property.''

The blue eyes flickered only slightly, less a movement than a darkening of the color, a graying out, an emotional recognition of failure. Veiled hostility. Suddenly the blue eyes were not quite so attractive.

"What are you? Reporter? Not television, the hair's too short and the uniform fits too poorly. Press?" I nodded. *"The National Enquirer? The Globe?"* I let the questions sound like the insults they were intended as.

One fist tightened on the arm of his chair. Hostility unveiled as a slow smile spread over the lower half of his face. He didn't like me and wanted me to know it. Most people couldn't carry on a conversation with facial expressions alone. This guy could.

"Why the charade? I mean, just for argument's sake, until security gets here to escort you away."

He blinked. Slowly, he moved his eyes toward the phone-intercom and let them rest on the brightly lit red button that showed our conversation was being monitored. For an instant, the threat of violence sizzled on the air. His mouth snapped closed, blue laser eyes stabbed me in sudden fury, and Lieutenant Montgomery Leander simply got up and left.

Not a word, not a single denial, just a quick exit, thick rubber soles silent on the waxed floor. By the time I circled the desk and reached the hall, he was rounding the hallway and out the door. Anne leaned toward me, her mouth pulled down in a "well, would you look at that" expression.

"Security?" I asked as I jogged to the door and pushed through.

"I beeped him as soon as I heard you say the word, but he hasn't called," Anne said to my back. "A.m. rounds take him to the nursing center, so he'll be a while." I sprinted to the ER air lock and outside.

The man—not Lieutenant Montgomery Leander, I felt

sure—was pulling away in a red pickup truck. Ford. With a crushed back left bumper and side panel. There was no plate. The lieutenant had a driver, though. Young, white, crew-cut, male. Not much to go on. I sighed. Wasn't it illegal to impersonate an officer of the military? If the press had wind of our little *wet germ,* there could be problems I hadn't even considered yet. Before leaving for the day, I called the hospital administrator's desk and reported the encounter with the fake Lieutenant Montgomery Leander. And then I went home, in search of a dress suitable for high mass, or whatever Episcopalians called Easter services.

13

PEARLS, SWINE AND MUSTY DRESSES

At home, my big dogs prancing around me as if my closet was a new play space, I found a dress. I had left two hanging in the darkness for the past year. The black, knee-length cocktail dress, cut short to show my legs, slit up the back for the same reason, had long vertical creases where gravity had pulled the fabric out of shape. It probably wasn't appropriate for church, and it needed ironing at the very least. The iron on the top shelf of the closet beckoned like a huge hideous steel tooth and sent me back to search again.

Almost invisible in the black depths was another choice. The navy dress and blazer were in better condition—and were perhaps more appropriate to Easter Sunday. I found a pair of leather pumps that needed only a damp sponge to uncover the almost-new sheen beneath the dust and make them—and me—presentable. That and panty hose. Exhausted at the very thought of wearing the outfit, I fell back on my bed and closed my eyes. I had managed a whole year without panty hose. A personal record I was about to break.

I woke an hour later when Belle jumped onto the bed and rolled me toward her with pounding front paws. The duvet and sheets were still in place following Arlana's most recent ministrations, and Belle thought of a made bed as an invitation to roll and play. Arlana, who thought dogs in the house were practically a sin, always kept the bedroom and living room doors shut when she left for the day to keep the furniture looking nice. It didn't last long after I got home, but it looked good for a while at least.

"Down, Belle," I muttered. "Stop. Down."

The big mixed lab-setter settled in a false-humble crouch, chin on paws and her soul in her eyes. She wanted to go for a run. Checking my watch, I decided there was time and rolled out of bed. Belle whuffed and danced happily, claws clicking on the wood floor as I reached for the leash. In the closet door mirror, reflected across the room, I saw the blue suit and pumps and froze.

Something about the suit. So like the uniform the man wore... My fingertips tingled as they did when something was important, but this time ineffectually. I rubbed my palms down my bare legs. Nothing came to mind and the sensation faded.

Belle stuffed her wet snout into my hand, demanding. Pushing her away, I bent into the first of my warm-up stretches. Ecstatic, Belle whipped her body around a dozen times and clattered up and down the hallway leading to her doggy door, snorting and whuffing and making various dog noises of delight. Pulling on my shoes after a minimal stretch to warn my tired muscles they were about to be moved, I grabbed the leash.

"Okay, girl. Let's go." Yellow Pup whined and sulked, knowing he was being left behind, but he wasn't leash-trained and I had no time or energy for a tug-of-war today. I really had to train the guy. He was big enough, or nearly so, to keep up.

It would be a fast run, I decided. Belle seemed to sense my urgency, nose turned to the sky, scenting, breath already a pant when we started out. The weather had cleared, the storm runoff was long gone, and blue sky sparkled overhead between the fresh green of opening leaf buds. Hickory and oak trees were still in bud, while maple and poplar were struggling to catch up with the faster-budding dogwood, which cast blossoms in wide sprays across my path. Temps were mild, in the low sixties, as I jogged a quick warm-up and then ran.

A faint breeze in my face brought the scent of horses and cattle from the farm not far away, the underlying odor of last autumn's leaves moldering on the ground, the breath of newly opened flowers in gardens I passed, and the ever-present diesel and gas fumes from the highway. Like Belle, I had my nose turned to the sky for spring. Pounding along the path beside the creek behind my house, little more than a trickle once again, I covered ground quickly, homes flashing by, children in backyards searching for eggs left by a mischievous rabbit, a glimpse of street, and then under the barbed wire fence into pasture as I followed an old cow trail now used by dirt-bike riders and a few intrepid horsemen.

In the distance, I could hear the lowing of cattle as they left the barn for green pastures still wet with dew. The excited screams of the searching children fell away, and I stretched out, legs pounding, breath a steady bellows. Beside me, Belle increased her stride, matching mine, long black hair flowing back, rippling with each dual step as she ran.

The earth had needed a warm day to dry, and was now a perfect surface for running, better than any Olympic packed-clay arena man ever devised. Belle glanced up at me, tongue lolling to the side in ecstasy. I knew just what she was feeling. This was as close to heaven as I ever expected humankind got. The worries of the strange disease fell away, my concerns for a possible epidemic, my sadness over Marisa's inability to communicate as she once had, my now-ancient grief over John, who was probably dating again as if we had never been engaged, and my confusion over Mark, who perhaps wanted something more than I could give. All were whipped away by the wind.

When I slowed and turned back to the house, I was a new person. And Belle was elated. She stopped at the creek and drank long draughts of the clear, cold water while I again stretched my legs, pulling at loosened, relaxed muscles that would stiffen back up in minutes without the stretch. Checking my watch, I found I had just enough time to shower, run a comb through my hair and despair over makeup before it was time to pick up Marisa for church. Perfect.

We were almost late to the service Marisa wanted to attend. But it wasn't my fault. Not exactly.

My suit, while flawless as far as I was concerned, needed something, according to Miss Essie and Marisa. I had no more than knocked on the door when Miss Essie, Marisa's housekeeper, healthcare worker and former nanny, started tsking.

"Shame. Shame, shame, *shame*," she said through the door, the words growing clear as she undid the locks and swung it open. "The way you treat your clothes." She shook her head, gray curls unmoving above a seamed, dark-chocolate face. "Look at this child, Miss Marisa," she said, though Marisa was not in the room. "Clothes all wrinkle up and shoulder dusty. I know your mama didn't teach you to dress that way, her bein' a Rheaburn an' all. I know for shore *she* appreciate good clothes."

"When she was sober," I agreed, determined not to be baited.

Miss Essie's head went back and she clutched her shawl by the ends, a sure sign she was riled. "Watch your mouth. She still your mama, and her dead, and this the Lord's risin' day. Come in and see the pretty thing Miss Marisa wearing. And take that dusty dress and coat off so I can put a damp cloth and a iron to it. Ain't no woman leaving this house looking like that. Out of it."

"I like the shawl, Miss Essie. Purple is a good color on you."

As she always wore a purple shawl, Miss Essie's eyes narrowed. She held out her hand for my clothes.

"I'm not undressing, Miss Essie."

"Oh, yes you is. You can take it off by yourself or I can pull it offa you. My friend Esmee be shaking her head at me, you leave here looking like that."

"Esmee won't see me, Miss Essie."

Miss Essie reached up and pulled the shoulders of the coat off. I didn't fight. Miss Essie was all of five foot three, and though I towered over her by a good six inches, there was no doubt that she was in charge. "Esmee's people be going to the church. They come home talking all about my baby and the wrinkled thing what brung her to services on the Lord's-risin'-from-the-tomb day…. I be shamed to my bones."

Meekly, I followed her to the back of the house, the smell of a hot iron pulling Miss Essie like a magnet. Marisa stepped from the master bedroom, a peaceful smile glowing. Her face was a bit puffier today, the child seeming to ride a little lower, as if pushed down by the weight of Marisa's hands resting there.

"Rhea-Rhea!" she said. "Sunshine!" She took my hand, placed it over the baby at her own navel and held it until the baby kicked. "Legs," she said proudly.

"Football or soccer?"

"Running. Like you."

I smiled. Melted, if the truth be known. And the kid kicked again. Miss Essie picked that moment to unzip my dress and yank. And of course she tsked again. This time her "shames" were more pronounced.

"I was wearing the coat. And no one was supposed to see me naked," I defended, holding my arms over my chest. I hadn't worn a bra. A cardinal sin in Miss Essie's eyes. Especially on the Lord's risin' day, as she informed me. And this time she was really mad, her eyes spitting sparks.

"Shame on you, child. Just pure shame, goin' into the Lord's house like that. I be dead I roll over in my grave if I knowed it."

"It's lined, Miss Essie," I said desperately. "And you're no help, Risa. Go away or quit giggling."

"My little Marisa look like a princess in her dress, with the flower all over it. Her look plum pretty in lavender and pink and orchid." Essie hurled my dress across the ironing board and wiped it down with a damp cloth, her strokes so strong I feared for the seams. "And you come to take her to the Lord's House—" she slammed down the iron and speared me with her eyes "—*the Lord's House*. Looking like that."

I stood in silence, arms crossed over my chest as she finished freshening the dress. Moments later I was clothed. Properly. The suit did smell better. Less musty. And it did hang better. As she hurried us out of the house, I assured Miss Essie that I was thankful. That she was a dream and a wonderful woman. That I had worn panty hose, rather than go bare legged, just for her. But Miss Essie had decided not to throw pearls before swine—her words being pearls, me being the swine—and had stopped speaking to me. She kissed Marisa as we left, told her to keep warm for the baby's sake, and ignored me as if I were something slimy that had crawled into her house. So much for good impressions.

In the car, Marisa continued to giggle, stealing glances at me. I had worn lipstick, damn it. And panty hose. And *heels*. Why couldn't that be enough for them? The farther I drove, the closer I came to the church, the more I steamed. I didn't want to be here. Going to church. In a dress and heels and lipstick. And I couldn't understand why Marisa still wanted to go to church at all.

As we entered the church, we attracted more attention than I wanted, voices raised and calling to Marisa, some jumping up from seats and rushing to her, greeting us both as long lost and returned to the fold. I smiled and nodded and replied where I could, all the while urging our way forward through the crowded aisle.

I knew some faces, former patients, one or two who were familiar from summers spent in Dawkins at the Stowe farm. But the sense of welcome was uncomfortable. I didn't want to be here. I certainly didn't want to come back.

We finally had the Stowe family pew in sight when I spotted him. Eddie Braswell. Sitting on the front row of the balcony. Leaning forward, lips parted. Eyes fixed on Marisa.

In the instant before he spotted me staring, I identified a torrent of emotions in that piercing gaze. Shame. Loneliness. Longing. And then he saw me.

As our eyes met, there was a single moment of recognition. His eyes widened with shock. His lips tightened, slammed shut. Firmed with an emotion that could have been anything. And he sat quickly back, his head disappearing behind the balcony railing.

We had reached our place. I moved Risa in and we sat. Around us the crowd hushed. Glancing back, I still could not see him. Almost forcibly, I put Eddie Braswell from my mind.

Sitting beneath the high gabled ceiling in her old pew, the one she used to share with her Aunt DeeDee and me during the summers I spent in Dawkins County, and later shared with Steven and Eddie, Marisa turned her face to the pulpit and simply glowed. Her skin, her clothes, even her blond hair took on a pearly sheen I had never seen before. Risa was…happy.

It wasn't the sunlight through the stained glass windows. It wasn't the people, though practically the entire crowd—congregation—knew and loved her. It wasn't the sermon, because that hadn't even started yet. It wasn't pregnancy increasing blood circulation to her epidermis. It was being where she was, in this church with her God. It was being who she was. Injured. Damaged. And still *happy*.

And suddenly I was angry. Not simply mad, but raging.

As if the anger had been there all along, for months, tamped down and smoldering.

The crowd hushed. Settled. The organ began to play. Rich, deep strains filled the church. Risa's smile widened.

Fury flamed up in me, pounding in my temples, stealing my breath, taking me to some place within my own brain I couldn't even identify. My hands began to sweat, respiration came in useless little puffs. I put my head down, stared at my fingers fisted in my lap. Took a few slower, deeper breaths, trying to regain control before I embarrassed Risa and myself. Tried to identify the reason for my own anger so that I could defeat it. And it all came down to one throbbing, stupid thought.

Risa was happy. Happy in spite of her injury. People weren't supposed to be happy after suffering such an injury.

Beside me, she stood and opened a hymnal. And she started to sing. She opened her lips, and words—real words, sensible words—came from her mouth. She never missed a line as she sang some song about glory on high. But the words she had for me weren't even full sentences. They were broken and often incoherent…. And yet she could sing to her God. *Selfish, silly thought.*

Brain damaged. She was brain damaged, some reasonable, trained part of me whispered as I sat in the pew, shaking, the only person in the church not standing, not singing. And brain-damaged people had weird reactions to things. She could sing a hymn she knew but not form thoughts into sentences. It made medical sense.

But there was no medical reason why she would be so damn happy. And she was. Blissfully so. Joyfully so. Beside me, her voice reached some impossibly high note and slid down into an alto minor. Glory on high.

A single note escaped me, soblike, though I was dry-eyed, the sound lost beneath the music. Rage pent-up, seeking release, and glory on high all around me.

I wanted to hurt something. To kill something. A red haze

burned into my sight. My fisted hands looked as if they were caught in a heated glow, as if I were on fire.

Marisa was damaged. Forever damaged. And there was not a damn thing I could do about it. *And her God had let it happen.* The God she worshiped. Praised. Sang to. *He* had let her be hurt. And Marisa had the gall to be happy in spite of it.

I fought to regain my sanity, to slow my heartbeat, to find a single full breath in my chest. A breath without pain.

Brain damaged. That did strange things to people. It wasn't her fault that she could sing just as she used to, and yet not speak as she used to. That I knew.

It was not Marisa's fault.

Slowly I found a semblance of calm. One breath. Two. Gradually, the sound of music replaced the sound of roaring in my ears. Organ music rose above the sound of Marisa's voice, sounding triumphant. Voices around me rose. Singing amen. That meant the song was over. My vision had cleared. My chest didn't ache. I could breathe.

Marisa sat and took my hand as if I needed comfort, not her. I let her hold it, staring at our hands, fingers interlaced in her lap, next to her big baby-belly. Mine olive-skinned, Risa's a pale, pale, Dresden pink.

I could count on two hands the times I had lost my temper. Today almost made number eight. And for such a stupid reason. Because Marisa was happy. Because Marisa could sing.

No. That wasn't it. I almost lost my temper because her God had let her be injured. Stupid, stupid, stupid. I concentrated on breathing. Tightened my hand on hers. Held on.

The service seemed to fly by, the hour over before I could sense it. I stood, sat, knelt, held a hymnal—whatever Marisa did, I did. But I felt nothing. Heard nothing but the beat of my heart and the sound of Marisa's voice. Singing.

14

OWL CALLS AND ANGELS

After the service, I escorted her down the aisle and to my little BMW, pausing every step or two so someone could speak to her, tell her they were thinking about her, praying for her, asking about the baby, whatever. Eddie never approached her. I didn't see him, though I looked. It was slow progress, but we finally made it from the church down the street to the car and away, joining the crawl of vehicles as they left the parking lot and curbs and headed to Sunday dinner in a favorite restaurant.

I took Marisa home. The glow she had worn in church had faded into a tired sort of serenity and she needed a nap. So did I, for that matter. The lack of sleep and the anger I had fought for the last hour had drained me, left me feeling like I was rolled in cotton batting. Isolated. Alone.

The silence of the car was odd as I maneuvered through the slow traffic, and when I pulled at last onto a side street that would wend a quick way to Marisa's neighborhood, I glanced at her. She was staring at me.

I have no idea why a guilty flush stained my cheeks, but I could feel the burn of it. "What?" I asked.

"You tell me," she said calmly.

"You sound good. Better and better every day." It was

a lame line and she knew it. I could feel her thoughts churning beside me. "You're making full sentences sometimes."

"Tell me," she said again. "You got mad. Why?"

A prickle of the now quiescent rage touched my mind. I thought about lying. I thought about evasion. I thought about denial. But that would have been a denial of my friendship with Marisa. So I settled on the truth. "You sang," I said, after a long moment. "Every word, every note. Perfectly. Never missed a beat. And you were happy." The last word broke, as if it were too heavy to carry across the air from my mouth to her ear. I cleared my throat, embarrassed, though whether it was embarrassment at the broken word or my feelings, I couldn't tell.

Marisa nodded. "Therapist says I will—" she struggled with the word "—discover…things I can do. And singing is a…help…to my brain."

"Okay. Medically I can accept that. But…" I took a deep breath. "How can you be *happy?*" I slowed the small BMW as the rage I had forced down seeped into the edges of my brain. All around, dogwoods had burst into bloom, seeming to appear since just this morning. White cascades of blooms like snow on green hills of branches. I had always loved the sight of dogwoods in Dawkins. Now all I wanted to do was cry. And tears had always made me mad.

Marisa smiled, the glow she had worn in the church back in full force. "I need God. He makes me—" she searched for a word, and finally settled on mine "—happy."

"*Happy?* He let you get *hurt!*" The words burst out, louder than I intended, more brutal. "He let *that* happen!" I jabbed a hand toward her head. "He let her do that to you!" And the dam broke. Tears I had resisted for months burst. Rivers of tears. And sobs like the sound of nails being forced from old wood. Pain I had pushed away, buried, refused when I first discovered she was hurt, erupted. Slammed into me. Out of me.

For an instant, my breath burned. The beat of my heart ached. Every nerve, every cell twisted with suffering. All I could think of was Marisa as I first saw her after the injury. A vegetating mass beneath the covers, stinking of old urine.

Unable to see, I pulled the small car over and shoved it into Park. And I cried. Like a baby. Like a child who had lost everything. I cried. Sitting in the front seat of my car, Marisa beside me, calm and unmoved by my misery, as the agony and grief poured out of me. Misery that did nothing to ease my pain.

Long minutes later, I rested my hot head against the cool window, seeking solace, my back to Marisa. "How...how the *hell* can you be so damn happy?" I managed to say at last.

Marisa pulled at my jacket. Repeated the nonverbal command. Finally I turned to her, though she was blurred by my tears. "Not happy... Peaceful." She shrugged, the motion altered, fluid, like a vision seen through a window on a rainy day. "God didn't hurt me. He...got me through." She rubbed her belly gently through the cloth of her dress, scratching. "Get me through every day. An' don't curse," she admonished, as always.

"I don't understand. I don't see how you can forgive him."

"God? Or Steven?" she asked.

"Either. Both. Pass me a tissue." I pointed to the little package in its slot in her door. I blew my nose and patted dry my burning skin. Too much salt. When I took a breath I shuddered, as if my lungs were loose, flapping inside. "How can you?"

Marisa smiled and took my hand. The warmth was a comfort, just as it had been in the church. Did she know how much of a comfort she was? She smiled, a tender expression.

"I heard you. When I was in the hospital." Her hand made a pillow motion beside her face, like a child miming the need to sleep.

"Unconscious?"

Marisa nodded. "I heard you. Singing. For me."

"Hymns." I remembered. In an effort to bring her back after her injury, I had resorted to everything. Reading to her, even singing the hymns she used to sing in medical school every morning as soon as she woke. Used to drive me nuts. But I had hoped it would reach some part of her brain entombed beneath the clots and infection.

"I heard you. You helped. My Sunshine."

"I sing like a dying cow," I said through fresh tears.

"Bad," Marisa agreed, nodding.

I laughed, a short, quick spurt that seemed to take some of the pain with it. "And I still hate that nickname."

"Tough," she said with a grin. "God let you bring me back. For you and for…" She patted her belly, rising like a beach ball hidden beneath her dress. Tilting her head, she said, "If my baby a boy baby, I name him Rheaburn Lynn Stowe Braswell," she said distinctly. Practiced words. Not something unplanned, but something premeditated, deliberate.

I hiccuped with surprise, but she wasn't finished.

"If a girl baby, then Rheane Lynn Stowe Braswell."

My full name was Rheane Rheaburn Lynch. Marisa was naming her baby after me. I laughed again, the sound half manic, half shock, covered with fresh tears.

"Peace," she said, "because I'm here. With baby. With Sunshine. And Miss Es."

I turned down Easter Sunday dinner with Miss Essie and Marisa. I was too drained, I needed sleep and had very little time left in the day to get it. Still wearing what little makeup hadn't been cried off, I stripped and fell into the bed, Belle and Pup on the floor beside me.

It was near five when I awoke, bleary-eyed, stiff, suffering from a stopped-up nose and a headache. Too tired for a run, I made the dogs go out, put on a pot of bourbon vanilla coffee, took a hot, steamy shower and dressed for work. I felt miserable, certain now of why I so seldom indulged in a good cry.

Just after 5:00 p.m., Mark knocked, opened the door and shouted, "Haven't I taught you anything, woman? Locks only keep you safe if you use them!"

"Be nice," I shouted back without standing, my hands cupping my mug. "I feel awful and may be PMSing."

"Yeah? And the difference would be what?" he asked, walking in with the dogs. When I didn't reply to the insult he bent and looked at me closely. "You look sick. Your nose is all swollen, your eyes are puffy, and your skin is flushed. Can I have coffee?" he asked as, without missing a beat, he went to the pot and poured himself a mug.

It was a good thing my self-image wasn't dependent on his compliments or I'd be in tears again. "Help yourself."

"Got any of them hard, cold doughnuts lying around?" he asked, his voice dripping country sarcasm like fresh honey on the comb.

I would have sighed had my nose allowed it. Mark knew very well what "them hard, cold doughnuts" were. He was practicing his redneck, dumb-hick, good-ol'-boy routine on me. The Winn-Dixie sold several bagel brands, even one kosher brand, and Mark ate them here with some regularity. "Bagels are in the fridge, and a couple tubs of cream cheese. Blueberry and honey-nut. I think." I sniffed and sipped my coffee, watching him make himself at home in my kitchen, washing his hands, getting out the bagels and cheese tubs. Slicing and heating.

John had displayed that same kind of competency, back when we were together, planning our future. John, who taught me to really appreciate the novelty of being loved, the joy of living with another human being, and the delicacy of fine food. Me, who had been raised without a loving hand, on frozen dinners and canned ravioli. I had loved

John's expertise and competency in the kitchen. Somehow, Mark's presumption annoyed me.

"And what is that for?" I asked as he brought a third mug to the table. "You think Belle wants coffee?" If I intended it as humor, it fell flat, but my annoyance was quite clear.

Belle, curled up at my feet, thumped her tail. Once again, whatever she had been rolling in had been dead. I could smell her even through my occluded nose.

"Actually, I have a favor to ask, if you're not too sick. You really do look awful." He returned with the pot, the bagels and cream cheese, a knife and plates.

"Help yourself to anything in the kitchen. Just make more coffee. I feel too bad to start another pot. And for a man who wants favors, you sure know how to flatter a girl."

"I'm sorry you feel bad." He kissed the top of my head as if I were twelve. "I'm sorry your nose is red and your eyes are puffy. I'm sorry you sound like you're in a fifty-five-gallon drum."

"Uh-huh." I pushed my mug over for a refill, not rising to the bait.

"I have a friend."

"Fancy that. You must not insult him and then eat all his bagels." I broke off several pieces, hot from the microwave, and fed the dogs.

"He's outside."

"Because you ate all his bagels?"

"Will you be serious?" he said.

"Why?"

"He's sick. I want you to take a look at him."

I lifted my brows and drank the fresh coffee. "What's wrong with the emergency room? I'll be on duty in less than two hours." When Mark didn't answer, I said, "Put on a new pot. What's wrong with him?"

"He's a fire investigator."

I put down my cup and met his eyes. Mark hadn't sat

down, and his face was troubled. His hands fidgeted a moment, as if needing something to do. He settled on rearranging the bagels on the serving plate.

"Hiram worked the Killan's Mill warehouse fire. Word is that one fireman may have picked up something at the scene. And now Hiram has this rash...."

"Bring him in before his coffee gets cold."

"Thanks, Rhea." As he stood and headed for the back door, Mark flashed me a smile, all white teeth below green eyes and lashes any woman would die for. A warmth started just below my ribs. It could be the flu, but more likely it was the green eyes. "Thanks, Rhea."

"Get my bag? In the hallway, I think. And put on that fresh pot."

"Got it." The door opened. "Hiram, she'll see you."

"I don't feel good about disturbing her," a strange voice said softly, country in the inflection. Not mill-hill, which had its own stretched-out vowel sounds. But rounded and shy, like a man who didn't talk much. "She's a doctor—"

"Get your butt in here. If she wasn't a doctor, would I be dragging you over here?" Mark asked, exasperated. "You won't go to the emergency room."

"I'm not sick," Mark's friend said stubbornly.

"It's okay," I said as the two men came into the house. "Mark has volunteered to bathe my dogs as payment."

"That's right," he agreed as if we had discussed the subject. "Tonight. Belle stinks. You can smell that even with your nose?" I nodded. "Hiram, this is Rhea. Rhea, Hiram Kellett."

Hiram blushed as he was introduced. Stout at about five six, one-eighty, with florid, freckled skin and a shock of red hair, Hiram lived up to his voice, shy and country as an old pair of barn boots. And he had a rash I recognized from earlier today. Reddish, flat, irregularly shaped splotches beneath his skin.

Standing, I held out my hand. "Rhea Lynch. Have a seat."

Taking my hand and shaking, he released it quickly, his flush deepening with embarrassment. "I don't like doctors," he blurted.

"Me neither." Retaking Hiram's hand, I pushed up his sleeve. The rash started above his wrist and ran proximal to his body, on the underside of his arm, in the tender flesh. When pressed, the rash seemed to disappear and then reappear darker than before. "Bunch of know-it-alls with too much education and no real-life experience." I shoved Hiram gently into a chair, watching his eyes grow round as I spoke. "Don't talk English so's you can understand them." I handed him his coffee and opened my bag, moving slowly to build his confidence. Or at least not send him running.

"Too much money, too much power, and people who go to the doctor seem to die faster. Seems like most folk'd be better off if they just stayed home and let a body heal itself. And half the time it's true—they'd be better off if they did." Hiram started to relax, darting amazed glances to Mark as I worked. I pretended not to see, jotting down numbers on a paper napkin as I worked, and told Hiram about specific cases I had heard where doctors made mistakes, cases that had made news across the country—wrong legs removed by surgeons, wrong breasts removed, wrong medications given. "And most of the time it's all because the doctors didn't take the time to listen to the patient, or to check the chart." I shook my head. "They should know better."

"They sure should," Hiram agreed. "Uh, can I have a bagel?" Mark spread cheese on one and turned the plate so it was close to his elbow. Hiram took a bite and actually smiled.

I checked his blood pressure and pulse as I continued to chatter about all the things doctors do wrong, counted his respiration, listened to his chest, told him to breathe. Hiram sipped his coffee as I moved and grew calmer by the moment.

"Of course, occasionally I do discover something that needs my attention." I began a basic neurological check, starting with his pupils. "A heart attack. A kidney stone. Ever have a kidney stone, Hiram?"

"No, ma'am. But my brother had one few year back. Pain 'bout killed him, he said."

"Uh-huh. They take it out or blast it with ultrasound?"

"'Sound," he said as I hit his elbows with my little hammer.

"Infection. I can help that. Can't do much for some kinds of stroke yet, but medicine is getting better, and someday we'll be able to treat them in the ER, speed up rehabilitation. Sugar problems, prostate problems. We can do things with that. Tell me, Hiram, you ever smoke?"

"No, ma'am. Well, the occasional Punch or Partagas."

At my lifted brow, Mark supplied, "Cigar."

"Umm. Ever had heart problems? High blood pressure? Stroke?"

Hiram shook his head no, drank his coffee and answered my questions, which were lengthy and fairly detailed. Except for the rash, Hiram was as healthy as a horse. And suddenly much more kindly disposed toward doctors. This doctor, at least.

Mark grinned into his mug, his green eyes amused but admiring. He made coffee and kept us all supplied with dark brew as the hands on the clock crept toward seven and the time I needed to be at work.

My exam completed, I said, "Tell me about this fire. The warehouse fire."

"It's still under investigation. I can't talk about it. Sorry, ma'am."

"She's not a reporter. She's a doctor," Mark said blandly. "She'll keep it under her hat. 'Sides, it might help."

After a moment's thought, during which he looked me up and down, taking in the scrubs, running shoes and red nose, Hiram nodded. "Okay. Privileged information."

"Deal," I said, and sat across from him to sip at the bourbon-vanilla-flavored coffee. As he spoke, my sinuses cleared a bit, and I fancied I could smell the fine whisky scent.

Hiram's knowledge was fairly detailed, and considering the fire was still under investigation, he shared his information freely. Once a family-owned mill where cotton was spun into yarn, the hundred-year-old building was made of heart-of-pine and oak, post-and-beam construction behind a brick facade, some of the timbers larger than a man's waist. It was well constructed, with a better-than-usual roof system, insignificant rot, running water still piped in, though the old iron pipes were rusted and flow was minimal. Because it made the owners money, they kept it up better than most of the abandoned, overgrown mills in the county.

There were several families living in the old Killan's Mill-turned-warehouse at the time of the fire, squatters who had hidden from the owners and those who rented the space as storage. Best as the investigators could determine, a cooking fire had taken hold and spread through the heart-of-pine timbers like a wildfire in drought season. Old heart-of-pine was tall and strong, but resinous, and using it was like building with kindling wood; its flames spread incredibly fast. And once the old oak caught, the fire was both fiercely hot and long burning.

The firefighters had pumped water from the nearby creek in an attempt to keep it under control, but even with the flood-enlarged water flow, there was little anyone could do. Only part of the brick shell and floor system remained, the old wooden planking being below the heat of the fire in some spots.

"The families all got out," he concluded, troubled. "Don't know where they'll go. Ain't got a county shelter.

Church is looking for ways to use the gym, but we ain't got showers. Can't just send children and babies into the cold.''

I smiled and bit into a bagel, talking around the small bite. ''Ethical men are hard to find. I'm sure you'll find something for them.''

''Compassionate. Not ethical,'' he said staunchly. ''Anyone can be ethical, that's easy. Compassion is a different thing entirely.'' Hiram looked up at me suddenly, eyes piercing. ''Once we get a place for them, they'll need medical checkups. You willing? Free of charge?''

My first reaction was that I didn't know if my liability insurance would cover seeing patients out of the hospital. A friend with a rash was one thing. Homeless people with nowhere to turn might be different. I shrugged uneasily and Mark laughed, the sound faintly mocking. Which made me mad. It implied I was ethical, the easy thing that anyone could be, but not compassionate.

After a sharp, uncomfortable silence during which I swallowed my bagel, I said, ''You get a place. I'll get the liability insurance to cover the exams and see if the hospital will cover the cost of tests and supplies.''

Mark grinned and Hiram smacked the fist of one hand into the open palm of the other as if he'd just won a point in a game I didn't know I was playing. Had I just been snookered? I glanced at Mark, who stood and went to the sink. I couldn't see his face, but I knew he was trying not to laugh.

''Tell her the rest,'' Mark said over his shoulder. He rinsed his mug and set it to the side to dry. ''She's got to know.''

''I'm as compassionate as the next gal, but I'm not letting a homeless family move in here, if that's what you're planning on asking next,'' I said, more than half serious. ''I know when I've been railroaded, and I'll do what I can for any homeless program you come up with, but I'm not *that* gullible.''

"He means about the fire," Hiram said.

"Or what happened after," Mark said, returning to the table.

"Okay. I'm listening, as long as you don't plan to take away my car or make me share my toys." Both men laughed. I wondered if they knew I was serious.

"The warehouse remains were raided after the fire. Someone pulled in a ten-wheel truck, off-loaded a forklift, lifted something into the truck and drove away," Hiram said.

"Several somethings, actually. Looks like they made maybe five trips." Mark pulled out his chair, whipped it around backward to the table and straddled it. "Only thing left is some leakage all around a dozen round circles. Unburned places in the floor 'bout this big." Mark made a circle with his hands to show me a foot diameter.

"Canisters?" I asked.

"That's what we're guessing. About the size of a big oxygen tank."

"The owners didn't know anything was being stored in that part of the warehouse. It's close to the water. Could have been brought in originally by flat-bottomed boat."

"During the fire, that's where I was working, downwind of that site. And I've been all over the mill since it cooled. And I got to feeling a little funny while I was there after the canisters got moved. Like I wanted to get asthma or something. My son's got it. I know the feeling he gets when an attack is starting, all tight and clogged." Hiram rubbed his chest with an open hand. "But when I left, the feeling went away. Could have been something else, but then Lyle got sick...." His voice trailed off. He looked at his rash, questioningly. "You know. The other firefighter."

Until then I hadn't known the name of the patient, but even as I blinked, I remembered the way he looked, when I saw him last, flaccid, unresponsive, the victim of a massive bacterial attack, pneumonia and stroke. I nodded. "Your rash looks like his."

Hiram's face paled. He made a fist. Hid it beneath the table.

"While you don't have any of his other symptoms, I want you in the hospital. In fact, I want you to pack a bag and drive to Columbia to Richland Memorial tonight. I'll get you admitted."

Hiram didn't argue. It seemed his aversion to doctors was temporarily inactive.

I glanced at the clock. "But I do have a few minutes to spare. Why don't you let me follow you to the warehouse site. Just to look around."

"Why?" Hiram asked.

"Why not? I may spot something there that will help me diagnose you."

Hiram nodded. "I guess you want me down to Columbia in a hurry. Can I use your phone?"

"Sure. Mark can show you where it is. I have to get a few work things together."

I left the men alone and packed my overnight bag, gave the dogs water and made sure the doggy door swung freely. I didn't want them caught in or out, unable to move around. I shut the bedroom and living room doors in case Mark remembered to bathe Belle and Pup. Wet dogs on her furniture would not please Arlana, who would be by before school to check on the condition of the house. I wrote her a note to see about buying a guest bed. Besides keeping the place clean, bossing me around as if she were the employer and I was the housekeeper, and fast becoming a close friend, Arlana was my personal decorator, escorting me through the perilous act of settling into a house. I was sure she made a bundle on the stuff she picked out, had delivered and then arranged for me, but it saved me the time of doing it myself. And her taste was better than mine.

The long driveway from the main road was chained, marked with yellow crime-scene tape, and heavily rutted.

My little BMW moved through the gathering darkness at a slow crawl, left behind by the bigger Jeep with its high undercarriage. Trees to either side had grown in close, feathery tips of new leaves brushed the windows and cast twisted shadows, and I could see both my car's undercarriage and the five-layer paint job being damaged in one fell swoop.

It was twilight when we got to the old Killan's Mill warehouse site, the evening air silent and heavy with the scent of fresh ash and sour water. Tall brick walls and a partially caved-in roof were dark and fire-scorched, marked with black shadowed windows, like empty eye sockets with sooty brows where flame had licked out and upward. Somewhere, an owl hooted sadly, as if he had lost his home, too, when the warehouse burned. Seeing the mill, I understood why empty, burned buildings made such great sets for horror movies, though this place seemed more lonely than terrifying.

I got out of the small car, pulling my bag with me. I have never come across an accident where a victim was stranded and in need of medical help, but I kept PPEs in the back of the car so they'd be handy if needed. Most doctors did. South Carolina law allows for any passerby to stop and help an accident victim with no regard to personal liability. In other words, if I stop and help and someone dies, anyway, I can't be sued. Many states are not so agreeable, and medical doctors are often afraid to stop and help, for fear of future lawsuits. My personal protective equipment was rolled into an old grocery store bag.

Quickly I dressed out in a yellow paper gown, paper shoe covers, a paper hat and hepa-mask. Lastly, I double-gloved. The two men leaned against the Jeep and watched, though it was too dark to see their expressions. If part of the contagion that was attacking patients' lungs and tissues came from here, I wanted to be prepared.

As I dressed, I could hear nightbirds calling on the breeze. Cool air touched the skin of my face like a lover's touch, riffled my hair. My clothing rustled as I moved, the sound odd, like dead leaves in a silk bag. It fit the ambience perfectly. I shivered. It would have been a wonderful night for a run. I wasn't so sure about mucking about in a deserted, burned building.

I moved toward the men, noting that Hiram was wearing a pair of thick latex gloves and some form of rubberized shoe covers. Smart move. I hoped he had worn something stronger when he was working the investigation of the site.

"Mark, do you have your own PPEs?"

He held up a paper coat, shoe covers and mask, his eyes dark sockets in the moon-touched, pale oval of his face. I couldn't see his expression, but I could sense his tension in the way he moved, pulling on the paper coat, bending to slip on the shoe covers.

"Have you been inside yet?" When he shook his head, I said, "Your PPEs will be contaminated when you get done. I can take them with me to the hospital for proper biohazard disposal. Speaking of which, Hiram, you should burn the clothes you wore to the fire and when you came back to investigate. Make sure no one handles them."

"My fire-retardant suit was hosed down and stored after the fire. And my wife already washed the clothes I wore when I came back after it got cool enough to work." I could hear the incipient panic in his voice. "Is she in danger?"

"Probably not. She have a rash? No? Then I'd say she's fine." It was possible that I was lying through my teeth. I had no idea how this germ was being passed, and while few forms of bacteria remained viable in cloth or could be passed by simply touching cloth, this bacteria was a constantly evolving area of study. "Just get the docs to watch her in Columbia. First sign of any problems, they can give her something. In fact, when I get them to admit you, I'll write her a prophylactic prescription." At his blank look I explained, "Antibiotics, just in case. I don't usually give antibiotics until someone is already sick, but I'll make an exception for you.''

"Thanks, Doc." Fear and relief in equal proportions vibrated in his voice. "It's this way. Step carefully. There's still a lot of discarded equipment and standing water."

I glanced at Mark, his face close enough for me to see the worry there. Worry for me. "You don't have to do this," he said. "It could be dangerous."

"And treating these patients isn't?" I asked gently.

He shrugged, shook his head and took my doctor's bag from me, holding both it and the flashlight he carried in one hand. Flicking on the flash, he indicated that I should follow Hiram into the blackness of the ruined building.

Stepping carefully, I moved through the blackened doorway. As we passed through, the wind seemed to die away. Nightbirds fell silent. The only sound was our feet shuffling on the ground.

I could smell the burn, even through my stuffed-up nose. Sour. Harsh. A smell like the scent of sickness in diseased flesh.

I had no flash, but the men's two were enough to light up the broken interior. The beams danced across the darkness, picking out strange shadows and dark-on-dark silhouettes. Shapes I couldn't identify seemed to move of their own will.

As my ears adjusted to the absence of the breeze, I heard water dripping slowly somewhere, a soft, irregular patter. Things slid and crackled in the night, like rats hiding from the light. I shivered again, and Mark took my arm above the elbow as if he sensed my discomfort. Together, we moved after Hiram.

Fallen, charred spars blocked our way. We bent and went under. Stepped high and moved over. There was no floor. Walking was treacherous. The uneven ground hid pools of wet left from fire hoses. Blackened earth was mired slippery mud. Mangled, blackened engines, machinery, unknown debris littered the space inside the walls. I moved closer to Mark, several times putting a hand on his shoulder for balance as we wended our way through the hazardous clutter.

Quickly, I was lost. Glancing back, I couldn't see the doorway where we had entered. Off in the black, something big and heavy shifted, groaned softly as if dying. My heart rose and lodged high in my throat. My breath grew hot, blowing back at me from the tight mask. The sound rose, almost at the edge of hearing.

It was a damaged beam. Had to be. Not someone moaning, left here after the blaze, burned and dying. With a sharp report it snapped. Fell. Echoing like a rifle shot. Startled, I jumped, slipped. Mark caught me, his hand steadying.

It would have been a perfect place and time for him to banter with me, teasing me about my reaction to the place. He didn't. I took his hand, our gloved fingers interlacing as he lifted my arm and tucked it securely against his side.

Hiram had moved far ahead. Mark stepped faster, following the fireman's flash.

Minutes later, I spotted a lighter space, and then another, as windows peeked onto us from the night. We had reached the far side of the old mill. Here there was a floor, and Hiram had climbed a fallen girder, a two-foot-square wooden monster, lying at a sharp angle, several feet onto the floorboards. They cracked under his weight, all the strength baked out of them. But it was a floor. And behind were unburned walls picked out in the glare from the dual flashes. I didn't bother to hide my sigh of relief.

Mark released me, handing up my medical bag and his own flash. Hiram positioned the lights to best advantage on the girder and held out a hand as Mark boosted me up. Using his shoulder to steady myself, I slid my feet in their muddy protective covers up the incline until I could grip Hiram's hand and step onto the floor, sighing once again to be on a firm foundation. Behind me, Mark jumped and cat-walked up the huge timber, bending forward and pulling with his hands for balance.

Though I had done nothing strenuous, I was breathing heavily, heart pounding a bit unevenly as it does when I am tired or try to run with an inadequate warm-up. It was the darkness and stench, which I could taste through my open mouth. Sour, wet, burned, aged.

Hiram seemed unfazed, his hands steady as he handed my medical bag to me. Moving with more speed, he led us through a hole into a second room. The floor was more stable here and resounded oddly, half muted, as we walked. In a corner were rolls of cloth. A pair of pants hung on a peg. A dress hung on another. Plastic dishes, warped by heat, sat in the center of the floor, a sleeping bag nearby. The detritus of living, left by the homeless squatters who had now lost everything to fire.

"This is where the fire started?" I asked. My words were muted by the open space and my hepa-mask, the question dead-sounding. The former echoes were left behind in the main warehouse area. Behind us, something else shifted and fell, groaning as it settled.

"No. There was a family living here. Took good care of their fire." Hiram turned the flash a few feet left, illuminating a small brazier to illustrate his meaning. "Fire stared at the center of the mill, near a support wall. Idiots. Heart-of-pine that old could be set aflame with a matchstick."

Directing the light to the end of the building, Hiram exposed a hole that had been torn in the wall. Beyond the black of the warehouse, I could see the beam's faint reflection on moving water. "This way," he said.

I followed him to the corner, my eyes picking out the circles of lighter wood in the slightly seared flooring. There were a dozen, each twelve inches across. Several showed dark places in irregular patterns around the outside diameters. Long-term leakage.

Deep gouges had been torn in the blackened flooring,

evidence Hiram interpreted to mean that the canisters were heavy, and had been hauled away with a forklift. In several of the grooves was the darker shadow of increased leakage. At least one of the canisters had been ruptured. My shivers returned. Something dangerous had been stored here. Something so valuable the owners had returned under cover of darkness and removed them while the ashes were still too hot for the investigators. Thoughts of the Twin Towers, the anthrax scares, Middle Eastern terrorism, flickered through my mind.

Pushing my hepa-mask more firmly in place, I said, "Why don't you two stay here. No point in getting close more often than necessary." I held my hand out for a flashlight, and after a reluctant moment Mark transferred his to me. Above his mask, I could see worry reflected in his eyes. Though it was obvious that I would be in no immediate danger, he didn't want me to go alone. "I'll be fine," I said. He shrugged, not liking it but acceding. I crossed the space to the circles.

Putting down my bag, I opened it and used the light to find what I needed in the black depths. Sterile culture collection swabs, the kind that came with their own gel-like media tubes for transport. I had six. I thought I had eight, but six would do. Carefully, I opened the first swab and knelt in the circle of light. With delicate motions, I dabbed a dark, leaklike area, then inserted the swab in its plastic tube and capped it. As I worked, my fear receded, dulled by the simple measure of doing my job.

Duck-walking, I took a culture of another area. Duck-walked again to the corner of the room near the wall, and took a third. The darkness seemed to have puddled quite heavily in the corner, near blackened oak posts that had once held up the roof. Cracks had opened in the mortar. Had the fire created the holes, or had the settling of the building during its hundred years made the holes? My breath was hot again, steaming up around my eyes, down around my chin. I knew that meant the hepa-mask was not completely secure, but my hands were contaminated now and I couldn't adjust it.

"I need to see this wall from the outside," I said, standing.

"Door there." I found Hiram in the dark and followed his pointing finger to the right to a rectangular hole. "Steps down are pretty steep. Don't meet code 'cause they were built so long ago. But there's a ramp. That's the way the forklift got in." Mark moved to retake the flash.

"Stay away," I said, more sharply than I intended. I swallowed down my reaction to the thought of Mark touching me just now. "I've been in contact with this stuff. I don't want you close." With an uncontaminated thumb, I pushed the flash toward him across the floor. "I haven't touched that. It's safe. And Hiram, I think you need to call in the DHEC Health Hazard Evaluation team, perhaps bring in CDC. I have a friend—Dr. Shirley Adkins—who is a CDC investigative officer. She can help. You were right about this place, something was stored here. It leaked and was hauled off. I don't like the look of this."

Hiram and Mark exchanged a glance but didn't respond. Silently, they followed me at a distance, shining the light ahead as I left the warehouse. Outside, the wind had stiffened and grown cold, the unpredictability of early spring bringing in a cold front. The paper of my coat flapped in the gusts. Nightbirds sounded again. It was eerie how they couldn't be heard from inside. The owl hooted far off, an answering sound coming from nearby, multiple sounds of short and long notes followed by a few quiet clicks.

I shivered again, though my breath was hot and labored. Fear. I was afraid, but not of the deserted and blackened building. I was afraid of what I had found. The leakage. The thought that it might be a biohazard. Some manmade horror. Some modern-day plague that had been released into the environment.

Finding the outside wall that corresponded to the place where the canisters were stored inside was difficult. Sooty water had drained through the sievelike brick. But Hiram seemed to know what I was looking for, pointed the flash without a word and led me to a spot. I took two more cultures from the brick, and my last one from the earth a few feet away. The ground sloped sharply to the creek below, a wide expanse of water reflecting back ripples of moonlight, giving no indication that virulent bacteria might have made its way to the water during the storm and was now infecting people. Manmade bacteria. Biological terrorism. My shivering worsened in the cooling breeze.

Deep ruts scored the soft soil, wheel tracks and footprints, some showing signs of plaster casts having been made as part of the investigation. Hiram shone his flash into one, showing me a print with sharply demarcated ridges. "Whoever they were, they all wore new boots," he said. "And all the same kind."

The freshening breeze blew through my paper coat and the thin scrubs beneath it, chilling my skin. My nose had clogged up totally in the minutes it took to collect the cultures and look around. "Track them?" I asked. It came out "Twack dem?" with my nose so stopped, but Hiram understood.

"Shoes are the same kind issued by the military with standard gear. Manufacturer sells them to the general public, too. Must be millions out there. Only odd thing about these is that they're all new. No old wear patterns on any of them."

Still shivering, I dumped the plastic culture tubes with their possibly deadly samples into my bag and snapped it shut. The owls hooted again in chorus, causing me to look up at the old mill. For all the danger of the old burned building and the deadly contamination, I liked this place. It was peaceful and remote. No traffic sounds or security lights pierced the canopy of trees and scrub, nothing but nature and silence and darkness. It might drive me nuts after a few weeks to live in a place like this, but I could like it for the short term. The owls called again, the sound taking with it some of the tension I was feeling.

"I'm done," I said. "Can we get back by walking around?"

"Don't recommend it. It's pretty grown up and we came farther than you think."

I sighed. "Back through the cadaver, then."

Mark laughed, the only sound he had made in what seemed like ages. His eyes grinned at me above his mask. Hiram looked up, startled in the moonlight. "Ma'am?"

"The burned building. It's like a dead body."

Hiram shone the light slowly across the brick facade, illuminating arched windows, brick turned in upright soldier courses at each window base and again above the arches. Decorative brickwork marked each corner, rising from the ground all the way up to the dark sky at what must have been a second-story roof. "Umm," he said, the tone appreciative. Overhead, wings flapped a strong three beats as an unseen nightbird launched its flight from the walls. An owl?

"They don't make them like this these days," Hiram said, the cliché wistful, mournful as the owl calls. He studied the building, light moving over the scorched surface.

Standing in the cold, I followed the light playing on the old brick. I wondered if it was mating season for the big predators. Wondered what time it was. If I was late to work. None of us moved, standing in the dark instead, putting off reentering the mill.

"Only because no one will pay for it," he continued. "The skills are still out there, being used here and there for restoration work. The occasional rich man's house. Labor-intensive is what this building was. These days; most folk only want the bottom line. 'How cheap can I get it?' And cheap is what they get. You see that brickwork there, where the mason made a pattern, two bricks one way, two another, two back, and so on? That was skill, pure and simple. Made this old mill a showplace.'' Finally, Hiram stomped off, taking the light with him but leaving me with an appreciation for the structure, which I hadn't had only a moment before. And I was grateful, as the mill was suddenly an abandoned work of art, not a dead body I was about to travel back through.

Mark gestured me forward, taking up the rear as Hiram paused and leaned back. "Watch your step," he said, holding out his hand.

I almost took it, before I remembered. I held up my gloved hand, fingers splayed. "Can't."

"Oh." He slowed his pace. "Well, be careful."

I smiled. Hiram was being bossy. I figured his fear of doctors had suffered a major drop in severity. I wondered how long it would last once a few specialists got hold of him at Richland.

Back at the hospital, I sent the cultures to the lab with the request that they be refrigerated until a courier could pick them up for CDC. Or until I heard from Shirl. As long as the bacteria was not temperature sensitive—and I didn't think it was or it would not be easily spread except by intimate human-to-human contact—it should keep well enough in the media-gel in the plastic tubes.

Preparing to ship Hiram to Richland Memorial in Columbia, I lanced one of his lesions, took the sample to the lab, gram-stained it myself and looked at it under the microscope. It was gram-positive cocci. Not that I was surprised.

Back with Hiram, I told him what I had found. "Hiram, the rash under your skin is caused by a special bacteria. A dangerous one."

"Is it that stuff I been hearing about?"

I nodded, seeing the fear in his eyes.

"I already told the wife. She ain't happy 'bout it."

"She's worried about you," I said as I wrote out a prophylactic antibiotic prescription for his wife and tucked it into his shirt pocket.

"No. She'll miss her angel program on TV. She loves that angel of death," he said sourly. "Maybe I should tell her I'm so sick she'll get to meet him personally. Just stick around a few hours. Damn doctors and hospitals both, 'scusing your presence, ma'am." .

"I'll call and check on you," I promised. "And Hiram?" He looked up. "You're doing the right thing."

He made a sound halfway between a snort and a splutter. It was clear he did not believe me.

I quickly called Richland and got Hiram admitted to the general practitioner on call, with a suggestion that she consult with an epidemiology specialist and liaise with CDC and DHEC about the case. Hiram left the hospital looking glum and muttering under his breath about how he was going to get his wife away from the angels. I advised him, "Whatever you do, do it quickly. I want you there in less than two hours."

15

GOD-AND-COUNTRY AND GUTSY WOMEN

I was nearly late for my shift, attracted to ICU by the scurrying of employees through the heavy double fire doors. And then by the smell. The stench of necrosing human flesh, especially when it is still attached to a living human being, is beyond description. Strong enough to pick up through my stuffed-up nose. The homeless mother and child I had helped Douglas Byars admit before I left work only twelve hours past were the source of the scent and the cause of the bustle. The patients' small, flat, reddish rashes had developed into open, distended, pus-filled lesions.

Douglas was masked, standing at the foot of the mother's bed, moving frantically as the nurses worked around him. She was conscious, alert and terrified. Hands grasped at the bed rails, eyes were wide and flashing, and she grunted and coughed and called for her child as she thrashed. As she moved, the flesh seemed to ooze from her. Tearing with each motion. Ripping each time she fought against the soft restraints holding her in the bed. It was horrible. The pain must have been unbearable, and through the glass doors to her room, I heard Douglas order a dose of painkiller IV, enough to calm the woman almost to the point of paralysis. I would have done the same thing.

In the next room, the child who was the object of the

woman's fear lay unmoving. Damp stains marked the sheets that covered her. Padded bandages showed as rounded lumps. A nurse checked the level of fluid in the catheter bag hanging beside the bed and shook her head at the color. The child's urine was a vibrant brown, proving the vitality of the invading organism rather than the host it was killing. Had she stroked-out? Had the bacterium mutated into a strain that attacked brain tissue? I wrapped my arms around myself and moved on.

I looked in on the firefighter in Mel Campbell's old room. He was hooked up to a ventilator, his flesh suppurating and purpled, looking like a plum pudding gone bad. He was totally limp, and if the ventilator had not been rising and lowering his chest, I'd have thought him dead. I wondered how long it would be before the machines could no longer give this perception of life.

Repelled by the stench, I left the unit. And carried with me guilt. I couldn't even remember the patients' names.

As I walked to the ER, I heard the rotors and engine roar of a medical helicopter. I passed Trish and was informed that the mother and daughter patients in the unit were being shipped to Richland Memorial Hospital in Columbia. Filling me in without pausing, Trish talked fast before she reached me, as she passed me, and continued as we moved apart, walking backward. "Somehow, Dr. Byars and Dr. Reeves found a doctor willing to take two uninsured patients with systemic infections of flesh-eating bacteria.

"They even found financing in the form of a grant to pay for additional negative-pressure units. He got the Reverend Lamb of God to ante up. Can you believe it?"

"Okay, I'm surprised," I said with a half grin.

Trish was manic—the kind of mania that results from too much caffeine and too little downtime. "Dr. Reeves has been amazingly helpful. He found us three respiratory techs who were willing to help us part-time through the crisis, and unearthed two additional negative-pressure units that are being shipped in by morning. God, that man is gorgeous!'' Her blue eyes glittered rapaciously.

I laughed at her non sequitur.

''And CDC has been called in on the problem. Administration and DHEC made the call around noon, and, thanks to you, we had a contact who already knew about it. I don't know what the latest is on it, but at least we have help. Gotta go, Doc. Later.'' I waved, but she had turned and was gone.

In my own department, there was no such excitement. The usual Easter Sunday crowd had thinned early and I was alone to call Shirl at CDC. Things were progressing too fast, and though I hadn't been the one to make the official request to CDC for assistance, Shirl could update me on the latest. I wanted to know who had been called in on our worsening situation.

Shirl was still on duty.

''Rhea,'' she said, relief evident in her tone. Groaning, she stretched, throwing her head back and her arms over her head. I didn't see it—it wasn't a psychic moment—but it was what Shirl always did when she was exhausted: groan and stretch, her thick hair falling down the back of her chair or over a shoulder like a river of spiraling flame. ''This has been a bloody, buggering, ballsed-up, cacky day, and I'm bleedin' knackered,'' she said in street-slang at the end of the stretch. ''What a soddin' mess you've given us.'' A faint thump told me the routine was finished and her feet were now crossed at the ankle on her desktop. For a well-bred, God-and-country Englishwoman, she had habits that might have looked mannish had she not been so small and delicate.

''What is it?''

Dropping the worst of her slang, she said, ''It's what you were expecting. A gram-positive beta-hemolytic strep, perhaps a new subgroup of group A, that is bloody awful to get to grow, though the bacteriology blokes have it plated on a round dozen different media and in half that many different broths. It seems to like some rather unusual nutrient factors, and your wild guess about potato is actually paying off rather well. It *was* a wild guess, wasn't it?''

"Does my reputation have to stand forever?'' I had been a poor microbiology student, much of my dislike of the subject matter due to the fact that Steven Braswell had been teaching the course that semester.

"You would surely have failed that class had you not asked for tutoring, and you are not a stupid woman,'' Shirl said.

"Thanks. I think.'' In conscious imitation of my memories of Shirl, I propped my feet on the desk at the MODIS terminal and rubbed the tips of my fingers through my scalp, feeling the short hair riffle. "So, what's the bottom line. Can we treat it?''

"I really don't know. We're already geno-typing the strain, and that will take a bit yet. Perhaps by morning we'll have found something concrete to track on. Sternes and Company have been working on a new antibiotic, and while it isn't ready for trials, the FDA might make an exception if it hopes to avert an epidemic. Of course, if an epidemic *isn't* in the making, then your patients may be royally buggered. And there is the possibility that one of the bio-tech companies specializing in genome-based R and D might be interested in an opportunity to test some of their latest theories on targeting specific organisms, cell-wall proteins and— Am I boring you?''

I answered with a soft snore and Shirl laughed, that ladylike tinkle that seemed to lilt, in high contrast to the London gutter talk she often cultivated. Next to her and Marisa I had felt like a not-too-well-bred horse all through med school. My laugh was like a whinny, not that anyone had ever been cruel enough to say so. And perhaps it was simply my own poor self-image left over from childhood with a mother who spent her days in a bottle, alternating between vicious verbal assault and treating me like a doll. My mama had been nothing if not inconsistent.

"But we're not going to get anything soon, are we? Shirl, we're losing them," I said before she could respond. "And this thing is changing its MO."

"How so?" Her voice sharpened, making me almost want to salute.

"It started out attacking lung tissue and preexisting skin lesions—"

"I've seen the charts," she interrupted.

"And now it's acting like flesh-eating bacteria, forming flat lesions that look as if small hemotomas are developing just under the dermis. Then just hours later they erupt, bleeding and pus-filled, and the stench is really bad." I paused. "In fact the smell is similar to the smell we were finding in the necrotic-lung patients. But these new patients are breathing fine. Could it be mutating?"

"Not sodding likely. If so, it's evolving at a rate I've never encountered before."

"Well, let me boggle your mind."

"Oh goody, bedtime stories?"

"I hope so." I told Shirl about the warehouse, the twelve circles of unburned floor, and the evidence that something heavy had been moved. She listened without comment, totally silent as I spoke, though I could hear keys tapping and assumed she was contacting someone else via the Internet as I talked. When I finished, she was silent for a long moment.

"Rhea," she said finally, sounding just a bit odd. "I'm coming. I'll be there by midafternoon."

"I'm buying a guest bed. You can bunk with me."

"That may not be necessary, CDC may be picking up the tab."

"Your other choices are a well-used inn, or no-tell-motel frequented by truckers, or a forty-five-minute drive from Ford County."

"Not the motel Cameron Reston was telling me about?"

"One and the same. He stayed there when he was helping with Marisa, and though he didn't complain, it wouldn't be up to your four-star standards. When did you talk to Cam?"

"I talk to him quite regularly. We've been seeing each other for the last few months."

I didn't react. Except on the inside. Cam had dated almost every attractive woman in his graduating class at medical school and worked his way through the ranks of the classes ahead and the ones that followed. With the exception of a very few like Shirl. And me, of course.

"Now, before you start remonstrating, please note that I am *not* the cause of the breakup with his latest lady-love, and I am *not* shagging him, and I don't intend to. Though he assures me that the experience would be life-changing, and I'd be beggin' for it after the first time."

I laughed. I couldn't help it. Cam was a scamp. Irrepressible. And I was an idiot.

"Exactly," Shirl conceded, and for a moment I wondered if I had spoken aloud, but she was only agreeing with my laughter. "So I'll be dossing at your place. Shall I bring towels and disinfectant?"

"I'll have you know that my house is clean enough to please even Marisa."

"How much do you pay your poor, abused housekeeper? A small fortune?"

"Don't be snide. You have my numbers."

"I'll ring for final directions when I reach the outskirts of town. And I may be bringing a few other EIS officers with me. They can stay at the no-tell. However, *you* can take me to that lovely restaurant you mentioned, put me up for the duration, feed me three meals a day and generally treat me like the queen. I do get my own lav, don't I?"

"Thank you so much," I said. "And yes, you do."

"You're quite welcome." The connection ended. Before I left the MODIS room, I called Arlana and prepared her for visitors and a buying spree. My housekeeper-cum-decorator was ecstatic at the thought of spending more of my money.

The ER was still empty of patients, with Ashlee, my favorite nurse, on duty behind the desk. Because I hadn't seen her in a while, I stopped to speak. "Been on vacation, Ash?"

The pert blonde looked up at me and grinned. "A whole week on a cruise to Jamaica and sundry islands." Holding out a tanned arm, she compared her fair skin to mine. "I even got some color. Not as golden as your olive skin, but not bad for my own. Of course, my cousins have had a word or two to say about my attempt to look like a *real* Chadwick, but I like it."

Ash was really Ashlee Chadwick Davenport, widowed and land-wealthy. As a Chadwick, she was a member of the large, near-legendary biracial family living in the county. The family had claimed one another since before the Civil War, and was multitudinous enough to have perhaps started their own county, had they wished. My titular boss was Ashlee's cousin several branchings back in the family tree.

"Do you have any trouble being a Chadwick?" I asked. "I mean, this is a small Southern town, and mixing the races is still looked upon as…socially inappropriate." Inadequate phrasing for an action best described as exploding a bomb in an enclosed space.

Ashlee shrugged. "I've been called the *N* word a few times, and had to defend a cousin or two in junior high school when they got picked on. But most of the well-bred, upper-class Dawkins citizens, especially the ones who attended Miss DeeDee's social graces classes back in high school, like to point at us and say, 'See. We aren't racists. We let people like the Chadwicks into our club, or church or whatever.'" She placed a hand over her heart for a moment. "'We are Christians and Democrats to our very roots,'" she quoted, tilting her head, short blond curls sliding with the movement. "Why?"

"That man, Leon Hawkins, who was lynched. Did it make you…" I paused, rephrasing my words. "How did your family react?"

"Madder'n hell."

"And what did they do about it?"

"Nothing. Except call in a few favors from law enforcement. We'll be notified when they catch that Ellis fella. And my nana will make sure he stays in jail this time."

"How?"

Ash leaned back in her chair. "Old women in this county have more power than you can imagine. You want something done, just tell a man's grandma. It'll be done a lot faster than if you tell the man. Nana is looking to see who she has to call to get this handled."

I nodded, my thoughts far away, my fingertips tingling just a bit. Something twittered in the back of my mind. Something about Leon Hawkins and his racially motivated method of death combined with the timing of the new illness. It was far-fetched, but… The ER had no patients, so I was still free. I could go back online. I could do a bit more research….

"I'll be in MODIS, Ash. Call if you need me." She nodded, grinned and returned to her paperwork. I moved down the dark hallway back to the MODIS room, punched in the code and reentered. I didn't have a grandmother to call in favors for me. Okay, technically I did, but she wasn't one to acknowledge the likes of me. I was on my own.

MODIS—Medical Online Diagnostic Interface System— was a high-tech, partially closed Internet hookup that allowed doctors to confer about difficult cases in real time without having to travel to see the patient. X rays could be sent over the digital system, as could test results and surgical photographs, and even microscope photographs. The system had all sorts of potential, only half worked out yet, but I used it most for a simple Internet hookup. I could have walked to the doctors' lounge for the same computer capability, but I preferred the quiet and certainty that I wouldn't be disturbed, at least at night.

An hour later a soft tap at the door disturbed me. Because I was no closer to understanding what was going on, I closed down the system for the second time that night and stretched to the doorknob. I was getting nowhere. I didn't know where to look or what to look for.

Mark poked his head in as the door cracked open for him. "Got a minute?"

I yawned and nodded, pushing a chair toward him with one toe. Instead, he leaned against the doorway, one shoulder holding it up, his arms crossed, hands tucked beneath the opposite armpits, booted feet crossed at the ankles. "What?" I asked when I saw his expression.

"DHEC brought in a bacteriological monitoring team. They're quarantining the warehouse site, working downstream to track the enteric pathogen released from Mac's hog-waste lagoons." His voice was stiff, the words abrupt, as if he were saying one thing and meaning another. I nodded slowly when he paused. Suddenly he burst out, "Look Rhea, do I have to be worried about this thing?"

At that, I understood. "You mean about catching it?"

Mark nodded.

I sighed, stood and gestured him out of the small room. The hallway was empty and dark and I pulled the MODIS door shut, pausing near him, my voice low. "Mark, I don't know its method of contagion—how it's passed," I clarified. "So I can't answer for sure. But I can say that the only people who have come down with this thing were exposed through direct contact or immediate water-based contamination. The Campbell couple by being in the water where it was leaking. Most of the homeless people by direct contact. The rest of the homeless and the firefighters by being in the vicinity when contaminated water was sprayed over the fire. Either they breathed it or were drenched with it. You don't fit either of the above-named situations, do you?"

"No."

"Then so far, my guess is you're fine. None of our patients seem to be transmitting this thing. No secondary infection. I've had multiple exposures and I'm infection free. Douglas Byars is healthy, same thing with him."

Mark nodded, his body language only a little less stiff than his words. "Can you tell me anything new about it?"

"Unofficially," I agreed. "It seems to be the same type of organism that causes strep throat, glomerular nephritis and other common conditions. Similar to the organism that is commonly called flesh-eating bacteria."

"They have to amputate when people get that."

"Sometimes," I said. I could see him thinking about Hiram, his mouth turned down, face drawn. Mark was fiercely loyal to his friends. And if Hiram died, Mark would carry unearned, unjustified guilt. That kind of guilt I understood. Doctors felt it often.

"Off the record," Mark said slowly, his eyes not meeting mine, his body tensing.

"Okay."

"The ten-ton truck. The boot prints in the ashes." When I said nothing, he looked up, green eyes meeting mine. "They match some worn by U.S. combat troops. The kind worn in regular soil conditions, not swamp, not desert. They show enough wear to be just what they look like. And we had an official visit by an FBI agent in to observe. Just after you left tonight, I called in the Health Hazard Evaluation team from DHEC and before they could even get to the site, this guy shows up. Like he was monitoring the call, waiting, and he didn't seem surprised to hear about the canisters. If DHEC hadn't shown up to take over the site, he might have kicked us all off it and taken it over for the federal agents. As it was, DHEC claimed jurisdiction. And there were more of them than he expected so he backed down gracefully."

I didn't know what Mark was trying to say. Didn't know if he knew himself. Without breaking eye contact, I said, "I had a visitor…this morning?" I asked myself, thinking back, "just before I got off. A guy in ill-fitting navy dress blues. I thought he was a reporter."

Mark nodded. Suddenly he uncrossed his arms and stepped forward. Taking my neck in one callused hand, he leaned in and kissed me hard, fast. He tasted of coffee and heat. An answering fire kindled deep inside me. As if from far off, I heard a soft moan. His grasp gentled. His lips softened.

Lifting my hands, I gripped his shoulders. My joints felt suddenly loose. Rubbery. My breathing was out of sync with my heartbeat.

Holding me close, mustache moving against my lips, he stared into my eyes. "You take care. Hear me? The men who got away during the jailbreak? Richard Ellis and his cronies? They are…" He paused as if filtering through what he wanted to say and what he was allowed to say. Finally he settled on "dangerous. Bad. Real bad. And they're still out there somewhere."

"How bad is bad?" I asked, and felt him stiffen. "Don't scare the little woman," I drawled in imitation of his own hick lingo. "Don't let her know the truth, 'case she couldn't handle it. She might get a case of the vapors and pass out in the hallway."

He chuckled ruefully. "Vapors? I'd like to see that." He looked up at me from under his bushy brows. "So you caught me being protective. Sorry."

"I can live with you being protective. I just want to know what I'm up against. So how bad is bad?"

Mark's eyes hardened. "One of the men we flew out after the jail takeover was a black guy accused of raping a white teenaged girl. Ellis's men, they…they castrated him." His voice dropped on the last two words.

"Oh," I said. "That bad."

"Worst thing I ever saw in my life, Rhea. He might not make it. It's been in the news for days."

I nodded slowly. "I haven't seen or read the news in days."

Mark pressed his lips to my temple, his hands warm through my scrubs. "That's why I want you to be a good little woman and call me if anything, and I mean anything, looks hinky."

We both smiled at the word and the tension between us eased. "Okay. Hinky. Is that an official word?"

"It is now," he said. "It is now."

"Mark?"

"Um?" he said, eyes on my mouth, a wicked gleam in them.

"Do you really think it's possible that the military is in on this thing, whatever it is?"

The sparkle left him, leaving his eyes the flat green of cold stone. "Don't know. Involved, or already monitoring it, somehow. There's so much going on, so many rumors flying. No one's speculating. Not officially."

"But unofficially?"

He pulled away and watched me closely. "If your navy visitor, or any other person who looks a little too military shows up, call me."

"Half the men in this town have military experience. How am I supposed to tell?"

Suddenly, Mark released me and stepped back. His shoulders went rigid, his chin dropped. His eyes, which had seemed cold only moment ago, were glacial. I nearly shivered. "Ma'am?" he said. Even his tone was different.

"How'd you do that?"

The Mark I knew reappeared, lazy grin, mustache quirking. "It's called command presence. Any officer worth his boots will demonstrate it. Even without trying."

"But how did you?"

"I spent four years at Citadel," he said, winked and spun

on a military heel, heading down the hall. "Call if you need me." He was gone, leaving the hallway dark and empty.

Quietly, I reentered the MODIS room and shut the door behind me. Had I known Mark went to Citadel? I didn't think so. Was it important?

Probably not. The important thing was that I had a disease I couldn't classify. Not to mention a hint that something was stored at a local warehouse, and that particular something may have contributed to the medical picture I was seeing. The presence of military and FBI... And before it all, Leon Hawkins.

Moving blindly, I sat in front of the computer system and hit the reboot button. For the third time that night I went online, my fingers moving of their own will on the keyboard. I checked my own e-mail, and then, because I couldn't get into my e-address book, I e-mailed Charlie Goldfarb, a friend from med school, for his father's address.

At loose ends, I began to scan the recent state news, expanding my search, when I couldn't find what I wanted, to include past news. I found what I was looking for in the State Newspaper, back in the nineties. A sidebar recounting a series of hate crimes carried out by a small group of neo-Nazi military men based at Camp Pendelton, South Carolina. A tight-knit group of U.S. soldiers in marine boot camp had metamorphosed into something else entirely. A white-power, Aryan-based, violent, secret gang. One of the men in the gang had once attended Citadel, but been kicked out for unacceptable behavior.

The State didn't speculate on what kind of behavior, at least not in this scanty article, but what if it had been the same kind of thinking that affected the group at Camp Pendelton? And if so, what did that have to do with my problems in Dawkins County?

At that point, the use of the Internet to discover what I needed to know was beyond me. Stymied, I closed down and went back to patient care. At least I was good at that.

I wandered down the hallway toward the ER, my thoughts trapped in a haze of misty facts, returning again to Mark and the things I didn't know. Mark didn't wear one of the garish graduation rings all Citadel men wore. Or flaunt the connection. He hadn't ever talked about Citadel, but then Mark and I didn't talk on a deep level. That thought was sobering. I had dated him on and off for a year, and I knew very little about him.

I entered the office I claimed while working and shut the door without turning on the light. Leaning my back against it, I closed my eyes. My relationship with Mark wasn't exclusive—not in the sense that we were *going steady*. There had been no ring or pin or declaration of intent. One couldn't be monogamous with a man one had never slept with. And there was as much competition between us as there was romance.

When I met him in the ER one night over a year ago, Mark was just another cop with a wound obtained when chasing down a criminal. Since then, I had met his mother Clarissa, had met his dogs, walked the family farm, seen his house, studied the photos hanging on his walls. I knew he had been in the military for a few years. I knew he had been engaged once and the girl had died in an auto accident. I knew he was a few years older than my twenty-nine years, drank coffee the way I did—by the gallon—and drank bourbon neat on the rare occasions when he indulged. But I hadn't known he had attended Citadel. And that seemed important, though I wasn't sure why.

Citadel was part of Southern tradition. It attracted many of the best and brightest; many future and past politicians and high ranking military officers were Citadel grads. There was a Citadel mystique, a slowly modifying girls-keep-out, boys-only, clublike secrecy that bound the men to one another. If a Citadel grad wanted a job in any business, anywhere, and a Citadel man was on the board, all he had to do was flash that Citadel ring, and he was suddenly the best man for the job.

And Mark was a part of them, that insular, isolated crowd. I wasn't sure I liked that. And wasn't sure why I didn't like it.

Except that Citadel had a long tradition of being only for white males, not Jews, not Asians, not Native American, and certainly not women and African-Americans. Something teased at the back of my brain, some small thing I should have known or remembered. And then it was gone, like a candle in a cavern suddenly snuffed.

Quickly I flipped the switch, lighting the room in harsh fluorescent white. Sitting behind the desk, I dialed Mark's cellular number and waited until it rang.

"Yceellow."

"Green," I said, remembering his mutable eyes. "Listen, Mark, I have a question. Do you know what HazMat found at the farm where the Campbells were held prisoner?"

"Your enteric pathogens. Lots of salmonella and some *E. coli*. A few other things I can't pronounce."

"But no streptococci?"

"Hang on. I got a list here somewhere." I heard papers rattle in the background. "Don't see anything like that. Why?"

"Just curious," I said, adding that little bit to the list of questions and curiosities I was building in the back of my mind. "Thanks." Hanging up the phone, I wandered back to the ER and poured a cup of coffee. Drank it sitting silently in the break room, alone. Something was hinky here, all right. I just didn't know what the hinky thing was.

I was halfway through my night, sewing up a toddler who had fallen in the dark and cut his lip when it hit me. And I felt like an idiot for not thinking of it sooner. Two a.m. on a Monday might not be the best time to go waking up a not-exclusive boyfriend, especially when the parameters of that relationship were yet to be decided, and when one was working a hunch, so calling Mark was out. Instead, I dialed dispatch of the local LEC and asked for a favor. Fortunately, an EMT I knew personally answered the phone.

"Dawkins County Sheriff's Department, Buford Munsey. How may I help you?"

"Buzzy, you answer for 911 and the sheriff's office, too?"

"Umm," he said.

"It's Dr. Rhea."

"Oh, hi, Doc." The professional-sounding "I have an important job" tone left his voice. "Yep. In a county this poor, sheriff and city *po*-lice lines route over to 911 after midnight and I get them all."

"I'll bet you get some real interesting calls after midnight," I said, feeling no sense of haste. After all, there was nothing I could do about my suppositions now.

"Aliens, drunks asleep on strangers' front porches, helicopters flying overhead shining bright lights on the ground, gunshots in the woods, more aliens, a few cars parked in the wrong places, and the occasional dead body found on the side of the road."

I laughed dutifully, though I guessed he wasn't joking. "How often do you get strange doctors asking to have a picture of a wanted felon faxed over?"

"Dating service? I get that all the time. Though most times it's johns who've been stiffed by one. Oops. That came out wrong."

This time I laughed for real. "Not quite. I just had a visitor in the ER on Easter Sunday morning and I'm wondering if it might have been the escaped guy, Ellis."

"No kidding?"

"No kidding."

"I got a picture right here, what's the fax number?"

I gave it to him, disconnected and waited. Moments later,

the ER fax rang and beeped and I had a picture of the state's most wanted in my hand. My fingertips began to tingle sharply. It was my navy man in the ill-fitting suit. Now I had a reason to call Mark. I needed privacy. I went back to the MODIS room and shut myself in, grateful for a light workload tonight.

"What," he croaked when he answered.

"Sorry to wake you up, but you wanted to know if anything got hinky."

"And? Down, boy. Get off the bed."

I heard a sliding thump-thump, the kind a large dog makes when pushed off a bed while still half asleep. Another dual thump followed, and I wondered how many of his hunting dogs had crawled into the sack with him. "Ever since you demonstrated command presence, I kept remembering something about my navy visitor Easter morning. He was forceful, charismatic, just like you indicated. I got dispatch to send me a fax of the wanted poster. He was Ellis."

"Ellis is in Savannah. Last I heard. He's got a girlfriend there and he called her. Told her he wanted to see her."

"Well, he was here Easter morning." I checked my watch, trying to calculate the hours. "Less than twenty-four hours ago."

"Doesn't make sense," Mark muttered. "Feebs know where he is to within a half mile. Who'd you talk to at dispatch?"

"Buzzy Munsey. Who's Feeb?"

"FBI. I'll make a few calls, see what I can see. And Rhea?"

"Yeah?"

"For a smart woman, you sure took long enough to figure this out," he said, sounding sleepy, amused and vaguely challenging.

"Be nice. I could have called the *Feebs* myself. Instead, I'm letting you have all the glory. Ellis drove away in a red

Ford truck with a dented left rear bumper and wheel panel. No license plate. Had a driver, buzz cut, male."

"I'll be nice. Anything else you can remember?"

"He was interested in the bacteria infecting my patients." I paused, not sure if I was being overly alarmist. But my fingertips were tingling, and they seldom let me down. "He kept calling them wet germs. I think he knew something, Mark. Did you say he was in the Middle East at some point?"

"Yeah. I think so. Served in the Gulf War. Been over there since. Sorry, I'm still half asleep. Why should that matter?"

"Chemical and biological warfare. Things that might be stored in canisters."

The silence on the other end of the phone was suddenly sharp, brittle.

"I was thinking that maybe he brought something home, or heard about something for sale on the black market while he was over there. Got it delivered over here. This stuff can be easy to grow and easy to keep alive, once you know its nutritional needs. You said he had some anthrax when he was caught that time in D.C. Well..." I ran out of ideas. At least the ones I was willing to suggest at this point.

"Don't stop now, woman." I could hear Mark moving in the background, the sound of clothes sliding over his head, perhaps.

"What if someone, somewhere, figured out how to store vital bacteria for extended periods and shipped it over for domestic terrorism. Maybe marked in oxygen canisters or propane canisters. Maybe someone involved in genetic engineering with viruses found a way to insert a virus into a specific bacteria to prolong its life, *and* found a way to make it more virulent. Or maybe the two things weren't being experimented on, but were a lab accident. A dangerous one or a fortuitous one, depending on how you look at it." My fingertips were tingling so hard they itched, and I held the phone with a shoulder so I could rub them against my scrub pants. "I can't see how radical Muslim groups would give away their secrets, but maybe someone stole it…"

"Anyway, all they would have to do is release it into the atmosphere, in aerosol form. Real damp aerosol form, if my guess is correct. Every one of the infected patients was exposed to it in connection with large amounts of water, even Regina Hawkins, who found her husband hanging from a bridge over Prosperity Creek and cut him down."

"This could be done? Making and storing a germ for extended periods of time? Those canisters were stored in the warehouse for weeks, Rhea."

"I wouldn't bet against it being done."

"I'll be in the office. You know my number. And look, Rhea, don't say anything about this to anyone else. Not until I can make a few calls. This is important."

I sat up straight. "Well, heck, Mark. I thought I would shout it from the hospital roof. Maybe call in a few reporters and tell them my suspicions, send out an Internet alarm, go on late-night talk radio, and start a panic riot or two."

Mark chuckled into the phone.

"I'm not an idiot," I said, growing more indignant. "I have patients, Mark, and they're important. If I choose to tell someone, or ask someone a few questions, I'll handle it appropriately. You can't muzzle me on this."

"Sorry. But some of us were tossing around a few ideas like you just mentioned. We didn't think it could be done. Now you tell me it could be."

"*May*be. *Maybe* it could be done," I said, backpedaling to cover my backside. "As in, it's within the realm of possibility. I'll be on duty till seven," I said.

"I'll call before then. And I know you're not an idiot."

"Good."

We parted on that note, and I sat in the dark, nursing my ire. I had no idea why I reacted as I did to his suggestion. Okay, I did, but one can't blame everything in life on a mother who had problems with bottles. His comment had been a perfectly reasonable suggestion. *Look both ways when you cross the road. Don't take candy from kind-looking men. Don't pet wild dogs. Look where you step when crossing a cow pasture. Don't pick up hitchhikers. Don't talk to strangers.* All very valid reminders, coming from an ordinary person. But coming from Mark they irritated me in the same way they had irritated me hearing them from my mama. And that was stupid.

The competition that flared between us was fun up to a point. Maybe I really was PMSing. But that was no excuse.

Feeling uncomfortable, I dialed his number.

"And?" he said.

"And I'm sorry."

"Oh. I thought you remembered something else."

"I did. I remembered how to be polite."

Mark laughed. "I do love gutsy women. Later."

I looked at the dead phone. Had he said gutsy or gusty? I preferred the former, as the latter made me think of beans and cabbage.

Smiling, I put the receiver down and left the MODIS room, hearing the door lock behind me.

It was 4:00 a.m. before I could check my e-mail again, and I discovered I had heard from Charlie Goldfarb. Young, fresh-out-of-school-or-residency doctors got the worst hours and the most difficult rotation schedules, meaning that we were often working at hours most people would relate to industry or manufacturing, and for us working the graveyard shift was often a literal thing. Charlie was still working a residency in forensic pathology, and spent his time carving up dead bodies in various stages of decomposition. Graveyard in reality.

His e-mail was terse and to the point, telling me he was up to his armpits in the results of a bus accident, and giving me his dad's e-mail at the Pentagon. Rear Admiral Rufus

Goldfarb. Nothing like taking one's questions to the very top.

Before I could chicken out, I typed my letter to the admiral, whom I had met a few times at various medical school functions, and hit Send.

16

GOOD WITH THE BAD

It was eleven Monday morning when a crash notified me that I had company. My door was shut, and through it I could hear the quick, low barks that meant Belle was facing an intruder. As my house had been burgled only months before, I crawled from bed and grabbed the only heavy thing I could find. Holding the iron above my head, I opened the door.

Two men were wrestling a mattress up the hallway.

"Just a little more, then into the guest bath," Arlana said from the kitchen, her best bossy voice at work. When something fell and shattered in the bath she jumped, pushed past the heavy mattress and into the crowded space, glancing at me and the raised iron on the way past and lifting her entire brow at the sight. "You got no idea how to use that thing, so you might as well put it back where you found it. I didn't even know you had one," she said. Before I could reply, she was gone. My arm slowly fell to my side.

"Look what you done," she said to the deliveryman, her rising voice coming from the guest bath. "I just paid twelve dollars for that white swan. And it broke, now. You paying for that, I hope you know. Now, push on through to the guest bedroom. And don't break anything else, if you don't

mind.'' The man's apologies were lost beneath Arlana's ex-
asperation.

A cold nose nudged me, and I moved aside to let Belle
and Pup into the room. Belle jumped to the foot of the bed
and Pup curled under it. ''Smart move,'' I said softly. Belle
whined.

''No, not there,'' Arlana said. ''I got the bed frame where
I want it. You just put that mattress on top that box spring
and leave the placement to me.''

Feeling a bit abashed, I closed the door, put the iron back
where I had discovered it on Easter Sunday, and crawled
back under the covers. Belle paw-and-belly-crawled to me
up the far side of the bed, still whining. ''You can stay,'' I
told her. ''But Arlana will not be pleased.'' And Belle
whined again, eyes soulful, tail thumping. ''Yeah, I'll protect you, but I can't be here all the time.'' Belle put her
head down and whuffed once to let me know that she accepted the consequences.

I pulled the covers over my head and tried to go back to
sleep. Arlana had other ideas. Less than an hour later, she
opened the door and stuck her head in. ''Belle, you get off
that bed.'' The big dog moaned, pawed once at me and
slithered off the bed when she realized I was not going to
intervene. ''And you get out that bed, too. You got a phone
call. Dr. Somebody Adkins. That who coming to stay
here?''

''Yes,'' I said carefully.

''She got a given name?''

''Shirley. We call her Shirl.''

''Well?''

I moved an arm from beneath the covers and answered.
''Shirl?''

''I'm on the way,'' Shirl shouted gleefully, ''and it's a
jolly good day for a drive!''

I could hear wind rushing by and knew she was driving
with the windows down, or perhaps the top down, if she

had purchased a convertible. Shirl drove like a lunatic, her
hair plaited in multiple braids, all blowing in the wind. It
was like watching a happy Medusa. Unless one was in the
back seat; then it was like being beaten with soft red ropes.

"I'll be there by 2:00 p.m., if the sodding traffic will
cooperate, and you can feed me at that lovely restaurant you
mentioned. The rest of my group will be down sixish, and
I'll have to go to work after."

"Your room is ready," I said.

"That delightful woman who answered the phone said
she was your decorator?" A horn blew in the background,
loud for an instant then fading. Shirl was speeding. As usual.

"Delightful?" I poked my head out from the covers to
find Arlana still at the door, listening. She had braided gold
beads into her hair for Easter, and plaited the braids close,
giving her head the look of a golden cap or helmet. She was
dressed in a lavender power suit and four-inch heels, with
long gold hoops in her ears. But *delightful* was not a word
I'd ever used in conjunction with Arlana. "Yes, that was
Arlana. She decorates and does—" I paused and rose up on
one elbow, altering my phrasing "—arranges some house-
cleaning."

At Shirl's next comment, I grinned at Arlana and said,
"I'm sure she'd be happy to help you any way she could."

Arlana lost the grown-up dignity she had been sporting
and covered her mouth. A soft squeal escaped her hand. Her
eyes were brighter than the gold beads in her hair.

"As you English might say, 'she's frightfully expensive'
but worth every dime. Still in school, but with a solid client
base."

The squeal went up a notch. Arlana's feet began the
"happy dance," her spike heels making little tapping
sounds in the hall, hips rotating, arms and shoulders boo-
gying to unheard music. I had recommended Arlana to one
of the nurses, who had used her to decorate her living room.

Two clients made a solid client base, didn't it? Besides, I knew she'd do right by Shirl.

"I'll see you in a couple of hours," I said. "Don't get arrested speeding."

"All the coppers pull me over, expecting to find a rich old bloke with a long comb-over lacquered to his scalp, a gold fob round his neck, having a midlife crisis," Shirl shouted gleefully over the sound of an eighteen-wheeler passing close by. "Instead, they get a butchers at little old me, with my impish grin and my lovely accent and me fine bubbies, and they all want to take me home or to the nearest hotel room. I've yet to receive a citation."

"What are you driving?"

"A Porsche 911 Cabriolet in drop-dead red."

"No kidding. Well, be careful. We have a lot of deer on the back roads and you don't want to end up smashed."

"Splendid! Ta-ta."

I turned the ringer back on and hung up the phone, not quite sure what Shirl thought was splendid but knowing she had heard the warning about the deer. The moment the phone was down, Arlana jumped on the duvet, squealing louder, bouncing on her knees, up and down. The power suit did little for her at the moment except make her look young and vulnerable. And terribly happy.

"If you still intend to be a nurse, this is something you would not be allowed to do on a patient's bed," I said, trying not to grin.

"I got me another customer, don't I?"

"You do. If she likes your work."

Arlana settled, flipping her spikes off onto the floor and crossing her legs. "Oh, she'll like my work. What's not to like? This place perfect."

"You would make a dreadful nurse."

"You keep telling me. But I need a job that pays me what I'm worth, and nurses get paid well. No competition. Not a doctor or hospital in any town but what need a nurse."

"But now you have three paying customers. Think about switching majors and going to USC instead of Ford Tech. I'll still co-sign your loans if you need me to."

"I'll talk to Miss Essie." With that phrase, Arlana closed the subject, as she did with most of what I had to say. Miss Essie was Arlana's grandmother, or great-grandmother. I wasn't always sure. And Miss Essie had final say on everything in Arlana's life, as well as in the lives of her whole clan.

"I got you something."

I dropped my head back to the pillow with a moan.

"It was expensive, but you'll like it."

"I didn't need expensive for the guest bedroom. I just needed a bed."

"I got what you needed for company and I got it on sale." Arlana climbed from the bed and went to a low table that had once been empty. I couldn't see what she was doing, but the table was now loaded with something black that could have been electronics. "What I got that cost money is for you. Listen."

A soft sound filled the air, seeming to come from all four corners of my room. Music. Rich, full-toned music. Followed by the sound of Billie Holiday's low, vivid voice singing "Lover Man." I groaned in pleasure.

I lost my meager music system and dozens of CDs when my house was broken into and I had missed music more than I could say. Closing my eyes, I stretched beneath the covers and listened. I lay still through "God Bless the Child," "Porgy," and "All of Me" before the music changed to something raucous and just a bit naughty. Bonnie Raitt. Laughing, I raised my head. Arlana was standing in the doorway, a half smile tilting her full lips.

"How'd you know?"

"That you needed your music?"

I nodded and she went to the black electronics system, lowering the volume but not turning to face me. She took a deep breath, as if her words were hard. I tensed. "Miss Essie say you not been yourself since your mama's music been took by them thieves. She say to get you something to bring her back."

The pleasure I had felt at the mellow strains faded. "My *mama's* music?"

"She say your mama and you shared only one thing. Music. And when you lost that, you lost your mama and your past." Arlana said this with her back turned. Coward.

"My *past?*" My voice rose. "My mama was a raving maniac who drank herself into an early grave. Tammy Arnette Rheaburn Lynch was a selfish manic-depressive with the mothering instincts of a crocodile." Blood skittered through me, a rough rhythm of sudden annoyance. "My love of music is *mine,* not hers."

Arlana shrugged. "What Miss Essie say. She say as how I was to get this house wired for sound little by little and then get you a system. I done what she said. Got Malcolm and Steve to do the wiring. Finished it up last week. Labor didn't cost you nothing. Just the system and a few CDs Miss Essie say you liked." Arlana turned around, dark eyes serious, shoulders back as she spoke her mind, as she always did.

"We all got pasts. We all got things and people in 'em what we don't like. And even with the bad ones, there's things that are good. Your mama loved music. She give you that. You don't have to thank her, 'cause she dead. But you got to see it."

When I said nothing, she went on.

"I had this man in my life when I was twelve, thinking I was all growed and such hot shit and could take care of my own self. And Chico and me was seeing each other behind my mama's back, sneaking around, drinking and smoking. And he took me one night. And it was bad, 'cause of him been drinking. And it hurt. And the trial hurt worse, 'cause I sat there, a minor, and unidentified to the jury. But the judge say I got to talk, and I got up there and had to say what led up to the taking. And I knew I was a fool and my mama and Miss Essie sitting there hearing it all, shamed to the soul 'cause a me. Not cause I got took, 'cause that part not my fault. But 'cause I such a fool to go with him in the first place.

"All that bad. All that a shame to my mama, who taught me better. But the good I found later. Chico, he spoke two languages, him being half Mexican. And I learn enough offa him to take a class in school and make good grades. I'm pretty much bilingual now. I can use that when I get a job, most anywhere. And even if I don't like it, it be so.

"Chico, he'll be outta jail in a couple years. I got to deal with that then, 'cause I gone see his face, know he back in town. And him such a pretty boy, he couldn't a had a easy time in jail. And that all I got to say 'bout that."

Arlana turned the volume back up to reveal Carole King singing "Goodbye Don't Mean I'm Gone," and walked from the room. Just as the door closed, I said, "Arlana?" The door opened again, my friend's carefully blank face in the hallway darkness. "Thank you. For the music system. And for the lecture. I didn't much like it, but I'll think about it."

She shrugged, a twinkle returning to her eyes. "Know-it-all doctors got to have someone what keep them in they place. That why Miss Essie send me to you."

"So thank Miss Essie, too."

"That your job."

I nodded. "Can I see the guest bedroom now?"

"Whenever you ready. Just keep that mangy dog offa my furniture."

"Yes, ma'am."

The door closed gently. I rose to Carole's languid voice and headed to the shower.

The minuscule guest room was decorated in deep shades of taupe and stone, with hints of ecru and dark blue. The bed was queen-size, with a simple wood headboard, striped bed skirt, contrasting floral comforter and pillows, and not a frill in sight. A small slipper chair and tiny ottoman sat in one corner with a flea-market magazine rack and old brass lamp for reading. An inexpensive (I hoped) wool Oriental rug was beside the bed, a chest of drawers on the far wall under the window, which was covered with metal blinds and a simple draped swag of fabric through a brass hoop. Little knickknacks were situated here and there, a couple of candles, a few used books. The room was inviting, neither masculine nor feminine, but gender neutral, as a good guest bedroom should be.

I praised the room. Though I had shared little of my decorating preferences with Arlana, she had watched how I lived, studied what I liked, and somehow made my house look like me. The best me, not the slob me. "I love it," I said to her. "I really love it."

Arlana glowed. Closing the bedroom door, she showed me two brass hooks hung with thick, navy-blue terry robes on the back. "Because your guests will have to go down the hall to use the bathroom, which looks right nice, too." Opening the door again, she led me into the hall and gestured for me to enter the long, narrow guest bath.

Arlana had previously wallpapered the bath in a tone-on-tone embossed taupe stripe. Now the room had ecru-and-taupe towels, dark blue washcloths, an ecru rug and blue candles. I thought I might be smelling blueberries through my half-stopped-up nose, and Arlana agreed that the candles were scented. The mirror over the sink was old and spotted, but she had cleaned the wood frame around it and tinted it to match the room's ecru woodwork. *Ecru* was the proper term for the fixtures. Not beige, she had informed me.

"You gonna let me finish the master bathroom now?"

"You gonna do it up like this?"

"Better."

"Start small. I have to work overtime to pay for this first. What did the deliverymen break?"

Opening the bath closet door, Arlana handed me a large swan of blown glass in swirling shades of blueberry and taupe on white. It was broken in several pieces, but I could see how the glass water bird had been intended to tie the room together.

"I'll find you something else, but that swan I really liked. It was a soap dish or change-holder or whatever. But it was pretty." Arlana sighed in frustration.

"Yes, it was."

"Well, I gotta get to class. Later, Doc."

"Bye, Arlana," I said. Lingering in the guest suite as she let herself out, I touched the towels, the scented soaps, spotted a small floral arrangement tucked beside the toilet, holding the paper.

Back across the hall, I ran my fingers over the comforter, noting its nubby texture, sat in the slipper chair, which was a bit small for me unless I used the ottoman, and then it was a good fit. I liked the room. I liked it very much.

The fact that I could see Cameron Reston in it more easily than I could see Shirl Adkins was a problem I could live with.

Barefooted on the cold wood floors, I padded through the house. Arlana had made me coffee, and I knew my nose had cleared up when I caught the fresh-brewed scent. Beside the coffeepot was a plate of English scones and pot of peach jam. Carrying the tray and a mug to the living room, I settled on my couch to watch the news, legs curled beneath me, a knitted afghan over my lap. The dogs were outside, and the house was quiet, with the faint strains of Carole King coming over the speakers. But what I saw on the TV made me lose my appetite.

Charlotte, North Carolina, less than fifty miles from Dawkins, had an outbreak of a virulent form of pneumonia. There had been twenty-five cases of pneumonia in the last twelve hours, twenty-three of them African-Americans who had been at a club near Pinkney Street on Saturday night. The two other cases were white males. Anyone who had been at the club on Saturday night was being asked to go to the health department, call their doctors or go to the emergency room at Carolinas Medical if they developed a cough or flulike symptoms.

CDC had been brought in on the North Carolina cases, and officials there were calling for calm.

Reaching for the phone recently installed beside the end table, I called Carolinas Medical Center. Telling the switchboard that I was an emergency room doctor who had seen some virulent pneumonia over the weekend, I had my call routed to a Dr. Smiley. He was skeptical of my story, but at least he listened.

After explaining my interest, I was put on hold while Smiley called Dawkins County Hospital and verified my credentials. I wasn't surprised or insulted. I was sure the press was going nuts, trying anything to get the latest story. When he came back on the line his first words were rapid-fire questions. "Is it a gram-positive cocci? And how is it spread?"

"Yes, to the first question. A form of group A beta strep. Hard as heck to grow in vitro but eats into the alveolar tissue, causing necrosis. The closest thing that could compare to it is a fast-acting tuberculosis. We had patients coughing up tissue in the end stage," I said, offering as much information as I could. "But so far no patient-to-patient contagion."

"Big thanks for that. But what you're describing doesn't sound like what we're seeing. What we're looking at appears to work less like a bacterial breakdown of tissue, and more like a vesicant."

"Vesicant? Like mustard gas?"

"Somewhat. No external blistering like with mustard gas victims, no blistering of eyes or soft tissue, but the membranes of the trachea and bronchial tubes are covered over with blisters that shed and suppurate." Smiley exhaled heavily. "On X rays, the alveoli show sudden accumulation of fluid. Their lungs are filling up. We put in chest tubes in the first two, with the result of uncontrolled bleeding into the chest cavity and the lungs."

I sat back during his description and bit into a scone to think. When he finished, I said, "You're right, it is presenting itself differently, but if this strain of group A is mutable…" I let the phrase drift to an uncertain end.

"True. It may be changing how it attacks in vivo."

"CDC is geno-typing our strain now. Perhaps they could do yours and compare." I heard papers shuffling again. Voices in the background saying things I couldn't make out.

"How many did you lose?" Smiley asked.

The question jolted me. I hesitated, then said, "So far, ninety percent of them." When Smiley didn't respond, I said, "We had less than ten, but we lost most of them. Some combinations of antibiotic cocktails seemed to slow it down, but nothing has stopped it. This thing is just too fast-acting for the meds to have time to work. You want the list, anyway?"

"Yes." The word was terse. But then, Smiley had twenty-five cases to contend with at once. I would have been terse, too. Papers were shuffled in the background. "Go ahead."

I gave him the list and told him which patient cases seemed to advance slower than others, and we discussed some alternatives. The man had some good ideas. I wished I had had Smiley to talk to when Douglas and I were first combating this bug. We might have saved some patients.

"Dr. Shirley Adkins is coming to Dawkins with a team of CDC officials, and she has seen some luck with several growth media in the lab. When we get some reliable culture media to work with, we can experiment with other antibiotic combinations."

"We had been informed that CDC knew of a problem, but no one told us—well, no one told me—that it was so close geographically. A team is supposedly on the way here also but I have no names. And nowhere to put a team, if they want space to work."

That was something I hadn't considered. Dawkins County Hospital was small and overcrowded, and the wings where there might have been room to put a makeshift lab might not have reliable electrical power or running water. My call room had been on the fringes of a remodeling job for several months in late winter. It had been uncomfortable and noisy. I wondered if anyone else had thought about CDC lab space. Did CDC even *need* lab space?

"Something else you should know," I said. "PT results are slightly elevated but not life-threatening. High teens. The DIC work-up shows some changes, but nothing major. And the bacteria seems to spread by way of moist air, like in an aerosol," I said.

"That was what we thought. It seems that during the big storm a few days back, a leak developed in the club roof where some shingles blew off, and on Saturday night there was a sudden deluge of collected rainwater that showered over the dancers. Some of it trickled through an air-conditioning vent and was coming out in a spray. So far, the majority of our cases are from party-goers who were under the leak and got drenched, or who were dancing beside the AC vent for extended periods of time. The State Health boys are taking culture samples now and the club is shut down."

"And the two white men?" I asked, finally biting into a crumbled bit of scone.

"Well, that's where my story gets to be a bit confusing."

I sat up in my seat, uncurling my legs to the floor. "Let me guess," I said gently. "You have two young, white, skinhead, male members of a white supremacy group, possibly with military backgrounds." I heard a sharp click. The background noise changed, became louder and brighter-sounding. "Are you still there?"

"Yes. Would you say that again? I want my colleagues to hear you." His voice was tinny and echoing, and I realized I had been put on speakerphone.

"Sure." I repeated my speculation and sipped coffee to moisten my suddenly dry mouth. "You might want to speak to Captain Mark Stafford of the Dawkins County Sheriff's Department. He can fill you in on the possible connection." I gave the man and his unidentified listeners Mark's work number and his cellular number. Mark wouldn't thank me, but he would understand. Besides, officially it was someone else's job to mention Ellis, the warehouse fire, biological warfare and any military tie-ins. At least until Rear Admiral Goldfarb got back in touch with me.

Smiley and I shared other names and phone numbers of common interest, speculated on treatments and guessed about outcomes. During the last few minutes, I told him about the possibility of the same strain of bacteria mutating into flesh-eating bacteria, and no longer only attacking lung tissue. After I finished, there was a lot we didn't say about where such a bacterium might have come from, and what it might eventually mutate into. The possibilities were simply too frightening.

The only new information I gleaned from the phone call was the name of the hate group. The young infected men called themselves the Hand of the Lord.

Dismayed by the phone call, I changed into running clothes, warm sweats to compensate for the Monday afternoon cold I could feel coming through the floorboards. An Arctic front had blown down, swatting spring in the face with a vengeance.

Belle and I ran along the creek in back, and for the first time, I left the leash off the big dog. Looping it around my neck, under my hood, we ran side by side through the crisp leaf mold and over hard-packed ground. I had no idea how

Belle would react to the lack of leash; I was still learning the parameters of her training. She was a found dog, rescued by Mark and me in the dead of night while she was delivering puppies in a graveyard. I didn't think Belle would run away, but she might not stay close, and chasing a dog through the rough was not my idea of fun.

Polite and well trained, Belle ran steadily beside me, pausing only twice, once when nature called and when we came upon a dead squirrel that appeared to have fallen from a tree. The scent of the freshly dead rodent was more than her training could bear and she swerved off the path, looking at me with longing when I called her back to me. Her expression seemed to say, "But, Mama, I'm *supposed* to roll in it. God made me this way."

I assured her that God would not care if she stayed fresh-smelling, and only then realized that Mark Stafford had indeed washed my dogs. Belle smelled almost pretty. We went home by a different path to avoid temptation. I loved dogs, but the scent of dead things was forever associated in my mind with medical school or grief. It was why Belle was bathed so often.

While I pounded the narrow path through the woods, I spotted two other runners in the distance, moving with a speed I never attempted, long legs stretched out as if they were training for the Olympics. One was Taylor Reeves, wearing skin-tight Lycra running pants and a hooded sweatshirt, the hood thrown back, his leg muscles bunching and relaxing with athletic zeal. A girl could tell a lot about a man from the way he ran, and I liked the way Taylor moved, serenely and smoothly, though he was covering ground with a brutal pace. Beside him ran another man, bundled and hooded in dark brown sweats. He seemed to be straining to keep up the pace a bit more than Reeves; he ran back on his heels rather than forward, on his toes, but his feet pounded the ground steadily.

The two men were sweaty and fully stretched into the

motion of the run, as if they were right in the middle of a daily ten-mile competition, yet I had seen neither man on this trail before. I'd have remembered the movement of bodies at this level of training. They appeared to be perfectly in sync, as if they ran together often. And then it occurred to me that perhaps Reeves was single because he had a boyfriend.... Trish would be devastated.

I grinned, glad I had not asked Taylor Reeves to run with me. I surely would have embarrassed myself, either because I would have been unable to keep up his pace or because I was the wrong sex.

Taylor spotted me just as he rounded a curve in the woods and lifted his hands. One hand gestured to his running partner, who sprinted off on a tangent path, the other hand was to me. I put on a short burst of speed as I waved back, then felt silly for the sprint as Reeves followed his partner into the woods.

The lyrics *Anything you can do, I can do better,* ran through my mind, and I was reminded of Mark and our long-standing competition. Something about our constant rivalry wasn't entirely healthy. Perhaps I should think about that someday.

Belle, her head close to my knee, matched my pace changes and ran happily, tongue lolling. She was the perfect running partner, not needing to speed past me, prove her machismo or provide a running commentary. I clicked in approval and she whuffed softly, her big yellowish eyes grinning up at me.

After my run, feeling alive, better than I had in several days, I let Yellow Pup out of the house and walked through the gathering cold to Marisa's. In the backyard were three new long raised beds, marked with railroad ties and lined with black plastic. The soil was tilled and dark, rich with manure, compost and mulch. Miss Essie had been at work.

Though the older woman had kept a small vegetable garden in the past, this looked different, and I wondered what she was starting. Miss Essie grew the best tomatoes in the world, and I could suddenly taste the sweet, tart flavor of a tomato sandwich on her homemade yeast bread. Fresh basil always lined the bread, mired in the mayo. Sometimes there would be fresh oregano or lovage between the bread slices, too. Or the bread would be whole wheat bread, thick and tough and slightly yellow, just a bit nutty in flavor. I adored almost any kind of Miss Essie's homemade bread, even rye and pumpernickel, though my favorite was her seven-grain bread.

I realized I was starving, and hoped there were leftovers from Easter Sunday dinner. And if there were, that I would be allowed to eat. I *was* wearing a bra....

As it turned out, Miss Essie had forgiven me and served up a fine afternoon lunch. Feeling lighthearted for the company, the dogs and I lingered, eating treats off Miss Essie's table and visiting with our people. A particularly Southern saying—our people—it covered so much territory, and so many emotional connotations. Miss Essie and Marisa were my people. My family.

I tried not to think about the people missing from the cozy tableau. Eddie, his face filled with longing as he peered over a balcony railing at the woman who had helped raise him, and whom he had betrayed. Miss DeeDee, languishing away in a barred hospital room, no three-star chef, no whirlpool, no company on Easter Sunday. No family.

17

I WISELY KEPT MY MOUTH SHUT

When Shirl arrived midafternoon, my house was still clean, the dogs were still fresh-smelling, and I had even made up my bed. Feeling very homey, I had lit some of the candles Arlana had placed around, brewed up some fresh black tea in Shirl's honor—an autumnal called Margaret's Hope, which I could actually smell, as my nose had opened up—and made the requisite phone calls to the necessary people. Lastly, I had put on music.

I hated to admit just how much I had missed music in my life. The sense of comfort I felt as I listened lent weight to Arlana's theory of my attachment to my past. I didn't need reminders of my mama. I didn't. The memories were crisp and cutting enough. But I did need music. And Mama had needed music. Even when she was sober...

The dogs alerted me to visitors and I went out to watch as Shirl roared up in her new bright red Porsche, its top down, her dozen thick, tousled braids lying like well-worn scarlet lariats down her back. Her cheeks were plumper than I remembered, and pink from the cold wind. Shirl sparkled. "Cheerio, luv!" she called, smiling the impish smile I remembered from med school. She cut the motor, hopped over the door, dropped from the car and caught me up in a bear hug.

"Now, don't rib me about the extra stone," she said, referring to a few reserve pounds around her middle, her face buried for an instant in my shoulder. "I know I'm a bit plump, but it's a genetic thing. I'm mutating into me mum."

"Hello to you, too. Down, Pup."

Shirl giggled and pulled away, looking up at me. "Allow me to greet you with a proper 'Good afternoon, Dr. Lynch.' And hello to your dogs as well."

"Good afternoon, Dr. Adkins," I mimicked back in her precise tones.

"Crikey, it's good to see you. It's been simply years! And what huge hounds!"

"Three. And a half. Years, that is. And yes, this well-mannered one is Belle and that obnoxious one is Pup."

"How do you do, Belle and Pup. It's a pleasure to make your acquaintance." Turning back to me, Shirl said, "I say, aren't you a bit taller? Have you grown since I saw you last?"

"No, Mommy," I said, deadpan. "Neither up nor out."

"Cruel girl," she slapped at me. "I know I'm a bit large, but I'm not a moo. At least not yet. Speaking of huge, when can I see Marisa? Cam says she's absolutely precious."

"After you get settled and we go by the hospital. I called to see about an office for you. Space is at a premium, by the way."

"Not to worry. I won't need much," she said, releasing me and reaching over the door for her luggage. "Just an office cubicle and telephone. I'm used to making do with little. CDC loaned me out to soddin' World Health Organization for a few months last summer, and I ended up in Nairobi. Space consisted of a bleeding thatch hut and a petrol-run generator.

"Lovely house," she said without segue. "I always did like bungalow-style homes. Is it paneled inside?"

Chatting of inconsequentials, we entered the house and I

gave the grand tour. Bungalow homes often have rooms arranged in a circular shape, with each room opening into another. Mine followed that scheme through the kitchen, dining room, living room, and study, but the living room opened onto the hallway leading to the bedrooms. So did the kitchen.

Shirl made the appropriate appreciative noises in the rooms Arlana had finished, and was polite about the dining room, the windowed study off the living room and the other guest bedroom. They were either dusty, musty and empty, or dusty, musty and filled with unpacked boxes. I had lived in the house for a year, but getting unpacked was still a task to be accomplished.

I bragged about my decorator and promised Shirl an introduction, helped her unpack and climbed back into her sports car for the hair-raising trip to the hospital. I had forgotten that Shirl drove with such abandon and speed—hence the tired-looking braids. The few miles through the winding country streets reminded me, and I resolved to drive myself for the duration of her visit.

When we arrived, Shirl and I both donned white lab coats and name tags, and I took her to administration for introductions. It was late, but the office suite was still unlocked, lights blazing. Rolanda Higgenbotham, the second-in-command of the hospital, a pert, slender, African-American woman of indeterminate age, looked up in alarm and yanked on her tight-fitting jacket hem. "Oh, thank *God,* it's just you."

I lifted a brow, trying not to smile at her relief. "Who else would it be?"

"You're not press, are you?" she demanded of Shirl.

Oddly, Rolanda was wearing makeup. And the jacket was brand-new. For the press? I let the smile loose and checked out her shoes. According to Miss DeeDee, one could tell a great deal about a woman by her shoes. Mine were well-worn running shoes. Rolanda's were new pumps in a shade to match the jacket. Easter Sunday finery for a workday? Maybe she was waiting for Bryant Gumble.

"No, ma'am. I'm not from the media." Shirl presented her credentials with a proper English smile and handshake. "I'm Dr. Shirley Adkins from Center for Disease Control and Prevention in Atlanta. How do you do?"

"Not well at all." Rolanda threw herself back into the leather swivel office chair she had propped behind the door. The computer usually manned by Abigail Staton, the hospital administrator's secretary, was on and the operation menu pulled up, but Abigail was nowhere to be seen.

"Why is that?" Shirl asked, appropriately concerned, hands in her lab coat pockets. Shirl's coat was ironed. And perhaps even starched. I wanted to reach out and finger the material, but thought it imprudent to do so during an interview.

"The press." Rolanda's eyes opened wide, as if stating the obvious. "You would not believe the trouble we have had in the last three hours with them trying to sneak past the guard and into the hospital. We had to call in backup security, on overtime," she emphasized, "to handle the bunch of them." Rolanda yanked again on her peplum jacket hem in frustration. "Honest to God, I think they would just walk into a patient's room, camera and all, and try to interview them as they choked on their own lungs. Poor Abigail has had to spend the entire day fielding questions and—" The phone rang shrilly, cutting her off. "And that's another thing. These blasted phones." But when she answered her voice was honey-laced and professional. It was the press and she cut them off with a quick "Please speak to the press secretary, Abigail Staton. I'll have her return your call."

Not Bryant Gumbel.

"I'll be brief," Shirl said when Rolanda was free again. "Chancel Martinson, Eliza Meeks and I—all EIS officers— are investigating the origination site for the causative agent of the purulent pneumonia you reported, and request full access to your hospital records, personnel and patients where appropriate.'' Shirl smiled and ducked her head ingenuously to take the edge off anything that might inadvertently have sounded like a command. CDC worked only when and where requested, and EIOs were fully cognizant of the politics in such situations.

Though I had seen her in medical school more times than I could count, I had never seen Shirl being the professional, and was impressed with the transformation. No jeans and sneakers, no *crikey,* or *sodding,* or the rarer *bugger off* to mar her aristocratic English-accented conversation. Shirl's father was a wealthy industrialist, and though there was no title to go with the fortune, she had been raised with all the trapping of wealth. The street slang she affected was just that—an affectation. This was the real Shirl. She had changed at the house out of her scruffs, as she would call them, and into neat slacks and sweater with sensible black walking shoes. And she spoke like a member of the queen's own family.

"Drs. Martinson and Meeks will be stationed primarily in Charlotte, while I will be primarily here in Dawkins County. CDC and your DHEC state bacteriology laboratories will handle all in-vitro testing, doing duplicate workups in the interests of speed and reliability. It is my task to find the source of the contagion, isolate it and decontaminate it. I will need a spot of office space, and a minuscule area to work in the microbiology lab. I hope that meets with your approval?''

"I thought you would be bringing in a whole team to track down and identify the organism,'' I said.

"It was a possibility that several officers would join me, but I received a call from my superior just prior to my arrival. DHEC has a good start on the actual site work, and our usual practice is to keep the Epi team on site in Atlanta. With DHEC so close, we will find a quicker response time leaving personnel as they are. We're close enough to send a courier with fresh samples back to Atlanta or to DHEC in Columbia within two to four hours, and it would take much longer than that to set up here.''

I could have added that a rural, backwater hospital would not have the specialized media and equipment used by a crack Epi team. Wisely, I kept my mouth shut.

Leaving Shirl to receive the official guided tour—sans access to the media-filled front lobby—I went to the MODIS room to check my e-mail.

Rear Admiral Goldfarb had replied. And he wasn't happy with me. It seemed I was spoiling his retirement and it hadn't even officially begun yet. Goldfarb had made a few discreet inquiries into the possibility of biological warfare canisters, and within hours, agents for the CIA, NIS—Naval Intelligence, which took care of legal matters for the navy and the marines—and NSA had paid him a call. There had also been one from the president's Homeland Security czar. Now some of them were coming here. To take a look at our *situation*, and possibly to talk to me. Goldfarb wanted to know all the particulars and a timeline of events.

I sat in the windowless room, reading the letter from the admiral, wondering what I had gotten myself into. Wondering just how virulent the bacteria infecting my patients was. Wondering if the MODIS connection was as secure as it was touted to be, if it was good enough to keep out prying eyes interested in national security. MODIS was designed to provide for patient confidentiality, but this might be of greater vulnerability than medical records.

Feeling wary, I typed out a sequence of events, including some of my speculations, and sent it on to Goldfarb. Then, as an afterthought, I highlighted, copied my words and sent a copy to Shirl and to Mark, updating them on the pentagon, Homeland Security, NSA and CIA interest. Moments later, Mark called, the connection patched through from the ER.

Cellular phones had become taboo in hospital situations, and my cellular stayed in my bag while on duty. Instead of responding to my hello, he opened with a salvo across my bows.

"Now you got the big guns in on this? How'd you manage to make my life more miserable than it was before?"

"I'm talented that way. And don't be so grouchy. I didn't ask Rufus Goldfarb for help, I just asked for information."

"Why didn't you tell me you knew someone at the Pentagon? And why didn't you tell me you were calling them in?" he demanded. I could hear the fatigue like a steel rasp against his vocal cords. I'd bet money he hadn't gone back to sleep after I called him last. "I could have used some help from the boys at Fort Detrick and the Interagency Command System and you could have gotten me in touch with them faster."

"Fort Detrick?" I asked. I'd never heard of it.

"Yeah. 'At's where the Pentagon has its biowarfare labs. They might know something about all this. I sent them a query and they took all day to get back to me."

"I didn't remember about Rear Admiral Goldfarb, and though I appreciate your predicament, I didn't need your permission," I said gently, "just like you didn't need mine to contact Fort Detrick."

"Contacting them was part of my job. I'm a cop, Rhea. I'm looking for bad guys."

Oh, indeedy, I thought. *And because you get to carry a big ol' gun and act all macho, you don't have to share any of your ideas, but I do.* But Mark was tired and so was I, and so I kept the words inside where they belonged. Instead I said, "And I'm a doctor, trying to save lives. We've been over this a dozen times, Mark. Sometimes our jobs overlap. We have to cut each other some slack."

When Mark didn't reply, I said, "At least you can sit back and watch as the CIA or NIS boys run roughshod over the Feebs."

"There is that." Grudgingly mollified, Mark yawned hugely into my ear. "Sorry I jumped all over you. I was going to call you in a few minutes, anyway. Figured I'd be the one with the biggest news and you beat me."

"I'm talented that way," I repeated, smiling into the phone.

"Yes, you are. And you were right. Ellis was spotted at the Wal-Mart just an hour ago, buying ammo. Feebs are trying to save face, saying they knew he was here all along. The guys and I figure they were hiding their agents in the woods till they caught sight of him. Feebs are sneaky that way. Of course, it seems strange they ain't come out from hiding yet. Almost like they have to drive back from Savannah or somewhere."

Before I could laugh appreciatively, he said, "Hold on," and covered the receiver. Behind the muting of his palm I heard him curse before speaking to me again. "Rhea, the Feebs are on their way over to the hospital to interview you."

"About what?"

"Ellis. And why it took you so long to tell anyone about talking to him. Someone thinks you may be sheltering him. Where are you?"

"I'm in the MODIS room."

"Stay there. I'm on my way."

The phone went dead, and I stared at it. "Well, ain't that just dandy?"

In the few minutes before the Feebs and Mark could get to the hospital and find me, I arranged the playing field to my satisfaction and made a few emergency e-mails. By the time they arrived, I had the room situated to suit me. I was sitting in the only chair, having pushed the two others into a waiting room around the corner, and while physically being on a lower level sometimes is a power-play negative, my indolence, jeans, sneakers and comfort level actually gave me an advantage.

My feet on the desk, hands locked behind my neck as though I hadn't a care in the world, I looked over the three FBI agents as they hurried down the hallway, trying to pick out which one would have been good cop to the heavy's bad cop. I decided the woman would play Pollyanna. She was wearing a plaid skirt and one of those silly blouses that tie around the neck in a jabot, making her look like a misplaced Salvation Army worker. The smaller man was in charge, and the third guy was just for show, and to take notes. At least that was how I pictured them. Mark jogged around the corner to catch up to them.

It was a very short conversation. Mark and the agents crowded into the MODIS room, the Feeb in charge looking very annoyed at both me and Mark. Clearly he had anticipated getting the naive doctor alone for a thorough grilling.

"Rhea," Mark said, face intense, trying to tell me something with his eyes, "these are Special Agents Jim Ramsey, Emma Simmons and Howard Angel. They want to ask you a few questions, but you might want to have an attorney present. In fact, I would recommend it."

"There is no need for the lady to have anyone present. This is simply a fact-finding session," the larger man said as he looked for an outlet for his equipment.

"Gentlemen," I drawled as they shuffled around, trying to find a place for the tape recorder and all the briefcases. There simply wasn't room. "Ma'am. Welcome to Dawkins."

I nodded to the only papers on the desk. I had placed them dead center in the small clear space just as I'd heard footsteps marching down the hall. "Rear Admiral Goldfarb said you could have a copy of that, with his compliments. I sent it to him, to Captain Stafford and to CDC. It says all I intend to say about this medical condition, the timeline, and what I knew at any given moment. Now, unless you intend to charge me with something, go away."

Short man started. "Miss Lynch—"

"That would be Doctor, to you," I interrupted, deliberately losing my pleasant expression. "*Dr.* Rheane Rheaburn Lynch." I tossed in the Rheaburn just in case one of the agents was from Charleston. I wasn't above using the name I was born with. "And I meant what I said."

"You have no idea what you are dealing with here. You could be charged—"

"On the contrary." I sat up fast, slamming my hands down on the table, feeling the first hint of anger, quickly bridled. "I know *exactly* what I am dealing with here. I've lost several innocent patients, the youngest still a toddler." I glanced quickly at Emma and away, still trying to determine who was in charge; no hint of compassion marred her stiff features. "I stood and watched them cough up chunks of lung and then drown in their own blood." I leaned closer to the nearest man. "I *do* know what I'm dealing with, a lot more than you do."

An agent's phone chirped in the startled silence. I stood, shoving the chair back. It rattled as it hit the wall.

"That will be your superior at FBI headquarters telling you to treat me with utmost respect and kid gloves or face stepping down from this investigation. I have Rufus Goldfarb's word on that. That would be Rear Admiral Goldfarb at the *Pentagon*."

The bigger man spoke into the phone and handed it to Emma Simmons. I was impressed. A woman in charge, not a Pollyanna. I never would have guessed. My own sexism jumped up and kicked me solidly in the butt. The woman lifted narrowed eyes to me and turned away to insure her privacy. She was royally PO'd.

I stepped around the desk and left the room, winking at Mark as I closed the door. His expression was worth a thousand lost games of handball. For once, I had won, and won

hands down. I had actually startled Mark Stafford speech-
less.

Hands in my jeans pockets, wrinkled white lab coat
pushed back, and feeling almost jaunty, I wandered to the
ER. Mark found me there later, in the break room with
Wallace Chadwick, Taylor Reeves and two nurses, watching
the news. Wallace had brought in a television and we were
seeing, through a camera in a circling helicopter, hordes of
panicked people at Carolinas Medical Center in Charlotte.
Like ants, they swarmed to the emergency room door,
knocking over a makeshift triage table and stampeding to
get inside.

"You have a setup that can survive that kind of desper-
ation?" I asked my boss.

"Not yet," Wallace murmured, mesmerized. "But I will
within an hour."

"We'll have every asthma patient, every COPDer, every
panicked mother with a coughing child, within miles,"
Reeves said. "And maybe some wash from the larger hospitals' waiting rooms. If the terrorists strike again while the
panic is taking place, the hysteria will only spread it faster."
His voice was tense, mouth tight. Lips that, under different
circumstances, could have been called sensual were held in
a hard frown. Moody man. I still wondered if he was gay.
I looked back at the TV.

In Charlotte, the helicopter news camera focused in on
the beating of a hospital employee, his white lab coat van-
ishing beneath a wave of flailing arms and kicking legs.
Moments later, police in riot gear and the SWAT team
pulled into the parking lot and raced from their vehicles. I
didn't think their timely arrival would help the poor soul on
the pavement. His attackers ran, leaving a blood-stained
body, unmoving.

"Bunch of unthinking savages," Taylor said.

I glanced at him again, his face still set in hard lines.

"No discipline. No planning. No idea what they would

do if they actually got inside the hospital except destroy everything in sight. Just senseless panic. Primitive, lower-brain, reactionary animals.''

"I think I'll ask for National Guard protection,'' Wallace said.

"Make the call. It'll take a day or so. Volunteers from my unit can cover things until the unit the governor calls out gets here,'' Taylor said, his eyes never leaving the screen.

"How fast can you get your boys here?'' I asked.

"Soon enough. I hope,'' he said. "But that leaves us shorthanded. You're off tomorrow, aren't you?''

I nodded, not taking my eyes from the screen, even when Mark joined us in front of the tube. "For the next forty-eight hours. I have to take Marisa shopping for baby stuff.''

"You?'' I could hear the disbelief in Wallace's voice. My antipathy to shopping was well known.

"Yeah. Me. Unless you have urgent need of my services?'' I didn't turn, but with my peripheral vision, saw Wallace grin.

"Consider yourself called in as part of a, um, let's call it a civil service emergency.''

"Thank you.''

"You're welcome.''

"We've got some off-duty and part-time men and women who could come in and provide security for a while. Until you get your Guard unit called up,'' Mark said to Taylor Reeves. "They could be on hand in an hour.''

"Thanks.'' Wallace swiveled and shook Mark's hand in delayed greeting before the men turned back to the TV screen. From their absorbed gazes, I deduced that this was better than football or boxing. They were bonding over the TV, male-style. "You know where this bug came from yet?'' Wallace asked.

"Yeah. Thanks to Dr. Lynch and her contacts at the Pentagon.''

Wallace glanced the question at me, and Taylor lifted an interested brow. He seemed almost amused.

I shrugged. "I went to school with Charlie Goldfarb, the son of a navy rear admiral. I e-mailed him about the bacteria." I was aware of Taylor's eyes on me for a moment. He was smiling, his full lips softened.

On screen, police were pushing back the milling crowd, helping emergency workers to reach the fallen man. Someone threw a bottle. It bounced harmlessly off a riot shield.

I spoke slowly, pedantically, as the scene unfolded in Charlotte, a scene that could be repeated here soon. "He e-mailed me back just now. Richard Ellis was a marine in the Gulf War, and when the American advance took place, he ended up near a little town that didn't even show on a map at the time. There was an underground factory there, where biological and chemical warfare agents were produced and stored." My hands were suddenly cold, and I shoved them back into my pockets. "There's no question that he had access to the inventory, though no one seems to think anything went missing in the field.

"We know that the BW agents and the men who created and stored them were captured. What sort of bacteria was made at the site is still open to debate. That's still classified and Goldfarb wouldn't tell me even if he knew, but my money is on a virulent gram-positive cocci. After he went AWOL, Ellis went back to the Middle East several times. We can assume that Ellis got something or someone back to the States or made contacts to get something shipped back over later."

The hovering news crew focused in on a white male waving a gun. The crowd scattered. Though there was no sound, we saw three police officers dive for cover, roll, lift their arms. The man fell.

Mark took over the narrative. "And we can assume that Ellis and his hate group stored the canisters in Dawkins, picking the county because it is largely rural, with a widespread, sparse population. Some of it was released accidentally in the warehouse and again after the fire, infecting some of our people. Then he released more at the club in Charlotte. Trying to precipitate his race wars. An Aryan version of Jihad. Either way, now that there is both an overseas and a military tie to the BW agents, naval investigators, CIA, NSA, Homeland and maybe Customs will be swarming all over this like flies on a dead dog, beg pardon, ma'am,'' he finished automatically, his eyes never leaving the screen. ''Jeez, would you look at that?''

In Charlotte, another man fell. He was carrying a child. The crowd trampled over him. Rolling, he tried to protect the child with his body. A police officer led four others forward, moving back to back, shields surrounding them. They reached the fallen man, pulled him into the center and carried the two back to safety.

''Race wars my black ass,'' Wallace said. ''That's why there won't be race wars in this country. Four white officers rescuing a black man and child.'' He crossed his arms, the possibility of such a war laid to rest.

Taylor Reeves was watching me, something in his eyes I couldn't decipher. Curiosity? Interest of a more personal, and less medical, nature? Mark glanced between us and I returned my attention to TV. Moody men were definitely not my type.

''Admiral Goldfarb warned me that CIA and NIS may be on their way here to take over the investigation and coordinate the search for Ellis and the canisters,'' I said.

''Now, there's an oxymoron for you. Naval Intelligence…'' Taylor said half under his breath. Mark snickered softly.

''Maybe NSA, too. The military from Fort Detrick can fly in some of their specialists and medical equipment. We might need it,'' Mark said.

Mark pushed past Wallace and turned up the volume. The reporter was shouting into a headset over the sound of the rotors. "…believed to be agents of biological warfare brought into the States by a radical right-wing hate group called the Hand of the Lord."

Taylor snorted.

"Unconfirmed sources say that the Hand of the Lord's purpose is to engage in domestic terrorism." Long blond hair swept across the reporter's troubled face. With one hand, she gathered up the strands, pulled them back, battling the wind.

"Other sources claim that the manmade agents come from the long-denied U.S. stores of biological warfare agents. Back to you, Ted."

On the split screen Ted appeared, a local TV news personality with piercing blue eyes and wavy black hair. "Renee, wherever the source of the bacteria that is making people sick, the United State's culpability cannot be disputed. It has never been denied that, in the sixties and seventies, the U.S. used any and every means to secure its oil supply." Ted turned away from Renee, who was agreeing sadly, and faced directly into the camera.

"In the seventies, the U.S. offered freely its knowledge of biological and chemical warfare methods, tactics and agents to Middle East countries. Most of these were run by moderate, western-thinking men. But when those countries fell into the hands of anti-American fundamentalist Islamic groups, the technology fell also. And the U.S. lost control of its oil, and its warfare resources.

"With the demise of the Soviet Union, the specialists of that country entered the black market, bringing with them their expertise, skills and perhaps their wares as well. Add to that the advances made in the field of gene splicing, and we have a situation that was waiting to happen. A pot simmering, ready to boil over. These Hand of the Lord terrorists may have brought it to our attention, but they didn't create 't. We did. We, and the uncontrolled powermongers of the 'venties."

Taylor muttered an obscenity beneath his breath.

"Peace," Mark, said, holding up two fingers of one hand, eyes still on Ted's face. "Power to the people."

"What's your sign?" Wallace asked, his lips barely moving.

"Libra," Mark said. "Black Label. Yours?"

"Aries, ninety proof."

"You guys are nuts," I said. "One hundred percent nuts."

"Thank you," they said in unison.

"I have two questions," I said. "The man, Leon Hawkins. Who did he work for at the time of his death, and did he participate in the Gulf War? Like maybe in Ellis's squad, or company, or whatever they're called? If so, then maybe he knew too much about what happened over there or something."

Taylor jerked his head at me. For the first time, he focused on me, really seeing me, dark eyes intense.

"I mean, a black man lynched, canisters stored here, Hand of the Lord terrorists around…" I let the sentence fall away, feeling uncomfortably warm beneath Taylor's direct gaze. "I've been wondering if he had one of those tattoos."

Mark's eyes stabbed me like jade knives. "Good questions. I'll have to find out." He glanced from me to Reeves and back, his face unreadable. "And I think I heard a comment about a tattoo on the man."

"A six-sided star?"

"Maybe." I could see Mark reevaluating the puzzle, with Leon Hawkins exposed as a major playing piece instead of a lone incident.

In the hallway, a child coughed. Wallace and I jerked in unison and stepped together out of the break room, into the trauma room. Taylor followed. The cough came again. Raw and ripping. That distinctive sound I had come to know. There were four boys in the room with a teary-eyed woman. She had seated the boys on the gurney and was touching

them, wiping their faces, hugging them, murmuring soothing words with a smile. But her eyes held worry, as if she
knew how sick they really were. Two of them coughed. I
kept from flinching. Barely.

The boys were stair-step kids, no more than a year apart
at any point. The mother looked like she might have been
forty, but was likely my age. Each child had a rash. One of
them was curled on his side, holding his head as if it pained
him. A simple headache, unrelated to the bacterium? Or
another stroke?

"You the doctor?" she demanded.

"Yes," Wallace said. "I'm Dr. Chadwick." He moved
into the room. Over his shoulder he called to me, "See you
in the morning. At seven."

"I'll be here," I said.

"Have the boys been near Prosperity Creek in the last
few days?" Taylor asked, moving past me into the room.

"They fish in it all the time. We all do. Why?"

Mark pulled me away from the scene in the trauma room,
back into the relative privacy of the break room. Every time
I blinked I could see the stair-step image. Four little boys
who were going to die. And soon. Mark shook me slightly,
and when I looked up at him, his face was somber. "They
got it?"

"Yes. They do."

"Shit."

I nodded and pulled away, turned down the volume on
the television set, kept my back to the hallway and the rip-
ping-wet-linen sounds. Taylor Reeves's voice murmured
down the hallway, low and compelling. I remembered his
eyes only moments before. Trish was right. The man was
gorgeous, but in a way that was uncomfortable, not engag-
ing.

"You really ticked off Emma Simmons. She's amending
your file as we speak."

"The FBI has a file on me?" I couldn't keep the incredulity out of my voice. When I turned, Mark was standing braced in the door, back against the jamb, watching me, arms crossed, jeans-clad legs braced. A serious expression on his face. All thought of Reeves vanished. "You're kidding, right?" I said, half question, half statement.

"FBI has a file on everybody."

"So when patients come in complaining that the FBI is after them, listening in on phone calls, flying over their houses in helicopters, sending them messages through their dental work, they're serious?"

"Could be."

"So what is Miss Pollyanna putting in my file?"

Mark grinned at the appellation. "She thinks you're calculating."

A rush of anger flared. "I get paid to tell people that they are dying. Or their loved ones are dying. Or already dead." I walked directly toward Mark, invading his personal space, stepping between his spread legs, lowering my voice to make certain he understood what I was saying. "I get paid to tie up bullet holes and knife wounds and stabilize trauma patients. I'm *paid* to be calculating. It's part of the job."

"I'll pass that along," he said, lips barely moving, his eyes on my mouth.

"You do that. You pass that along to that calculating, bow-tied little woman, and while you're at it, tell her I wondered just how freaking devious her job has made *her*. Ask her if she gets paid for it."

Mark grinned slowly, deliberately misinterpreting my last line. "I'll do that. First chance I get."

When I left the ER, my icy fingertips were tingling, the sensation scarcely stronger than the angry buzz in my head.

18

THERE WENT MY CHANCE FOR FAME AND GLORY

Shirl wasn't ready to go when I found her again in her new headquarters, a headset phone on her head, tangled in the myriad braids, laptop computer online to CDC, two conversations going at once. Three-way calling had nothing on Shirl. The tiny space was a cubbyhole off the administrator's office, the nook where the fax machine and the coffeepot usually went now converted hastily into office space with a small desk and chair, and the sink covered with a plank for use as bookcase and work space. Shirl waved me off.

Bored, I went to the cafeteria and bought a Diet Coke, settling in front of the TV there along with a small crowd. No one was talking; all were watching the taped replay of the small riot at Carolinas Medical. Ted, the good-looking news anchor, was rehashing the scene, talking to another media-Ted, this one nationally known.

"A panic is building," local Ted said. "So far local police are handling things, but there are unconfirmed reports that the National Guard has been called in to deal with the populace, and to help with the medical aspects of the rare pneumonia."

"But you say that so far, the disease is not catching from person to person?" national Ted asked.

"That's what we're being told, Ted, but of course, local

hospital officials are keeping this close to the chest, sealing off the hospital to media, so anything may be happening.''

Keep the story big enough to glue watchers to their TVs, but not big enough to close down the country and restrict international travel and flights out. Big enough to raise ratings, but small enough to be manageable. Local Ted was doing a good job.

''What about the outbreak in the little South Carolina town? Same disease?''

''It appears so, Ted. But again, little is being released to the media. All we have been told is that the disease came from a creek in the area, but how it got there, what tie-in it has to the Middle East, and what this means to the populace downstream we don't know. Carolinians are being kept in the dark.''

''The creek is called what?''

''Prosperity Creek, Ted. Ironic name, especially now, in light of the pneumonia.''

''Thank you, Ted. We'll be monitoring the situation, and hope that you'll apprise us of any changes in the Carolinas.''

Local Ted flashed a big smile that didn't seem to conflict with the concerned air he wore. ''We're here for the long haul, Ted, no matter how bad this situation becomes.'' Local Ted was milking his national TV airtime, hoping for a bigger contract next time around, or a bigger market to come calling for his services. New York? Seattle? Los Angeles? The sky was the limit in cases like this. Local Ted was headed for the big time.

''Media types. They all suck,'' someone in the crowd muttered.

''What do you think, Dr. Lynch?''

I drank my cola, pondering what I would answer. There were a few faces in the group I didn't recognize, and I didn't want to be misquoted by any media types, sucking or otherwise. ''I think it's true that not a single case has come to this facility with a person-to-person secondary infection. I think it is safe to say that the local and state DHEC officers and law enforcement have pinpointed the location where the outbreak originated. And I think it is fair to say that any and all means, including utilizing CDC microbiology specialists, have been exercised to identify and treat the bacterium responsible for the outbreak. And I think any other speculation is tantamount to screaming 'fire' in a crowded theater.''

"You go, girl," a voice said. "You tell 'em. It's about time someone started talking straight and stopping all the rumors.''

I didn't know precisely what rumors I had stopped, but I took that as my cue and left the room. On my heels pattered a woman in dress slacks, skipping out the door into the hallway behind me.

"Dr. Lynch?"

I turned. "Are you the sucking media or the nonsucking media?" Someday my mouth was going to get me into big trouble.

The woman laughed. "I'm Anne Evans with the *Charlotte Observer*. You tell me."

I shrugged and grinned. "I don't know. I haven't had time to read a paper in days."

"Because of the outbreak?"

"Nope." I stuck my hands into my jeans pockets and watched her. When I didn't elaborate, she went on.

"Would you like to talk off the record?"

I sighed. "I don't have the authority to talk off the record or on. I'm just a lowly doctor, trying to take care of patients.''

"So where do I go to get the real story?"

"The story about where this thing came from, which I don't know and don't know if anyone will ever know for sure, or the in-depth human interest story about what we're doing to combat it and prevent a state of panic in the county? About our total commitment to patient care, with no thought to hospital profits?"

She looked at me speculatively. She had brown eyes and a page-boy haircut, tousled into untidy waves as if by nervous raking. "Either."

"You want to talk about the latter, you call Dr. Wallace Chadwick. My guess is he'll give you all you want to know about that aspect."

She flashed me a smile, uneven teeth in a gamine face. "Thanks. Can I use your name when I call him?"

"Will that make you a sucking media type?"

"Probably," she laughed.

"Sure. Go ahead. Honesty always did have a disarming effect on me."

"Maybe I'll call you later, when this blows over. I'm interested in why a charming, bright, female doctor would settle in a small rural place like Dawkins County."

With a bite of sarcasm I said, "Now, that'll make for interesting reading. I think you just graduated at the top of the sucking media class."

"I try to keep my hand in. Thanks again." Still laughing, Anne Evans turned and walked back to the cafeteria, pulling a cell phone from her pocket. She was about to be disappointed. The walls in this part of the hospital were too thick to allow for microwave transmission, and if a security guard caught her trying to use it, she'd be tossed out on her backside. Cell phones could occasionally cause problems with delicate hospital machines and were disallowed. Oh, well. There went my chance for fame and glory.

When Shirl was ready to leave, we walked back toward ICU to the back door. I assumed that the media, sucking and nonsucking alike, would have the exits covered, but that the doctor's parking lot would be safe simply because Security could see it from their office. Peeking through the windows at the nurses' desk, we discovered the press was absent, held at bay by the uniformed police officers Mark had promised. We headed out, waving to nurses too busy to speak. Just as I reached the outer door, a cough sounded, echoing down the hallway. Peculiar, specific, familiar as an old wound.

Jerked like yo-yos, Shirl and I stopped. Backed up.

Gloris was standing in the center of the long space, one hand over her full lips, eyes wide. She was frozen, white pants stationary, uniform top printed with little bears immobile. She turned to me, the motion bringing on another cough. Little bears danced with the motion.

Shirl raced past me. Nurses stepped from every room, leaving patients without a thought. I moved toward Gloris, her eyes on me, stunned and pleading.

"Come with me, ducky," Shirl said gently, turning Gloris to the desk and a chair. "Sit down. Have you been in proximity to Prosperity Creek?"

"No."

"To firefighters or the warehouse fire at Prosperity Creek?"

"No." Gloris slumped for a moment, her well-padded middle stretching against the seams of her uniform. The motion made the little bears on it move. One had a caption reading Nurses Are the Best. "No. Nothing. Only patient care." Her eyes narrowed with the first spark of anger. "Only here. On the job."

"I'll call your husband," one of the other nurses said. She was new, young, and I couldn't remember her name. I was frozen inside, a block of frigid fear. I liked Gloris. A lot. My eyes took in the stout figure, the bleached hair teased up in a modified beehive with rigid stylized curls over the surface.

"I've got his work number," another voice said.

"Let's not have a tante," Shirl said, unconsciously using the London slang for *tantrum*. "I think it would be wise to wait until after an X ray. We'll take this one step at a time.

No phone calls in or out about this situation until after we are quite certain exactly what is transpiring. Is that understood?''

"And just who are you?" the young nurse challenged.

"This is Dr. Shirley Adkins, CDC. And she's in charge from this point on," I said, stifling my emotions and reaching for the phone. I made the calls to the nursing supervisor, to infection control and to X ray. But Shirl and I both knew it was all academic, anyway.

Gloris was our first case of person-to-person contagion. In the blink of an eye, in the space of a breath, the entire picture of what we were facing had changed. It was now much more than a terrorist act with limited victims. This thing was capable of spreading. We were facing an epidemic. And health care workers were the first targets.

Though Gloris's X rays did not present exactly the same picture as the previous patients infected with this manmade microorganism, she clearly had a buildup of fluid in her lungs, her bronchial tubes looked swollen, and even her trachea looked odd. Gloris was admitted to an ICU room just down from the patient she had been caring for. A negative-pressure unit was installed, pulling the air from under the door into the room, through a hepalike filter and back out. Blood work was ordered. And Gloris withdrew into herself like a balloon collapsing, her eyes wide with fear.

A visit to Sottise for a late supper was out of the question. It was my guess that every restaurant in town would be closed indefinitely, until this bug burned itself out.

Shirl and I spent the next few hours implementing basic quarantine measures. No visitors to the hospital except immediate family over the age of eighteen or under sixty. No visitors with compromised immune systems or compromised respiratory systems. Immediate triage and X rays of any patient with shortness of breath or coughing. And the press was moved off hospital property.

Security was beefed up. The governor approved use of the National Guard, and Taylor Reeves had his local unit in place within two hours, until a unit from Charleston could be called up and arrive. This was a full-fledged epidemiological emergency. Ordinary civil rights could be abrogated at will. If a patient was diagnosed with the atypical virulent pneumonia, now called simply AVP, then he could not sign out of the hospital, could not refuse treatment and isolation, and could not leave against medical advice.

The situation in Charlotte was worse. With the advent of Dawkins's newest problem, Charlotte city and state health professionals and CDC had created a lockdown. No one in or out of the hospitals except the patient, with the exception of one parent for all children under the age of twelve. And once admitted to the hospital, no one could leave without approval of the medical review board, now convened once a day. All elective surgeries were canceled. Health care workers were vetted before they could leave each day. And any employee who called in sick was required to appear at a triage station for evaluation. False sick-outs were cause for immediate termination.

A Mecklenburg countywide voluntary curfew was announced, with a mandatory one for children, and a comprehensive curfew being considered by the mayor. The National Guard and county emergency personnel were out in force. Similar precautionary measures were being considered south of the state line in both Ford County and Dawkins.

By midnight, I was exhausted, and Shirl drove home at an almost sedate speed, indicating that she was nearly as tired as I. The streets were silent, deserted. The top was still down and the tires of the Porsche hummed along, icy air and an occasional braid beating me in the passenger seat. The dogs barked as we pulled up, their pitch changing and tails wagging as they caught our scents. In dog-think it meant that the rest of the den was back, and all could bed down. For them, all was right with the world. For Shirl and me, it meant a few hours' sleep then back to the hospital and a panic that would surely build.

The Porsche went quiet, leaving only the ticking of the motor and dog woofs to mar the perfect silence. Neither of us moved. Cold air no longer battering me, I began to warm. Shirl removed the keys and tucked them in her pocket.

"We will chitchat or gossip," Shirl said, still using her doctor-in-charge voice, but sounding tired and wan. "We will arrange each other's hair or paint each other's fingernails or talk about sex or tell outrageous lies. But we will not discuss this problem tonight. What there is left of the night. Is that understood?"

"How about dinner?"

"I shudder to think what you might serve. However, I was born a brave and stalwart Englishwoman. My countrymen tamed the entire world. I myself lived in Nairobi for months with a cholera outbreak all round me. I suppose I can risk eating a meal prepared by you. Bugger it all."

I laughed through my frozen nose. "This isn't exactly what I envisioned when you said you were coming, and I'm certain that you didn't plan on spending your days off in the midst of a crisis."

"I said, 'Not a word.' And I meant it."

So I didn't add, *Instead of a visit, we'll both now be working, and any free time will be bought with the lives of the innocent. You might die. I might die. I'm sorry I got you into this.* But I thought it. Okay, I was maudlin and weepy and worn to the bone. Gloris was sick. I deserved to grieve. Gloris had nursed Marisa back when I thought my best friend would never even begin to recover. Gloris had been the start of Marisa's healing.

Wondering just how congenial a hostess I was going to be, I opened my car door and led the way into the house, flicked up the heat and washed my hands under scalding water. Prepared us a snack. The kind of thing I would make when I was alone and too hungry to go out for a real meal. While I worked, Shirl settled into her room and got to know the dogs, talking to them in baby talk and feeding them bits of dog treats I gave her. They loved her. But then, they loved anyone with food.

As the cold from the open-air ride seeped from my bones, I began to feel homey, and heated two cans of Campbell's tomato soup, with an added can of spicy-hot Rotel tomatoes and a second can of chopped Italian tomatoes. I even grated Cheddar cheese on top of the thick soup, after carefully slicing off the mold on one hard end. Served with cheese crackers that were only slightly stale, it was a tasty meal, though not up to Sottise's standards.

Chitchatting as Shirl had ordered, we sat at the old table that had once belonged to Miss DeeDee and ate. Belle and Pup munched on their suppers, lying at our feet, content. I should have put on music to complete the ambience, but now that I was still, I was too tired to go to the new system in my room. Instead I enjoyed the quiet and conversation about nothing and everyone, and the satisfaction of having a guest in a house that was presentable. And the soup was pretty dang good after the long day.

We sipped—okay, Shirl sipped, I slurped—and talked about friends from premed and medical school, about Josh and his plans to work in India for a year in a small provincial hospital. About Amelia's mother and her diagnosis with colon cancer. About Wes's sister, who had finally gotten married to the slimeball she lived with. Wes hated the guy and made no bones about it. Finally the gossip died down, and a companionable silence settled between us, broken only by the sounds of humans eating and dogs crunching.

"You acquired the china and silver," Shirl said into the silence, her eyes on the meal.

A small electric shock seemed to pass through me, as though lightning had struck close by. I focused on the heavy, engraved soupspoon in my hand, the red soup beyond in the white-on-white Rheaburn Royale china. Any pleasure I had felt melted away. I forced myself to bite into a cheese cracker and chew it, swallow, before answering.

"What good would the Rheaburn china have done John Micheaux, of the South-of-Broad Micheauxs?" I tried to speak lightly, but the underlying bitterness slithered along my tone like a blade on stone. "I don't even know how he managed to have it made. According to John, even Old Lady Rheaburn has a hard time getting this pattern."

I took a sip, aware that neither of us looked up. My use of the words *Old Lady Rheaburn* indicated so much about the nonrelationship between my grandmother and me. In fact, I had never met the Grande Dame of the Rheaburn clan. And my tone... Well, that was pretty clear, too.

Belle snorted and yawned, exposing huge curved teeth and a black-spotted tongue, and went back to her food. I took another sip, this time chewing a solid tomato chunk. The spicy food was suddenly tasteless, but there was a gnawing pain in my middle. If I filled my belly, perhaps it would go away.

"Do you want to talk about it?" Shirl asked, again breaking the silence, her eyes on the soup, her spoon tracing little swirls in the melting cheese.

"What's there to say? John's uncle died, leaving the Micheaux Clinic void of a physician family member. John took the position. Simple as that." When Shirl said nothing, I went on, constrained by some weird compulsion to speak. "We had plans, and they didn't include staying in Charleston forever. He changed those plans without so much as a by-your-leave from me. Just came in one night and presented it as a done deed. I left about two weeks later and came here."

"People do change," Shirl said gently, her silver spoon ringing once against the china. "Plans change. You could have stayed. You were bloody good together, you two. We could all see it."

"Yes. We were." I took a bite, swallowed past the lump forming in my throat. Somehow managed to speak again. "But it wasn't the first time John had ordered our lives without my participation. Without my input. It was part of a…pattern." The word came out whispery, and I cleared my voice. "I don't want to live my life at the mercy of another person's whims." *Like my mother's whims,* a small voice whispered, ignored. "I want some control over my life." When I said the last words, the lump in my throat seemed to melt, as if I had spoken some magic phrase that leveled the building emotion.

I looked up, surprised at what I was about to say. "And you know what, Shirl? I like it here. I like my little house. I like country living. I like this rural county. I made the right decision." A hint of pleasure returned to me, warming me like the soup should have, and I grinned at my old pal. "I really did."

"Are you…happy?" I could hear something in Shirl's winsome voice, and in her eyes was a darkness I hadn't seen before, uncertain and a bit bewildered.

"I think so." I shrugged, my discomfort returning. Contentment was one thing. Happiness was another entirely. "I'm not sure what happiness is now, any more than when I was in med school."

"Do you remember that night all us girls sat up late in your apartment, having a giggle? It was just after Marisa left school to get married, and we were making pigs of ourselves on s'mores, cold pizza, messy butties, stale Cheerios, and drinking beer."

I lifted a slightly limp cheese cracker and Shirl grinned at the comparison. I had never been very good in the kitchen. "You had somehow gotten a case of something Irish. Harp's maybe? And Cam crashed the party," I said. "Drunk and raving about Marisa and Steven and how life wasn't worth living."

Shirl smiled faintly and nodded, sipping her soup. It was

hard to follow the pace of her eating, but for the movement of the dozen windblown braids bending slightly forward and back with each bite. Dainty, she took a sip of tea.

"You never talked much about your childhood back then," Shirl said. "I don't think any of us even knew you were a sodding Rheaburn. And certainly we didn't know your mother had passed on. But that night, you had just met John. You had stars in your eyes. And for some very odd reason, you rent an opening into your life. Just a tiny crack.

"Cam was raving and whining on, and storming 'round all to cock like a silly little boy, and you slapped him, quite soundly, as I recall. You said something about life then that I've never forgotten. You said—and forgive me if I misquote—you said, 'You don't have to enjoy life, you simply have to do the best you can at it. Because every day you wake up and see yourself in the mirror, and that reflection is something you can never get away from. Not ever.' And Cam became quiet. As did we all. You finished it up with 'You always have to live with yourself.' That last is the line I remember most clearly. 'You always have to live with yourself.'"

Uncomfortable, I shrugged and scratched Pup's ears when he put his front paws on my leg and stretched. "I was taking a philosophy course. Had my head full of other people's words."

"Crikey, you're stubborn. All right, perhaps it was some long-dead philosopher. But I don't think so. I think you were stating your life philosophy. Your personal advertising jingle." Shirl's lips crinkled on one side. "I think you were being totally and completely honest for one bloody moment. And I listened. I think several of us did. It's why Cam sobered up and started studying again. It's why I didn't go home to England to practice. It's why I applied for citizenship here in the States."

I looked up and met her eyes, surprised. "You did?"

"Yes. I did. My family was furious until I offered to house my sister here and pay her way to school."

"Good for you."

"Umm," Shirl said, as if she didn't exactly agree but was leaving the door open for later consideration. "I'm not so sure about the sister part. She's a bit of a handful. Gobby, you see?"

I nodded, remembering the term from med school—mouthy, verbally offensive.

"Anyway, what you said? It really is why Cam finally got over Marisa and settled down to chatting up every other woman on the campus. And it's why you left John. You were being true to yourself."

"I was being selfish. Pure and simple."

The smile widened. "Bugger that. You always were hard on yourself."

"When did you discern the secrets of my soul, oh wise woman?"

"I do have a trace of Romany blood back a few generations. But what I'm trying to say is that I think you will be happy wherever you are. Always."

"Do I have to cross your palm with silver?" I asked, joking to keep the effect of Shirl's words at bay. I had never liked serious talk. And I wasn't good at it.

"Not my pattern," she said, glancing at the spoon. "A simple hot shower and bed will suffice. Do you mind if I turn in now? I know it's beyond rude to leave you with the dishes—"

"Go on. I'm not doing the dishes. I'm a big important doctor now, remember?" I teased. "We doctors don't do dishes. We have people to do them for us."

"Oh, I beg your royal pardon," Shirl said, standing and offering what must have been a full court curtsey. "Or should I say, 'Oi beg ya royal arse's pardon?'"

"I've been called a royal arse a time or two. Go on. Shower. I'm not sure how the hot water holds up with more than one shower running. Come to think of it, I'm not sure how big the hot water heater is. I'll have to find out. But go ahead. It won't take me but a minute to stick these dishes in the sink and straighten up."

A moment later, as I bent to put the leftover soup in the fridge, water thudded into the guest tub, echoing down the hallway. Belle padded to investigate the new sound. Then, suddenly, the water shut off and Shirl was back, Belle's claws clicking in a fast jog to keep up. I rose up from the fridge, the door held open.

"I say, Rhea?"

She was standing in the doorway in a T-shirt and leggings, half of her windblown braids unplaited, her hands stalled midway through a braid. "Didn't that bloke from Charlotte... What was his name?"

"Smiley?"

"Yes, that's the one. Didn't he say that his patients were presenting a different picture, a different set of symptoms?"

Standing, I closed the fridge door and moved to the tall stool at the bar beside Shirl. Suddenly my fingertips were tingling, and I dragged the tips against my jeans in a slow, clawing motion as I sat. "Edema, blistering. Like mustard gas," I murmured. "Not like end-stage tuberculosis." I repeated the motion. Again. The refrigerator hummed to life. Somewhere outside, an owl called, reminding me of the warehouse. The fire.

"And the canisters had been subjected to heat prior to being moved...." I said, my voice a bit louder, surer. "Prior to being used in Charlotte at the club."

"Gloris's X rays looked a bit different from the previous patients'. You mentioned that," Shirl said.

"What if hers looked like the X rays from the Charlotte patients? Like mustard-gas blisters. X rays we have yet to see because we didn't request them through MODIS."

"Oh, indeed." Slowly Shirl dropped her hands, the braids forgotten. "I think we're bloody brilliant."

"I think we need to go back to the hospital."

"No," she said in her doctor-in-charge voice. "We *need* to place a few calls to the physicians now on duty. And we *need* to get some sleep. Tomorrow will be bleedin' hellish."

"But do you think that heat alone could create changes like we're seeing?"

Shirl shrugged, the hallway light shining through the thin fabric of her T-shirt. "I don't know. But it *is* the only thing different between the North Carolina outbreak and the South Carolina one."

The tingling in my fingertips became an itch. "Not quite," I said, my words hissing, a whisper of excitement. Belle, hearing my sudden animation, barked in response. Her long claws scraped on the hall floor as she ran from the kitchen to the unused front door and back. "There's also the little factor of Mac McHewell's hog farm." I turned in my seat, the high stool squeaking shrilly. "What if this bacterium *needs* enteric pathogens—" I took a shaky breath "—to mutate."

"Oh, bloody hell," Shirl murmured. "I'm gobsmacked."

"What if we can make it grow in the lab by mixing it with the same specific pathogens recovered from the first patients?"

Shirl pulled her cell phone from a hidden source—where did she keep that thing? It was always on her somewhere—and hit a speed-dial button; the phone hummed a ten-digit tune. Pup had joined Belle in her mad dash up and down the hallway, both yelping happily. I called them to me and quieted them as I listened to Shirl confer with Atlanta, with her colleagues in Charlotte, and then call the lab at Dawkins County Hospital and request that several of the group A cultures be subbed to new media, each with an added single streak of an enteric pathogen recovered from the wounds of the deceased patients. Lastly, she requested CT's of Gloris's lungs be compared with CT scans of previous patients.

When Shirl's phone calls ground to a halt—most of the world was asleep and therefore she couldn't call *everyone* she knew—she looked up at me and spoke a single word. "Symbiosis."

19

YOUR LITTLE BUG

My alarm went off and the phone rang in the same moment on Tuesday morning. Way too early. I punched off the alarm, flicked on the bedside lamp and picked up the phone, feeling the chill in the air on my bare skin. "'Lo." My voice sounded as if I had swallowed gravel instead of soup for supper and I tried again. "Hello."

"Breakfast on the table in twenty minutes. I got home-made biscuits, eggs and bacon, that maple-sugar-cured kind you like so much. And fresh squeezed orange juice." A pan banged in the background, the stove exhaust fan a muted roar. "I got baked apples and yeast-bread toast, a fine mess of cheese grits, and fruits swimming in honey. Miss Marisa up and dressed and she a waitin' to see that Docta Miss Shirley. You want coffee or black tea?"

Shirley appeared at the door, her hair looking as if it had been in a riot, her mouth open in a yawn.

"Miss Essie says breakfast is ready if we can be there in twenty minutes," I said.

"Oh, Blessed Mother of God," Shirl said, cutting off the yawn in mid-breath. "I could simply *die* for some of Miss Essie's yeast bread. I'll be appropriately attired in ten," she said, heading for the guest room.

"Tea for Shirl, coffee for me, Miss Essie. We're on our way."

Shirl and I dressed in minutes, tossed our bags into our respective cars and walked across the runnel-of-a-creek to Marisa's backyard, frisky dogs trailing and preceding us by turns. We blew cold clouds of vapor as we moved, little puffs of white dissipated by the chill breeze.

Miss Essie met us at the door, her bustling authoritative self, purple shawl flapping with the movement of her arms. "You put them jackets on the hooks behind the door. Make them dogs be still or I make them go back out where they belong. And you come here, Docta Miss Shirley. I ain't seen you in near 'bout three year."

Hugging Shirl, patting her vivid red hair, Miss Essie stared into her bright eyes for a long moment, as she always did upon meeting a new friend, or seeing an old one after a long separation. "You still the same, yes you is," Miss Essie said, patting Shirl's cheeks, holding the contact, "but you got you a new young man in your life. Oh, my Lord above." Miss Essie stepped back, disapproval on her features. "It that Cameron Reston. Shame, chile, don' you know he bad for you. He hurt you shore as I'm standing here."

"We're just friends, Miss Essie. Really." But Shirl's apple cheeks burned with chagrin as much as the cold.

Miss Essie made a harrumphing sound of disbelief. "That boy ain't never been a friend to no woman in his life. 'Cept my Miss Rhea." Looking over me critically to make certain that I was properly attired, she narrowed her eyes. I had worn a bra under my scrub shirt, and a sweater over it. I wasn't giving her any ammunition to withhold her maple-sugar-cured bacon and scrambled eggs. I was salivating already. "Good morning, Miss Essie," I said politely, and shushed the dogs. Belle sat upon command, and for once, so did Pup, pink tongue dangling comically.

"How did she know?" Shirl mouthed to me, eyes wide. *"Did you tell?"*

"No," I mouthed back. I had no idea how Miss Essie knew most of what she knew. Sometimes she just looked at a person and knew more than she had been told. It was uncanny. If the government could bottle the talent, there would be no secrets left.

"Hello, Shirl."

Marisa stood in the doorway, huge belly foremost, stretching the pink floral dress she had donned, the baby clearly dropped lower than on Easter morning. Her face was puffy, swollen ankles encased in soft pink slippers. Scrubbed neat, with her hair pulled back into the signature chignon she had worn since premed.

Squealing, Shirl ran to Marisa, wrapped her arms around her, then put her hands on Marisa's middle, cooing like a dove or an English farm wife. "Look at you, you darling, dear thing. You're going to have a *baby.* Is it kicking yet? Can you feel her move? Is it a boy or a girl? What does your doctor say? Are you effaced yet? It's dropped, hasn't it? God's blood, when are you due?" Shirl went into full doctor mode then, her hands roaming, checking pulse and temp and counting respirations.

"Stupid doctors don't know," Marisa said, grinning at me unrepentantly. "And don't curse."

I sighed, sat at my usual place at the table and poured coffee for myself and Miss Essie. For Marisa I poured a cup of decaffeinated, in its own carafe, marked Decaf in big yellow letters. Shirl got tea, in a yellow teapot, a short and stout one with a handle and spout. The childhood rhyme rumbled through my mind, and I smiled as I poured and watched Shirl with Marisa.

"About fifty percent e-fface-d," she stumbled over the word. "And I don't know about the baby. Boy or girl." She shrugged at the joke, which Shirl caught.

"As opposed to something bovine, I suppose."

"I'm bovine," Marisa said, the word coming easily. "I'm a cow." She was getting better. Day by day. I hoped the delivery wouldn't set her back. I had recommended a C-section, but Marisa had refused and her doctor had concurred. Nothing Marisa had experienced would necessarily preclude natural birth.

"Balderdash. You are utterly beautiful, and I will not hear a single word to the contrary. All pregnant women are beautiful."

"All cows," Marisa said, disagreeing.

It couldn't have been easy on her, trying to find words in her damaged speech center, yet she handled herself with all the social aplomb of a Stowe, born and bred.

"Sit youself down, Miss Risa. These doctas got to get to the hospital. They in a hurry, what with the plague being upon us."

"Shopping?" Marisa said plaintively.

"Docta Missy Rhea got no time to take you shopping this morning." Relief shot through me, until I belatedly heard the "Missy." Not Miss... Missy. A sure sign of trouble. "'Sides, you too far along now to shop. That baby coming in the nex' two, three weeks. Missy Rhea jist have to take them pictures you got and go shopping by herself." I knew it. "Here them pictures and the list, Miss Rhea. That baby coming soon, so you get them things tonight, you hear?" Miss Essie said, stuffing a trim stack of magazine photos into my unwilling hand. "She got the old Stowe cradle, but she need them other things pretty fast, especially them cloth diapers. We not using no diaposable ones, no ma'am.

"Miss Marisa, you sit down. She having them Braxton-Hicks contractions. Miss Shirley, you help with this pan of eggs, you ain't no guest around here, and jist because you a docta don't mean you too good to do your share. Miss Rhea, you cut that yeast bread. Here's a new wood bread slicer and a knife, and I'll bring up the biscuits and bacon. Miss Marisa, you dish up the fruits and pour on some a that local honey, you ain't a invalid, you jist pregnant. That honey from over to Dunstan Ferry Farm, it is. Good clover and herb honey, from they herb garden.''

Rambling, chiding, bullying, Miss Essie got us to the table and served in only minutes. If I had not now been looking at a solo shopping trip for baby items, it would have been a perfect meal, but with the trip to Charlotte malls hovering over me like death's sickle, it was all I could do to stuff myself with the food, coffee and familial feelings before heading out.

Shirl and I arrived at the doctors' lot to find a scene reminiscent of the televised one from the day before. Police, sheriff's deputies and National Guards had erected barricades in the long drives. Patient parking had been roped off in the grass near the medevac helicopter pad. Physician parking had been expanded to include space for cop cars and two army-green, camouflage-painted transport trucks. And a triage table with patient seating and a portable screen had been set up under the covered ambulance port. A child and mother sat there, shivering in the cold.

Inside the glassed-in waiting room, there were already at least twenty patients waiting to be seen. Only patients themselves, or children and a single parent, were allowed to wait inside. All others were politely escorted to the parking area by an unarmed guard wearing a hepa-mask and gloves.

"I must say, that will surely help to keep panic in the populace to a minimum," Shirl murmured. "A military man in mask and gloves. How bleedin' lovely."

"Isn't it?"

Shirl and I split up at the door. Shirl went to her office and then to the bacteriology department of the lab, I headed to the ER. The TV was still in place in the break room, against all rules and regs, with a haggard Wallace Chadwick standing two feet from the oversize unit, holding the remote, flipping from channel to channel.

On the screen, there were shots from hospitals all over the region, head shots of officials calling for calm, yesterday's taped replay of the near-riot at CMC hospital doors, and commentary by sober-faced reporters back on the scene this morning. In every case, the reporters had hepa-masks hanging around their necks, ready for immediate use if an opportunity came to interview a dying patient.

They enumerated instances of patients being dropped off—literally—at the ER by family members. Cars driving up, doors opening, people rolling to the concrete, cars driving off. They talked with doctors and with officials at DHEC and CDC. They talked with on-duty Guardsmen, with patients waiting to be seen, with school officials who had closed the schools in compliance with the quarantine. Schools would be prime breeding grounds for an epidemic, as would churches, grocery stores, public offices. There was a mass sick-out all over the upstate in South Carolina, from the state capital, Columbia, to the north boundaries of Mecklenburg County in North Carolina. The sun was barely up and the media frenzy was running full force.

Wallace paused his surfing on a local religious channel out of Charlotte. The Reverend Shackleford Lamb was preaching before a packed audience, the show taped the night before, as he proclaimed death, destruction and the fall of civilization, his suit sweat-soaked, tie askew, arms windmilling. "The *plagues* of the Last Days are upon us!" he shouted, pulling his tie further to the side. "The ultimate thrust of the *Antichrist* is upon us! Prepare ye for the final battle of Arma*ged*don, when the earth will be rent a*sun*der!"

Armageddon I had heard of. Plague I had heard of. But Lamb should have been among those arrested for his antics in shouting "Fire!" in a crowded theater. He was inciting to riot, at the very least. Face mottled, his breath coming fast, Lamb looked like he needed to lose a few pounds and be put on blood-pressure meds. He looked ready to "bust a gasket," as my patients might have said.

"The book has been *opened* and the seal *broken!* This is God's punishment to the un-Godly evildoer and the luke-warm believer. Death and destruction are *upon* us! Bring all your worldly *possessions,* your *families* and *loved ones* to the compound of the Lord. There you will find *sanc-tu-ary.*" He paused. "Then *together* as the world dies around us, we will *finish* the compound. *We* will become the 144,000 who survive the onslaught of death. And the 144,000 will finish the compound—" his voice rose again "—and the *promise* of Zion will be *fulfilled!*"

I realized that I had heard part of his speech earlier when he was practicing on the woman from admissions. I had to admit, the man had a sense of style and timing. The kind that drove my mother to drink herself to death, though it wasn't fair to blame anyone but Mama. She had known what she was doing, all the way to the end.

"Sisters and brothers," the Rev. Lamb continued, "are you living a life of purity? Are you keeping the races pure, immaculate, as God intended? For we each are precious and valued in his sight, to be kept unadulterated and uncontam-inated by chaste sexual practices inside the bounds of mar-riage. Are your bodies and hearts pure? Your souls pure? Are you in step with—" But Wallace turned down the vol-ume and moved on to the next channel. "Fool," he mut-tered.

"Maybe so, but I bet good money that he has a line of cars waiting to get into his compound right about now," I said.

"He's nothing but a con man and a coward. Hiding be-hind the protection of the Constitution to spout his claptrap, masking his personal racism by claiming all races are pure and should be kept that way. He circumvents laws against hate-mongering by a margin so narrow you can see through it."

"Man wants money. Pure and simple." I shrugged. It

seemed obvious to me. He'd found a niche and was milking it for all it was worth.

"And you notice that he didn't join the other ministers who are dressing out and going from room to room, praying for people who have this thing. No, he's shouting racist obscenities from the safety of a soundstage."

Surprised, I glanced at Wallace. "We have ministers in this hospital? I thought we had a lockdown."

"They insisted. 'Bout four of them. Signed papers releasing the hospital from liability, agreed to wear hepa-masks, gowns, gloves. Agreed to stay out of rooms unless a nurse approves. Had one helping with bedpans. Honest to God. Say it's their duty as Christians." Wallace left the TV and poured himself a cup of coffee. "I don't like it from a medical standpoint, but they agreed to a medical check before they come and go each time. And I admire their dedication. Especially as Preacher Billings is the pack leader."

"Your preacher?"

"Uh-huh."

My cell phone rang and I pulled it from my bag as Wallace drank down a half cup of hot coffee and went back to patient care. Down the hallway a patient coughed, the sound insistent. I fought down a sense of foreboding as Wallace changed course to intercept the cough. The day was starting with a bang. I shut the door to protect the department equipment from cell phone microwaves and punched the call button. "Hello," I said.

"You had good instincts about Leon Hawkins," Mark said.

"Good morning," I said, pulling out my hepa-mask and slipping the elastic bands over my head.

"Yeah, whatever. Miss DeeDee is in jail. She can't call up Clarissa and complain, now can she?" Clarissa Stafford was Mark's mother, and a good friend to Miss DeeDee in her preinstitution days. Clarissa expected her son to exhibit the finest social graces at all times, and his being a cop was neither an excuse nor a detriment to her expectations.

"I suppose not," I said, laughing, "but I'd never put anything past Miss DeeDee. She wrangled a call to me near midnight the night of the storm."

With bad grace, Mark said, "Good morning." Miss DeeDee was a big stick to carry in these parts, even now. She would have been considered by the locals as a PTB. Slyly, he added, "You want to hear what I got to say, *Sunshine?*"

Marisa had been blabbing to someone. "I do, but if you call me that again, I'll have no choice but to beat you next time we play handball."

"Fat chance. Be nice, woman. Leon Hawkins, the guy who was lynched, worked at the Killan's Mill warehouse. He was a part-time clerk, keeping up with rentals. Worked weekends, when he was off from his job as shift supervisor at Violet Mills."

"So he would notice if something new was moved to the site. Like a bunch of canisters." My fingertips were already itching.

"And I discovered what his participation was in the Gulf War. Part of Desert Storm, but not part of Ellis's platoon. At the time, Hawkins was a Guardsman, not a marine, but he did go in-country. Part of a group that accepted surrender of several enemy installations. You need to check with your source to see if he was near the town where the underground factory was located."

I paused. Hawkins's wartime history sounded familiar, but I couldn't place when I might have heard it. Putting the half-memory aside, I said, "I can do that." I turned to the TV, which, though still muted, was showing a scene from Dawkins County. A burned warehouse, placid water of a creek flowing nearby. Figures in hip boots and yellow bio-gear were working on the bank near the warehouse. Some of them looked military. Rear Admiral Goldfarb's spy-boys? Homeland Security types?

"Good. Oh, and that tattoo I said he may have had? A fresh one. Six-sided star on his left pec. Just like the ones applied to some of the men in the jail takeover. God, I don't think I'll ever get caught up on my sleep," Mark groaned through a yawn. "Call me if you think of anything else." The phone went dead. So much for polite goodbyes.

Before my shift officially started, I went to MODIS and sent a message to Goldfarb asking the question posed by Mark. And adding a few of my own. Not that I thought they were important. My fingertips didn't seem to be tingling for any particular purpose. Perhaps they itched just to annoy me. Or remind me that I had patients still dying.

Fortunately, I was still alone when the ER patched through a call, and a woman asked me if I would please hold for a Judge Goth. Nonplussed, I hesitated. "Goth?" I asked, feeling stupid.

"Yes. Will you hold for the judge?"

"Um, yes. I'll hold," I said, feeling suddenly clammy. Muzak filled the phone, Barry Manilow piano without the vocals. It seemed like weeks since I had talked to Miss DeeDee, and she had promised to have her judge call, although it had only been a few days. But Goth? I wondered if he had jet-black hair, black nails, purple lips and bizarre body piercings hidden beneath his robe. Maybe he even sat at the bench with his feet resting in a bit of soil from the old country. But I didn't ask.

"Dr. Lynch?" a deep voice asked.

"This is Dr. Lynch."

"I appreciate you taking my call, Doctor. I understand that you have been fully briefed on Miss DeeDee Stowe's request for transfer to another facility."

Transfer to another facility sounded like a pretty tame way of saying *change of incarceration from one loony bin to another,* but I didn't say that, either. I wasn't sure what

I was supposed to say to this judge who held Miss DeeDee's future in his hands. I settled for a simple "Yes."

"You realize that she desires to be moved to an upscale private facility, one that might better accommodate her preincarceration lifestyle."

"I understand. But her preincarceration lifestyle included gambling away her fortune and killing people. Someone will be monitoring her activities, I hope."

"Rather more stringently than the state has managed to," Judge Goth said. "That woman is supposed to be under lockdown with no phone access, no visitors and heavy medications, and yet she has somehow tracked down my home number, my cellular number and even my club number. She has called me nonstop for days." Judge Goth sounded perturbed. I pictured him shaking his long black hair and checking his vampirelike canines for sharpness as he considered possible avenues of revenge. "And I have been reliably informed that she called you to notify you about this request."

"She did. She have Internet access?" I asked.

"We did allow that. Monitored, of course. Her legal rights were abrogated when she was incarcerated, but her doctors have suggested that we slowly return a few privileges as she improves her mental functions. Until she is deemed mentally competent to stand trial, of course, she will not be allowed return of full legal rights. Is there a problem with her having Internet access? Did she try to contact her family?"

"No. She didn't. But you can find out anything about anyone on the Internet. That's probably how she tracked you down. And if she had access to a pack of playing cards, then she likely lulled unsuspecting night attendants into an innocent game of hearts and then proceeded to fleece them in return for phone access. She's good."

"I'll pass that along to the proper authorities. What are your feelings about her request for transfer to another facility?"

"She's paying for the move and the costs of the new place?"

"Yes, and a right smart monthly expenditure that is." He named a price per month that made me wince. "I have made it clear to her that this is not a customary practice, allowing someone with her history the luxury of Silver Lakes. But as her move saves the state a hefty amount monthly, and she is underwriting all expenses, I'll allow this, on a trial basis. Miss Stowe also understands if she misbehaves or fails to make a single payment to Silver Lakes on time, she will be carted back to the state facility immediately."

I sighed. "Let her have her transfer, Judge Goth. I'm willing to let her move laterally, but if she ever asks for removal to a halfway house, or to home incarceration and bail, that I'll fight tooth and nail. Even if she is deemed able to stand trial, I don't want her free. I hope you understand."

"Perfectly, Dr. Lynch. I will then approve Miss Stowe's transfer request to Silver Lakes, to be effective immediately." I could hear papers rustle in the background, and a soft, feminine voice murmuring. One of Goth's thralls offering him a little blood snack? I wanted to giggle. "Thank you for your time, Dr. Lynch."

"You're welcome, Judge Goth." When Goth clicked off, I sat in the darkness, seeing the shadows with faint surprise. Even now, in the safety of the hospital, miles away from Miss DeeDee, she was working her magic on my life, pulling strings, affecting my emotions, my daily life.

My reactions to Miss DeeDee were mixed, confused. It was because of her that I was practicing medicine. It was because of her that I survived my childhood mostly intact, was a person of some refinement, and not some multitattooed, angry ruffian. She had taught me to ride horses, identify trees and plants on her farm, given me some manners and sense of social ease. My kitchen table had come from her attic. And then, of course, she had tried to harm me. I sighed again, lustily, the sound of the breath forlorn.

A knock on the door pulled me from the edge of despondency. "Yes?" I called, sitting upright, adjusting my lab coat.

In a blast of fluorescent light, Shirl joined me in the dark little room, her eyes glittering with amusement and information. "Two things," she said by way of greeting. "You simply will not guess what we learned about your little bug." She closed the door behind herself and parked her butt on the desktop before me, palms flat by her thighs, her legs swinging.

"The geno-typing results are complete, by the by, and though the strains are different now, the Dawkins strain and the one recovered from the patients in Charlotte appear to have started out as the same organism. While it likely was never *quite* stable, the bacterium has indeed become mutagenic, perhaps due to its exposure to extreme heat in the warehouse fire. The result is two main strains of the microorganism—" Shirl's hands made a V in the air between us "—with little branchings still taking place as we speak." Her fingers separated and wiggled.

"There have been at least three small mutations here in Dawkins that are not manifesting themselves in Charlotte, accomplished by swapping of proteins in the DNA structure. Neither here nor there, I know, but I was fascinated. Can't wait to get back to the labs and play with it a bit myself. But first... Your bacterium is a nasty little fellow indeed. Are you familiar with staphylococcal enterotoxin B?"

I had no idea where we were going with the switch from "my" little strep bug to a staph, but I was intrigued, as much with Shirl's babbling excitement as with her information. "It's a toxin produced by staph B," I said, "most commonly seen in food poisoning. I had a patient in Chicago with toxic-shock-like symptoms from it, but that kind of reaction is rare."

"Right-o. But SEB has been used in terrorist attacks also, most often delivered in aerosol form and inhaled by victims, in which cases, the toxic-shock symptoms are not uncommon. In mild cases the effects of the enterotoxin are mediated by the victim's own immune system. The toxin binds to the victim's histocompatibility complex, which subsequently stimulates production of T-lymphocytes. These T-lymphocytes then stimulate the production and release of various cytokines, which are thought to mediate the toxic effects of SEB."

"Meaning that the disease produces its own cure. It's self-regulating."

"Exactly. You weren't asleep *every* day in class! But in severe cases, the body's histocompatibility complex isn't big enough to bind all the toxin—" her fingers twisted together in a snarl "—and we see massive toxic-shock symptoms. While your bug—"

"I really wish you wouldn't call it *my* bug."

"—does not have the same kind of proteins in the cell wall that allow the staph to produce *its* enterotoxin, the strep seems to have been engineered to produce something like it. But instead of binding with the histocompatibility complex, our theory is that it binds with several coagulation factors and proteins, primarily in an oxygen-rich atmosphere. The particular proteins inhibit the body's ability to release calcium, among other things. And the effect is greatly increased in the presence of several different enteric pathogens."

"That's why our patients who were downstream of both the pig farm and the warehouse bled to death. And why the PT results were increased. Because some of the coagulation factors were being used up outside of actual blood-clotting processes."

"Precisely. And because the bacteria needs increased oxygen, the site of the bleeding is primarily the lungs. Someone is looking into whether the spreading petechiae in the dermis of the latest patients is taking place in the arterioles. If so, it adds confirmation to the theory. Brilliant, isn't it?"

My mind was whirling with the possibilities of Shirl's news. I felt my fingers drag along the fabric over my knees. "I should get back the preliminary postmortem reports this week on the first patients."

"Actually, CDC already has them," Shirl said, managing to look shamefaced. "Someone pulled strings. You'll receive copies of your own, eventually, through the usual channels. But if we are right about the protein-binding activity of the enterotoxin, we can mediate the effects—"

"Fresh frozen plasma," I said, slowly coming to my feet. "Albumin. Things we keep in the blood bank every day." I focused on Shirl's wide-open eyes in the gloom. They were manic with excitement. Her hair, still in its wild morning travel braids, seemed to move with a life of its own. "Things we would have given to bleeding patients, anyway, if they had lived long enough."

"Crackin' brill, I say! But now we give them prophylactically. To anyone with a cough. Allowing the body and the antibiotics to do their job before the bug kills off the host. And assuming that the enterotoxin itself is stable, as the SEB toxin is, we draw blood on every patient, ice it and send it to CDC for analysis, to see if we can recover, isolate and study it."

I moved to the door and opened it, stepped into the hallway. "I'm having Gloris typed for FFP."

"It may not work, you know. It's a sodding theory."

"Better than any theory we've had so far. And FFP won't hurt her even if it doesn't help her."

"Aren't you interested in my other news?"

"Yes." I paused, the door open, lighting the room. But I wasn't. Not really. I was interested in passing along the information I had just received and creating a treatment protocol for patients with AVP.

"Liar. But you will be. Cam is coming."

"Here?" I asked stupidly.

"Here. He'll stay at your no-tell-motel. Isn't it splendid?"

"He gets put to work. Just because he's gorgeous doesn't mean he gets off lightly."

"Axiomatic. I never coddle good-looking blokes. It goes to their knobs. Both of them."

I grinned at Shirl, still sitting on the desk, her legs swinging. "I'm glad you're here."

"Me, too. And we *will* eat at Sottise, I promise." She hopped off the table and bounded into the hallway to do whatever it was that epidemiology intelligence officers did. I went straight to Gloris's room, and to work.

The door to her room was closed, the quiet hum of the negative-pressure unit pulling air from beneath the closed door, keeping any possible contagions inside. With Gloris. Hepa-mask firmly in place, I knocked and entered. The room was dark, blinds closed, lit only by the flickering of the television mounted high on the wall. Replaying on its silent screen was the near riot from the day before. Panic in the streets. Gloris was curled in the bed, facing the window. "Gloris?"

She rolled toward me and instantly I could see the edema around her mouth and eyes. Swelling that could easily become blisters, the kind seen in mustard-gas poisoning. "Hi, Doc," she croaked, her breathing sounding like a broken bellows.

"Are you willing to be a guinea pig?" I asked.

Her eyes opened wide. "You found a treatment!"

"Maybe," I cautioned, moving closer to the bed as Gloris punched the bed controls and sat up higher. "It won't hurt you even if it doesn't help you. I want to ask your physician to give you diuretics and fresh frozen plasma, and maybe a little albumin." Quickly I outlined the new information about the strep that was infecting her, and offered the possibility that simple measures might slow the progress of the disease, allowing enough time for the antibiotics to actually kill the bacteria.

Gloris was not only willing, she picked up the phone before I left and called the lab. As I closed the door behind me, I heard her telling them her blood type, demanding that they thaw a unit of the blood product and ready it for her. They wouldn't, of course, not without a doctor's order, but that was only a few minutes away.

Douglas Byars, looking like death only slightly warmed over, was sitting at the Dictaphone, Gloris's chart in front of him on the desk. Worn and wan, he looked up at me, focusing slowly. Something must have shown on my face because he sat up straighter, eyes wide. "What? *What?*" he demanded.

When I told him the news, Douglas Byars dropped his head into his arms, his shoulders shaking. A moment later, he laughed, the sound not quite steady.

With a small cadre of medical personnel and Shirl's theory of protein binding, Douglas and Wallace and I devised a temporary protocol for treatment of the AVP. Taylor Reeves came in off Guardsman duty to assist. The Charleston boys were here and he was ready to go back to doctoring.

Because the bacterium needed an oxygen-rich atmosphere, we took the patients off oxygen or turned down the oxygen being administered to the most ill. Because the initial onset of the disease created interstitial edema between the alveoli, we ordered massive diuretics. And we instituted a comprehensive program of fresh frozen plasma and albumin to every patient who presented symptoms of AVP or its sister disease, now called ACS, or atypical coagulation syndrome.

Gloris received her first unit of FFP and two vials of twenty-five percent albumin on Tuesday afternoon, within the first two hours of Shirl's announcement. Within three hours, she reported a decrease in her shortness of breath. It wasn't wishful thinking; her O_2 saturation went up, even without the O_2 she had been receiving. Using her improvement as a baseline, we administered fresh frozen plasma to all the patients—including the two surviving stair-step little boys and their mother—sent a courier to the Red Cross in Columbia for fresh supplies of plasma and administered more. And crossed our fingers.

Only a few hours later I visited Gloris in her room and found her sitting up, playing a hand of hearts with a hepa-masked, bearded man wearing a too-small Harley-Davidson T-shirt, who had to be her husband. A big, barrel-chested man, he looked up guiltily over the brim of his mask and sighed. "Busted," he said softly.

Closing the door, I stood in front of it, crossed my arms over my chest, assumed my most severe doctor-in-charge face, and glowered at them both. Anger isn't an easy emotion to communicate when half of one's face is hidden. Gloris was noticeably smaller, the edema around mouth, nose and eyes decreased. She had fixed her minibeehive hair and was wearing lipstick, a good sign, I figured. The man had flushed under my scrutiny. "And just who sneaked you in here against all quarantine regulations?"

Gloris's husband dropped his cards and wiped his palms down the front of his jeans, as if his hands were suddenly sweating. "Um, Gloris, maybe I better—"

"Don't go snarling at my hubby," Gloris said with an unrepentant grin. "I am a certified hero. A guinea-pig hero. Get it?" Laughing, she pinched a few inches of spare tire at her waist and elbowed her husband. "Elmer, this is the doctor who figured out what to do to save me. You—"

Elmer whooped, bounded off the bed and did a little touchdown dance, fists pumping. Before I could react, he grabbed me up in a bear hug, which proved to me beyond any doubt that the massive chest beneath the Harley emblem was all muscle, not fat. My ribs protested, and all the air whooshed out of me in a hard grunt. Holding me off the floor, Elmer looked me right in the eye, his beard pressed against my mask. "Doc, you want anything in the world I got and it's yours," he said. "*Anything.*"

"Doc might want the old Indian motorcycle you're fixing up, Elmer. She looks like an Indian, don't she?"

Elmer dropped me and stood back, holding me by one arm as I found both my balance and my breath. "She got that olive skin, all right, and black hair."

"No, Elmer, I mean her legs. She'd look good on that old bike, all them legs wrapped around it."

"You want a Harley, Doc?"

"No," I managed. "Thank you. But no."

"You even ever been on a bike?" he demanded.

"No," I said again, pulling my arm free.

"We'll go for a ride on it and then you decide."

"Fine," I said, resuming my dignity, readjusting my mask. I had no intention of riding on a motorcycle but this wasn't the time to say so. Instead I said, "Because you were willing to try the new protocol, I take it you're a hero." Gloris nodded, a satisfied grin on her face. "And you can have anything you want." Gloris nodded again, preening, one hand in her stiff hair. "And what happens if this is only a temporary improvement? What happens if we find that the antibiotics still don't have enough time to work and you still get real sick? And so does Elmer?"

Gloris looked abashed for an instant, but it didn't last long. "Dr. Lynch, I know my body. I know what it feels like when it's sick, pregnant or dying, 'cause I been there. And what it feels like right now is healin'. I'm getting better. You found the cure."

"Dr. Shirley Adkins and the people at CDC found the treatment, Gloris. Not me." But Gloris clearly didn't believe me. Neither did Elmer, who eyed me with a look that was a combination of hero worship, Harley speculation and gratitude. I left the room quickly, worried that my ribs couldn't take another grateful hug.

By late afternoon, the hospitals in Charlotte began a similar program of plasma administration and they, too, reported improvement in many of the milder cases within a matter of hours. Officials there were predicting mortality rates substantially lower than the near ninety percent we had seen in Dawkins to this point.

The press was all over the story. News vans swarmed like fleas across hospital grounds and back and forth to Charlotte, reporters interviewing anyone and everyone they could find, from the average man in the street to retired epidemiologists to self-proclaimed specialists in bacterial warfare to the county sheriff. It was a Dawkins County media blitz.

One intrepid woman, whose description sounded a great deal like Anne Evans with the *Charlotte Observer,* made it into Gloris's room and interviewed her before being thrown off hospital grounds. Which is how Shirl's and my name made it to the next morning's front page of the *Charlotte Observer* and was picked up by the AP. It seemed my chance for fame and glory had not been lost. But that was a problem for the morrow. There was still the panic of today to deal with.

20

AUNTIE MAUDE AND KITCHEN PRIVILEGES

During that long Tuesday, there were five more cases of patient-to-patient infection, one was a hospital employee who stopped me in the hall, one an emergency medical technician who had brought in Regina Hawkins and another of the early patients, and the rest were family members of sick patients. And even with the media coverage of the possible treatment to mitigate the panic, the ER was a madhouse.

Usually there was only one doctor and two nurses on duty at any one time, sometimes with an EMT who worked the desk, handled the paperwork and took vital signs. Today we had two doctors on hand at all times, three nurses and an EMT. At first, we were tripping all over one another, but with the large numbers of patients, we finally settled into a rhythm that moved patients through the ER speedily.

"Greet 'em, treat 'em and street 'em," was the ER mantra at Miami Valley Hospital in Chicago, where I did my internship. Today, Dawkins County Hospital ER followed that advice. I worked triage with Ashlee, seeing patients under the ambulance hood, in the cold wind, while Taylor Reeves, the other doctor pulling ER duty, worked with patients sick enough to be sent inside immediately. When one of us took a break, an extra physician came in to help. Once it was Michelle Geiger, back from her conference, then while Taylor went home to grab a couple of hours of sleep, Chris Russell took over for a few hours. His specialty in nuclear medicine and radiology was no hindrance to his helping out in the ER.

It was during Reeves's only break that the Hand of the Lord struck again in Charlotte. No one knew about the release of more deadly bacteria into the ventilation systems of a mosque and a black church during afternoon prayer services until a Hand of the Lord spokesman called local Ted, the television reporter vying for a big-time posting, and read a prepared statement to him.

Local Ted had managed to tape the entire statement in the caller's own voice and then replayed it over the air within minutes. His face appropriately grave, local Ted broke into regular programming and played the statement.

"The Hand of the Lord has struck again at the lesser races, the less-than-humans who pray for safety and deliverance. They will *not* be delivered," the gravelly voice said. "They will all die. All the lesser beings masquerading as human or praying to false gods will be destroyed. In keeping with this intent, the Hand of the Lord has struck at the Cornerstone of the Spirit Church and the Islamic Center Mosque approximately forty-five minutes prior to this communiqué. The final plagues have begun." The Charlotte church had held more than one hundred twenty of the faithful, the mosque fourteen men and boys.

The FBI swarmed in and took over, removing Ted's tape as evidence, at the same time that another group of agents wearing HazMat biohazard suits closed in on the attack sites. Taylor Reeves was called back to work, looking bleary-eyed and worn.

The panic resulting from the attacks swamped the emergency facilities in Charlotte and brought out nearly two hundred people to Dawkins County Hospital, most of whom had phantom illness or SOB from other causes. However, there was a rising number of patients with real problems.

Primary contagion AVP and its sister ACS was spreading among firefighters who had handled the warehouse fire and among people who lived along the banks of Prosperity Creek.

Following the attack, local churches either suspended services or hired off-duty cops to provide security. Some smaller churches had deacons walking patrol twenty-four hours a day. Schools in nearby counties were closed and nonessential government offices closed. The FBI had set up command posts in strategic areas all over the piedmont. The National Guard was on standby in several areas to assist should the public panic.

Thanks to the presence of the National Guard, triage in the hospital ambulance port was relatively easy. Even in the cold. Even with more than fifty patients waiting to be seen at any one time. Ash took vitals, listened to patient complaints, recommended lab work or X rays and dispensed medications. I worked in the open air or in the waiting room, using the actual triage room for patients who needed shots or privacy. If I hadn't been constantly on the alert, listening for the ripping cough, some aspects of it might have been pleasant.

We admitted two dozen patients during my shift, far too many for the number of nurses available on the halls of the small hospital, but we couldn't turn anyone away. When we ran out of beds, we shipped patients; nearly a dozen went to Richland Memorial, several to Carolinas Medical in Charlotte. EMS service ran like rabbits. By midafternoon every health care worker in the county was past exhaustion, but the panic seemed to be subsiding.

Taking a moment when all the waiting patients had been evaluated and no new ones were standing in the cold, I turned over my triage work to Dr. Geiger and had a late lunch with Shirl in the darkened, deserted cafeteria. She was as exhausted as I, her now-unbraided hair in a drooping bun, strands hanging in shadowed straggles around her face, her shoulders tight, pulling the seams of her starched lab coat. She had been to the burned warehouse, visited the county health department, talked with members of the Hazardous Materials Team and the Interagency Command System, and been on the phone all day.

Beyond filling each other in on our activities, we were both too tired to talk. In companionable silence, we each ate a bowl of the hospital cafeteria's vegetable-meat surprise soup and homemade cornbread. The soup was a surprise because one never knew what one might find in it. All left-over vegetables from the week's cooking were tossed in the pot along with beef scraps, chicken and pork, so that one might find the more common string beans, carrots and on-ions floating alongside soggy broccoli and cauliflower, dis-integrating spinach or turnip greens. With the addition of vast amounts of pepper, and the sweet, crumbled, bacon-drippings cornbread, it was delicious.

"How do you not slurp?" I asked when my spoon hit the bottom of the plastic Melamite bowl.

"I'm English," she said without looking up. "We never slurp."

"Your hair is in your soup."

"I'm English. We never let a little thing like our own hair get in the way of filling our bellies."

Curious how she would continue the theme, I sat back and said, "You look exhausted."

"I'm English. We didn't conquer the world by letting a little thing like being fagged to death stand in the way of a goal," she said, her tone growing lofty.

"I thought you were applying for citizenship in the U.S."

"I'm English. We *built* this country, and but for the inept-ness of a certain monarch, who shall remain nameless, we would own it still. If we want to live here, we can."

I laughed and so did Shirl, but when she finally looked up something sad glinted deep in her expressive eyes. "I was always jealous of that between you and Marisa."

"What?"

"The byplay. The easy conversation."

Pain stabbed deeply for an instant. *I would never have that with Marisa again.* "Risa and I have known each other forever. I think we sometimes read each other's minds."

Shirl set her spoon in the bowl with a soft rasp of sound. She kept her gaze on it as if unwilling to meet my eyes. "Exactly. That is the part I envied. The *friendship.* I wanted that friendship. Wanted to be a part of it, or at least find a similar relationship of my own. You were bezzy-mates. Like sisters, like…the way sisters were supposed to be, I mean."

"I didn't know," I said, uncomfortable with Shirl's confession.

"You wouldn't have. I had other friends, you understand. I wasn't lonely. And I'm—" I said the word with her, *"English."* And Shirl dissolved into giggles.

"Or anal," I said.

"Bugger off," she said, proving my point. "We English are quite adept at hiding our emotions. 'Stiff upper lip, buck up, hold the line,' and all that."

I didn't know what to say and so I chuckled obediently, watching Shirl.

"What I'm trying to say," she said, moving her spoon off the bowl to the tray, straightening her folded napkin, "is that my two-year hitch with CDC is up in a few months, and I've been offered a teaching position at Carolinas Medical Center in Charlotte. I'm thinking seriously about taking it."

"Shirl, that's wonderful," I said, understanding suddenly. "That's not so far away. We could see each other."

Even in the dim light I could see her fair skin flush with pleasure. "You could find me a dog like your Belle. And a suitable college for my pierced-and-tattooed sister. And we could eat at Sottise," she said, the words tumbling out as they always did. "And I could help with Marisa. If you wanted me to."

"Find me a bilingual, well-bred English nanny," I said instantly. "She needs to be proficient in French or Spanish as well as speak with that upper-crust accent like you do. Marisa's orders."

"Crikey. Upper-crust? Me?" Shirl splayed her hand over her chest, looking up and meeting my eyes. "Does that mean I can't use words like *karzy* anymore?" she asked, employing an extremely rude word that would more politely have been *loo* or *the ladies* in England, or *restroom* in America.

"Yeah, you. And no, not around Marisa's kid."

"I can do that."

"Not your pierced-and-tattooed sister."

"Never. Heaven bleedin' forbid. I was thinking of my Auntie Maude. She retired last year from the Home Office after thirty years on the continent. She speaks four languages and reads three more. She's bored."

Behind Shirl, a Guardsman entered the dark cafeteria and went to the ice machine on the far wall.

"Likes kids?"

"Adores them. Especially the ankle-biters—the little ones. Never had any of her own, and so used to pamper us all quite to death. Not that she can't bark an order like a brigade colonel. Made us all mind our p's and q's, did Auntie Maude."

As we talked, the Guardsman bought a cola and crackers, glancing toward us several times as he made his purchases, change, can and wrappers loud in the empty room.

"Will she defer to Miss Essie?"

"No. But she'll compromise. She'll want her own rooms, lav and kitchen privileges."

The Guardsman left the cafeteria. I hadn't seen his face, but his buzz cut caught the dim light as he went out the door. *Ellis?* It couldn't have been Ellis. But I held up a hand to Shirl in warning. She immediately fell silent and swiveled in her chair, following me with her eyes as I walked to the hallway door, opened it and looked out. The man was gone, and I felt stupid in my paranoia. Ellis would have to be a fool to come back here. And there were buzz-cut Guardsmen all over the place.

"Sorry," I said as I returned to my place and picked up my spoon for a last bite of soup-soggy cornbread. "I thought I recognized that man. The kitchen privileges will be a problem. Miss Essie is in charge of the kitchen."

Shirl's lips curled up in an unwanted, guilty smile.

"You've already talked to her, haven't you?"

The smile quirked up higher. "And if I have?"

"Will she come on a six-month contract?"

"I'll certainly ask her. Marisa told me she wanted a nanny this morning over brekkers. She's just as obstinate as ever, isn't she."

"Headstrong, stubborn, pigheaded," I said, pleased that I could say such mean-but-true things about Risa, as opposed to vegetating, comatose or dead. "Take your pick. She is. The trauma didn't change her personality at all."

"In return for Aunt Maude, I want a dog. Where did you get Belle?"

"Found her in a graveyard giving birth. Long story."

"Tell me later? Over a cuppa?"

"Absolutely. If mine can be coffee."

"Dreadful American habit, that. Good thing I'm going to stay in this country. I find I have developed a passion for coffee, especially in the middle of the night. And speaking of passions, we need to talk about—"

Overhead, the speakers blared to life. "Code 99, ICU. Code 99, ICU. Code 99, ICU." Sharing a smile, we pushed back our trays and stood. Time to go back to work. In the same voice we said, "Later," and laughed over the unintentional harmony.

Trouble, or perhaps I should say more trouble, descended on me at six-thirty, just before I got off work. I was checking a child with persistent cough, my hands and stethoscope bell on his warm, moist back, listening to the chronic bronchitis that rattled his upper respiratory system and brought him to the ER often. I had seen the child eight or ten times in the year I had been in Dawkins, which meant that he had likely been to the ER twice as many times, seen by other doctors. His anxiety-ridden mother, who was only a kid herself, perched on the edge of the stretcher, body stiff with fear. "It's not the pneumonia, Ms. Young," I assured his mother. "His cough is just a bit worse than usual, probably because of the weather, like you thought. Have you been able to move out of the apartment, into a newer place?"

"No. The Assisted Housing peoples say we nex' on the list, but they ain't no new places. And wid Damson's mold allergy, we need us a new place, not no old one what been lived in and got other people's mold on the ceilings and such. But soon's we can, we be out that old 'partment and in a new one, we will. Then Damson's cough be better."

I cooed into Damson's face, his big blue eyes and pale skin testament to his mixed-race heritage. There were a dozen such mixed-race children for every Rebel flag displayed in the county. And there were hundreds of flags. Damson giggled up at me and tried to grab the stethoscope, chubby fingers chasing the swinging bell. "You're a pretty boy, aren't you, Damson. Yes, you are."

"Pretty like his daddy," Ms. Young said, her tone proud.

"And his daddy is where?" I asked, curious. I couldn't help it, I always wanted to know where family was and where support systems were. In cases of single parents, there was seldom any aid except that provided by government.

"Gone. Don't know where." Ms. Young shrugged, unconcerned.

Behind me a throat cleared and I glanced over my shoulder, rose and patted the small back. "His X rays are clear," I said as I studied my guest, "and like you said, with all the wet, cold weather, mold is aggravating his chronic condition." The man standing in the doorway was a long, lean military man wearing a khaki-colored, naval officer's uniform and carrying a briefcase. It wasn't Richard Ellis.

"Just keep up with the meds you already have at home, and when the weather clears, he'll be fine." I glanced at the officer's shoes, pleased to see polished black lace-ups instead of the boots Ellis had worn. He carried a hat beneath one arm, and the uniform fit, unlike my last visitor's. I noted that he was studying me as closely as I studied him. "If his cough changes, you bring him back."

"I do that, Doctor. You know I will."

And, of course, I did know that. Damson was a regular. With a final baby pat, I turned to the man, extended a hand, halted and pulled it back all in one motion. "Just a moment." Using near-scalding water, I washed my hands at the sink in the corner and dried them carefully with the rough towels provided by the hospital. It was necessary, but it also gave me time to compose myself.

The man was entirely too good-looking for my tastes. The ladies-man glint in his eyes reminded me of Cam, but this man's bearing was more composed, more authoritative, and the command presence demonstrated by Mark and Ellis was more subdued. Not less present, but more controlled, as if he reined it in with a firm hand. I tossed the towels into the garbage and nodded to him as I stepped from the room. "I'm Dr. Rhea Lynch."

"Dr. Rheane Rheaburn Lynch," he corrected me with a smile, "as I have been assured by my friends in the FBI. Lieutenant Gilroy Adams. Call me Gil."

"Feebs have friends?" I asked as we shook hands. His grip was firm, the palm uncallused.

Adams laughed easily, fine lines at his eyes. "A few. Some of them don't even have knife handles sticking from their backs."

"You have ID?" In a louder voice I called to Ash, "I'll be a few minutes."

The officer flicked a black leather case from a chest pocket and held it out to me. Taking the ID, I motioned him through the side door, which he hastened to open and hold for me. I wasn't accustomed to that kind of chivalry on the job and nearly bumped into him, feeling clumsy with my own exhaustion. "Thanks. This one looks real. I wonder what the other man's would have looked like."

"Other man?"

"Richard Ellis. He paid me a visit, dressed a lot like you are, but his uniform was dark blue and it didn't fit. I have a timeline in the back to help explain, but he came here looking for information. Said he was trying to help us with our *wet germs.*"

"Erudite of him."

"Um," I agreed, amused at Adams's tone. "And his uniform…" I let the words trail off with a negative inflection as I gestured to Adams's clothing, which fit like a fine glove.

"Shame," he said dryly. "Properly tailored, a naval officer's uniform can do wonders for a man's image."

I laughed, impressed with the man's humor in spite of myself, and handed back his ID. Adams was aware of his impact on women and found it amusing. And useful, no doubt.

My estimate of the lieutenant's looks was confirmed when we passed Trish in the hallway and her jaw fell open. She quickly snapped it back in place, noticing all the medals on his chest and the ringless left hand in a single glance. I knew it was only a matter of time before she found my visitor for a more thorough look-him-over session.

Knowing better than to stand between Trish and fresh man-meat, I paused and said, "Trish, we'll be in the MODIS room. Would you mind getting a couple of colas for Lt. Gilroy Adams and me? Trisha Singletary is our nursing supervisor."

Trish stopped as if she had all the time in the world, bosom outthrust in a motion that was definitely not military.

"Lieu*ten*ant," she purred. "Well." She took his hand, testing its grip, much as I had only moments before, but with a decidedly predatory gleam in her eyes that I hoped had not been present in my own. "Welcome to our little hospital." In a gesture that was patently female and feline, she cocked her head, exposing her throat. Blond hair slipped back, framing her face.

I could never hope to copy such a move. Either you were born with it or you weren't, and, sadly, I was not.

"Will a Coke be all right? And you take Coke, right, Dr. Lynch?" she said without looking at me once. She flicked back an imaginary strand of hair.

"Right. In the MODIS room," I said, out of my depth in this posturing, mating dance.

"That would be great, Trish. Thanks." Adams flashed her a smile that was all white teeth. The estrogen and testosterone were flying around the two as if whipped by a blender, their hands were still nestled together in a greeting that might not end any time soon. I was totally extraneous to whatever subliminal preintercourse ritual was going on between them. "You're a nurse?"

"Yes, a nursing supervisor."

"Do nursing supervisors have time to be waiting on simple military men?"

"I can make a few minutes," Trish said, ducking her head, withdrawing her hand and strolling on, her hips in the tight white dress moving seductively.

When she was out of hearing I said softly, "I see what you mean by the effect of a properly tailored uniform, Lieutenant."

He laughed, the sound strange in hallways that had been marked only by fear and dying for so many days. "That is a dangerous woman," Adams said, looking back at Trish's retreating form once more as we rounded the corner. Facing forward, he took in the scuffed wallpaper at stretcher-rail height, the unwaxed floor that had seen far more traffic than usual in the last several days, the prints hanging on the walls, one or two at not-quite-horizontal angles. And me. He shook his head, trying to regain his equilibrium.

"If by *dangerous* you mean intelligent, educated and pretty, she is that," I agreed, trying not to laugh at his reaction to our hospital femme fatale. "And speaking of pretty dangerous women, do you need to speak with Dr. Shirley Adkins now?"

"Later is fine. I'll be talking with all of you at some point."

Keying open the door to the MODIS room, I flicked on the lights and pulled out the swivel desk chair at the keyboard. The other chairs were back in their places and the lieutenant sat, opening his briefcase. "What can you tell me about Richard Ellis?"

We talked for ten twice-interrupted minutes before I was paged to return to the ER to finish up my shift. Still weary from the fifteen-hour shift he had pulled the night before, Wallace Chadwick came in early for the late shift as ER doc, and I was able to go home on time. That meant leaving Lieutenant Gilroy Adams in the willing and capable hands of Shirl and Trish. I was certain that he was well pleased.

I could have sworn that a car followed me home. Headlights pulled out behind me when I left the doctors' parking and made the first four turns before taking a right. And a different set of headlights followed me the rest of the way, not close enough for me to be able to identify the make or model, but close enough to make me feel uncomfortable. I had a hand on my cell phone when I turned off onto Starlight Lane. But when the lights turned off in a neighbor's drive I relaxed. Since seeing a buzz-cut head in the cafeteria I had been just a bit paranoid. Half the county had family or friends waiting to be seen in the ER, and the last set of headlights could have joined the short cavalcade at any point.

I showered, changed from scrubs into jeans, fed the dogs and climbed back into the car. I had moved so fast that the interior was still warm. A cold, light rain had begun to fall, misting over the windshield. With a turn of the key, my car roared to life. I had a shopping spree to take on, and a list of items, complete with pictures. God, I hated shopping.

By the time I got to South Park, the upscale Charlotte mall Marisa frequented, I had only an hour to shop. There was no way I could get the French-style crib Marisa wanted into my little toy-size car so almost everything would have to be delivered, which could become an expensive proposition. Unless I managed to do all the shopping in one place. The thought brightened my disposition considerably.

On the mall diagram, I located a baby store on the lower level and a second one on the upper level, oriented myself with the little red You Are Here X and jogged down the wide mall. Luck was with me and I found a French crib at the second store. It was displayed prominently near the front window, with a mattress, pillow, bed bumpers, sheets, and a draping thingy that looked vaguely like mosquito netting. While it wasn't a perfect match, the crib closely resembled the bed Marisa and Miss Essie had picked out. With Marisa so far along, I didn't think I wanted to spend the time shopping for the exact bed in the picture. And if a little voice whispered that I was lazy and hated shopping and would have bought whatever bed I found, I was safely able to ignore it.

In the store, appropriately called Baby2Baby, I found almost everything on Marisa's list, and set the happy owner to pulling items off shelves and out of inventory. She was an observant little imp of a woman, with a name tag that read BARB in caps, who perceived instantly that the list wasn't for me, and that I hated doing the shopping. With the voluntary curfew in place, business was slow, and though Barb was alone in the store, she was able to give me her total attention.

I sat in a squishy chair, sipped decaf tea, and ate crispy cinnamon cookies set aside for the pregnant shoppers needing a break, while pointing out additional items I thought Marisa could use. Barb's smile grew the longer I sat, and even when the mall lights began to dim, she didn't suggest closing up the store. I wasn't stupid. I knew I was buying out the place, but it wasn't my money, it was Marisa's, and she was rich as Croesus. And somehow sitting and shopping when money was no object was kinda fun.

I was halfway through buying out the place before I realized the list was in Marisa's handwriting. Her sure, strong cursive was almost unchanged from before her accident, a penmanship I had envied all our years growing up together. Not even med school had an impact on her handwriting, while mine had started out crabbed and gone from nearly illegible to totally illegible in under six months. I held the list, fighting back unexpected tears. Took a shuddering breath. Choked on a cookie crumb.

Coughing, turning my head away from the manager, I glanced out the window. And spotted a man with a buzz cut. I froze mid-cough. Shrank into the squishy chair. Dropped the crisp cookie.

He angled his head as he ambled by, hands clasped behind his back, and glanced into the storefront across the mall. I couldn't see his face. But I could see the beer belly pushing out against his windbreaker. Fear whooshed out of me and I coughed uncontrollably. *Not Ellis. Not Ellis. Just a late husband looking for his shopoholic wife.* Still, something made me hunch deeper into the upholstered chair and watch for his return, sipping tea and fighting the cough.

Moments later, following another shopper who was studying every window carefully, he came back, still relaxed and casual. The beer belly was sitting a little lower on his hips this time, as if a load had shifted. And when he turned his head, just so, to peer for a moment into Baby2Baby, Ellis's crystal blue eyes swept the place and moved on. Richard Ellis was in South Park Mall with me. And I had no doubt he knew where I was.

21

My fingers found my cell phone in the front pocket of my jacket and I dialed Mark's number from memory. I didn't have it programmed into speed dial but knew I would do so at the earliest possible opportunity. Behind me, Barb rattled paper and grunted as she climbed down from the ladder she used to reach the top shelves. Out in the hallway, Ellis passed on, expression indifferent, seeming to be bored. My irritated throat constricted.

Mark's home number rang. Rang again. On the third ring he picked up and growled in a sleep-clogged voice, "It better be pretty fucking important."

"Richard Ellis is following me in South Park Mall. Important enough for you?" I knew he must be beyond exhaustion to answer the phone that way, but I was scared.

"Jeez, woman. Where the hell did you say you were? Get off the bed." There followed the now familiar sliding thump of a dog hitting the floor.

"I'm shopping for Marisa in a store called Baby2Baby on the upper level of South Park Mall."

"You sound weird. He know where you are or is this a chance encounter? Not that I think that's possible."

"I choked on a cookie crumb. He knows."

"Marisa with you?"

"No. She's having Braxton-Hicks contractions and—"

"No is fine. Are you alone?"

"The store owner is with me. Her name is Barb. Why are you asking me all these questions? Why aren't you doing something?"

"Yeah, let me talk to the sheriff. I am doing something. I got a cell phone, too, remember? Hold on."

I sipped more tea and swallowed convulsively while Mark told his superior what was happening to me across the state line in Charlotte. Then there was silence while I watched the mall, whose lights were dimmed for closing, answered questions by Barb, and waited. "I'll tell her. Rhea, tell the owner to close and lock the door. Security is on the way. Give them a description of Ellis, what he's wearing as well as physical characteristics. When we get it all set up, they'll take you and her to your vehicles, where you will both find marked cars waiting, which will follow you home. Well, follow *her* home. Follow you to the state line, where I think an FBI unmarked Crown Vic will take over. The agent will see you home, and then most likely come inside to talk. And this time be nice."

"I am nice."

"You're a pigheaded, stubborn, troublesome pain in the butt, is what you are. Why in hell is Ellis interested in you?"

"I don't know. I've got to go," I said. "Security is here." I punched the end call button on the cell phone, terminating the connection. Two could play the be-rude-to-friends game. Besides. I had to cough. And I wanted to listen to it carefully. Just an ordinary strangled cough? Or something more underlying it?

Two men, one short, black and stocky, the other tall, white and stocky, entered the store. "You Dr. Lynch?"

"Yes. And am I ever glad to see you guys."

"You say Richard Ellis was spotted in this store in the last few minutes?" Taller, white and stocky asked. Shorter, black and stocky took the keys from Barb and locked up for her, telling her what was going on, but that she was safe.

"Out in the hallway. He passed by several times. Well, twice. He was wearing khaki pants and a black windbreaker and he had padded his middle, like with a rolled towel to look like a beer belly." I almost said *like yours* but covered up the near gaff by coughing. The sound was coarse and broken. Not like tearing linen. I was sure of it.

Barb took the arrival of Security in stride, her good mood at the nearly $4,000 sale too strong to be punctured solely by the appearance of a neo-Nazi national terrorist. She flashed her imp's grin when she told me the total and rang up the final sale with excellent grace and high good humor. I paid with Marisa's credit card, which had been placed in the neat wad of photos and list, made arrangements to have the load delivered to Marisa's the next day, pocketed the last of the crisp cinnamon cookies and finally followed the uniformed Charlotte cops from the building.

The two men, who turned out to be off-duty Charlotte policemen, walked with us sandwiched between them, Shorter in front, Taller in back, hands on their gun butts in their utility belts, eyes watchful for a man with crew-cut hair, wearing a windbreaker. But the mall was empty. No sign of Ellis anywhere.

It was their own cars they led us each to, the marked cars parked in the center of the empty lot, and then they drove us to our separate vehicles, turning us over to two new marked cars, which followed us just as Mark had suggested. I pulled into light traffic, the marked car behind me, and drove at a sedate pace toward I-77. The whole thing was over in minutes, leaving me with a case of the shakes and a hunger headache.

A mutating, lung-eating, brain-mushing, skin-dissolving, contagious bacteria wasn't enough. I had to have a terrorist come courting.

I started feeling stupid on the way back and wanted to

wave the Charlotte cop off, wanted to slink right by any unmarked Crown Vic and sneak home to my bed. But Mark's question haunted me as I drove. What *did* Ellis want with me?

The marked car blinked its lights when my short caval-cade reached the border at Ford County and pulled off through the grassy median, then an ugly brown car pulled in after me. The Feebs. I wondered if it was special agent Jim Ramsey or Howard Angel, because I couldn't see bow-tied Emma Simmons pulling baby-sitting duty.

Suddenly angry at the intrusion of cops, military men and female 007s into my life, I sped up to just under seventy and put on music. Meat loaf. It seemed fitting. When we reached Dawkins County, I took the two-lane road off the interstate and whirled the steering wheel into the nearest fast-food joint. I hadn't eaten since the bowl of vegetable-meat surprise and was starving. The smell of sizzling meat and grease made me salivate as I ordered a Quarter Pounder with extra onions and had the girl make it a biggie, meaning extra-large fries and drink. And just to show my good breed-ing, I ordered the same for the driver of the unmarked brown Crown Vic, squealed my tires over to the car and held the bag out to the closed driver's window.

After a long moment while I watched my patient reflec-tion chew fries, the window came down and a man's hand reached for the food. "Are you Angel or Ramsey?" I asked as the hand withdrew, taking the meal.

"Ramsey," he said. It was the taller agent from the aborted interview in the MODIS room, now clearly identi-fied as low man on the totem pole. "Thanks."

"Thanks for the baby-sitting job."

"Why is Richard Ellis interested in you?"

"That's the question of the moment, isn't it? I hope one of you guys figures it out for me while I'm still alive."

When I finally got to my house, tired and cranky and

greasy-fingered, there was another car waiting in my drive. One with government plates and a military tag on the back window. I hoped that Shirl had brought Lieutenant Adams home for a quick bonk, as she would say, but with Cameron Reston looming large in her life I didn't think it was likely. The Lou was here to see me.

Ramsey raised a hand out his window as he drove off, and while I didn't see his face, I figured he was grinning. If only I had made nice-nice with Emma I might not be talking to the military now. So much for my big mouth.

I was surprised to find Shirl and Mark sitting at my old battered kitchen table with Lieutenant Gilroy Adams, eating Texas Taters and fried chicken from the Blue Dot store and drinking from sweating bottles of Mike's Hard Lemonade. I carried the scent of onions and burgers in with me, dumped the paperwork from my hard hours of shopping onto the bar and went to brush my teeth. I might not mind offending the Lou, but I wasn't going to insult Mark Stafford. At least not unintentionally.

Belle and Pup writhed through my legs as I bent over the bathroom sink, for all the world like two cats, but big enough to knock me down if I hadn't steadied myself with a hand. "I didn't bring you anything," I said through the foamy paste. "Sorry."

Belle sighed and returned to the kitchen and table treats she might be able to con from visitors. I didn't often let her have food from the table, not wanting poorly behaved, begging dogs, but guests had no such compunction. Pup gazed at me with hopeful hunger, not quite ready to abandon a new source of edible delights.

"No," I said gently. "No food." Drying my hands, I gazed with longing at my bed, the covers still rumpled from the morning. This was to be no early-to-bed night. Not after this latest incident. And the look in Mark's eyes as I came in the door had been more than clear. His being awake was all my fault, and if he didn't get to sleep, then no one else did, either. He was so exhausted that he looked severely hungover. I was sure he hadn't slept more than a few hours at a time since the night of the storm.

The rectangular kitchen table was a bit too large for the place it occupied, pushed up against the wall between kitchen and living room. Not a problem for my usually solitary existence, but with more than two people actually using it, there was a space requirement not being met. Mark was sitting across from Adams, occupying the presumptive head of table, which left the Lieutenant's back to the hallway and door, and Shirl sitting partway into the kitchen proper.

I pulled the remaining chair around and sat next to Shirl, smiled genially around at them all and helped myself to their Texas Tater fries. They were still hot from the frying grease, slightly limp, heavily peppered, even better than my fastfood fries. Probably fried in lard, like all the really good fries had been until the discovery of cholesterol. Heaven on earth.

"So. I hope you aren't all planning on staying over tonight," I said, unabashedly licking my fingers. Shirl placed her thigh along mine and pressed steadily in warning. I smiled in acknowledgement without glancing her way. Preempting the Lou, I said, "Lieutenant Adams, I have no idea why your man is following me. I saw him up close precisely once, when he tried to pass himself off as a navy officer. When I called his bluff, he walked. He told me nothing."

Adams leaned back in his chair, his coat unbuttoned to reveal a taut, lean chest beneath his khaki shirt. Lacing his fingers across his stomach as if it were very full, he studied me as I ate and licked, my brows raised in curiosity. I assumed the posture-and-stare combo was an effective interrogation technique when used on the average prisoner, but with the spot of ketchup on Adams's chin, the result was somewhat diminished.

"We know," Adams said finally, "that Ellis has been in this county for some time, has numerous contacts, acquaintances, followers, hangers-on." He pursed his lips as if thinking, but I doubted what he was saying was extemporaneous. There was something about his tone I didn't like, but I couldn't put my finger on what exactly was so annoying.

"We have traced some of them, following their actions. And most of them, well, at least two of them, have also spent time with you."

"Here? That limits the numbers to Mark, Shirl, Arlana, Marisa and Miss Essie. And the dogs." Taking a paper napkin from the Blue Dot store, I stood and reached across Shirl to the Lou and wiped the ketchup off his face. Adams froze in place, trying not to react as the coarse paper scraped down his chin. "Ketchup," I said, sitting back down. "And I don't think any of them are involved with your bad guy. Other than that, we have work. And I see whoever comes in to be seen."

Beside me, Shirl was working to keep her face straight. Mark was chuckling softly through his nostrils. Slowly Adams sat forward, the pleasant-but-disbelieving expression gone now from his face. "Dr. Lynch—"

"Rhea. Call me Rhea. And if your bad-guy pals were patients, then I'm sure you can tell what I know by issuing a subpoena for the charts and talking to the nurses on duty at the time." I ate a big Tater and watched him react.

"You let days go by before you told Captain Stafford about your visit from Richard Ellis." The lieutenant's voice was less than controlled, less than calm, but at least the tone was real, and not the staged lawyer voice whose timbre I didn't like. "You could be charged with harboring a criminal, with accessory after the fact of any crime he committed after you saw him and didn't report it."

I shrugged and swallowed, licking a finger. "It'll get thrown out of court. I had no idea what Ellis looked like.

And you can't prove I did. A 911 operator will document the day and time when I requested a photo of Ellis, and Mark can document when I called him about the ID. Any charge you come up with has to be hinged upon my knowing who he was before that time. You can't prove that I knew who he was earlier, because I didn't. Now, why don't you tell me what you really want from me so I can hit the sack. I'm tired.''

Adams unlaced his fingers and placed his palms flat on the table. "We want Ellis. We want him back in stockade for the remainder of his natural life. We want the canisters of engineered streptococcal bacterium under the control of the proper authorities and then destroyed. We think you are part of the key to achieving all this. And you aren't cooperating.''

I shrugged again. "If I know anything, I'll help, but if I know anything, I don't know what it is that I know. Did that make sense?'' I asked Shirl.

"Quite. A bit convoluted, but sensible. May I please give Belle and Pup a tater?''

Hearing the delicate English-accented question end with the word *Tater* brought a smile to my face. "You'll give them bad manners.''

"But I'll be gone and not have to live with evidence of their deficient training.''

"You are a cruel woman.''

"This I've been told by better bred, more highly educated, blue-blooded royalty.''

"Dr. Lynch,'' Adams sighed.

"Sorry.'' I faced him again, but continued speaking to Shirl. "Go ahead. Feed the dogs. But only one Tater apiece. Listen, Gil,'' I said, using his first name for the first time in an effort to seem chummy and cooperative, "I don't know anything. Seriously. But if I think of anything, I'll call you. Now, I really have to go to bed. If you have anything else to ask me, can't it wait until morning?''

Adams looked at his watch. "It *is* late. I'll see you at the hospital in the morning, Dr. Lynch. Please don't try and leave town like you did today."

I held up a hand, Honest Injun style, politically incorrect though it was. "No more shopping, I promise."

"And if Ellis contacts you?"

"I'll call," I said, a faint groan of irritated insistence in my tone. "I'll call."

"Tomorrow," Gil said, standing and buttoning his coat. "Could you give me directions to the motel you mentioned?" he asked Mark.

"Yeah. I'll see you out." Mark sent me an unmistakable look as he stood. He wasn't finished with me.

"I'll straighten up in here," Shirl said. "You have a few messages. I heard one as I came in." Her voiced dropped. "And I quite thought I would have an eppy when you wiped his face and then kept nattering on as though you hadn't."

"Eppy? Some esoteric English message in that?"

"Have a fit, like a grand mal epileptic. A tante." She slitted her eyes at me. "Are you codding me?"

"Never." I left Shirl putting greasy napkins and bags in the garbage and feeding the dogs leftover Taters despite the one-Tater ruling. The message Shirl referred to was from Rear Admiral Goldfarb. He wanted to talk to me no matter what time I got in. Feeling a bit of trepidation, I dialed the number on the machine and sat on the rumpled bed.

The person who answered identified their location as a Holiday Inn Suite. Surprised, I asked for the room number the Admiral had left. Goldfarb was still up, answering the phone with a bark of a greeting. When I identified myself, his tone softened. Slightly.

"Dr. Lynch, my son is a bright man."

"Yes, sir, he is," I agreed, puzzled at his opening.

"And he has some bright friends."

I sighed, understanding where he was leading. "Yes, sir.

He also has some friends with bizarre problems, is that where you were going?''

"That is precisely where I was going," the admiral said, a trace of amusement in his tone. "You're familiar with NIS?"

"Naval Investigative Service? Naval Intelligence Service? Something like that? You mentioned them earlier." Belle jumped up on the mattress beside me and I scrubbed her ears gently in the way she seemed to like best. She sighed long and deeply and settled her head in my lap.

"Close enough. We know who the FBI is looking for, and Richard Ellis is someone we need to contact."

"Contact?" I said, surprised. "As in talk to, as opposed to apprehend?"

The admiral hesitated. "Richard Ellis is currently responsible for working with Patriot groups in your area, and for allowing use of a weapon of mass destruction, a bacteriological warfare agent, in pursuit of racist ideology. Terrorism of that nature is an FBI responsibility, Dr. Lynch. However, Ellis didn't import a ready-made batch of strep. He's involved with those responsible for bringing the creator of the strep into the country from the Middle East. Ellis is a secondary concern."

"And so," I concluded, "although Ellis is *your* man, a soldier who got away from you, he's small potatoes. At this point, you're willing to leave Ellis to the Feebs if he leads you to the bacteriologist who constructed the strep in the first place."

"We are indeed more interested in other guilty parties," Goldfarb said carefully, "however, we are not leaving him to others. We simply want him free to lead us to the creator of the strep and the person who is bankrolling the operation in Dawkins County."

I considered the deliberately worded statement. Something clicked in the recesses of my mind. "Did Ellis kill Ron Hawkins because Hawkins was black?"

"While in the service, Ellis issued a manifesto calling for the massacre of every non-Caucasian being on the face of the earth," he said. "What do you think?"

That wasn't exactly an answer. "Maybe he knew Leon Hawkins from the Gulf War," I said, trying to put the pieces together. "Ellis and the Hand of the Lord hate group."

"Patriot group," Goldfarb corrected me. "Groups, to be more precise. For the last few months, there have been three or four different groups operating out of Dawkins County. Some more violent than others."

"Um," I said. "Whatever." It didn't fit. Something was missing.

"We are close to finding and capturing Ellis, Dr. Lynch. But if he slips by us or contacts you before we have him in custody, we want you to lead us to him."

"Do what?"

"For some reason Ellis is interested in you. We want you to be available to him when he contacts you, and to set up a meeting. Then we will be at the meeting, waiting for him. And hopefully he will lead us to the others in his organization."

Confused questions bubbled just below the surface of my mind. And Goldfarb's answers had stimulated more questions.

"Now, if you would be so kind, take down this number. It's my cell phone number. If at any time Ellis contacts you, please call me immediately. Me. Not anyone else. Not your friend the cop, not the FBI, not Lieutenant Adams. Will you do that?"

"I could do that," I said slowly. "Do you want to tell me why I should call you and only you?"

"Because you are a law-abiding citizen, with the best interests of this nation at heart." When I didn't respond, Goldfarb added, "And because you have patients who are dying. Calling me first is the best and fastest method to their eventual healing."

When I hung up several minutes later, I was no closer to understanding what was going on. In fact, I was more confused. Why shouldn't I call Adams? Wasn't *he* their man, too?

"Are you going to tell me what you just learned?"

I looked up to find Mark leaning in the doorway, wearing his exhaustion like a mask. His shoulders drooped, his hair was lank; even his skin seemed to sag just a bit on his frame, as if too tired to hang on to his bones. "The navy doesn't want Ellis. Not primarily, anyway. He's small potatoes, there to lead them to the bigger guy."

"The man who actually engineered the bacteria," Mark said. When I looked surprised, he said, "The bacteriological warfare canisters weren't pirated from stock seized in the Gulf War, or at least don't appear to have been shipped over from there. We found some of the homeless who were squatting in the warehouse—" he yawned hugely, the back of one hand over his mouth "—and they described the canisters pretty accurately.

"According to three people we interviewed, the markings on the canisters were English, not Arabic, though of course, no one can remember what was written on them. That indicates that although Ellis may have met the guy in the Middle East, perhaps in that town where the BW factory was in the Gulf War, he didn't take the inventory. Now it looks like both Ellis and his BW biologist are somewhere else. Like here. And I'm guessing the navy hopes you will lead a path right to them both."

"But I really don't know anything," I said, sounding as honest as I could with the admiral's words and my own half-baked questions ringing in my mind. I pushed Belle off the bed, hearing a familiar thump-thump sound, the same dual thumps I heard over the phone when Mark shoved his own dogs off the bed. Action-reaction.

I sat up straight in the bed. An action requires a reaction. What goes up must come down. Bacteria-antibiotics. Was *that* what Goldfarb wanted? The formula for the antibiotic that would combat the strep enterotoxin?

No bacteriologist—unless totally insane—would make a bacteria he couldn't combat. He had to have made an antibiotic, too... And Goldfarb wanted it more than he wanted his own man. Wanted me to call him first if Ellis contacted me...

To give the antibiotic to us? To make enough to save the patients who were dying? Goldfarb had said he was the best way to my patients' *eventual* healing. Just how eventual did he have in mind?

And what was it the prisoners had said about Ellis and his men beating up the other prisoners in the jail takeover? No, that wasn't quite right. Ellis's men. Not Ellis. Why not Ellis? He liked to watch, they said. And Mark had said something similar....

"What?" Mark asked. "You got a weird look in your eyes."

I explained my concerns about Goldfarb's possible interest in the antibiotic. And knew as soon as the words left my mouth that they sounded dumb. Conspiracy theories with a distinct *X-Files* flair.

Mark sighed in disgust, squared his shoulders slowly and said, "If you think of anything *serious,* would you mind calling me first, before you call Adams? And while you're at it, call me before you call the admiral. Just for kick's sake."

Still looking stooped and worried, Mark left the house, shaking his head.

Not *because you care for me and trust me,* but *just for kick's sake.* Somehow that bothered me.

And why call Mark first? Why call the admiral first? Did they each want credit for bringing Ellis in, or did they each have a hidden agenda for the man?

I fell over in the bed, fully clothed, pulled the covers up to my chin, and lay in the darkness, a jumble of questions tumbling in my brain. And then one of the admiral's statements came back to me.... The NIS wanted the man bankrolling the bacterial warfare terrorism operation. A man with money. A man with racist ideals...

Was it possible, this thought I was contemplating? Could a person hide such a thing as hatred for all races except white? I'd heard the Lamb of God once say something about the "purity of the races." Was that the key to Hand of the Lord hatred? Why would Lamb want to hide his hatred in the first place? Were the canisters hidden on the Lamb's compound? Was he bringing about the modern-day plagues even as I curled safe in my bed? And the most important question, why? It didn't fit the man's public persona. The conspicuously humanitarian side seen by the world. This was the man who donated $200,000 to indigent care. Who had given the hospital a grant to fund the purchase of more negative pressure units. I had seen him pray over Shareeka before she died, and Shareeka was half black....

And Ellis... Where did he fit in?

I had no answers, and curled tighter into the warmth of the covers as sleep claimed me. I didn't wake until the alarm went off in the morning.

Miss Essie didn't call at daybreak Wednesday, offering breakfast and coffee and wake-up treats. Instead, Shirl and I crawled out of bed, took hot showers one at a time, as the hot water slowed to a trickle when both showers ran simultaneously, and headed to work. Or tried to.

I left the house, aware of a strange tickle in my throat, climbed into my dew-covered BMW and backed out, only to be stopped after about twenty feet. Half a dozen news vans and twice that many cars blocked the drive and spilled out into Starlight Lane. The only reason I made it back into the house before I was surrounded was that no one expected me to be up so early. I slammed the back door and secured the doggy door flap just as three reporters in various stages of makeup application pounded on the frame.

Shirl raced from the nether regions of the house, the left side of her head a flame of curls, the right half plaited for the trip to the hospital. "What? *What?*" she demanded.

I looked at Belle. "You didn't warn me we had visitors."

"Visitors?" Shirl ran to the kitchen window and peered out. "Bloody hell."

"And for some reason the dogs didn't bark." Belle's thick tail was swinging slowly, a canine grin in place. She looked sleepy. Pup rose up and put his paws on her back, requesting dominance play, but she ignored him.

"Neglecting him, too, are you?" I asked, looking up at Shirl. "We have a pileup of news people out front, too. Must be about thirty vehicles." I swallowed. My throat itched.

Shirl looked down at the dogs. "Shame on you. What kind of hound are you if you don't bark a bit? How are we to get out of here?"

Glancing at her with a "like this" expression, I picked up the new kitchen phone for the first time and dialed the police, identified myself and requested that someone clear my drive. I could have called Mark, but the fact that I hadn't completely told the truth about the phone call from the admiral weighed on my mind.

Shirl, listening, fingers braiding automatically, nodded when she understood. "I'll be dressed in a jiff." Still running, she disappeared into the guest room.

The kitchen phone was Arlana's idea. It was a cordless model with a headset, which would allow her to clean and keep up with gossip at the same time. Walking from window to window, I described the circus that had become my front yard and was pleased to see two marked cars pull up while I was still on the line.

"Now, that's great service," I said.

"We aim to please, Doc," the man at dispatch said.

As the cars and vans were moved, creating a trail to the

street, I called the hospital and told Wallace what was going on.

"Well, I should have guessed," he said. "And it's partly my fault. Some woman from the *Observer* got inside last night and found me in the lounge. I had fallen asleep with my mouth open, and I'm sure I was snoring. A bright light that was probably a camera flash went off just as she poked me and started asking questions. Before I could get awake, she asked if it was true that you were responsible for finding the treatment for AVP and ACS. And I'm pretty sure I said yes."

"Wallace!" My exclamation exacerbated the tickle and I coughed again.

"I know. I know. But I was asleep. Before I could explain that it was a joint effort by CDC and several others, she was outta there."

"Anne Evans," I sighed.

"You know her?"

"Sucking media. Blood-sucking media, you ask me. I think I can get clear now, but I'll be a bit late to work. Thanks to you."

"I guess I don't get to dock your time?"

"Correct," I said, watching as the last of the vans pulled out and parked along the street. "Under the circumstances."

"But I do get to set up a press conference with you and Dr. Adkins."

"Do what? No."

"We need to make certain that the proper people get credit for giving plasma as a treatment for the AVP and ACS, and we also need to put out a call for Red Cross blood donations. Columbia ran out of plasma last night, and although they can have some flown in, it'll be a long while before supplies return to proper levels. You get to make the appeal for donors."

"Wallace—"

"It's been set up, Rhea. And approved by administration."

"Crap."

Wallace laughed. "See you soon."

"Wallace," I called to keep him from hanging up, "make that press conference as early as possible and still give time for Shirl's people to get here from Charlotte. Meeks and the other one. And make sure someone from administration is there, too."

"Chancel Martinson and Eliza Meeks. It's been handled, Rhea. Relax."

"You owe me one, Wallace."

As he disconnected, I could hear his laughter. And I started coughing.

22

KEEP IT LEVEL

The press conference was a madhouse. Hospital administration was doing its best but had never been accosted by national media and didn't have the PR skills to run things smoothly. They set up in the nursing center dining hall, the only room big enough to hold the reporters and cameras, too. Abigail Staton, the hospital administrator's secretary, and the de facto press secretary, had set up the site with a portable podium, microphone, table with pencils and notebooks, and chairs for the interviewees, all backed up against the hallway wall next to the cavernous, damp room where laundry was done. Behind the table were two doors that we could escape through when our part of the fiasco was over.

Rolanda Higgenbotham, the hospital's second-in-command, chaired the news conference, which was covered live by CNN and had representatives from all the major networks. Rolanda, graduate of a state university, a local-girl-made-good, and tough as nails under pressure, was dressed to kill. In purple-tinted lipstick and matching eye shadow that did wonders for her dark skin and tinted, slicked-back hair, she was wearing a teal-and-blue pantsuit and matching teal flats. Shirley was hidden under a crisp white lab coat that showed only the pointed collar of her hunter-green blouse, her hair up on top of her head in a single, smooth, curled bun.

Chancel Martinson, Eliza Meeks, Mike, the director of Dawkins's laboratory and some man from DHEC also wore starched lab coats and professional airs. They looked like cookie-cutter copies of one another, with their hair combed, makeup neatly applied. And then there was me. I sat at the distant end of the table, as far from the center of the excitement as I could get, drinking coffee to soothe my scratchy throat, dressed in my scrub suit and wrinkled lab coat over long johns, with running shoes and a smear of lipstick. I had smoothed down my hair with one hand seconds before sitting down. I was pulling triage under the hood again, and windblown was the best I could manage.

The news conference swirled around me, questions being directed to specific people or to the table at large, and I was able to sit and doodle on the notebook so kindly provided, and not look at the cameras. Twenty minutes into the conference, the officials had described the onset and spread pattern of the disease, the investigation into possible vectors and site of initial contagion, all in very technical lingo that had the reporters asking for explanations of vocabulary and the interviewees looking a bit smug. And I heard my name called by a familiar-sounding voice.

"Um, yes?" I looked up from my doodle into the bright lights, and spotted Anne Evans. She looked as though she were undergoing a mystical, heavenly experience, her color high, her eyes sparkling. News conference orgasm.

"Can you tell us what you think about the claims made by the Reverend Shackleford Lamb Sexton that this is the beginning of the last days and the time of Biblical plagues?"

"Drivel." The word slipped out of my mouth before I could stop it, and I could have sworn I heard Shirl giggle into the instant of silence that followed.

"Would you elaborate?" Anne asked, delighted with my slip.

"Well, Ms. Evans," I said, casting back in time, searching for information of plagues-past to compare with this one. "The black death of the Middle Ages killed off two-thirds of the population of Europe, leaving entire cites empty of inhabitants. The viral flu of the 1920s killed off something like twenty million people. Ebola, when it strikes, is almost universally fatal and there is no treatment or cure for it. We have a treatment for this bacteria, and antibiotics that can eventually kill it. Doesn't sound much like a plague to me." Of course, there were parallels to the concept of plague, especially as plague used in biological warfare, but I wasn't about to admit that.

"You were the one who came up with the treatment, weren't you," she persisted. "The use of blood products to cure the disease?"

"Not alone. Dr. Shirley Adkins can address the question of who at CDC figured out what the strep was doing to the patients. After that it was only a tiny leap to come up with the treatment idea. I was just one of a team of three or four who helped put together a specific protocol for use in this hospital of the fresh frozen plasma to control bleeding. And the FFP doesn't cure anything. It just controls the symptoms of the disease until the antibiotics do their work. Dr. Adkins?"

Shirl took the spotlight off me, and addressed the concept of team effort used by CDC to control and combat disease. I glared at Anne Evans and returned to my doodle, a nice profile of Belle, considering my nonexistent artistic skills.

"Dr. Lynch?"

I looked up again, having lost track of the questioning in the shading of her droopy ears. "Yes?"

"We understand that you control the desk beside the emergency room, is that correct?" I nodded. "There have been complaints by some patients that you practice preferential treatment. That you let in some people and make others wait, instead of taking first-come, first-served. Would you address that issue?''

I found the fellow asking the questions about halfway through them. He was an average-size man about forty, with perfect dental work and soft, pudgy hands. Slowly I sat upright, took a sip of cool coffee and leaned forward.

''It's called triage. The theory of triage has been explained repeatedly. But since you don't seem to get the idea, let me put it in terms you can personally understand. Let's say you are around forty, with a few extra pounds around the middle, don't get much exercise, eat junk food, have a high-stress job and live a sedentary lifestyle.'' The reporter scowled at me, correctly calculating that I was describing him. ''And you come to the ER complaining of severe chest pain.

''In front of you is a kid with an earache, a man with a cut finger and a postal worker with a nontraumatic dog bite. Now, if I let you go in first, someone else has to wait. If I make you wait, based on the first-come, first-served notion, then while I'm stitching up a finger, you blow a hole in your heart and die.''

My throat tickled. I sipped again. *I was not coming down with AVP. I wasn't. I simply had an irritated throat, scratched by a cookie crumb....*

''Now,'' I said. ''What I do out in the cold is evaluate patients. And I send to the emergency room the patients who are the most ill, yet stand a chance of being treated and surviving. I send them back in order of more urgent diagnoses, not in order of age, race or whether they are wearing a press badge.''

That brought a tittle of amusement from the crowd. And that was when I spotted him in the back of the room. Richard Ellis. Watching me. He stared for a long moment, his piercing blue eyes holding me in my seat. Then, moving like a cat, he turned and left the room. I didn't have my cell

phone with me. I couldn't call to anyone. But there were
police and armed Guardsmen all over the hospital perimeter.
Surely someone would spot him. Apprehend him. I tried to
remember what he had been wearing. Khakis? Jeans? The
only thing I could remember were his eyes, the blazing blue
of a cutting torch.

Richard Ellis wanted something from me. That much I
understood.

And then I thought about the people gathered in this
room. Sitting ducks. With air vents above us, blowing in
cooled, humidified air. But the hospital didn't have humid-
ifiers. The air was always uniformly dry and miserable, even
during the Carolina-damp, humid-heat summers. My fingers
curled into fists as I fought the urge to cough.

Looking up, I saw one grill, covering a vent, placed directly overhead. While Shirl was speaking, being captivating
and English in a room full of Southern accents, I rose and
slipped out. My running shoes squeaked on the damp tile
of the passageway behind the Nursing Center dining room.
Bleach-scented steam billowed and curled around my ankles, pulled by cool-air vents into an artificial downward
flow, rising slower than seemed normal in wisps toward the
ceiling.

The dampness in the next room could come from here.
Of course. The laundry. The one place where the moisture
content of the air might be pleasant. But what if I was wrong
about the humidity, and right about the vents? I coughed
hard and my throat eased.

Looking around carefully, I saw no one. No Richard Ellis,
no housekeeping personnel. I found the laundry-room phone
on the wall beside a low desk and dialed nine, followed by
Mark's cellular number.

"Mark Stafford," he said on the first ring, his voice
booming.

I jerked the phone away from my ear. The volume was
turned up all the way, perhaps to compensate for the noise

of the machines nearby when they were running. Holding the phone at an angle in front of my face, I said, "There's a press conference in the Nursing Center dining room." My words ran together, my voice pitched low. "I looked up and spotted Ellis. This was a big deal, this press conference, and what if Ellis did something to the air supply? That would make a big impact, terrorist-wise, maybe make a statement."

"What the hell is it with you and this guy?" he thundered. "I'm on my way." The phone went dead.

"Talking to your boyfriend?"

I whirled, holding the phone out before me like a barbell-shaped shield. Blue light caught my eyes. I sucked in a breath. Backed away from Richard Ellis.

He was standing in the passageway, hands holding an envelope by its edges, looking vaguely medical in a lab coat and slacks, totally nonthreatening. Except for his eyes. I reached the end of the phone cord and lurched to a halt. "What do you want?"

"I want you to get a letter to your lieutenant friend. The one who was at your house last night."

I clutched the phone, drew it close, the cord taut. "You know he was at my house last night?" I repeated stupidly. Fear settled in the pit of my stomach, leaving me thick-headed and nauseous, as if I were under the effects of anesthesia. Soft gusts of steam billowed up around Ellis as an engine somewhere hummed to life, disturbing the air currents. The stench of bleach worsened. "How do you...?" My words trailed off.

Tender flesh around Ellis's eyes crinkled with amusement, the blue of the irises becoming even bluer. "Because I was at your house last night, watching through the kitchen window. What did you do to his face when you stood up and wiped his chin?"

"Ketchup," I said, still sounding half-witted. I pressed the phone to my stomach as fear-induced nausea rose.

"Good move. Threw him totally off base. Who is he?"

"Who?"

"The lieutenant," Ellis said patiently. "His name?"

"Gilroy Adams." I tried to swallow past my dry throat.

"Get this to him for me, okay?" Ellis stepped closer and held out the large manila envelope, one of the thick, padded kind used to mail delicate, though not necessarily fragile, items. I reached a hand forward, dropping the phone. It landed with a plastic crash that made me jump.

Gingerly I took the envelope. Held it as he did, with two fingers of each hand. It started to droop.

"Anh-anh-anh," Ellis said, showing teeth now in his grin, lifting the drooping end with an outstretched finger. "You want to keep it level. Use both hands."

"Level?" I swallowed, fighting my cough, my throat burning with bleach fumes.

"Le-vel," he said, as if teaching a child a new vocabulary word. "And don't set it down. Understand? You'll know what to do with it later."

I held the envelope in both hands as directed. Tears of bleach accumulated in my eyes, making Ellis blur. Someone in the laundry must have spilled bleach. A lot of bleach.

"I would have given it to him last night, but your boy-friend hung around too long. Sent him to a really shitty hotel on the outskirts of town, by the way. Even the hookers don't hang out there."

I didn't know what he was talking about, but I managed a deep breath. The nausea and cough receded slightly. "Did you sabotage the ventilation system in there?" I asked, nodding to the news conference still ongoing, the envelope held out in front of me.

"With the strep enterotoxin? No. But it would have been a good move, if I had known about the press conference in time." His eyes crinkled with a smile again, as if he had made a good joke. "World would be a better place if about half those bloodsuckers bit it. Except for Connie Chung. I like her."

I flinched hearing my own terms on his lips. Bloodsuckers. Wasn't that what I had called them? "Connie Chung is Asian. I thought you hated Asian-Americans."

"Propaganda. But then you already knew that, didn't you?" With that, Ellis turned on a heel, ran into the steam of the laundry room and disappeared around a corner. "Rhea?" he called softly.

I jerked, hearing my name on his lips. Sweat trickled hotly down my spine. "What?" I whispered.

"You can open the package when I'm gone. But till then, remember... Hold it just like I told you. Level." The gentle words echoed softly. I heard a door open and close on the far side of the room, the sound resonating, blending into the warning. I could see against the blackness of my eyelids as I blinked, the form of the man as he ran into the fog. Again. Again. Running. Disappearing.

I focused on the envelope in my hands. *Level,* he said. It wasn't heavy. That meant it wasn't a bomb, didn't it? Bombs were heavy, weren't they? Bombs didn't have to be kept level, did they? Nausea rose again in a tidal wave as bleach fumes and fear knotted my stomach. I swallowed repeatedly, fighting for calm as I saw again Ellis running and disappearing against the blackness of my eyelids. My fingertips itched. My throat ached.

Carefully, I squatted and hit the plastic receiver hook with an elbow; a dial tone sounded from the floor. Scooting backward, I found the receiver in the swirling mist. It was an old model, with only two nonnumerical buttons on it, Hold and Redial. Being careful not to shift the package, I freed a finger and hit Redial. From near my feet I heard the phone ring. Heard Mark pick up, irritation in his voice.

"Mark," I called in a voice almost too dry to speak. "Mark, he was here. In the hospital's laundry room. Ellis was here.'' My voice broke on the word. ''Can you hear me?''

''Yes, barely. Rhea?'' I didn't answer. If I opened my mouth, I would throw up. ''Why did you call me back?'' The voice was tinny and far away, even with the volume turned up so high. ''Blast it, Rhea, are you there?''

My lips stuck together as if coated with plaster. I pulled them apart. ''He told me I had to keep it level.''

''Keep what level?'' Mark's voice had dropped, grown deeper with the one line.

''The package. The envelope he gave me.''

''Shit,'' he said, the word explosive. ''Rhea, don't move. Do—*not*—move. Are you holding the envelope?''

''Yes. He said not to put it down. But he said I could open it when he left.''

''Do not move,'' Mark repeated. ''Do not put the envelope down and most certainly do not open it. Understand?'' Mark's voice migrated from the phone a moment, the tone full of authority, bellowing orders in the background.

''Oh, yes. I understand,'' I whispered to the faraway phone. ''But Ellis walked with it. I saw him.'' That was important, wasn't it? That meant I was all right....

''I don't care what Ellis did. Ellis knew what he was holding, just how he should handle it. You don't. Rhea, if that *is* a bomb he gave you, even a bacterial warfare aerosol bomb, it could be triggered by anything. By pressure changes, by changes in its center of gravity, by setting it down. *Do not move!* Help is on the way.'' When I didn't answer, he shouted. ''Rhea?''

Pressure changes? Changes in gravity? I fought the urge to giggle and cough wildly. A tingle had begun in my hands and feet, a crawling sensation, as if fire ants were nesting on my skin, ready to strike. Signs of hyperventilation. I was going numb.

A tinge of darkness at the outer edges of my vision warned me the effect was far along.

"Rhea?" Mark shouted, panic now in the sound.

I was passing out. "Oh, shit," I whispered.

"What was that?" Mark said, still with me.

"I'm passing out," I said louder, the words gasping, "from hyperventilation. Which means I'm sitting down. I have to move. No choice." I shifted my bottom to the side, changing my center of gravity. "If you hear a loud boom, don't worry about finding anything but little pieces of me." Giggles burbled near the top of my throat. I tried to slow my breathing. "And don't you dare bury me next to my mother. You hear?" I held my breath.

Carefully, my eyes glued to the envelope, I dropped the few inches to the damp floor. Cold steam billowed up around me like a cloud. The smell of bleach irritated my nostrils, my voice, tears of discomfort filling my eyes. The scent of ammonia was clear beneath the smell of bleach. Bleach and ammonia mixed together? Had Ellis mixed up a vapor bomb using chemicals in the laundry? That could be deadly.... I needed to get out of here.

"I'm not spending eternity next to my mother. Are you recording this? I'm *not*. You understand me?" I was rambling. Babbling. Mist swirled around me, exposing a swath of fresh air. I sucked a breath that actually seemed to fill my lungs. The cough receded.

"I hear, Rhea." His tone was tender for a moment, then it toughened. "Do me a favor. Don't be such a *woman*."

"Woman?"

"Yeah, women always pass out. Something about all those female hormones make them weak. And then they have those stupid panic attacks. Like the one you're having." Tears finally fell from my eyes, easing the sting. I knew what he was doing. Challenging me. I could hear it in his tone, on the floor two feet away. I almost laughed, it was so obvious. But I had to admit, it made me feel stronger on some weird level. The fear-and-bleach-induced nausea receded to bearable.

"Mark? You want to take my place? Come on and be a man, save the poor, weak female. Come carry my bomb for me, you dumb cop."

"Hey, I'm not the bright lady who took a gift from Ellis. You want to reevaluate the dumb part?"

"Good point. But could you tell me please when someone even dumber than you is coming along to save me?" My vision brightened as the faintness retreated.

Mark chucked gently. "Not long now, baby. Not long now."

The "baby" part told me just how worried Mark Stafford really was. I couldn't remember him ever using an endearment for me. A serious endearment and not a jesting one. I suddenly felt icy all over.

Cold and wet seeped through the lining of my scrub pants, my long johns and my underwear. My butt started to chill down drastically on the wintry red tile. But at least the blackness had begun to recede. "Well, they better hurry, because now that I'm not going to throw up or pass out, I really, really, *really* need to go to the bathroom."

He laughed. And I laughed with him for a moment, before coughing took over. Outside, the wail of sirens split the day. Three Guardsmen and two uniformed sheriff's deputies converged on the hallway. All five had weapons drawn. I hoped they really were all good guys; through the tears pouring down my face, I couldn't have identified them.

"Deputy Darby here, ma'am. Which way did he go?" one asked.

Some deeply buried, halfway insane part of me chortled at the old line. I nodded through the laundry room to the far wall. "I heard a door shut through there." I almost added "pardner" to my response but didn't. Again, I could see Ellis run, disappear, run, disappear, the motion replicated each time I blinked. Artificial rain had begun to fall from the ceiling in echoing plops. One of the deputies ran through the wet and the steam. I coughed, fighting to hold the package level.

"Are they there, Rhea?" Mark asked from the floor.

"Yes," I said, finding my voice. "But I thought you were going to send the stupid ones so I could get out of here. These guys look too bright to take my package."

"Thank you, ma'am," a Guardsman said. I thought I heard a hint of laughter in his voice.

The other deputy motioned the Guardsmen toward the news conference. "Stay away from her. She's got the cough. Come on. Let's get those people out of here."

"I'm going now, Rhea. I'm on my way," Mark said.

"Okay." I sniffed at the tears rolling unchecked down my nose. "Mark? Thanks."

"Anytime. Hang in there."

Overhead, a speaker came to life. "Code Blue to the laundry. Code Blue to the laundry. Code Blue to the laundry." I coughed hard, but it wasn't AVP. *It wasn't.*

In the next room, I heard the deputy announce an emergency and tell the assembled to vacate the premises. The acoustics were amazing, or maybe one had to sit on the floor near an intake vent to take advantage of them. I could hear the anger of the reporters and cameramen as they were told to leave any equipment they couldn't carry, and get out. When they resisted, the Guardsmen moved in and attempted to enforce the order. A crash sounded, and a curse. Scuffling followed. I wondered if all this was going out live.

Finally someone—it sounded like Rolanda Higgenbotham—mentioned the Code Blue, which they had all heard, and informed them that a bomb threat had been called. Somehow, suddenly, the presence of a bomb made it all okay. Equipment they had not gathered during the argument was abandoned and left in the building. A deep silence ensued, and I realized I had been left alone with Ellis's package and my cough. My standard, ordinary cough.

My hands had grown icy, the bones aching. My thighs

cramped where they touched the cold floor. My scrubs were soaked through. I was crying and coughing steadily, the tears displacing the acrid fumes, deep breaths dragging in caustic air. But now my skin burned where the tears touched, the bleach fumes seeming to worsen again.

I couldn't imagine working in this place. But then, the laundry workers probably seldom sat on the floor near the vents; they were up and moving around on the far side of the room, the fumes pulled away. Dumb place to put a phone, I decided as I cried.

Yet, I knew it was not always this bad in the laundry. This level of fumes was unusual.... I reconsidered my thought about a possible vapor bomb. Ellis said he had not expected the presence of the news conference. He must have come to the hospital to deliver his envelope and been trapped by the crowd. To get away, he had mixed laundry chemicals together and added an accelerant of some kind. Which meant he had come prepared. Toxic clouds billowed up around me.

I was having trouble breathing, my throat coarse as burlap and burning. The ammoniac smell grew. Ammonia and bleach mixed together with something added to speed the reaction.... Had to be. Both chemicals would be present in a laundry. It certainly explained the caustic effects of the fumes.

I sat on the wet floor for what seemed like an hour, the envelope in my hands as fumes swirled around me, growing stronger then weaker by turns. Finally a man came back in. I took a shuddering breath at the presence of another human being, even one in black padded clothing that looked as if it belonged to a giant. He lumbered as he walked, the motion wavering through my tears.

"I'm here," Mark's voice said, close and strong and in the room with me. I hadn't known the moving pile of black was Mark until he spoke, so swathed in protective clothing was he. "You okay?"

"I'm fine."

"You're crying." He sounded amazed, as if he had never seen a woman cry before.

"Fumes," I said. "Bleach fumes. Really bad." I coughed, fighting to hold the package steady. "I have to set this thing down, Mark. I'm cramping."

"No. No positional changes," the black-padded suit told me. "You have to hold it steady."

"It would be a lot more steady on the floor."

"Yeah, but it would be setting on its flat side, not supported by the edges. If it's a bomb and if it has a trigger on the bottom…" His voice trailed off, the end of the sentence clear without his words. "You have to sit still, and you have to hold it, Rhea."

So I did, though the cramping crawled steadily up my body in the form of shivers, and my coughing worsened, tearing at my throat. Nearby, something clicked, the sound of white noise filled the room, and then Mark described the package to someone, giving its dimensions, color, apparent method of sealing.

The man on the other end of the connection asked, "Can she tell you its weight?"

"About two pounds?" I suggested. "It feels like twenty right now."

"Roger that. Hold tight, Cap'n."

"So when do the dumb guys get here?" I asked. "The ones who take this away from me?"

"They're here. They're out in the parking lot. They have a robot they're sending in. He has no sense of self-preservation. He'll take it."

"Dawkins has a robot?"

"On loan. Remember the toys we talked about? That listening device you wouldn't let me use?" I nodded, the burn on my face and down my breathing passages much worse. "Well, they also lent us a robot, a high-explosive, miniature, mobile, electronic, robotic device called a Hemmer." I assumed the designation was derived from initials, but it sounded personalized, the nickname of a new pal. "He's about three feet long, and eighteen inches high, all black and gray, on six rubberized wheels. Has a camera and portable X-ray device, a set of claws to grab packages, a small explosive chamber on the back. Used to transport, identify and destroy certain types of bombs. Cute little thing."

"Cute? Like R2D2? Only a man could find a bomb-robot cute. I'm burning, Mark." A cough followed on the last word, racking. I struggled to keep the package level.

"The fumes in here are bad. Are they always this bad?"

"No. I don't think so. I wondered if Ellis dumped some bleach onto the floor. But chlorine gas smells like this, too. So maybe he added some ammonia."

"You're just full of interesting info and possibilities today, aren't you."

Footsteps sounded in the back of the room. "Ellis got away, Cap. Found an eyewitness, a grave digger. He indicated a man jumped the creek behind the hospital, ran through the graveyard and drove off in a beat-up red truck."

"Shit," Mark spat. "Where's the damn perimeter?"

"Didn't see anyone till I was on my way back. Then a suit ran up, weapon drawn. Told me to stop or he'd shoot."

"And did he shoot you?" Mark asked, making a joke even in the face of the loss of Ellis.

"Everyone knows Feebs can't shoot, sir." Darby sounded young and cocky. "Jeez, it's bad in here."

"Someone want to tell me what's going on here? Mark, I'm really burning. It's getting worse."

"Will water disperse chlorine?"

"Yes," I said, and fought the cough that rattled deep in my lungs, "in enough quantities. But your best bet is to get us out of here and a HazMat team in."

"Darby, go get a fireman for a consult. Tell him we might need HazMat. And open that back door you came through, and any door you pass on the way. We need ventilation."

"Yes, sir." Darby's feet pounded off, splashing as they went. "I'll bring back some O_2, sir."

"Thanks," Mark called. "The FBI set up a perimeter around the hospital," he continued, answering my request for information. "But my guess is that they assumed no sane criminal would approach a building with so much activity. They pulled some men and left only a few to patrol. It must have been a cakewalk for Ellis to slip past them." Mark's voice was bitter. He cleared his throat, the sound becoming a cough.

A sharp click sounded. Mark said, "214. I have to get the doctor out of here. Ellis may have released some kind of chemical. Our eyes are burning, and it's getting hard to breathe."

"325 to 214. If that's a bomb and she moves, it could go off. We have Hemmer on the move."

"ETA?"

"Five minutes?" The answer wasn't sure, but phrased as a question, uncertain.

"I don't think we can wait that long," Mark said. We were both coughing, struggling to breathe.

"O_2 on the way, Stafford. Hang in there."

Mark didn't answer. He couldn't.

The oxygen arrived after hours, delivered by different-sounding boots. My eyes were swollen shut. I couldn't see if it was the same deputy. I was blind. The boots were joined by another pair. I could hear words, but make no sense of them through my coughing until someone spoke beside me.

"Okay, ma'am. This'll help. Don't move the package, though, okay? I don't feel like being splattered all over the place."

I nodded. Something heavy-feeling and solid settled beside me on one side, so close it touched my elbow. Protective barrier, looming over me. So that if I exploded, the damage to the man beside me would be minimized. But it blocked some of the rising caustic mist and for a moment I could almost breathe.

"Easy, Doc. Relief coming."

Something cold splashed on my face, bringing the burn to a fierce peak for an instant. Then sudden ease. Blessed cool as I was splashed again. It washed into my eyes. An oxygen mask was put over my face. A soothing bandage was gently pressed over my orbits, and something wrapped around my head to hold it in place.

But all I could think was that I was blind.

I was blind.

"Bleach, ammonia and a chunk of dry ice in a metal bucket, Cap'n," Darby's voice called. "Sorry I didn't see it the first time. It's neutralized now. The fumes should dissipate in a li'l bit."

In the distance, a small whirring sound emerged. Over Mark's and my coughing, I placed the position of the noise. "The robot?" I asked.

"Yes. In the room," a radio voice answered. "Cap'n, have your men fall back while Hemmer retrieves the package." Typical males. They had made a bomb-destroying robot into a fetching pet.

"Guys, out of here. But I'll stay with the doctor."

A red haze filled the darkness of my sight. Was that a good sign? "Clarissa would kill me if I blew you up, Mark. Go."

"My mother would kill me if I left a lady in distress. You guys *get out of here!*"

There wasn't much I could say to that one. It was true. "So, back off a bit?"

"I'd rather be dead than maimed. I'll stay close. You guys still here?"

"Cap'n…"

"Go."

"Yes, sir. Here's your radio. Hang in there."

Mark knelt beside me. I was so cold I could feel his nearby body heat like a blaze. The whirring grew closer.

"214, you have to remove to the far side of the shielding. Hemmer can't get close to her," Mark's radio said. Mark shifted, removed the heat.

"That thing radio controlled?" I asked.

"Yeah. This good enough?" he asked the man handling the remote.

"Fine. Doc, can you hear me?"

"Yes."

"Good. Okay, now. I need you to relax. You'll feel the device at your knees. Then Hemmer will take the package. But you are not to let go of the package until Hemmer pulls it from your grasp. Understand?"

"Yes," I said. My trachea and bronchial membranes were scalded. My voice sounded raspy and dry. And there was a foul taste in my mouth.

Something bumped my knees. Startled, I joggled the package.

"Hold it steady, Doc."

"Sorry."

The package moved slightly. There were little whirrings and faint scraping sounds, as of metal or plastic against paper. And the envelope slowly slid from my grasp.

"Rhea?"

"It's gone. The package is gone."

"Stay still," Mark said.

Footsteps pounded down the passageway, slowing as they neared. Two strong hands gripped my arms and lifted. I tried to stand, but my legs failed to move. They were totally numb. "I can't—"

"It's okay, Doc. I gotcha." I was lifted, hefted into a fireman's hold, and carried down the hallway. The pain of the motion was so great that I couldn't contain the moan that escaped from me.

"Hey, Doc," the fireman said, his voice entirely too conversational.

"Yeah?" I said warily.

"Anyone ever tell you not to take gifts from strangers?"

I sighed as I was carried into the light. I had a feeling I was going to be picked on about this incident. And I could only agree that I deserved whatever I got.

I was carried directly to a waiting ambulance where I was doused with something wet. My clothes were stripped unceremoniously from me, and I was doused again. It was chillingly cold. My shivers increased, teeth chattering furiously. A hot blanket was wrapped around me, easing my cough. Another. Heat burned into my frozen bones. "Oh, God," I whimpered. "Oh, God." I was strapped to a stretcher as the ambulance chugged to life.

23

A SPLENDID EXAMPLE OF STALEMATE

I learned about my bomb and the hospital's reaction to it much later—long after Taylor Reeves had diagnosed my eyes as severely irritated but not blinded. Long after my X rays ruled out AVP. After Mark, Gil Adams and the sheriff finished grilling me, an interrogation that took place in front of God and everybody in the middle of the ER while I was examined, prodded and probed. And long after I was home, cloaked in an electric blanket on the living room couch, a fire blazing in the gas fireplace I hadn't known worked, a mug of Kenyan coffee in one hand, Marisa's hand in the other. She wouldn't leave my side.

Marisa and Miss Essie had been watching the news conference on CNN live and had seen me get up and leave the room. And Risa had panicked when the bomb threat was called, the Code Blue picked up by the camera boom. Miss Essie informed me that I nearly caused early labor, and told me in no uncertain terms that I should show more consideration for her old heart and Miss Marisa's baby. Sounding like a heavy smoker, I agreed that I had been unforgivably rude, and squeezed Marisa's hand when she smothered a giggle.

As we watched TV, Miss Essie and Arlana bustled around the house, putting on a pot of stew, baking cornbread, drinking coffee, answering the phone and sharing with their long list of family and friends the latest inside gossip. About me, natch.

CNN replayed the bomb scare for hours, describing how the nearest section of the Nursing Center had been evacuated, the wing emptied. Patients in wheelchairs and on beds had been piled into hallways. Outside, fire crews forcibly pushed aside vehicles that were blocking fire lanes and wreckers towed violators, many that belonged to the media themselves.

For the hour during my ordeal, and the several hours that followed, news crews fought to find access onto the premises, worked to contrive exclusive interviews, or find sources that would give them the inside story. They were clearly pains in the hospital's collective butts. If I had been in front of the ER trying to triage patients and keep reporters from getting in the way during an emergency, it would have been more than infuriating. I was sure that they drove the employees nuts until the news conference reconvened in the parking lot much later that day.

According to an exclusive interview with an FBI spokesperson—Agent Angel, looking official and downplaying the entire incident—no one had made it to the roof. Strep enterotoxin had not been spilled into the ventilation system by neo-Nazi terrorists. Of course not. Not with the FBI on the scene. The only chemicals involved were the mix of ammonia, bleach and dry ice, a quick and easy way to keep us occupied while Ellis got away. And the terrorist used hospital cleaning supplies for most of that. Empty bottles of Clorox and household ammonia were found in the laundry. A small insulated box was found nearby, the words Caution, Dry Ice on the side. Ellis had mixed the bleach and ammonia together in an empty, heavy-duty biohazard waste container, then, as he approached me while I was on the phone, dropped in the dry ice. I was lucky I hadn't burned out my lungs on his vapor bomb.

The package Ellis had given me, which I tried so hard to keep level, was x-rayed in the parking lot by Hemmer, the area deserted except for members of the bomb squad perched behind heavy-duty protective screening. The picture revealed something delicate and metallic, yet nothing that looked like explosives, either traditional or chemical-based.

To be on the safe side, the bomb squad soaked the envelope in a bucket of water for an hour before Hemmer slit the package open. This part I saw on the late news, filmed with a telescopic sight.

My burned eyes were able to see for short periods of time between bandaging. I made the most of that time, grateful for the light. *I wasn't blind. I didn't have AVP.* The words were a whispered chorus in my mind.

What CNN didn't cover or didn't know, Mark told me. When the contents of my package were handed to Lieutenant Adams, they turned out to be a page of disintegrating paper, marked with water-damaged and illegible script, two driver's licenses, a wad of soggy cash, credit cards and some jewelry, including two necklaces with gold and silver angels dangling. Traces of blood were found in the chain links, blood that would later be identified as human. Some of the jewelry was engraved with initials, L.Y. or M.G.C. Jr., initials matching the driver's identification, proving that everything in the envelope had belonged to two people.

I never saw the jewelry. Only heard about it from Mark after he identified the contents of the envelope as belonging to Mel and Lia Campbell.

Richard Ellis had sent the belongings confiscated from my first two AVP patients. The man responsible for the kidnapping and torture had found it necessary to brag about it. To me. And my theories about the man blew away like a pile of ash.

The question was growing, looming large in the silence of my mind. Why did Richard Ellis single me out for his attention? I had no idea.

Over Wednesday night supper, Mark, Adams, Shirl and I tossed around possibilities while Marisa and Miss Essie listened. She served up asparagus casserole, chicken tenders, lima beans swimming in butter, salads, biscuits and raspberry cream cake, most of the ingredients carted over from the Braswell house. After my bomb scare, I wasn't particularly hungry, and my throat hurt to swallow, but I knew I needed calories to replace those lost to fear and stress. And so I ate the casserole—well-cooked, mushy vegetables, eggs and smoked oysters in Campbell's mushroom soup. It was Miss Essie's secret recipe.

The group of us sat at the table Miss Essie had pulled into the center of the kitchen and loaded with my good linens and china, silver and serving dishes. To save my eyes, candles had been lit throughout the kitchen, and the dancing flames bounced off glittering surfaces, the effect made sharper by the damage to my corneas. For once, my house looked almost festive. Outside, a Guardsman patrolled the grounds, weapon at the ready for a reappearance of Ellis, and to keep away any pesky reporters who wanted an exclusive.

"Maybe Ellis has a crush on you" was Mark's slightly snide answer to Ellis's interest in me. "Maybe he likes women who take candy from strangers."

"No, she's important to him somehow. Either she knows something, or she personally *is* something significant to him," Adams said.

"I never saw the man before," I croaked past my burned larynx. "I'd remember if I had. He has eyes like hot flames. Creepy."

"Not your type?" Mark asked.

"Not hardly."

"Perhaps Rhea prefers men who are the stolid and dependable types to the tall, blue-eyed and deadly ones. I know I do," Shirl said. "This Ellis sounds like a bit of an aggro."

"So where do we go from here?" Mark asked.

"Call Miss DeeDee," Marisa said, the words slurred.

"Whatever for?" Shirl asked. "I thought she was all to cock."

Beside me, Marisa shrugged helplessly, the words to explain her plea gone.

"I'm not calling Miss DeeDee," I said. "Not now, not ever."

"We'll figure this out without the help of that demented old bit—woman," Mark said. "She wasn't around this time. She couldn't have helped Ellis. She couldn't have directed Ellis to Rhea."

"Well, someone done sent out trouble looking for my Miss Rhea, that for shore. And you mens better be thinking on just how to stop 'em."

"Until your girlfriend thinks of a connection, we've got nothing," Adams said to Mark, his eyes slit with irritation.

Girlfriend? Stolid and dependable? I hid a sigh and put down my fork, what appetite I had now totally gone.

"What we have here, lads and lasses," Shirl said in her perpetually happy tones, "is a splendid example of stalemate. Fortunately, we have you keen and delightful gentlemen to solve it all for us."

Though my eyes were closed, I knew Shirl was fluttering her eyelashes at Gil, and laying a delicate and feminine hand on Mark's arm. I could have groaned.

Marisa stayed with Shirl and me that night, sleeping— what little sleep we got—on the far side of my bed. We three girls sat up most of the night, talking about boys. Literally. Though I was exhausted, I was too wired to sleep, and the unexpected jolt of caffeine in Marisa's system left her in a similar state. She had snitched a cup of the good stuff when Miss Essie wasn't looking. And as for Shirl, her excitement about moving nearby, taking a job with Carolinas Medical and seeing Cam in the morning when he flew in from Duke in North Carolina, had left her in a more manic condition than either of us. So we talked about boys. Or rather Shirl did.

Cameron Reston for the most part, but also the stiff-but-charming, Lieutenant Gilroy Adams, the available but somewhat distant, "stroppy" Taylor Reeves, and the "cheeky but charming" Mark Stafford, who was now confirmed as my hero-boyfriend. I knew Shirl. Now that Mark had brought the cavalry to save me and stayed by my side while an apparent bomb was taken from me, he had been elevated to hero status. And official boyfriend status. She would announce the relationship to all our friends via e-mail first thing in the morning, and by nightfall I would be inundated with queries and demands for details.

Up until a few days ago, it would have bothered me, having everyone know that I was dating again. Especially someone so different from John. And also, I realized on some level I wasn't particularly proud of, someone who wasn't a doctor. But every time I blinked, I could see the man, hulking down in the ill-fitting padded bomb clothing, staying with me and my package up to the very end.

Okay, so I was more trouble than I was worth. I could live with that. And that could change. Unlike John, who had tossed our plans in the crapper the first time his family came calling, Mark was his own man. And he let me be my own woman. Somehow, in the dark of night—with Shirl and Risa curled up on my bed, Shirl shaping and painting Risa's toenails, which she could no longer reach across pounds of baby, me sitting in the blindfolded dark—being my own woman was pretty important.

The next morning, I drank a Coke—sugar, calories, caffeine and all—for breakfast, as getting Marisa up, dressed and delivered safely to her door in the midst of an unexpected spring squall had taken a large bite out of my morning. When I got her inside safe and sound, Miss Essie gripped me by the collar and dragged me to the back of the house to change sheets. She had decided that Cam was staying with her and Marisa, not in some fleabag hotel, surrounded by press and reporters and such. My long arms were needed to help turn and freshen the mattress and linens that Mr. Wonderful would sleep on.

Miss Essie had made me change my own sheets when I had occupied the guest room. But then, to Miss Essie's mind, Cameron Reston was a hero for real. *He* would not lift a *finger* in *her* house. He had done the surgery and planned the rehabilitation that had given Miss Risa back to her. That made him deserving of being waited on hand and foot. At least for the first few hours of his visit.

While I wasn't last arriving to work, I was just barely on time. My lateness was becoming a habit. Wallace Chadwick had moved my triage equipment indoors, out of the blowing spring storm. The move was as much to protect the table as to protect the patients and my tender eyes from wind, but I appreciated the indoor air no matter what had precipitated the change of location.

And the first patient was a shocker.

She was brought in by ambulance, passed though the security cordon provided by the National Guard and sent on to the ER. Her accompanying cortege was kept off the property, though they abandoned cars at the barricade and waved raised fists in a vaguely threatening manner. Wearing sunglasses to protect my sensitive eyes, I stood at the windows and watched the odd group from the safety of the waiting-triage room. They were a curious mix, ethnically speaking. Blacks, whites, a sprinkling of Asians. But each appeared as a separate group, keeping a little apart from the others.

Wallace, looking morose, joined me at the window as the ambulance drove up under the hood. "Special patient of yours?" I asked. I couldn't think of another reason he would have left his packed ER.

"I guess she is." He shoved his new reading glasses up higher on his balding head and recrossed his arms across his chest. "Or at least her husband and that weird bunch of rabble-rousers out there thinks she is." The ambulance pulled to a halt and the driver jumped out. "Esmeralda Sexton. The wife of the Reverend Shackleford Lamb Sexton."

I remembered my confused questions from only two nights past. Questions about how a man could hide race hatred from the world. I was seeing how it could be done. By telling them to keep pure…

A tingling started in my fingertips…. Was this what the admiral had been alluding to and talking all around on the phone? Was the Lamb of God really bankrolling the production of the strep? If so, what was the connection between Ellis and Lamb? And if I opened my big mouth, would I ruin any plans set in place by Goldfarb? They had to prove that Lamb was involved in the creation and use of the strep enterotoxin. And here he was, the man they were all looking for. Were they ready for him? Had they expected him to show up here with a sick wife? Was Esmeralda Sexton ill with the strep enterotoxin?

I would have to sit tight and watch. And wait. Patience was not my best trait.

"Oh, goody," I said, rubbing my tingling fingertips against the rumpled cloth of my scrubs. "The Mrs. Lamb. Or would that be Mrs. Ewe? Sorry. Bad pun. Is she a television celebrity, too?"

"Bet she gets that a lot," Wallace chuckled, "and hates it. She has a daily children's program and a weekly women's Bible study program. Picture Tammy Faye Bakker without the looks." After a moment he added, "Celebrities suck."

"Want help?" Tammy Faye without the looks sounded entertaining. And if the admiral had something planned to bring in the Lamb, I wanted to see it take place. "It's quiet enough for the moment out here."

"Yeah, why not," he sighed, the sound as fatigued as I had felt only a moment ago.

"Have you had any sleep, Wallace?" I asked as we pushed through the doors into the ER proper.

"As much as anyone. I got two residents up here last night from Spartanburg Medical. They pulled twelve hours and will be back tonight for another shift. Then I have two new ones coming on."

"Everyone looking for a chance to see and treat the modern-day plague?" I asked, using the Lamb's own words.

"Something like that. I usually have to pull teeth to get ER coverage and now I have them coming out of the woodwork."

The stretcher carrying Mrs. Sexton bumped through the ambulance air lock and I turned to watch. The woman was covered with small purplish lesions, similar to but not exactly like the ones we had been seeing. And she was severely short of breath, breathing like a squeaking bellows. As they rolled, the EMS guys, all wearing heavy PPEs, spouted off vital signs, most of which were normal, though the patient's blood pressure was slightly elevated. Stress and fear would raise a pressure, so I didn't think that was a problem. It was possibly AVP and a form of ACS at the same time.

Standing back, I watched as the guys hefted the patient to an ER stretcher, broke their own down for cleaning and linen change and pushed it into the hallway. The RNs began to recheck vitals, hook the woman up to oxygen and attach EKG leads for a rhythm strip. Mrs. Sexton coughed again, pushing away the hands that tried to undress her. The cough wasn't the tearing-wet-linen sound, but something different. More like standard rales, as if her lungs were full of fluid. And her skin lesions were markedly different, too.

Approaching through the clot of people around the stretcher, I pulled the sunglasses off my nose to verify the purple color, and touched a lesion on the inside of her arm. Whereas previous patients showed flat reddish lesions, these were raised slightly, were definitely purplish, and when I applied a small amount of pressure to one, it moved, as if I had pressed on the skin of a water balloon.

"Wallace?" When I had his attention, I pressed again. Blood moved beneath the surface in a purple wave.

Our eyes met a moment, Wallace's deep brownish-green ones widening, darkening. The blood beneath the surface looked venous, not arterial. Had the strep mutated again?

"Let's get ABGs before she gets that oxygen," Wallace said, "DIC workup, blood cultures, CBC, a chem 18, a liver profile, and rainbow her if I left anything out. Rhea?"

"I can't think of anything else right now except do a chest film. And maybe a CT scan of her lungs. Her cough sounds different from most of our previous patients' and it may show something new."

"Do it," Wallace said. "And let's get this woman started on some FFP, two units of twenty-five percent albumin, and a standard AVP cocktail."

"Standard AVP cocktail? What's a standard AVP cocktail?" I asked.

"Antibiotic cocktail your friend Shirley came up with. It'll wipe out everything known to man. We started it on every one of the improving patients yesterday after you took off for the afternoon. By the way, how was your day off?"

"What a narky fellow," Shirl said from the doorway. "Is he always so bloody sarcastic?"

"He's the boss. He can get away with it."

"How are your eyes?" She moved into the room and pulled me out into the hallway. "You aren't wearing your mask, Dr. Lynch," she murmured.

"I can't wear a hepa-mask and sunglasses, too. They fog up."

Shirl gave a disbelieving please-try-to-come-up-with-something-original look of disapproval.

"Okay," I said contritely, pulling the hepa-mask from where it dangled around my neck up over my mouth and nose. "Better?" My glasses instantly fogged over.

"If it fogs, it isn't working. Come with me and I'll adjust it."

"But—"

"No buts. No excuses. You happen to be a champion in your own right at present. A rather foolish champion who takes candy from strange men and makes a bit of a martyr of herself, but a champion nonetheless. And that makes you a role model. You *shall* wear the mask and it *shall* fit."

Shirl pulled me into the waiting room, into the tiny room originally used for triage, and sat me down on the stretcher, much as she might have prodded a child. When did all my friends become so pushy? "You shove your sister around like this, it's no wonder she went in for piercing and tattooing. Sibling rivalry and childhood rebellion make a nice medley."

"Are you calling me bossy?"

"Yes, ma'am, I am."

"Well, hush." Shirl removed my glasses, tucking them into a pocket of my lab coat before she began pressing and pushing the edges of the hepa-mask into my jawline with bruising fingers. Finally satisfied, she reached into a pocket for the sugar-water used to test the fit, stepped aside and sprayed.

As she moved, I could see through the far waiting room window into the parking lot. An altercation was taking place between three Guardsmen and several followers of the Reverend Lamb of God.

I only saw the two together for a second, the Reverend Lamb and a young, buff, buzz-cut kid in camouflage and army-discard greens. But it was long enough. It was a familiar-shaped head. One I had seen very recently. And suddenly I understood why I was so important to Ellis.

The kid with the Lamb was the same head I had seen in church on Easter Sunday, bending over the balcony railing.

It was also the same head that had been driving the red getaway truck the day Ellis had tried the navy-officer stunt. His was a head I had seen often over the years since Marisa married. He was Eddie Braswell. Marisa's stepson.

24

Grabbing Shirl's wrists, I held her hands away from my face. "It was Eddie," I said. "Eddie all along, with both of them." She didn't understand the import, and I was too disconcerted to try to explain what the relationship meant to me. Still holding her hands, I slid from the stretcher to my feet.

"It fits. All of it," I whispered into her startled face. "The information that Rear Admiral Goldfarb told me about Leon Hawkins and the National Guard unit he was with in the Gulf War. The canisters in the warehouse…and the fact that Leon worked there. The tattoos the sheriff said have been showing up all over Dawkins County for several months. The fact that the Patriot groups keep splintering off, and 'some are more violent than others,'" I paraphrased Sheriff C. C. Gaskins. "Splinter groups. Random occurrences. Random bits of a whole," I whispered, "that weren't random at all."

"Rhea?" Shirl asked.

I dropped her wrists and ripped off my mask. "The fact that Eddie Braswell knows both Ellis and the Lamb. And is possibly a member of both groups. Mark told me that Eddie was spouting scripture…."

"Rhea! You saw something, didn't you? Crikey. Through the bleedin' window?"

I turned away from her, putting it all together in my mind. The groups intersected for years, beginning in the Gulf War.

And through Eddie to me. All this I understood in the instant I dove for my bag and the cell phone in the bottom.

Shirl watched me with wide eyes. "What did you see?"

The cell phone wasn't there. Where had I put it?

She looked through the doorway, which was empty. "What did you see, Rhea? Who is Eddie?" When I didn't reply, her foot started tapping. "Are you looking for your moby?"

I didn't bother to say yes. Moby equals mobile phone? Had to be. Dropping my hepa-mask, I dumped my bag onto the floor, its contents spilling wildly. Plastic, rubber-tipped instruments, medication samples clattering.

"Bugger it all, I am not a patient person, Rheane Rheaburn Lynch." Her feet tapped with increasing impatience. "At some point, and *soon*, you shall find the time to explain this to me. Nod yes." The tap tapping of her foot increased in speed.

Nodding, I found my phone in the pile, hit the power button and Redial for Mark.

"Sod you, what the devil is going on?" Tap, tap, tap.

The Lamb was raising a ruckus that I could hear through the heavy fire doors separating my little alcove from the ER proper. I ran to the doors and glanced through. In the hallway stood the Reverend Sexton. He had made it free of the security cordon, unaccompanied by Eddie, another buzz-cut youth, and the other man he had tried to sneak in. Blocking the stretcher holding his wife, he called on God to heal her, called on angelic protection. And damned himself all at once. It was a weird mix of language, and if I hadn't been trying to get Mark on the line, I might have slipped back again to enjoy the show. I let the doors swing shut.

Looking up, I saw Eddie Braswell standing at the window, staring in at me. He was wearing a small smile. There were no Guardsmen near him, trying to get him to move back.

Mark's line beeped a busy signal. My hands started shaking.

"Rhea?" Shirl asked, her strong voice unusually tentative. "Who is that?"

Wallace shouted, "Get those cameras out of here!"

Time seemed to drag, achieving that weird perspective of adrenaline overload where seconds seemed to take minutes, and minutes forever. I heard Guardsmen in the ER with Wallace, trying to restore order. That meant that no one was directly outside, protecting the ER entrance.

Eddie spun and headed to the doors. And he wasn't alone. The shaved-head youth was still with him. And the older white male, this one with a pierced lip and a tattoo of a snake crawling up his neck from inside his army-green jacket.

Mark's line was busy again. I dialed Lieutenant Adams's cellular as I once more stepped over and peeked through the ER doors. The Lou's line was busy. The two pals having a confab? I was shaking all over with sudden cold that had nothing to do with the frosty outside wet. I dialed the admiral's number, hoping I remembered it correctly.

The stretcher holding the Lamb's wife was still in the hallway, likely on her way to radiology for her chest film and CT scan. Lamb was laying one hand on his wife, gesticulating with the other, shouting. "No! *Goud*, hear me! Hear me! I called for your pro*tec*tion! Your *holy* protection, as at the time of the Angel of Death in Egypt. You promised that the death would *pass over* the true believers!"

The Lamb's God wasn't the same Divine Being that Marisa worshipped. I didn't know much about God, but that much I understood.

A recorded voice came over the phone telling me I had dialed incorrectly. Great. I dialed 911. The phone rang.

An unarmed Guardsman grabbed Lamb by the neck of his jacket, shoving him to the floor. Another Guardsman had swung his weapon forward, a big black gun that looked like it would do serious damage. Rubber bullets? Crowd control ammunition? I hoped so. The cameraman danced out of reach, still filming, his lips pulled back in a rictus grin.

Through the ER ambulance doors, I spotted Rear Admiral Goldfarb. "Yes!" I said.

"This is 911. Do you have an emergency?"

"Yes."

The cameraman wheeled. There was a reddish rash on the inside of his wrists.

As I turned, Eddie took the phone. Ended the transmission. With a single motion, he shut the ER doors, cutting off my vision of the admiral. Had he seen me? I didn't think so. Eddie was bigger than I remembered. Taller. Wider. The sickly, drugged-out boy from only a few months past was no more. Fear gripped me in ragged claws.

"Rhea-Rhea." His voice was pitched soft, full of warning. His dark eyes held a strange combination of pleading and determination. Metal glinted at his neck, a series of gold and silver angels, like those worn by the Campbells and given to me in Ellis's package.

"Eddie," I whispered.

He had a rough tattoo of a cross on his left hand, visible as he handed the phone to Shirl. "Ma'am," he said to her, "Dr. Lynch will be gone for a little while."

"She is going *nowhere* with you, you bloody bastard," Shirl said. Her eyes were the size of hubcaps, her few freckles vivid against her suddenly pale skin. "Rhea?"

Eddie took my right elbow in a paralyzing grip. My fingers went numb.

At Eddie's nod, the other young man took Shirl's arms and pushed her toward the small triage room. Shirl struck out, hitting him in the face. "You sodding—" With a quick shove, he rammed her into the room. I saw her fall back, her horrified eyes meeting mine for a bare instant just before she landed with a thump and he shut the triage door. The sound was a hollow thud of compressed air, cutting off Shirl's shrill scream.

Patients began to take notice; one man stood, eyes curious. If I shouted, would they help? Or would Eddie Braswell pull a weapon and start shooting? Did he even have a weapon? Did I dare take that chance?

I remembered the fear-laden eyes in his haunted face only a few months past. He had assaulted more than one woman…. I opened my mouth to call for help.

Eddie's grip on me tightened. "Don't," he said shortly. Fear rose in a wave of nausea. The other man took my left elbow, his fingers only slightly more gentle. Together, each holding me by an arm, they ushered me out through the doors into the blustery air. The unforecast rainstorm was gone and the sun broke through the clouds. Light coruscated painfully and I closed my eyes against the brilliance, stumbling. I thought to call out, but I had no breath. My scream emerged, a strangled whisper as I fell.

Eddie caught me. Righting me, his pace increased and I stumbled again. "Rhea, stop this," he demanded, his grip tightening on my arm.

"My eyes are hurt. I need my sunglasses," I whispered.

"Where?" he asked.

"Lab coat pocket."

A moment later, the glasses slid onto the bridge of my nose. And I was shoved into the dark recesses of a van, a hand on the top of my head to protect it from being bumped. Blinded from the too-bright light and the sudden darkness, I couldn't see but had the sensation I was not alone. As my eyes adjusted to the lack of light, the van started up, pulling away. Wheels squealed for a second, and I lurched into the aisle with the force of a turn. I jerked, sliding across the seat.

An iron-hard arm circled my waist and pulled me back

into the seat. Panic shuddered through me. The arm stayed in place around me, pulling me close to his heated body. His other arm crossed in front of me, fiddling at my hip. I tensed, ready for the assault that had to be coming. The man was fevered, his breath hot against my neck.

He pulled the seat belt across my lap and strapped me tightly in, the belt clicking sharply in place. He slid away. Fear whooshed out of me in a half-gagging sound.

"You are a troublesome woman, Dr. Lynch."

I knew that voice. Cold shivered up from my bowels. For a moment I struggled to breathe. All the things I thought I understood flooded into the forefront of my mind, arranging themselves into a rational pattern. I thought I now knew what was going on. But what if I was wrong?

My heart beat against my ribs like a caged animal fighting for freedom. I took a sustaining breath. "How so, Mr. Ellis?" My voice was so calm. So in control. So unsurprised. On some level, I was all those things. And I wasn't sure why. Stupidity? Bravado?

I closed my eyes, trying to give them time to adjust. Somewhere in front of me, someone lit a cigarette, the acrid smell following a click of a lighter and crackle of burning paper and tobacco.

"Turn here," he directed the driver, calm with accustomed command. The van swayed. This time I was prepared, and used the support of the seat belt to keep me in place. "Left here. Good. Circle through this area, but stay away from the highway." We hadn't gone far. We had to be within a few miles of the hospital, probably in a residential section of DorCity.

"You didn't open or deliver my package," Ellis said.

"You told me to keep it level. Told me I couldn't open it till you were gone. Sounded like a bomb to the police."

"So I gathered from the news," he said wryly. "And my note in the package with the Campbell couple's belongings?"

"Soaked down to pulp." I opened my eyes behind my glasses, took in my surroundings with peripheral vision. I was in a panel van, the side walls dark blue. There were three rows of seats: the front bench seat with a driver and Eddie as passenger, the half bench seat in the second row, where I sat with a fevered body beside me, and the full bench seat behind, where Ellis lounged. The only windows were at the windshield, driver and passenger doors.

No one would see me inside. Even if I unhooked the seat belt and tried to get free, no one would know I was in danger unless I actually made it out of the van. "You should have put it in a plastic bag," I said, and then wanted to bite my tongue. Big-mouthed woman, telling a terrorist how to do his business better. I was in trouble. Real trouble. It was time to watch my words. Carefully.

"Take off her glasses. I can't see her face."

The heated arm reached close and grasped my sunglasses at the frame around the right lens. Ripped them off my face. I got a glimpse of a snake tattooed around his wrist, emerald-green scales and scarlet forked tongue flashing. The brilliant green-and-red pigments achieved only in the Orient. Nothing like the crude stars I had been seeing.

Ellis studied me. My eyes were still red from the fumes of the previous day, my skin still blotchy. I had put some old moisturizer on the tender places and smeared on antibiotic gel. But I knew what I looked like. I wouldn't be using my looks to get out of this mess.

Ellis sighed, ran a hand across his flat-topped scalp. He was rumpled and worn, his uniform looking loose and in need of washing. My eyes had adjusted enough for me to see the blotches on the back of his hands as he replaced them in his lap. The blotches also moved out of his collar and up his neck, much like the snake tattoo worn by the other man. But these were no tattoos. These were lesions. Lesions caused by the bacteria he had released into the world. *Serves him right,* a soft voice whispered inside my mind.

Richard Ellis was a sick man. Very sick. And he had to know just how sick.... Why hadn't he used the antibiotic? Why hadn't the Lamb's wife? Was there one? Had it not worked? Or was I totally wrong in my assumptions?

He regarded me with tired blue eyes, their former light dimmed.

"Did Eddie send you to me?" I asked.

Ellis inclined his head in affirmation.

"The package was supposed to go to Lieutenant Adams, wasn't it?" I asked. "To explain what was happening."

"After you opened it. Read the note. Yes."

I put things together in my mind. "The antibiotic didn't work, did it? The one made by the guy who created the strep enterotoxin." Surprise flashed across his face, surprise and something else. Anger? Before I could identify it the reaction was quickly shuttered away. "Or there never was one," I speculated. But Ellis was prepared this time and didn't react. "And now you're too sick to wait. You need my help. Directly."

A smile quirked his lips. Without telling me whether there had been a failed antibiotic or no antibiotic at all, he said, "Troublesome, but perspicacious."

Fancy word, perspicacious. The word of a learned man, not a thug. Fear, which had been receding for the last several minutes, withdrew to the deeper parts of me. Not vanquished, but waiting. My hands, which had not stopped shaking, I balled into fists. Ellis needed me. Needed me alive. "You didn't kill the Campbells, did you?"

"No."

"And Eddie wears the necklace because…?"

"Respect," Eddie spat, turning his head. "And a warning to the guys who hurt them."

"And Leon Hawkins? Did you kill him?"

"No. Not personally. Nor did I order it done."

"But you knew about it...." It was only intuition. And not the kind of intuition I trusted. Medical intuition was based on training, a bedrock of knowledge, and years of experience. This was woman's intuition. Not a well-honed instinct with me. "You merged with a splinter group, a group much more violent than yours, and together melded with the Lamb's more violent followers. I assume he has violent followers? Splinter groups?"

"Oh, yes," Ellis said, amused at my thread of logic. "He has them. And they have been using him, and he them for years."

"You let all those things happen...the Campbells getting tortured, the castration in the jailhouse..." my voice trailed off to a whisper "—so you wouldn't expose yourself."

Blue eyes giving nothing away, Ellis inclined his head, adjusted his legs on the bench seat. Muscles bunched beneath his fatigues. "I knew the Campbells were being kept. But I couldn't find them. I'd have kept Leon alive if I had known he was in danger. I stopped what I could without giving myself away."

"Tattoos? The blue stars?"

"Not mine. A splinter group of the Hand of the Lord. And now that you've seen the sores on me you understand I need your help." Ellis extended his hands, exposing his wrists. Purple lesions crawled up the inside.

"Good deductions, Doctor. If you agree to do as I ask, then you will be put down at the side of the road, unharmed, with your phone, so you can call for help. And before you ask that clichéd line about how can I trust you, let me say simply that I have no one else to trust and I'm out of time."

I took another of the scarce breaths and said, "I think I'm beginning to understand. Tell me what you want me to do."

"He wants *what?*" Mark shouted, sounding stunned.

"He wants to turn himself in," I said as calmly as possible, stuffing a finger into my open ear to block the sound of Wallace ranting and Shirl shouting English imprecations, and Rear Admiral Goldfarb giving orders and demanding answers. The small office that ER on-call doctors used was far too full of angry people for me to hear well.

Through the phone I could hear a cacophony of sirens. Mark and most of the county's police force responding to the news of my kidnapping—which had been brief, pointed and totally lacking in ransom notes, shackles, small enclosed spaces, or any of the heinous, more romanticized aspects of popular kidnapping accounts. Thank God. "To you and to me, not to the FBI. He's sick. He wants medical treatment. I told him I could arrange that."

"And the canisters?" Mark shouted again.

"I'm not deaf," I shouted back, unbridled anger in my tone. My hands were still shaking. *I* was still shaking. I turned my head away from the others in the small room.

"Sorry," Mark said, softer.

"Ellis says he doesn't have the canisters, but he knows where they are. I think I can get him to tell me their location. All you have to do is bring in your listening equipment and set it up outside the room I put him in. But he was serious. No Feebs, Mark. And Goldfarb has to keep his men out of the way, too."

"That I can't guarantee. The FBI has to be present when that listening equipment is used. Supreme Court ruling. Maybe he doesn't know that. And I'm not going to tell him."

"All your talk at the restaurant about using the equipment was a scam? A reason to get a rise out of me?" The remnants of fear flared, feeding my anger. "I made a *promise* to him, Mark."

"And you did your best to follow through. It's not in your hands," he said even softer, understanding. "You didn't want us out playing cops and robbers without any restraint. The Supreme Court gave it to you. In spades. The FBI will have to be there.''

Shirl tapped me on the back, gripped both of my shoulders and turned me around, staring at me with mutinous eyes. I had refused to tell her the details of my abduction until I spoke to Mark. ''Ellis asked me to get Gil Adams on site, too,'' I said. ''He claims he needs to be debriefed about several Middle Eastern terrorist groups. I tried to call Gil, but I can't get through to him.''

''You tried to call Gil? Before me?''

''Don't gripe. Your blasted line has been busy for ages. Both of them.'' As I spoke, I sidestepped Shirl and strode the three paces from one wall to the other and back, ignoring the booted feet of my own newly appointed personal Guardsmen, Johnson and Sterns, dodging Shirl, who perched on the desktop to get out of my manic way, and moving around the admiral, who took up space the way a mountain takes up space. Immovable. Implacable. ''If they hadn't been, I might have gotten you *before* I was stuffed inside a van with a bunch of shaved-head Nazi types.''

Shirl tapped again. *What?* I mouthed.

Sod you, she mouthed back.

Grinning, suddenly exhausted, I sat down on the desk. She plopped back down again, her rump to the right beside me, pushing me over an inch. The two Guardsmen who had picked me up on the side of the road a half mile from the hospital and brought me in, appointing themselves my personal attendants, moved closer, along with Rear Admiral Goldfarb, who perched beside me on the left. Wallace stood farther back, watching, dark face grave.

''My ETA to the hospital is two minutes. Where are you?''

''My office.''

''Stay there,'' Mark ordered, and cut the connection.

Slowly, I dropped the phone to my lap.

''That sounded like it went well,'' Goldfarb drawled. I

snorted and met his gaze, which was in sharp contrast to his tone. The admiral's eyes were a shade of hazel that looked like pond water reflecting back the moon. A sort of yellowish brown that seemed to pull in all the light and cast it back. In his unsmiling face they seemed cold and hostile, sterile as the moonscape. "Charlie said you were a woman with a mind of her own."

"I'm doing my best to keep my word." Now that the kidnapping crisis was over, the remaining energy leached out of my system. The room around me darkened. I sank from the desk to the padded chair and put my head between my knees. The tiny office was too crowded for its size and the amount of fresh air it could hold. Goldfarb, Shirl, Wallace, Johnson and Sterns, all using my oxygen. "I made a promise."

Above me, Shirl took my wrist and counted, two fingers on my pulse point. I could have told her my heart rate was weak and thready.

"A promise made to a madman," Goldfarb said. "A promise you can't keep."

"Not mad." I lifted my head two inches and stared at the admiral from knee height. I didn't know the admiral well. Didn't know how he would take my statement. "But then, you know that."

After a moment, Goldfarb nodded. Turning to the Guardsmen, he said, "Resecure the perimeter. Notify your commanding officer that the doctor is back safely, and ask him if he would be so kind as to join me here, in the doctor's office."

Though they couldn't have been happy about being sent away from the excitement, they said "Yes, Sir," smartly, and left the room. A draft of fresh air blew in and I raised my head a bit more. The room no longer darkened, but Shirl did not release my wrist.

"NIS has a plan to bring him in."

"Did NIS expect the Reverend Lamb of God to be on

hospital property? Did NIS expect for Lamb to be infected with his own bacteria?''

The admiral's eyes widened fractionally as if he were suddenly processing information at a high rate of speed. "He's got the bug?"

"He's got it. I'm sure of it. And he hasn't taken any miracle antibiotic to cure himself or his wife.''

The admiral's eyes widened again. "I'm not in charge of this operation. NIS is. I'm only here as an observer, because you got me involved.''

I hadn't known that. "Maybe," I said. "But I bet you're the highest ranking officer here. And the fact that you know something NIS doesn't means that you could step in…. You have to let Ellis do this his way.''

"Why?" he asked, the sound explosive.

"Because he worked for it! Because he's ready to come in! He's sick. And there is no miracle cure. There never was one. You have to let him do what he wants.''

Slowly, the admiral said, "Maybe. Within reason.''

"He wants to come in.''

"He's been out far too long. He was ordered to come in two years ago.''

"He says he couldn't. He was too close.''

"Evidence suggests that he went over the edge before that.''

Shirl jumped from the desktop, dropped my wrist and stepped between my chair and the admiral, hands fisted on her hips. "One of you two bloody, blathering idiots will tell me what is going on, and tell me now," she shouted up into his face.

I sighed and sat up fully, resting my head on the raised back of the desk chair. "Richard Ellis was undercover with several hate groups after the Gulf War, trying to track down the biochemist creator of the strep enterotoxin, or the men responsible for conscripting him and sneaking him into the States. By the time Ellis found the man, he had died, and his job was taken over by someone else. Ellis went over the edge when he allowed the use of the bacteria in the club in Charlotte.''

''He went over the edge long ago,'' Goldfarb corrected more mildly, his eyes still pinning me to my chair. ''And I suppose you think it acceptable to discuss potentially dangerous, classified, United States defense secrets in front of a U.K. national?''

''You want to try to get her to leave? Help yourself.''

Goldfarb glanced at Shirl.

''Lay a hand on me and I'll scratch out your bloody, soddin' eyeballs, stripes and stars or no. And I'll lay odds that your son would assist me in that endeavor if he were here,'' she finished, her tone sizzling.

''Charlie would at that,'' Goldfarb agreed with a faint smile. ''But then, Charlie always was a rabid, tree-hugging liberal.''

''You going to help me bring Ellis in the way he wants?'' I asked.

''I am. Against my better judgment.''

A tiny thrill of success zinged through me, giving me energy where I had none. Putting a hand on the desk to stabilize my balance, I stood. ''Then we have work to do.''

Mark tracked me down in the room I had promised Ellis. I waved the cop away, not wanting anyone who might know him to see him. He motioned his understanding and pointed down the hall. I nodded my agreement and went back to work.

The room was a cramped, multibed ward unlike any this, or any other hospital, had seen for nearly twenty years. Long ago, when I was still in diapers, five or six patients might share a hospital room, toilet, nurse and, of course, germs. Now, with deadly patient-to-patient infections so prevalent, almost every hospital room in the country was a private room. Until now. The epidemic had changed that overnight.

Admitted against their will, the Reverend Lamb Sexton, his cameraman and his second-in-command were in the one narrow room. There were still two empty beds. And the Lamb was not happy with the accommodations.

"I will not be kept in this room," he said, his famous voice resonating against the walls. "I want to talk to my *own* doctor. He'll get me out of here. You hear me? I want Dr. Reeves!"

Most patients thought their personal physicians would give them preferential treatment, and so demanded that the physician appear instantly, like a rabbit in a magic show. From what I knew of Reeves, he would not be overly generous with anyone.

I tuned the Lamb out as the negative-pressure device came on and roared softly. Tired, overworked nurses and respiratory therapists came and went, starting IV lines, fluids, giving shots. In true nursing style, they, too, ignored the useless complaints, making soothing but unsatisfactory noises, promising nothing, abiding by the old nursing axiom, "If you can't fix it, pass the buck to the doctor."

At least two of the hospital personnel were undercover navy officers playing nurse, wearing the ID used by Staffers, a roving nurse-finder company out of Charlotte. They looked confident, if not competent. Waiting for their chance to nab Ellis. But Ellis was actually the secondary target. They also hoped to find evidence against the man Ellis had tracked for so many years. The man in the bed who was causing so much disturbance. Finishing with the new patients, I left the room, turning them over to Taylor Reeves, who nodded to me on his way in.

Following my out-of-uniform-cop-sort-of-boyfriend down the hall, I ducked after him into a niche created when the wing was added and the contractor didn't abide by the architect's plans.

"I told you to stay in your office," he said, glaring at me from the back of the niche.

My pleasure at seeing him died hard. "Well, excuse me for breathing." I whirled and started to leave.

Mark gripped my arm, stopping me. When I turned back to him, his eyes were closed against hidden emotions, his mouth tight with anger and fatigue, his eyes ringed with loss of sleep. "I'm sorry," he said carefully. "I'm…sorry." Opening his eyes, Mark let the official cop-face slide away, let me see inside for a brief instant. The exhausted vulnerability and foreboding mirrored there surprised me. "I know I took longer than the two minutes I told you," he said. "Gil Adams had some information he needed to give me. You know about the Lamb?"

"He was in the Guardsman unit with Leon Hawkins in the Gulf War," I said slowly, intensely aware of his hand on my arm. His palm was warm and steady through the layers of clothing. The hard core of my anger began to melt, revealing some other emotion. One I had no time to analyze. "It appears that he helped hide the strep enterotoxin. He probably knows the name of the biochemist who created it. And he surely has to know where the canisters are now, and who is making new strep. Goldfarb is willing to put Ellis in the room with the Lamb in the hope that we can get the Lamb to tell us more about what's going on. Ellis is undercover for NIS. Has been for years."

Something changed in the depths of Mark's eyes as some small click of information fell into place, like the tumblers of a lock when it finally opens. "How long have you known all this?" he asked, his hand tightening on my arm. Suspicion had replaced the vulnerability.

Anger and something that might have been shame made me jerk away. "I started figuring it out when I heard what the contents of Ellis's bomb package really were. Or did you think I knew from the very freaking beginning?"

Mark's face was still hard as he nodded. "Okay. Yeah." He stuffed the hand that had held my arm into his jeans' pocket. "I thought you knew something. Maybe. The way he kept showing up around you."

I laughed and the sound wasn't amused. "I confess. I was having a wild fling with Ellis, leading you astray, letting people *die*." The unreasoning anger I couldn't fully understand whipped through me like a small, hot flame. "You *ass*," I hissed.

Two lab techs passed the small niche, gossiping. At the word, they glanced in at us and hurried away.

A shadow of annoyed amusement quirked Mark's mouth beneath his mustache. "I'm not handling this very well." He scrubbed his face with his free hand, palm rasping against beard that was much more than a five-o'clock shadow. "Let me rephrase. Would you be kind enough to tell me what is going on and how you figured it out?"

I looked away, suddenly uncomfortable. This was the part that made shame squirm just under my skin. The part that prompted the anger I couldn't seem to control. Mark wasn't going to like what I had to say. "When Goldfarb first called me I learned that Leon was in the Guards with the Lamb in the Gulf War."

Instantly, Mark's eyes went flat and cold. Though he didn't move, he seemed farther away from me, and I crossed my arms, gripping them with my hands.

"And I didn't tell you. Actually, I only guessed it. Asked Goldfarb. And though he didn't exactly answer, he strictly forbade me to tell anyone. And then when Ellis, um, *requested* that I join him in his van, I found out the rest." Mark said nothing. "I couldn't tell you, Mark. Goldfarb said it was national security."

My anger was gone, and now that it was, I could see the emotion clearly. Anger had been a scam to cover my own sense of discomfort and uncertainty. I should have told Mark, despite what Goldfarb requested. I should have trusted him enough to know that he wouldn't screw up whatever Goldfarb had planned for bringing Ellis in. And I hadn't.

When I looked into Mark's eyes, he wasn't really there. He was shielded from me. I was aware that something fragile had broken between us, like the stem of a fine crystal glass in clumsy fingers.

Motioning me into the hall again, Mark escorted me back toward the room where Ellis was being admitted, and where the Lamb waited. I moved after him on legs that felt wooden. I had screwed up, and I knew it. Hot guilt engulfed me.

I opened my mouth to apologize but Mark cut me off, his voice containing no inflection. "The FBI, with the assistance of the NIS, has the listening equipment set up. You'll be glad to know that none of us lowly local cops will be involved in the acquiring of evidence or the capture of Ellis and the Reverend Sexton, only the bureau and Naval Investigative Service. And I assure you, ma'am, that no one's rights will be violated."

"Mark, I'm sor—"

Turning sharply on a heel, he wheeled away, severing my plea without a word.

"I wasn't sure about anything," I called to his retreating back. "I was *guessing* most of it." When he didn't turn around, I said, "Oh *hell*, Mark, it was *woman's intuition!*"

He stopped at the phrase. He knew how I hated it. A moment later, he moved on without replying at all. Still silent, he entered the room next to the ward where the Lamb was and closed the door.

25

SOMETHING FRAGILE HAD BROKEN

Overhead, the hospital speakers blared "Code 99, ICU. Code 99, ICU. Code 99, ICU." From doors everywhere, nurses ran, heading toward ICU and the patient whose heart had stopped beating, or who had stopped breathing. I should go. I should join the code, attempt to save a life. Instead, I stood in the hall, flat-footed and alone.

Moments later, Goldfarb emerged from the room where Mark had gone, Gilroy Adams behind him. Goldfarb motioned me over. Moving through the suddenly deserted halls, I joined the men and caught a peek into the room as the door swung shut. There must have been twenty people in the room, but Mark wasn't in sight.

"Ellis has reached the emergency room. He and two of his men will be given a swift admission to a Dr. Byars and brought here," Goldfarb said. "No one knows what we have planned except for Wallace Chadwick, a few local cops and you. Would you like to sit with us and watch on the equipment?"

I nodded. At least I'd be in the same room with Mark. I followed the officers into the room adjoining Lamb's. Beds had been pushed to the sides of the room and were covered with papers, briefcases, black equipment. Wires trailed everywhere. A table held more equipment, including a blank TV monitor and redundant recording devices.

The panel in the wall against which a patient's bed usually rested had been removed, exposing more wires and the workings of the nurse call button, the inside of the TV remote, the electrical wiring system.

"Almost have video, sir," a voice said as the door closed behind us. "Need another five minutes."

The admiral nodded.

Over the speakers I could hear Reverend Sexton arguing with Taylor Reeves. "I want a private room, Taylor. I can afford to pay whatever it costs."

"I told you earlier, there are not enough negative-pressure units to allow each patient his own room. Forget it." Taylor's voice was not a syrupy tone, but a hard, ungiving tone not used by most medical professionals. The doctor needed a lesson in bedside manners—not that the Lamb was complaining. Instead he seemed to be negotiating.

"I paid for those units. And I want one of them. You can make it happen."

"Maybe I could. But I won't."

"How about a semiprivate room with my wife? That would put two of us together. It's the very least you could do. Under the circumstances."

"And what do you mean by that? Under the circumstances..."

There was still no video, only a flickering screen and the slightly staticky audio, but I pictured Taylor Reeves standing beside the Lamb, looking down on the man in his slightly bored way.

"I prepared for it. Spent thousands on the necessary equipment. And you didn't handle it properly. You didn't do your job. There's no antibiotic. You said there'd be an antibiotic!" Lamb's voice rose. "And now I've got it!"

"And here you are. Happy coincidence. A treatment has been found that might save you. If your men hadn't killed your pet biochemist, you might have gotten an effective antistrep out of him instead of a dud.''

Beside me, the video screen flickered. A faint click came over the audio, a crackle in time to the flicker on the video screen, the sound harsh in the tense room.

''I'll see what I can do about putting you and Mrs. Sexton together. And I'll check on you shortly.''

The patient door opened and closed. Taylor Reeves leaving the room...

Goldfarb looked at Special Agents Jim Ramsey, Emma Simmons and Howard Angel. All three shrugged. The admiral looked at Adams and Mark. ''Did I just hear what I think I just heard?''

''Yes, sir,'' Adams said, his eyes narrowing with victory. ''I think you did.''

Mark didn't look my way. I might as well not have been in the room. Quietly, I stood and let myself out into the corridor, leaving behind the PTBs and the audio of the Lamb griping to his cameraman.

My fingertips were tingling.

''If your men hadn't killed your pet biochemist, you might have gotten an effective antistrep out of him instead of a dud.''

If your men hadn't killed your pet biochemist...

Standing in the hallway, I stared unseeing at the far wall. A print of a Charleston scene during a hurricane hung there, the Battery being battered by high winds and foamed waves. A squeaking sound echoed from the bend in the hallway and I turned slowly as a stretcher came into view, Ellis sitting up on it, a strange man in scrubs pushing, a strange woman pulling and guiding, opening fire doors as they moved.

I remembered the vision of Ellis running through the caustic steam and fog as I held his package level, a joke to scare the lady doctor. Evidence inside that should never

have been wet down. Running and disappearing. Running.
Disappearing.

If your men hadn't killed your pet biochemist…

Running. Disappearing. Running…back on his heels, not
up on his toes.

I had seen Ellis run before. Long before the day in the
laundry.

The three didn't see me standing in the shadows as Ellis
was wheeled into the patient-ward room. With the Lamb.

Long ago someone had told me something about Leon
Hawkins…. What was it?

My fingertips itched, tingled, burned. What *was* it?

As if the memory had been primed and waiting for me
to need it, I remembered. One of the cops had described
Leon. *"…good job, was in the armed forces, National
Guardsman—in that unit with one of the new doctors,
what's his name?"*

I moved down the hallway, my running shoes silent.

"…in that unit with one of the new doctors…"

Running. Disappearing… Running.

Taylor Reeves stepped into the hallway from the niche.
The small place where I had stood with Mark, where I had
broken something precious and fragile. Reeves smiled at
me. "May I have a word?"

"I don't think so," I said. My fingertips felt seared. I
pulled them across the seams of my scrub pants. I felt oddly
frozen, awkward. Unable to think clearly. Suddenly cold…
Except for my fingers. *Running. Disappearing. Running…*
Slowly, it all came together for me. "I have to get back to
triage," I heard myself say. "I don't have time—"

"Take time," he said, gripping my arm. The same arm
Mark had held. But Taylor's hand was cold, not warm
through the layers of clothing. "I'll walk with you. We have
a few minutes. And after all the months I've been here, we
still haven't gotten to know each other, have we?"

I shook my head.

"They were listening to that conversation, weren't they?" he asked as he pulled me with him down the hallway. "The Admiral Goldfarb and all the NIS people, the FBI. In the next room?"

I swallowed. The hallways were strangely empty. The code had claimed them all.

From somewhere, a door opened. Closed. I risked a glance. But the hallway was still silent and empty behind me. No one was around. And the admiral and Adams and all the PTBs were in the room up the hall. With Mark. I was alone.

The thought shocked me. Understanding ripped through me. The analytical part of my mind finally set free.

Up on one toe, I rotated, jerking my arm away. As if anticipating the move, Taylor caught me, whirled me back against him. Yanked my arm up high, behind my back. Tendons and muscles pulled, ripped. Pain sizzled down my arm, immobilizing it. I gasped as tears filled my damaged eyes.

Something sharp jabbed me in the back. Medical training shot the information to me. Right side of the spine, between the tenth and twelfth ribs. A knife was poised to pierce my right kidney. Already, my skin had been nicked through my clothes.

"I thought so," he said, reading my expression. "You can tell me all about it later," he said with a half smile, his lips bending close to my ear. "But make a sound right now and you'll go down. Dead in seconds. They would never get the bleeding stopped in time, not in this Podunk little place."

He was right. A patient with a severed renal artery would bleed out in less than four minutes. Silently. The pain from a kidney stabbing, properly done, made it impossible for the victim to draw a breath or scream. Military men were trained to kill with a kidney strike, weren't they? Taylor's weapon penetrated just a millimeter more. White-hot agony shot through me. Taylor held me upright as my legs tried to give way.

We passed the nurses' desk. A ward secretary sat behind it, her head bowed over a chart, computer keys clicking as she placed orders into the system. I prayed she would look up. Then I realized that Taylor would finish me and kill her before she could react, and I prayed she wouldn't. She kept her head buried in the paperwork.

Something cold pressed damply against my skin at my back. Blood, cooling in the cloth of my long johns. Something hot trickled down my spine into the waistband of my scrubs, down my thigh, my calf. With all the layers I had on, I must have lost a lot of blood.

I remembered the sound of the door opening and closing behind me. Someone would come along. And soon. As soon as they figured that Reeves might get away. If I could leave a marker…

Before I could scrutinize the impulse, I twisted slightly, and Taylor pressed the knife deeper. Pain was like a burning ember. I stumbled hard, and the blade moved again. Blood splashed the floor at my feet.

A blood trail. Scarlet on the pale gray tile.

Taylor maneuvered me down the corridor toward Surgery, an empty section of hallway as all electives had been canceled due to the emergency. His feet rang hollowly. Mine were silent, as if I were not really there. My knees gave way. Tremors ran down the long muscles of my legs.

More blood splashed. Too much? I was finding it hard to breathe.

"I heard the sound of the wire as they tried to thread it through the wall," Taylor continued as the nurses' desk fell behind. "Audio? Perhaps video as well? All it would take is a small fiber optic or two, run through from the room next door, hooked up to a video monitor. Yes or no." The knife twisted.

"Yes," I whispered. "Audio and video. Both."

"For some reason they didn't have time to get it all hooked up and running. Because they were waiting for Dick," he concluded, thoughtfully.

Dick.... Richard Ellis.

"Which means that until Lamb started talking, they didn't know about me. Correct?"

I wanted to lie and couldn't. Pain was bringing the truth to my lips. "Correct."

"And all this means that Dick is Naval Intelligence? All this time?"

I nodded.

"He hoped to get us all three in the room together. Smart move. The man always was too smart for his own good. He's got the bacterium, doesn't he?"

"Yes," I whispered, my breath too fast. Too shallow.

"Well, that's no longer my problem. You're going to get me out of here."

"I saw you. Running with Ellis," I said, my breath beginning to speed up, "in the woods that day." Rapid pants escaped my lips. "You were the other man they needed to pull off the terrorism. The man who would know how to keep the strep enterotoxin from breaking down. The man who could make more. And who could make the antibiotic…"

"Not bad, except the antistrep didn't work. Let's go, little girl."

Little girl… Patronizing and condemning all at once. "To the canisters?"

"Cute," he laughed. "This isn't some silly TV drama where the bad guy tells all to the heroine. Or where the heroine lives." His body tight against mine, Taylor slammed me against a door, the emergency bar bruising my hip.

Frigid outside air flayed my skin as Taylor pushed me through the door into the special parking reserved for surgeons. Down the ramp. A single vehicle waited there, a brand new SUV. A big one the color of old blood.

The world wavered around me. Nausea rose. I gagged. Blackness closed in.

The knife pulled from my flesh and I fell. Found myself sitting in a car. Alone. Sight struggled to return from a pinpoint of light to full day.

I was in Reeves's SUV, the old-blood hood reflecting back afternoon sun. Something white and red moved outside the window. Taylor Reeves's white lab coat stained with my blood.

He'd never get all the stain out. Miss Essie would have to help. I gagged again, vomiting all over the driver's seat.

Groggily, I looked up at the building, beige and terracotta brickwork and stucco, brown-painted trim. Mark's face at the door, mouth open, eyes wide.

Odd, sharp sounds. Muffled. Gunshots?

A hole appeared in the windshield. I closed my eyes. The window beside my face exploded. Round and sharp shards of glass blasted me. I turned my head and blinked.

Taylor Reeves, his face in a rictus of surprise and pain, gripped the door and fell in toward me, over the remains of the broken window. Blood ran from his nose. Slowly his pupils dilated. His face relaxed. The expression of pain floated away, leaving only an indication of mild surprise. Taylor's head fell forward and bumped mine. Hard.

I slid into the floor of the SUV and let myself pass out.

26

GAVE YOU A TRAIL TO FOLLOW

A needle stabbed me in the hip. Sharp, exquisite, a thin sapling of pain in a forest of heavier agony. I groaned, retched again. Bright light speared into my eyes.

Violent shivers took me and I groaned with the torment they caused. "I see you're awake," a familiar voice said. "That shot should make you feel better in a few minutes. You got lucky. Stayed unconscious for the entire exam." *Exam?* And then it came back.

Stabbed. I had been stabbed.

I tried to rise up. Pain wrapped its arms around me, a strangling vine of misery.

"It's okay, Rhea. I'm here. You're safe." Mark's voice. Tender with concern.

"I'm cold," I whispered, my jaw begining to quiver. The chilled covers were stripped off. A hot blanket enveloped me and I groaned with pleasure, the shivers receding slightly. Nausea curdled in the back of my throat.

A needle punctured my arm at the brachial vein in the bend of my elbow. "Just a little blood, Dr. Lynch. I'll be done in a minute."

"I left you a nice trail in the hallway," I said through chattering teeth. "If I'm empty, go scoop up some of that."

"'Bout a gallon, it looked like to me," the lab tech said.

Beth. I was proud I placed the voice. "Splashed all over the floor and walls, half dried. Housekeeping is having a fit. Say they ain't gonna clean it up if the cops let it get any drier. But they got it sealed off for picture-taking and evidence-gathering. Right awful mess, you made."

Someone put on a second blanket, and Beth removed her needle, leaving the room. "Good," I said, feeling some of the blanket warmth seep into me.

"Good?" Mark said shortly. "You nearly bled to death."

I could hear the anger in his voice. And the fear. I almost smiled, my eyes closed. The narcotic was beginning to work. "Gave you a trail to follow."

After a long second Mark said, "You did that on purpose.... Got yourself stabbed so we could follow you?" He sounded strange. Not surprised exactly. More like he had added a final, odd-shaped piece to a puzzle and was seeing the full picture for the first time.

I sighed as the agony began to flow away. *Nice, nice drugs. So nice.* Sleep whispered seductively to me.

From behind me, someone pulled at the tape near my wound. I made a soft sucking sound of warning, but the fingers that examined me were gentle and competent. Wallace spoke. "You're going to live. The wound isn't deep, only about fourteen millimeters, though you may have some nerve damage, muscle and or tendon damage, skinny as you are. Too early to tell. You'll need rehab. Of more immediacy, your hemoglobin's dropped to eight. You need blood."

"No," I said simply. "Not till it's six." I could heal with an eight-gram hemoglobin, albeit slowly, and not risk hepatitis. Or worse.

"I figured you'd say that." Wallace pulled the covers back over me and patted my arm. "And thank you for leaving me short-staffed in the middle of an epidemic. I expect you back at work in a week."

"Terribly sorry," I said as he turned away. But I wasn't

really, and I was sure he heard the lie in my tone. I slipped closer to the edge of sleep.

"Rhea?" Mark, calling me back. "I said, did you do that on purpose...? Get yourself stabbed so we could follow you?" Wonderment. That was what I was hearing. Weird.

"I heard you." I licked my dry lips with a dry tongue. I needed water. But I knew they'd never let me have any, not when I was nauseous. It would just make me sicker. "Wasn't my idea. He'd already broken the skin. I heard the door open and close up the hall. Knew someone would be coming eventually. Only thing I had to show where I was, was blood. I was in trouble. So, let him stick the knife in a li'l bit deeper. Lucky it was you. Jus' lucky," I mumbled half incoherently.

My pain was still there but had grown fuzzy around the edges. Mark held my hand, cradling it in his warmth. Against the stark blackness of my eyelids, I saw blood splatter from Taylor Reeves. Saw his head fall toward mine.

"Reeves?"

"Dead," Mark said shortly.

"The others?" Only it came out more like "Da obers?" and I wanted to laugh.

"Lamb and Richard Ellis are under guard. The FBI is rounding up their 'friends' from the various compounds for questioning."

I squeezed his hand to let him know I was still listening, even though my breathing had slowed, and my eyes would no longer attempt to open.

"Feebs and NIS think they got the more violent ones cornered in a barn Ellis told us about on the Patriot compound. Ellis says that's where the remaining canisters are located, so it makes sense that they'd be there, too."

I stretched my lips to make them work. They felt numb. "I been out a while?"

"A couple hours."

"Eddie?" I whispered, my question so soft I wasn't sure he could hear.

"Turned himself in. Says he'll turn state's evidence for immunity and dropped charges in any previous cases."

"And?" It came out, "An-duh." My tongue, like my lips, was no longer working.

"A long time ago, I told you Ellis had a religious conversion?" He paused.

I grunted softly in the affirmative when it seemed he was not going on.

"And Eddie, too?"

"Mmm."

"Well, Eddie was working with Ellis. Claims he went to Ellis with rumors about a bacteriological warfare plan put together by a group of white supremacists on the Lamb's compound. You still awake?"

"Mmm-hmm."

"Still want to hear this?"

I blew out a breath that parted my stuck-together lips. "Yesssh. Ah'm lishnen."

"Ellis was on the trail of the BW stuff and the people responsible for it. Had been for the last decade. And with the troubles in the Middle East, it became more urgent. Eddie joined up with him. Eddie claims he was one of the good guys, trying to find out who killed Leon Hawkins. Trying to discover where the BW canisters were. But it turned out the BW agent was something they couldn't control. Eddie thought you would know how they could stop it until they found the man making it."

All he was saying, I had long ago put together. All except the missing link. Eddie. The reason why Ellis had come to me. Distantly, I wondered why Eddie hadn't gone to his father.

"Reeves was a Lamb follower, and the final link," Mark said. "They just weren't absolutely certain he was the man doing the work. Now he's dead."

The odd tone was back in Mark's voice. Even through the drug-induced haze, I understood. He'd killed a man. It was over. Finally, it was all over.

Summoning my remaining energy, I squeezed his hand. And then tumbled into a drug-hazed sleep.

27

MENS WON'T DECIDE FOR YOU

Summer had come while I was out of work and taking rehab. I hadn't made it back to work in the week Wallace had demanded. Not even in the last month. Ellis's blade had severed muscles in my back that had to be compensated for by strengthening the surrounding ones. Blood loss had made recovery time slow, but my hemoglobin was back to nine, and every once in a while, I could feel a slow burn of energy as my body recuperated. While I was out of commission, the temps had risen, the birds had come home for summer, and the world had bloomed.

Even my long-neglected yard was bright with flowers: bulbs had burst through the untended soil, ground cover had sent up spikes of purple flowers, azaleas had opened purple, white and red trumpets, calling for early insects to pollinate them, trees had opened white and pink blossoms. I had called a nursery service for advice about what kind of fertilizers the soil needed and what kind of grass might grow beneath the heavy canopy of trees. I had a lot of work to do when I finally got my life back to normal.

For now, I was content to sit with Marisa in her backyard, smelling the herbs that had already sprouted in Miss Essie's raised beds, and watching Cam play with Belle and Pup. He was teaching Pup to fetch. Had taught the big, clumsy dog to heel and answer to a leash, sit and stay in the three days he had been back from Duke. And now he played with the two dogs as if he were still a little boy, laughter and yelping barks carrying on the still air. He threw a stick, his too-long black hair rippling with the motion.

Shirl would be here soon, hair braided and flying in the wind like a scarlet Medusa. She was coming from Atlanta for the weekend with the intent of house hunting in Charlotte, and to finally get treated to a meal at the little French restaurant. Dinner tonight was at Sottise. On me. Because I was unable yet to sit for hours in a car, Cam was going house hunting with her in the morning. And lately, he'd been making noises about relocating to Charlotte when he finished his residency. Another four years or so. Longer if he got a fellowship along the way.

I wondered if he was considering the move because of Shirl or because of Marisa. Either way, it brought him closer, and that was what mattered. Risa needed her family close by. I remembered her putting my hand on her tummy, telling me that family was all that mattered to her now. And we were her family.

Marisa laughed and clapped her hands, encouraging man and canines to further leaps of acrobatic endeavors and bursts of speed. Miss Essie adjusted the blanket that covered Marisa's legs, stepped to me and adjusted mine before walking back to her kitchen. For now, Risa and I were Miss Essie's charges, invalids under her care, to be fed nourishing broth, forced to drink vile herbal teas, be cosseted and babied. She even hired a town girl to take over the house cleaning so she could concentrate on us, Marisa under her own roof, me across the creek.

Life in Dawkins County was returning to normal. There had been fewer new cases of AVP and ACS as the disease died out. Patients who had contracted the diseases were being sent home from the hospital in varied states of health, some to require oxygen for the rest of their lives, others with little aftereffects of contracting the man-made bacterium.

The FBI had closed up the Patriot camp and the Lamb of God's compound, the Lamb's followers either stunned by his involvement in creating the BW strep enterotoxin or running for cover. And I had it on good authority that no new cases of blue, six-sided star tattoos had been seen. That authority being Mark, who had the men responsible for torturing Mel and Lia Campbell and lynching Leon Hawkins in jail.

He had made it a point to come by often since the day I had been injured and he had killed Reeves. And while I could sense a distance in him that hadn't been there before, we had begun talking, trying to deal with the fact that I hadn't told him all I knew. Had kept knowledge about Ellis from him that might have led him sooner to Reeves and allowed him to bring the man in alive. Because I had kept silent, Reeves had died. And Mark had to live with the knowledge he had killed a man.

Of course, it was all speculation. Perhaps if I had told Mark all I knew, he might now be dead. Or Reeves might have gotten away, taking the BW canisters with him, to resettle with a new white power group and start his terrorist activities again. I wasn't into second-guessing fate.

Richard Ellis had disappeared into NIS custody. Eddie was spilling all he knew in exchange for immunity. And Marisa was so huge she looked like she was ready to explode. All was returning to normal. Except perhaps me. Oh, I was healing externally. But inside, where my fears rested and bad dreams germinated like an evil weed, I was a mess. Post-traumatic stress, most likely. I had diagnosed myself, unwilling to seek counseling for the nightmares of Taylor Reeves chasing me down the blood-drenched hallways or falling toward me, dying. And I was uncharacteristically easygoing. Even Mark had commented on it. I wasn't my usual competitive self, and didn't want to be. Not today. Not yet.

Miss Essie came from the house carrying a tray and glasses of tea, sprigs of mint drowned in the bottoms of each. A snack of fresh hot bread and a bunch of red grapes, a hunk of pale cheese, and peanut butter settled on the table between Risa and me.

"You two girls eat," she said, settling into her chair with a satisfied sigh. "You gone need some real food before you go to that fancy French place and eat that foreign food."

"I thought you had decided to go to Sottise with us, Miss Essie," I said.

"Humph. I got me some fresh salad greens from the garden, with lovage and borage and mint and lettuce and spinach and sorrel. And a bowl of beans for supper. What I need foie gras for? 'Specially when you ain't gone get to eat it all." Miss Essie smoothed down her dress and folded her hands across her stomach as if settling all the world's problems with the gesture.

She had been warning me all day that I wasn't going to get to eat at Sottise. But the doctor had seen Marisa and told her it would be at least a few more days before she delivered, and a baby was the only thing that was going to keep me away from a great meal. "Never liked foreign food," she added. "And ain't gonna eat it tonight. 'Sides, *Jeopardy*'ll be on 'fore you get back and I don't want to miss it."

"Arlana and her boyfriend are going," I said, tempting her.

"And that mean you got to keep a sharp eye on my girl." Miss Essie's black eyes pierced me with purpose. "She got stars in her eyes over that man and she too young to settle down. It your job to make sure she keep her head on straight in that fancy place."

"Yes, ma'am," I said.

She turned her head to stare out at Cam and the dogs,

now moving back toward us across the lawn. "And your Mark. He going?" she asked, her tone deceptively mild.

I nodded.

"And Miss Shirley and my boy Cameron, too?"

Again I nodded, aware that she was carefully not looking at me, focusing instead on Cam's flushed face and the galloping dogs.

"You gonna have to decide between yourself and yourself what you want. Mens won't decide for you."

I looked away from Cam. I thought I had managed to keep hidden my interest in my old friend. It was foolishness, anyway. A woman had to be crazy to care for Cam Reston, especially when she had Mark Stafford nearby. A certified hero. A man who had killed to keep me safe. A man who filled me with contentment just by smiling at me.

"Oh-oh," Marisa said, her mouth opening in a huge O. "Oh-oh." She looked down. A dark stain was spreading across the cushion where she sat. "My *baby!*" She looked at me, amazement in her eyes. "My baby!" Her face twisted with a contraction.

"I told you not to make plans for that fancy French restaurant," Miss Essie said with satisfaction. "You gone be birthing babies tonight."

Cam ran up, winded and blowing, his dark eyes taking in all of us, especially Marisa's straining form and my frozen one. "What?" Then he grinned, the smile exposing all the expensive, glittering white orthodontia. "Her water broke!" he shouted.

"Now, Cameron, you go get my Miss Marisa's bag. It packed in the back entry. Miss Rhea, you go leave a note on the back door for Miss Shirley, and Cam, you come on back and help us into the car." A huge smile split her face. "We going to have us some babies!"

"Baby," Marisa said carefully, her wide eyes on Miss Essie.

"Nope," the old woman said with a jovial grin. "Babies. You is having twins."

We all stopped. "The ultrasound showed only one baby. There's only one heartbeat. One baby, Miss Essie," I said.

"One," Cam echoed.

"Humph. I been predicting babies for close on sixty year. Ain't never been wrong. Never. And we is havin' twins, one boy and one girl. And that all there is to say 'bout that. 'Cept Missy Rhea is gone have to go shopping again," she said with a sly grin.

___Author Note___

About Rhea:
So many of you have fallen in love with Dr. Rhea-Rhea Lynch. I love her, too! For me she is as alive as I am, as full of angst and energy, pathos and joy. Though Rhea and I are nothing alike, and she is fully fictional, I would recognize her if she walked into the room. I have heard the same comment from many of you.

For those of you who have asked, Rhea ages one year for every three books. After book three, she will permanently be listed in her mid-thirties. And no, I don't yet know how her romantic life will turn out! I am as ambivalent as Rhea about the two men in her life! And then…there's that small problem of John, the ex-fiancé….

Thanks to your help, Rhea will be around a long time! (And yes, I pronounce her name RAY, like a ray of sunshine—though she would hate that comparison!)

About medicine:
Our knowledge of medicine is evolving so fast that even the finest doctors have a hard time keeping up with the changes. When you read any medical novel, many of the procedures used by the characters will quickly become out-

moded, outdated and be put out to pasture! I hope you will keep this in mind when you read about Rhea Lynch, M.D.!

About Dawkins County:
There are still places in the South that are sparsely populated, having more cows and horses, chickens and turkeys, pigs and deer than people. The Piedmont of the Carolinas is pocketed with such mostly rural places. Places with little industry, where the average income is below poverty level, the opportunity for advancement is meager, and yet the people wouldn't think of living anywhere else. The reason... Roots. Family. Tradition. Generations on the same soil. Something many of us have lost!

About terrorism:
Since I finished this book, the world has been horrified by the events of September 11—the attack on the World Trade Towers and the Pentagon—and the following anthrax scare. In a desperate rewrite, I went back and added as much as I could about how the world is different, now. Before this book goes to print, there may be other such terrorist activities, other deaths, other horrors.

About the author:
If you wish to learn more about me, please come to www.gwenhunter.com or go to my author's page at www.mirabooks.com. I will answer quickly any letters that come via e-mail. Any letters that come by snail mail through the publisher will simply take longer! And if you don't send me a return address, they won't be replied to at all!

Thank you all!
Gwen Hunter.

GWEN HUNTER

66803   DELAYED DIAGNOSIS   ___ $5.99 U.S. ___ $6.99 CAN.
                   (limited quantities available)

TOTAL AMOUNT $_____
POSTAGE & HANDLING $_____
($1.00 for one book; 50¢ for each additional)
APPLICABLE TAXES* $_____
<u>TOTAL PAYABLE</u> $_____
(check or money order—please do not send cash)

To order, complete this form and send it, along with a check
or money order for the total above, payable to MIRA Books®,
to: **In the U.S.:** 3010 Walden Avenue, P.O. Box 9077, Buffalo,
NY 14269-9077; **In Canada:** P.O. Box 636, Fort Erie, Ontario
L2A 5X3.

Name:_____
Address:_____ City:_____
State/Prov.:_____ Zip/Postal Code:_____
Account Number (if applicable):_____
075 CSAS

 *New York residents remit applicable sales taxes.
  Canadian residents remit applicable GST and provincial taxes.

MIRA®

Visit us at www.mirabooks.com   MGH0402BL